ONE LITTLE KISS

THE WESTBROOKS: FAMILY TIES BOOK 3

AVERY MAXWELL

That's What She Said Publishing, Inc.

ISBN: 979-8-88643-996-0 (ebook)

ISBN: 979-8-88643-997-7 (paperback)

040922a

This book is for everyone carrying the weight of the world on their shoulders, and the friends that help lighten the load.

PLAYLIST

ONE LITTLE KISS

Ticket to L.A., Brett Young
Build Me Up Buttercup, The Foundations
Closer, Nine Inch Nails
Blister In The Sun, Violent Femmes
Peter Pan, Kelsea Ballerini
You Say, Lauren Daigle
To Be Loved By You, Parker McCollum
Feels So Good, Mase
I Need My Girl, The National
Gratitude, Big Red Machine
Open Your Eyes, Snow Patrol
Outnumbered, Dermot Kennedy
Lost Boy, Ruth B.
Rome, Dermot Kennedy
Gimme More, Britney Spears
Stay Stay Stay, Taylor Swift
The Last Time, Taylor Swift Featuring Gary Lightbody
Someone To You, BANNERS
Nightmare, Halsey
Be Still, The Killers

Please Don't Leave Me, Pink
Enchanted, Taylor Swift
We're Going to Be Friends, The White Stripes
What Ifs, Kane Brown Featuring Lauren Alaina

https://geni.us/OneLittleKissPlaylist

The WESTBROOK FAMILY

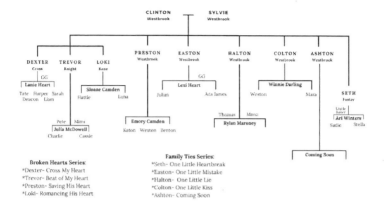

Broken Hearts Series:
*Dexter- Cross My Heart
*Trevor- Beat of My Heart
*Preston- Saving His Heart
*Loki- Romancing His Heart

Family Ties Series:
*Seth- One Little Heartbreak
*Easton- One Little Mistake
*Halton- One Little Lie
*Colton- One Little Kiss
*Ashton- Coming Soon

The Westbrooks: Family Ties is a spin-off series of The Westbrooks: Broken Hearts series. If you're looking for Dexter, Trevor, Preston, or Loki's stories, you'll find them in The Westbrooks: Broken Hearts.

Seth's story, One Little Heartbreak, is a bridge novella that connects the two series.

You can read The Broken Hearts series for free in Kindle Unlimited.

Happy Reading!

CHAPTER 1

COLTON

Eighteen months ago

"What flight ya on, Pan?"

Hearing GG behind me, I cringe. I don't know if Pan irritates me because it means GG's tarot cards have me in their sights or because my brothers think I'll never grow up, but neither option works particularly well for me.

"I'm flying out of Boston on Friday after my meeting," I tell her as pleasantly as I can. It's not the first time I've flown commercial, but it'll be my longest flight crammed into one.

GG cackles, and it's reminiscent of a sound that makes crows flock to the sky. "First time on a public flight, Pan?"

My family owns a couple of planes, but since everyone else is flying out on Thursday from North Carolina or Vermont, it made the most sense for me to fly commercial after my meeting. That doesn't mean I like it.

"It's not my first, GG." My eyes roll to the back of my head like I'm thirteen again.

"Ah, ha. On American?" she presses.

Nodding, I narrow my eyes as my brother, Easton, smirks behind her on his way out the door. My hair, a touch too long in the front, falls over my forehead, and I resist the urge to brush it aside. I know he'll give me shit about keeping up appearances if he gets the chance, so I focus on GG.

"Yes. Is there something I can help you with, GG?" Crossing my arms over my broad chest, I watch her every move.

GG is my sister-in-law's grandmother, and she's scary as fuck. She's a tarot card reading, truth wine connoisseur, matchmaking pot stirrer with way too much time on her hands.

"You boys are getting so suspicious of me these days. Tsk, tsk, Pan. I was merely going to mention that maybe you'll meet Wendy on that flight."

My brows nearly jump off my skin they rise so fast. "What do you mean, meet Wendy?"

She guffaws and walks past me with a gentle pat on my shoulder. "All in good time. You're not ready yet."

A groan escapes as I stare at the ceiling. *Thank fuck.* No, I'm not ready for anyone she might throw at me. But then, who's Wendy?

Peering behind me, I discover she's gone before I can ask.

Great.

GG's lodge has come a long way in the few years East has been here. I take a moment to observe the upgrades, proud of what we've accomplished. None of us could have imagined what life had in store for us when he followed Lexi here and never left. Now we all have homes on the backside of the mountain. East, his wife, Lexi, and Ashton live here full time, as do one of our adopted brothers, Seth, his wife, Ari, and their daughter, Sadie Sunshine.

A commotion at the door has me turning toward the sound. East and Halton barrel through with my oldest brother, Preston, right behind them. The family that follows is harder to explain, and as they filter into the room, I lose track anyway, but we're all here. Brothers by blood and by choice, and their families. There's a shitload of us now.

My mom unofficially adopted Dexter, Loki, and Trevor when we were young. They all have families that fill the space with more kids than I can count, and I smile when I see Seth's daughter, Sadie, frantically searching the room. I'm willing to bet she's scoping the space for my little brother, Ash, or Dexter's son, Tate. Maybe both.

I chuckle as she spots Tate first and takes off running. She has his hand in hers a second later and drags him around the room, no doubt in search of her second target. Ashton.

"I know Hatty's always called me his sunbeam, but I don't think anyone can shine brighter than that little girl."

A smile lights my face as I turn to my best friend, and soon to be sister-in-law, Rylan Maroney. She's probably the only one who can get away with giving Halton a girly nickname like Hatty.

"Ryguy! Where have you been?"

"Trying to round up the chaos you call a family." I understand Halt's obsession with sunbeams. Rylan is literally glowing with happiness right now.

"Another week and we'll officially be your family, too," I warn with a smile.

A very undignified squeal erupts from my friend, and I can't help but chuckle. Opening my arms, I wait for her to claim a Westbrook special. She's finally getting her happily ever after, and I'm not sure anything could keep her away from my brother. No sooner do I encase her in a hug than Halton is growling at my side.

"She was mine first, so take your crabby ass caveman grunts elsewhere." I love messing with him. Rylan may have been my best friend first, but she's always been his forever. That doesn't mean I can't fuck with the guy once in a while.

"Whatever, Colty. Just take your damn hands off my wife."

"You sure you want to marry this asshole?" I whisper to Rylan, but then raise my voice for Halton's benefit. "You're not his wife yet. You can still run."

3

I huff out a painful gasp when the jerk elbows me in the kidney. "Hands off."

"Jesus, Halt. I was only joking." Rubbing my now sore side, I release Rylan.

"Let's get this over with. We still have stuff to do." Rylan has softened him, but willingly social, he's not.

"Well, maybe you should have given everyone a little more warning that you wanted to get married in Mexico. A month really isn't much notice. I can't even find a night for Rylan's bachelorette party." I pout. As her best friend, I've been planning her bachelorette for years.

"Colty," Rylan sighs. "We told you, we aren't doing the parties. Neither of us wanted one, but we'll do a Jack and Jill party on the island. It'll be fun, I promise."

If she didn't look so happy, I'd fight her on this. But seeing them together makes my chest beat an uneasy rhythm that screams happiness and forever. We'll ignore the slight pang of longing I also get whenever I watch them too closely. I'm not relationship material, Peter Pan and all.

"Don't roll your eyes, Colton. This is what she wants. Family, the beach, and the great Mayan Ruins."

Halton's stern tone drags me from my thoughts. *Eesh*. He thinks I rolled my eyes because of the party. Well, good. Let him believe that. It's easier than explaining the yearning I don't want to acknowledge that sits just below the surface.

"I know. I'm sorry. It'll be great. Okay, let's get everyone on board with your instructions. I have to head out soon to get ready for the meeting in Boston."

"You doing okay with it?" Halt asks, suddenly all business.

"Yeah. I have this proposal. I know it inside out and upside down, but …"

"But Macomb is still fucking around."

My shoulders tense thinking about it. He hit the nail on the head. "I just don't understand why Ash hasn't taken him down yet."

Macomb is our arch-nemesis in the business world. He's a snake in the grass, and Ash has everything he needs to put the guy in prison, but he's dragging his heels and none of us knows why. My best guess is it has something to do with Macomb's missing daughter, and Ash has been through so much, none of us dare push him on it.

"We have to do something soon," Halton agrees. "The losses aren't happening as frequently, but we can't afford to keep absorbing them when they do. Since Macomb lost his inside man, he hasn't been able to hit us as hard, and we all know what happens when people get desperate."

"Things turn personal," I mutter. A chill goes up my spine thinking about how easily Macomb paid off a trusted WB advisor's significant other. He fed Macomb information that nearly crippled part of our company for months before we caught him.

Rylan and I nod because it's something we've both heard ad nauseam for the last two years.

"Do you really think he'd come after one of you with all that Ash has on him?" she asks, alarm showing in the frown lines that rarely appear on her sun-kissed face. Fall in Vermont looks good on her.

"Sorry," Halt mumbles, recognizing he went off on a tangent again. "With Macomb, it's best to prepare for everything. But we'll handle it. We always do. Let's get this show on the road, huh?"

Rylan places a hand on his bicep, and I watch Halton's demeanor change. I'd be lying if I said I wasn't just the tiniest bit envious of what they have together. Glancing around, I notice all the guys have it. Everyone besides Ash and I, but even he's calmer with Sadie on one side and Tate on the other. *Two tiny bookends protecting our protector.*

I zone out as Halt and Rylan gather the adults and give them the itinerary for Mexico. When the family meeting ends, I hug everyone, grab my suitcase, and head to Boston to pitch The WB marketing vertical to the Fenway Sports Group.

~

"*H*ow did it go?" There's no mistaking the smile in Halton's voice, even as the ocean breeze attempts to muffle the sound.

"It couldn't have gone any better, Halt. Seriously, I killed it. Ask Mason if you don't believe me. He's probably three bloody Marys in celebrating."

"Nah, I trust you, Colton. That's great. You're at the airport now?"

He has no idea how much his trust means. Sometimes I think my brothers expect me to fail.

"Yeah, I'm heading to the VIP suite to work on the pre …"

"Colt?"

I can hear Halton speaking somewhere in my universe, but it's not registering. Neither is the fact that my feet have stopped moving. My attention is singularly focused on a mass of blonde curls that bounce over delicate shoulders. While my gaze drifts down, my chest constricts as my memory attempts to map out curves that have my hands itching to squeeze them.

What in the fuck is going on with me?

I can't even shake my attention free from the woman across from me.

"Colton?" Halt tries again.

"Ah, shit. Sorry. Gotta go."

Cramming the phone into my back pocket, I'm suddenly aware of disgruntled passengers walking around me. No doubt pissed off that I stopped moving in the middle of a busy airport terminal where everyone is in a rush to get somewhere. However, I can't take my eyes off the pixie of a woman holding my gaze captive.

The thing is, she hasn't even noticed me. Her face is an

expression of determination as she stares into a book with her pen flicking the top at a nervous pace. My feet move closer to her, but she still doesn't glance up. *Does she not feel this magnetic pull? Is she not aware of the visceral reaction her movements cause?* When she frowns at the book in her hand, something lances my chest.

Shuffling to the side, I lean against an airport column to watch her in a completely stalkerish way, but I can't help myself. For the first time in my life, I don't feel in control of my body. Her attention never wavers from what she's reading and I'm beyond fascinated, but can't force myself to talk to her. Not with GG's words about Wendy and matchmaking on my mind.

Instead of hitting on this poor girl, I shake off the strange reaction. With great effort, I force all thoughts of her out of my head. The WB Group pays a membership fee for a private lounge at all major airports. It's generally reserved for celebrities, but we offer it as a perk for our top executives since we traditionally fly private. Today, I'm thankful for the space and the quiet it will afford me.

I last a total of twenty minutes before I push through the exit doors of the VIP lounge. The pop starlet and her entourage taking up one half of the private lounge have nothing on my mystery woman. Nearing gate twenty-two, I slow my pace and scan the now empty terminal.

Shit.

Raking a hand through my hair, I try to brush aside the uncomfortable pang that hits my chest.

She's gone.

It's for the best. That's what I tell myself anyway as I head to the bar for a beer. My flight leaves in an hour. I have plenty of time to blow off some steam. Plus, there's a four-hour layover in Miami. I might as well settle in for a long ass day.

≈

$\mathcal{W}$e touch down in Miami, and the entire plane breaks out in applause. I admit, the pilot deserves it, but the meaty paw of my seatmate clawing into my forearm has me hanging by a thread. You'd think the thunderstorm that caused turbulence would be the reason for my irritated state. But you'd be wrong.

What has me on the verge of an outburst is Jerry, who ate and spat Cheetos in my face the entire flight. I heard him berating the attendant before we took off, and he eventually bullied his way into a free upgrade. Right next to me.

I don't care what it costs. I'm buying the seat beside me for the next leg of this trip.

Jerry's squeals have finally stopped, and he releases me. I cringe when I glance down and find a Cheetos orange handprint on my six-thousand-dollar suit.

Listen, I'm not usually a jackoff. I know things can be cleaned and replaced, but it's this asshole's entitlement and his mistreatment of the staff that has me growling my displeasure.

"Get. Up." He has the gall to look offended, but does as I ask. Glowering, I shuffle into the aisle ahead of him.

I find Joanna, our flight attendant, and I apologize on Jerry's behalf while exiting the plane. She's an older woman with a warm smile. She held herself together well, but I could tell Jerry shook her up.

Asshole.

"Joanna? My name is Colton Westbrook. I'd like to apologize for the guy next to me. He was out of line, but I think you handled yourself professionally, and if you're ever interested in moving to the private sector, my family would be happy to have you." I smirk at her expression of shock. I can't help myself. "If you call my assistant on this card, she'll be happy to give you some information."

She gasps.

"We keep staff on retainer, but I have a feeling it's a lot less work."

Jerry pushes his way past us, and I don't hide the look of disgust on my face.

Pushing the card into her palm, I smile. "Just think about it. Google The Westbrook Group if you'd like to do your research, but rest assured, you won't deal with people like him in my family."

"W-Why?"

Flashing the flirtatious grin I was born with, I shrug. "We were taught to look out for people." Embarrassed, I glance away. "I heard you mention you'd like to spend more time with your grandchildren. I think we might be able to make that happen. If not, no worries. Have a good day, Miss Joanna."

Walking down the ramp, thunder claps above. It's loud enough to make the enclosure shake, and Jerry trip over his suitcase. He goes down with a heavy thud.

"Karma, Jerry, that's what that was," I glower as I step over and around him on my way to find another damn beer.

Pushing through the crowd, I catch the grumbling of unhappy passengers.

"Flight's canceled."

"Delay."

"No idea when we'll get out of here."

Stepping to the side, I search the screens overhead for my connecting flight, only to see the word delayed in red down the right side of every monitor.

"They've grounded all flights until the storm passes," someone says to my left.

"Wonderful." Closing my eyes, I take a deep breath and pull out my phone. It's already late. There's no way I'm getting out tonight.

"Hey, Halt," I sigh when he answers on the second ring.

He chuckles. "How was your flight?"

"The plane almost got hit by lightning. Twice." I don't know if that's actually true, but it sure as shit felt that way.

"Christ. Are you okay?"

"Yeah, but they grounded flights for a while. I need to check, but with the number of people milling about, I'm going to guess I won't get there until tomorrow."

"That sucks. Glad you're safe, though. What do you need?" I know he means well, but it's another example of my family thinking I'm incompetent.

"Nothing, just letting you know. I'll book a room for the night."

"I'll tell everyone else. Be safe and make sure you call when you get your new flight time. I'll send someone to get you at the airport."

"Thanks."

"You got it. See you tomorrow, brother."

"Yup. Love you."

"Love you, too."

He hangs up, and I move to the far wall out of people's way so I can check my phone without blocking traffic.

It doesn't take long. Flights are delayed, and so far, none of them are taking off tonight, so I text my friend, Lochlan. He has hotels all over the world. He can set me up somewhere for the night.

Colton: Hey. I'm stuck in Miami for the night. What are my choices for a place to stay?

Lochlan: Damn, mate. I was just there two days ago. We need to get our schedules synced.

Lochlan: I've got two hotels downtown. One at the beach. Any preference?

Colton: Nah, whatever you've got. Thanks.

Lochlan: My assistant, Jennifer, will send you confirmation in a few. It's all electronic now, so she'll also send a key code for your door.

Colton: Another new assistant, Loch?

Lochlan: Don't start. Not all of us have in-laws to hire. Expect it soon.

Colton: Thanks, man. Catch up when I get back from Halt's wedding?

Lochlan: Done.

Slipping the phone back into my pocket, I make my way to baggage claim to search for my suitcase. Another novelty I'm not used to.

People stand shoulder to shoulder, vying to get to the conveyor belt first like someone will steal their bags. Panic tightens my shoulders, and I grip my neck as I glance around. *Does that happen? Do people steal other people's bags?*

Watching the way people push and shove for the front row, I'm going to guess yes. Mentally, I do an inventory of the shit in my suitcase, and when I'm confident there isn't anything that can't be replaced, I relax and slip to the back.

I have no interest in elbowing my fellow travelers for a few bathing suits. Instead, I find an empty seat and let the lines clear out while I get lost in a game of blackjack on my phone. When I lift my head, my luggage sits beside the belt, but not stolen.

Internally, I smirk. Sometimes we can't help how out of touch with reality we are. We were born billionaires, but my parents did their best to keep us grounded. My mom didn't grow up with money, and she would kick my ass for my snobbery.

Thinking of my parents makes me sad, though, knowing all my father has missed. He passed away years ago. I was just a teenager. A baby. But I remember his love. His sense of humor. I remember the love he had for my mother. A once in a life-time love, he used to call it. It makes my heart hurt for her. And us.

Shaking my wayward thoughts from my head, I push forward, taking in the passengers and marveling at how stressed out everyone is. All in a rush to get to their destination. A hurry to get home. The thought has me slowing down and taking it all in.

Too many people rush through life. I've learned a lot from my older brothers. Mostly, that we need to make every opportunity count and live life to its fullest. Preston, East, and Halton all have their happily ever afters, but I'm not ready.

Someday.

Maybe.

"Don't be scared of love, Colty. Nothing will ever make you happier in life than love."

My father's words sound so clear in my head. It's like he's standing over my shoulder, and I think if I checked, goosebumps would cover my arms.

"Don't be scared of love."

I hear it again, and I stop to glance over my shoulder this time. I almost chuckle at the ridiculous notion I might see my father. Or worse, his ghost. But what I do see has my jaw hitting the floor, anyway.

My girl.

CHAPTER 2

COLTON

"*J*s anyone sitting here?"

My mystery girl doesn't even glance up from the book she's reading. "Nope. It's all yours."

I feel the frown form on my face, but I hurry to drop into the seat next to her. Leaning back in the chair, I observe her. Again. But she's unfazed. At some point, my leg bounces like it's about to take flight, and her attention finally lands on me. *Was that a sharp intake of breath I heard? Does she like what she sees? Does it matter?*

"Nervous flyer?" Her voice is as gentle as her gaze. She speaks like she's talking to a wounded animal, but it hits me in places it shouldn't. Not in public, anyway.

"No. Why do you say that?" My gaze lingers as the tip of her pen leaves her pouty lips. When I finally glance down, my leg freezes mid bounce, and a rough chuckle escapes with a deep, gravel-like sound. "Maybe a little. I'm not used to airports like this." It's not a lie since I rarely fly commercial, but I don't need to offer that tidbit up just yet. Something tells me a private jet wouldn't impress her.

"You'll be fine. Promise." She smiles, and my body leans closer. Her face flushes, and I wonder how much of her skin turns that lovely shade when she's aroused. I'm inexplicably drawn to her, but I can tell she's the most charismatic person I've ever met with just a few sentences.

"What's your name?" I almost don't recognize my own voice.

Her eyebrow quirks, and she flashes a fake smile.

"I mean, if we're going to make small talk, I'd like to know who it is I'm sharing my fears with. I was always told not to talk to strangers." I flash her a wink and hope it's sexy, not lascivious, but I feel out of sorts around her so it could look like a seizure for all I know.

Angling herself to face me, she crosses her arms over her ample chest as she shakes her head. I have to force myself not to do a quick scan of her entire body. "You're very—"

"Pushy? Nosy? Handsome?" I grin.

"Talkative," she finally settles on, narrowing her gray eyes that sparkle with flecks of gold and turquoise.

"Yeah, well, my family has a communication problem, so I've made it my mission to correct that. I might overcompensate for them sometimes."

Communication problem is an understatement I don't need to get into, either. All three of my attached brothers almost lost their girls because they didn't know how to hold a conversation, but I keep that to myself.

"Fair enough. You're not trying to hit on me, are you?" The sexy way her lips curl at the corners as she teases has me leaning even closer because, yes. Yes, I am most definitely hitting on her.

Playfully, I grab at my heart. "Ugh. I'm wounded. Why on earth would I want to hit on the most beautiful woman I've ever seen?"

"You're trouble, too, I see." Her eyes glint and her tone is mischievous. I realize with a start that she has no idea who I am. I'm not offended. If anything, I feel relief. When you're a Westbrook, it's hard to know if someone is into you for you, or your bank account. It's a rarity to meet someone that has no connection to my daily life.

"Always," I say with a crooked grin and hold out my hand. "I'm Colton." I hesitate for a moment, then decide to go with my middle name for now. "Colton Montgomery." Finally, my stuffy middle name comes in handy, but this way, if she Googles me, she won't get the gossip column full of half-truths. The thought of getting to know someone without preconceived notions is thrilling. I like it much more than I should. "It's nice to meet you …"

My mystery woman releases a breath neither of us realized she was holding and slips her palm into mine. "Wendalyn. It's nice to meet you, Colton."

The second her skin touches mine, time stands still. It's not a shock so much as an awakening. *Wendalyn?* I think my lungs just collapsed, and I swear I hear GG cackle. "Um," I swallow, and it sounds like a frog during mating season. "Like Wendy?"

She pulls her hand from mine. "Not if you expect me to answer you. It's Wendalyn. Not Wendy." She's not cold, but she's decisive. I like that. A lot.

"Thank God," I say in a whoosh.

"Not a fan of Wendy either?" She laughs, and it's a melodic sound I could grow addicted to.

"More like, I'm not ready for Wendy. So, Wendalyn, where are you off to today?"

I watch as her pen tap, tap, taps against her knee. She's watching me. Scrutinizing me. Evaluating me. I've never wanted to be a mind reader more in my life.

"I was headed to the beach," she says evasively, "but they rescheduled my flight, so I'm studying."

"Is it rescheduled soon?" Mentally, I remind myself to check my flight. *Will they actually fly out in this shit storm?*

Wendalyn sighs, and I greedily breathe in her scent. *Well, that's a new one. When have I ever been greedy about sniffing someone?*

"Not until tomorrow." My gaze is on her lips as she speaks, so it takes a moment to register her words. When I do, I snap my eyes to hers.

Caught red-handed, staring at her sexy, plump lips I'd love to taste, and I'm not the least bit embarrassed.

"Why are you sitting here, then? Are you waiting for a ride?" I'm already pulling out my phone, knowing I can have a car here in minutes. Why I feel the need to do this for her is beyond me, but I don't think about it too long.

Her pen pauses its assault on her leg and the confidence she carries wavers briefly before she slips her mask of indifference back in place. It was quick, but I saw it, and I'm invested.

"What? Am I missing something?" I ask, scanning the terminal. A few people mill about, but the crowd is rapidly clearing out.

She chuckles softly. "No, Colton. I'm not going anywhere. I'm going to sit here and study."

She's smart and beautiful, but my shoulders take up residence next to my ears again. I'm not used to feeling tense like this, and I know immediately that I don't like it. I don't know why Wendalyn's answers cause this reaction, but my heart beats against my chest like a colony of angry seagulls diving for a forgotten hotdog.

It's unsettling. This feeling she's causing is unnerving, yet I can't walk away from her.

Tilting my head, I study her and love the light shade of pink that lingers on her defined cheekbones. "What do you mean? Don't you want to get a room? There are a ton of hotels around here."

"No. What about you? Is your flight soon?" Her answer isn't curt, exactly, but I'm curious. Who, in their right mind, wants to stay in an airport terminal instead of a hotel?

Glancing to her right, I notice her suitcase for the first time. Navy blue. There's nothing remarkable about it except for the light blue and bright pink ribbon she's tied to the handles. It's old and worn. Threadbare in places, but sufficient.

When she notices me staring, she slings her jacket over it, and that light pink across her cheeks turns crimson.

Fuck. Did I just embarrass her?

That's when it hits me. She's not like the vapid women I usually date. This woman is real. No designer labels, no airs or pretense. She's someone you bring home to mom, and that intrigues me as much as it terrifies me.

"So," she drags out, "I should get back to studying."

I stutter, realizing I've been silent for an uncomfortable amount of time while studying her intently. I already know she has a tiny freckle just above her lip. That her eyes are the most unique shade I've ever seen. And her lips? Fuck me. Her lips were made for pure sin. "Jesus. S-Sorry, my mind wandered. I just realized I should let my brother know I'm going to arrive a day late."

She relaxes and gives a half smile. "No worries."

Unlocking my phone, I shoot Loch a text.

Colton: I won't need a room after all. Appreciate it, though.

Lochlan: If you're going to my competition, I'll kick your ass.

Colton: You can try, but we both know that wouldn't happen.

I chuckle, then put him out of his misery.

Colton: Nah, just hanging at the airport, hoping the flight will take off sooner than expected.

Lochlan: Right. Because that happens ALL the time. (eye roll emoji)

Lochlan: Who is she?

I forgot this asshole knows me almost as well as my brothers.

Colton: Not sure.

Lochlan: And you don't want the room because?

Colton: I already know she isn't a one-night stand kind of girl.

Lochlan: Good-bye, mate. It was nice knowing ya. Now who will be my wingman?

Colton: Whatever, dude. You're talking to Peter Pan, remember?

I hate the nickname, and it feels like a lie even as I type it. Now more than ever.

Lochlan: Right. Good luck with that.

Colton: (Middle finger emoji) (High five emoji)

Lochlan: Room's available if you change your mind.

Colton: Thanks.

Turning to Winnie, I feel my smirk slip into a full, toothy smile when I find her watching me. *Winnie? Where the hell did that come from?*

"All set, Peter?" Her smirk matches mine, and I know without a doubt I've just met my match. My equal. A trouble-maker disguised as a sexy angel.

My jaw nearly comes unhinged.

"You read my texts?" I ask aghast and a little impressed that she didn't even try to hide it.

"It's hard not to when your font size can be read from outer space," she deadpans.

Glancing from her to my phone, laughter erupts from deep in my soul. She's right. The font size is as big as it goes so I can read while on the rowing machine. I usually remember to adjust it after a workout, but I was in a rush this morning and must have forgotten.

"Guess Peter may stay a lost boy, but Colton is showing signs of aging."

I blink. And blink again.

Her laughter rings out through the now empty gate, and I swear to Christ, it's like angels singing. The last rays of sunlight filter in through the floor-to-ceiling windows and cast a glow around her, making it hard to breathe.

"Am I dreaming?" I don't know if the words even make it out of my lips until I hear the raspy sound that can only be my voice. Like an out-of-body experience, I watch as she tips her head back. Her shoulders shake as she laughs at me, and I can't help but join in. She laughs so hard a tear rolls down her cheek.

Without thinking, I reach over and cup her face. Using my thumb, I wipe away the single tear. She gasps, pulling away quickly.

So. Fucking. Inappropriate. And completely out of my control.

"No touching, Colton. I don't know you," she says huskily, and I get the first indication that she also feels this pull happening between us.

"What time's your flight tomorrow?" I counter.

She hesitates, biting her lip.

"TSA is all over this airport. It's not like I can steal you away, Winnie."

Now it's her turn to gape at me, and it takes a moment to realize my nickname slipped out. Attempting to make it less weird, I bump her shoulder.

"Come on, we've got," I glance at my watch, "tell me how long I have to make you fall madly in love with me." I'm kidding, of course, but it doesn't feel like a joke.

Closing her book, she laughs at my antics. "Thirteen hours. You have thirteen hours, Colton Montgomery."

CHAPTER 3

WINNIE

"*W*ait. Did you just call me Winnie?" I ask, coming to my senses. I'm not sure why I'm encouraging this stranger, but I have to admit, he had my attention the second he sat next to me and his undeniably sexy scent invaded my senses. Like the ocean, and a forest after a rainstorm, and something so masculine, it can only be him.

Colton's wolfish grin slips as he shrugs his shoulders. If I had to guess, I'd say I just embarrassed him.

"Truth?" he asks, rubbing his five o'clock shadow with his thumb and forefinger. His very, very long forefinger.

"Always," I gulp, tearing my gaze from his hand.

"Wendalyn seems like an old lady name."

"And Winnie doesn't?" I chuckle. At least he's honest.

Colton shakes his head slowly. His eyes never leave mine. "No. Winnie seems … honest. Wholesome. Sexy."

"Do you always find meaning in the names of strangers you're *not* trying to hit on?" I suck in a gasp as he angles his body toward mine and the heat from his leg causes an electric shock straight into my core.

Danger, Winnie. Danger. This guy could crush you if you let him.

"I don't think I've ever given a woman I was hitting on a nickname before."

"So what you're saying is, I'm your first?" It comes out suggestively, and he chuckles.

"I'm getting the feeling you could be the first of many things, Winnie."

His words are so honest, but they seem to trouble him. As he stares past me, I take the opportunity to study him. Again. When he was texting with his friend, I took full advantage of the chance to ogle him. Colton is stupidly handsome and obviously does well for himself. I don't know anything about expensive clothing, but I can tell just by looking that his suit probably cost more than my car.

His dirty blond hair is a little too long on the top, adding to the boyish charm his personality exudes. His eyes are what had my heart skipping a beat, though. They're almost a caramel color, but with a ring of navy blue around the irises. Colton could be on the cover of any men's magazine. Surely the women he dates match him physically. I have a healthy self-esteem, but Colton is god-like. It makes me question why he's hanging out here instead of the room his friend offered.

"Is your friend a hotel manager or something?"

Colton turns his quizzical gaze my way.

"In your text, you said you didn't need a room anymore. I just assumed he worked for a hotel."

A Cheshire-like smile slides across perfectly straight, white teeth. "Something like that."

"Is it not a nice hotel?"

Colton leans back in his seat, giving the impression he has all the time in the world. "They're some of the nicest hotels in the world, actually."

I feel my brows furrow in confusion. "Did you get a better offer?"

"That has yet to be decided." His seductive tone could charm a nun out of her panties.

I cross my legs uncomfortably.

Gah, the grin on this man could do serious damage to someone's ovaries. Someone else's. Not mine. "O-kay then. I'm, ah, I'm going to get back to studying."

I glance away quickly. Colton has me unnerved, and I don't get unnerved. Especially not by a man. I have a pretty good intuition for people, so I don't think Colton's dangerous, but I know better than anyone what misplaced trust can do.

With that thought, I'm suddenly scanning our surroundings for security, just in case.

"Hey," Colton says carefully. "What just happened? You look as though you're planning an escape."

"A girl can never be too careful," I hedge.

Sensing my unease, he angles his body to give me some space, which I appreciate, but it does nothing to calm the frenetic energy that seems to be super charged between us.

"I agree."

He agrees? With what?

"Are you planning to stay here all night?"

Yes. Yes, I am.

"Ah, that's the plan."

"Great. I'm Colton. I'm one of five boys, plus four more quasi-adopted ones. My family's made up of blood brothers and brothers by choice. Most of them are married now, with kids, which makes family gatherings completely insane and exactly how my parents always wanted it. My dad passed away when I was a teenager. As I mentioned, every single person in my family has a problem with communication. I've made it my goal not to follow suit. My family has a lot of really fucking amazing qualities, but none of them can talk through issues to save their damn life. They refer to me as Peter Pan because I'm not ready to settle down. That doesn't mean I never want to. I do. Someday. I'll be a kick ass dad someday, just like my father was. But I feel like I'm too selfish to achieve that level of greatness yet. I date. A lot, but I never lead anyone

23

on. I'm a loyal friend, brother, uncle, and son. And, for reasons I can't explain, I would rather sit here all night getting to know you, Winnie, than spend the evening alone in a five-star hotel."

He places his clasped hands in his lap, his sparkling eyes never leaving mine, and he smiles. Open. Honest. Devastatingly handsome.

"That's … wow. That's a lot of information." I feel jittery, and my gaze jumps anywhere but his face. My phone buzzes in my lap, and I nearly leap out of my skin. Glancing down, I see it's my mom. Hoping she made it back to Vermont after dropping me off at Logan International in Boston, I turn to Colton. "I have to take this."

He smiles and makes a go-ahead motion with his hands. Guess he isn't taking the hint. Turning away from him, I accept the call, and my mom's beautiful face fills the screen.

"Winnie." She smiles, and I can feel Colton's grin at my back. *Winnie*. "How are you, baby girl? I got a notification that your flight's delayed."

"Yeah, the storm really picked up, but I'm on the first flight out in the morning. I'm okay. I have so much studying to do."

"Win. You're going on vacation, even if it's a working one. Try to relax. Have some fun. Meet a boy." A shit-eating grin comes over her face, and I feel Colton's presence before I see his face on the phone screen.

Whipping my head over my shoulder, I hiss, "What are you doing?"

"Win? Who is that handsome boy?"

Good lord. I square my shoulders, knowing I'm not getting out of this one. If there's one thing my mother has a weakness for, it's handsome men. "His name is Colton, Mother. He's a stranger. A stranger who likes to talk. A lot. That's all." I peek over my shoulder to find him grinning wildly. Stupid, handsome boy. Stupid, handsome boy that has my tummy doing somersaults. *Gah!*

"Hello, Mrs. Winnie?" Colton calls over my shoulder, and I plant my free palm to my forehead.

Knowing my mother, she's reading way too much into this. Until recently, it's always been just the two of us. She's done the best she could as a single mom, and she always provided for me, but we couldn't be more different. She's the first to seek the fun in life, where I'm more cautious. I like things thought out. Planned. In some ways, I've always been the responsible one. I'll never be carefree like her. She says I'm an old soul, but she's a free spirit. The fun one. I'm the daughter she'll never understand but loves me endlessly, anyway.

"Well, hello there, handsome."

My mother suffers the same affliction as Colton. A helpless flirt.

"Mom!"

"Oh, Winnie, I'm just teasing—"

She's cut off by a wail of, "We-We."

"Someone heard your voice." My mom smiles and bobbles the phone as she bends down to scoop up my favorite person on the planet.

"We-We!"

"Hey, buddy!" I coo into the phone, and feel Colton's questioning stare, but he stays silent, watching me interact with the cutest little one year old on the planet.

Weston babbles, and I decide he's saying he loves me.

"Ah, I love you, too, Wessy. Be good for Momma, okay? I'll be home soon."

Before I can say anything else, he's wiggling free, and it's just my mom once again.

"Okay, sweetheart. I should get him a snack before he tries to climb the wall. Be good. Be safe, but have fun, sweet girl. That's what this trip is all about, right?"

It's not, actually. It's about making bank for a week and a half, but she wants me to have fun, so I agree. "I will. You're sure you'll be okay while I'm gone? Mrs. Fraser said she'll help out more while I'm away. We'll figure out how to repay her when I get home."

"Win. This isn't your problem to solve. You forget that I'm the mother here. I raised you, didn't I? Look how amazing you turned out. I can handle this. You worry about you for a few days."

I know it's not my place to problem solve, but I can't help it. She hasn't been herself lately, and I worry. "Love you."

"I love you, too, Win. Call me when you land." Leaning into the phone, she whispers, "Is your friend okay? Do we need to get security?" That's my mom. It's not that she doesn't worry about safety, but it's usually an afterthought.

I glance at Colton again. He's the picture of innocence with a spark of trouble in those mesmerizing eyes of his.

"I think I'm okay. I'm not leaving the airport."

Colton holds his hands up after I shoot him a pointed stare.

"Okay, good. I'll talk to you tomorrow. Wes. Hold on … gotta go. Love you."

"Bye, Mom." I barely get the words out before the screen goes black.

"So," Colton drawls beside me, "your mom seems fun, and Wes is cute."

CHAPTER 4

COLTON

Wes? Who the hell is that?

Glancing over Winnie's shoulder, I see her mini-me.

Shit.

Does she have a son?

Does it matter?

What am I doing here?

My gaze never leaves her as she talks with her mom. Their relationship is … different. I can tell Winnie's a fixer. Her mother's love is evident, but I wonder about their dynamic. Then again, what do I know? I come from a family full of boys.

As soon as she's off the phone, curiosity gets the better of me. "So, your mom seems fun, and Wes is cute."

"She is, and he's so cute."

That's it. I think she'll make me ask, but then she lets me off the hook. "Wes wasn't planned, but he's the best brother I could ask for."

Brother.

She doesn't miss the sigh that escapes me, but she doesn't comment on my noticeable relief, either.

Why does it even matter?

"So, it sounds like you help with him a lot?"

Winnie's quiet for so long I don't think she'll answer. When she does, her voice sounds strange. "My mom's a nurse." She peeks up at me through long lashes I want to feel against my skin. "I have no idea why I'm telling you this." She shakes her head like it's the most ridiculous thing ever, but I'm caught in her spell. She could tell me her mother makes bat soup, and I'd be enthralled.

"Hey, I gave you a rundown of my entire family, remember? We're not strangers anymore." I flash a smile that always works for me.

"Does that always work for you?"

Can she read my mind?

"Does what work?" I ask, with practiced innocence.

"Turning on the charm with that panty-melting grin?"

"I'm sorry, all I heard was panty melting. My brain is short circuiting. You'll have to try that again."

Winnie throws her head back and laughs. Her long, creamy neck is on full display, and that uncomfortable, erratic flutter happens in my chest as I watch her.

"I'll take that as a yes," she says with a melodic giggle that has my ears ringing. "Honestly, though. Is this how you go about picking up strangers? It seems like a lot of work for a booty call."

I don't want to tell her I never work this hard for a booty call, but for some inexplicable reason, I desperately want to impress her. As I speak, a low rumble happens in my chest, and I know I'm in trouble. "I only work this hard to get to know you, Winnie."

"Charming," she mutters, crossing her arms over her chest, putting up an invisible barrier between us.

Even scowling, she's beautiful. I don't know what it is about this girl that has me jumping through hoops. It doesn't make sense. I'm surrounded by beautiful women all the time, yet I'm willingly sitting my ass in an abandoned airport just to talk with her.

She lets out a long sigh, and it causes the curls around her face to flutter. My hands twitch with the need to tuck them behind her ear, but she set the rules. No touching. Instead, I ball my hands into fists, then flex them a few times.

"My brother wasn't planned, and my mother wasn't seeing anyone. She always wanted more kids, but my dad took off before I was born. My stepdad took off when I was a teenager after they struggled for years with infertility." She pauses, and my gaze tracks hers. With her hands in her lap, she twists her fingers around her left wrist, and this time, I can't help myself. My palm rests lightly over her hands, stilling them.

"Sweetheart? You don't have to tell me anything you're not comfortable with." Her expression morphs into confusion, but I see the determination behind her eyes.

"You probably won't understand this, Colton. It sounds like you come from a close, loving family."

"Appearances can be deceiving, Win. Yes, my blood brothers and I all had a relatively normal childhood, but my adopted ones? They each have shadows that lurk beneath the bed. My parents felt like it was their job to give them some normalcy, some stability, and at the same time, opened our eyes to life outside of our bubble. I think you'd be surprised by what I understand."

Winnie shakes her head, and those soft curls bounce against her flawless skin. After a few moments of silence, she turns in her seat to face me. Inhaling a large breath, she flashes a determined gaze on me and lets her truth fly. "My father's an alcoholic. A mean one. The only time he ever came around was to scare or embarrass me. He liked to yell to anyone listening that my mom had brainwashed me into believing he was the enemy. He didn't realize that I knew he was bad news from the time I was four. I don't have a single memory of him where I wasn't terrified. My stepdad, Dennis, was amazing, but he just left one

29

day. He gave my mother a note, saying the infertility issues they were experiencing were too much for him, but I never got a chance to say good-bye." Her voice wavers, and I gently squeeze her hand. I only now realize I'm still holding it.

Straightening her spine, she continues, "Mom and I ... well, we were both kind of blindsided by Dennis leaving. It really messed her up for a long time. I thought she was over it, but I guess my dad came around one night when she felt particularly lonely. She had tried for so long with Dennis, so I think she thought she couldn't have children anymore. Anyway, one thing led to another with my father, and Wes is the result. She found him a few months later to tell him, and he shoved her. Told her to get rid of it because he wasn't going to pay for another useless waste of space like he did with me." She chuckles humorlessly. "The funny thing is he never paid a cent in child support for me."

"Jesus Christ, your mother told you all that?" It slips out before I can censor it. A wave of irrational anger holds my breath hostage as I wait for the rest of her answer.

My words startle Winnie, and her mouth drops open in shock. The expression on her face tells me everything I need to know. She doesn't open up to anyone, definitely not strangers, yet she's sitting here with me and just told me something deeply personal.

A caveman instinct I didn't realize I had beats against my chest at that knowledge.

"She would never have told me that," she replies, aghast. "I had driven her, and we went in together. It wasn't the type of place either of us should go into alone. When she told me she was going to seek him out, I came home and made her promise to wait for me. I was standing beside her, and he didn't even recognize me, but Wes and I look just like him."

"You're so strong, Winnie."

"This really wasn't my story to tell." Her response is solemn, and I wonder if she feels like she betrayed her mom's confidence.

"I would have to disagree with that, Win. It sounds to me like it's just as much your story as it is hers. It also shows me how much you care *about* them and how much you take care *of* them. I think if my father had treated me the way yours did, I probably would be skeptical of all men."

"I am. I mean, usually I am. You must have caught me on an off day."

I feel her retreating before she even tries to stand. When she does, I know I'll have to let her go, but I'm compelled to say something.

Think, Colton.

Then it comes to me.

"I told you I come from a ridiculously large family of boys. Privilege was something my parents understood. So was consent and what the two could mean for all of us."

"Ah, okay?" She stares down at me with apprehension.

"My point is, I was in first grade when I had my first lesson in consent. My best friend, Rylan, was over. We were playing in the sand, and she had my favorite truck. It was mine, and I wanted it. As soon as I took it from her, my dad sat down next to us, removed the truck from my grasp, handed it back to Rylan, and explained consent. What it meant. Why it was important. Why we always had to ask, never take, and learn to walk away if someone said no."

"That was pretty progressive thinking back then."

I smile, remembering all the conversations I had over the years with my dad.

"It was, but it was important to my parents that we not end up the statistic of so many other entitled assholes. Listen, Winnie, I'm not expecting or even asking anything of you. I have no idea why it's so important for me to sit here with you tonight, but I'd very much like to spend this time with you." Raising my hands, palms facing her, I give my best puppy dog face. "No touching. Just talking. But if you say no,

I'll head to the hotel and leave you alone. I might cry, but I'll do it."

"I don't really understand what your lesson in consent has to do with me. Or why you would willingly give up a five-star hotel to sit in an airport all night just to talk."

"I'm telling you because it sounds like your dad and stepdad took something from you without your consent … your right to feel safe, and your trust in men. I don't know how to explain the connection I feel to you. But, on my father's memory, I promise, I'll never take something from you without permission. Now, if you want to give me your number tomorrow, I wouldn't say no, though."

Flashing her my best dimpled grin, I waggle my eyebrows, and she flops back into her seat, silently shaking her head. "I'm going to regret this, I think."

"I won't," I reply confidently, nudging her shoulder with mine.

She quirks an eyebrow, glancing down at where our shoulders touch.

"Shoulders don't count as touching, do they? If that's the case, we're going to need a seat separating us. I barely fit in this chair as it is."

Her laughter is the only response.

"Tell me about your family, Winnie. The ones who matter. You already know I come from a football team of boys that suffer from a communication deficit. What's yours like?"

She watches me for long moments, and my body heats under her curious gaze. Reaching up, I loosen my tie and undo the button around my collar. She regards each movement, causing the flutter in my chest to take flight.

"Well, my mom and I work opposite shifts so one of us can always be home with Wes." She smiles at the mention of him, her affection written all over her face.

"Can I see a picture of him?"

She eyes me curiously but pulls out her phone. My chest

32

tightens when I see her home screen is a shot of the two of them. When she hands me the phone, my lips twitch with a familiar happiness.

"You two look a lot alike," I comment. Staring at the picture, I find similarities between Wes and me, too. He could easily pass as our child, and that thought has me dropping her phone into my lap like it scalded me. Pulling myself together, I pick up the phone and hand it back to her.

"You think so? He has more of our mom in him, but most people think he's mine. I just assumed that was because of the age thing."

"Winnie and Wes. I like it."

I more than like it. I like her, and it feels dangerous. Flashes of first dates, holidays, and romantic getaways flit across my vision like a highlight reel, and I have to rein it in. Winnie could live in Hong Kong for all I know. Suddenly, not knowing all the details of this magical woman beside me feels like a safety net.

"Wendalyn and Weston, actually."

"Weston?"

"That's his name," she says, barely containing the *duh* intonation in her words.

"He would fit right in with my family," I remark darkly.

"Oh yeah? Why's that? The blond hair and obscenely good looks?"

Fuck me. I like knowing Winnie thinks I'm good looking.

"That," I say gruffly, "and his name. My brothers' names are Preston, Easton, Halton, and Ashton. My father's name was Clinton. There's kind of a theme."

"That's a *ton* of boys for sure." She giggles, and it makes my chest itch, but I chuckle along with her.

"It's definitely a ton of boys." My stomach growls, and I glance at my watch. "We need to find some food before everything closes."

Winnie's body shrinks slightly at my words. I immediately

hate it. Reaching into her bag, she pulls out some granola bars. "I'm all set, but don't let me keep you."

I place my hands on my hips and give my best Sylvie Westbrook impersonation. No one pushes food quite like my mother, and no one says no to her.

"Want to play a game, Winnie?"

"What kind of game?" she challenges. Her competitive spark speaks to my soul.

Well shit. I didn't think this through. I examine our surroundings to buy myself a few seconds as a plan forms.

"What time's your flight tomorrow?"

Her eyes dart everywhere but on me. She's nervous around me. Rightly so. I'm still technically a stranger, but hopefully not for long.

"Ten," she finally admits. "What time is yours?"

Chuckling, I shake my head. "I have no idea."

"What? How do you not know? Where are you going?" She's truly in shock at my indifference to my travel plans.

"I've been preoccupied. It's not the end of the world if I catch a different flight. For some reason, the only thing that mattered tonight was getting to know you."

"Charmer," she murmurs.

"Would it make you feel better if I checked?"

She furrows her brow, and her teeth sink into the right corner of her bottom lip. I widen my stance because staring at those lips makes me want to sink my own teeth into them and my lower anatomy is behaving like a teenage boy.

Tearing my gaze away, I pull out my phone and open the American Airlines app on my phone. When I see ten a.m. as my flight time, those hornets in my chest buzz again.

"I'm going to Puerto Vallarta, at ten a.m. Where are you going, Winnie?"

Her eyes widen in surprise, and I have my answer.

"Maybe you'll meet your Wendy."

The memory of GG's words startles me.

"Flight 1918. American?" she asks quietly.

Relief and fear fight for top billing in my emotional storage closet right now, but I push them both aside.

"Yup," I say, full of swagger I don't feel. "Looks like we're headed in the same direction, sweet Winnie. So," mentally, I calculate our timing, "we have just over twelve hours left to get to know each other. We'll alternate hours."

"Alternate hours to do what, exactly?" She's skeptical but curious, too.

"Whatever the hell we want. You choose during your hour, and I'll do whatever you want. When it's my hour, you do it my way."

"I'm not sleeping with you, a complete stranger, in an airport."

"Does that mean you'd sleep with me outside of an airport?" I can't help myself.

Laugher escapes, even though she attempts to suppress it. "Not happening, Pan."

I flinch at her words, but recover quickly.

"You don't like your nickname."

I shrug, unsure of how to answer.

"How'd you get it?"

"It's a long story."

"We have twelve hours," she says with a smirk.

Gripping the back of my neck, I give it a rough squeeze before placing my hand back on my hip. "Fine. I'll tell you, but over dinner, because I'm fucking starving. My treat because I think I'll enjoy watching you eat."

Why the fuck did I just say that? I sound like a perv. But it's also one hundred percent true.

"I've never been one to shy away from food, obviously." Her hands sweep over her body, and a low groan escapes. I pray she didn't hear it, but when her cheeks turn a delicious shade of pink, I know she did, so I go all in.

Taking two steps forward, I lean down into her space—not

quite touching, but too close to be polite. Electric awareness shoots between us.

"I love women, Winnie. I always have. But do you know how many have captured my attention enough to give up sleep, the one thing I love even more than women?"

She swallows. Then swallows again but says nothing.

"One. When I saw you, I was talking to my brother, ready to move full steam ahead to a luxurious hotel room. Your nose was scrunched up in concentration and the world literally faded around me. No one captures my attention like this. No one but you, and that scares the shit out of me. But I'm here. I'm all in. Your eyes drew me to you. Your curls that look soft as silk held me captive. Your curves scatter my mind in a hundred different directions, but it's your sass and strength that have kept me here. So, yes, I would very much like to watch you enjoy a meal with me. My body buzzes with awareness when I'm near you. I won't lie about finding you so fucking attractive that my brain is having a hard time focusing, but I also won't act on it unless you want me to. For the next twelve hours, all I want to do is learn everything I can about you." Licking my lips, I lower my voice. It takes on a gravelly nature that has me wishing I had a glass of water. "Is that okay with you, Winnie?"

My eyes dart back and forth between hers. Our connection is so intense I'm surprised sparks aren't shooting around us.

"Obviously," she croaks and tries again. "Obviously, you don't suffer the same communication barriers as your family."

A slow, dangerous smile spreads wide across my face. I feel it all the way to the corner of my eyes.

"Baby, I'll always tell you what I want, and right now, I want to find a place to have dinner before everything closes. Please say you're in."

With a look of determination, she returns my smile. That sense of danger. Competition. Finding my equal slaps me across the face as I stare into her sparkling gray depths.

"Your eyes are ridiculously sexy," I growl, but then step back, worried I'm going to scare her away if I don't get my shit under control.

Offering my hand, I hold my breath, silently praying she takes it.

"Twelve hours?"

"Twelve hours and then we'll renegotiate." I wink, mentally high fiving myself when she slips her hand into mine.

CHAPTER 5

WINNIE

*C*olton walks beside me, carrying our haul.

"So, are you meeting someone in Mexico?"

Why the hell did I ask that?

His smirk sets off butterflies in my stomach. "I may be Peter Pan, Win, but I don't have the moral compass of Captain Hook. If I were seeing someone, I wouldn't be working so hard to get to know you." He raises one eyebrow, and heat creeps across my cheeks. I work really hard not to roll my eyes. His deep belly laugh causes me to misstep, and even with his hands full, he manages to catch my elbow so I don't topple over. When he knows I'm steady on my feet again, he withdraws. "My brother's marrying my best friend. I'm meeting my entire family there. What about you?"

"My brother isn't old enough to get married."

His laughter echoes in the empty hallway and wraps my body in warmth.

"I meant, what are you doing in Mexico, smart ass?"

A genuine smile lights up my face. Our banter is easy. It's fun, and I'm afraid it could be addicting. *It's fine for this twelve hours, Wendalyn, but we are very clearly on different paths in life.*

The voice of reason that has always kept the fun at bay douses my joy. Colton notices before I do.

"I was just playing with you, Win."

Shaking my head, I force a smile into place. "Right, sorry. I was thinking of something else. Um, I'm actually going to Mexico to work for a couple of weeks. Some rich family is having a reunion and they're paying me to be their beck and call babysitter. The pay is so good, I'm willing to do just about anything to make it through the next two weeks. It'll help take some of the pressure off once I get to law school."

"I thought you were studying. Have you already applied to schools?"

"Yes, and I received acceptance letters to every school I applied to. I'm retaking my LSAT, though. I got into law school with the one-sixty, but I need to do better for me."

"Determined."

"Competitive."

"I can respect that. So, where are you staying while in Mexico?"

"Ah …" I hesitate just long enough for him to know he's made me uncomfortable.

Raising his hands, he shakes his head. "No worries if you're not comfortable telling me. I shouldn't have pressed."

What about this man makes me want to spill all my secrets?

"No, it's not that. It's just, I don't really know, and I probably shouldn't be outing the family I'm working for. I had to sign an NDA and everything. But I'm not technically staying in Puerto Vallarta. I think it's called Punta Mita."

A sly smile makes Colton's dimples stand out, and blood rushes to my cheeks. Suddenly, I feel the need to fan myself, so I quickly survey the surrounding area.

"I know Punta Mita well. Maybe we'll cross paths again, my sweet Winnie."

Of course he does.

"I'm going to be working. A lot. So, we probably won't."

"Mhmm." He stops walking, and I realize we're back at our original spot. "This is bullshit," he grumbles, staring at the food in his hands.

After learning all the restaurants in the terminal were already closed, he attempted to have food delivered, but TSA wouldn't let it through security. He could have left, but the agent informed him he wouldn't be able to get back to this side of the airport for a few hours. His options were to stay with me and buy out the vending machines or leave and get a good night's sleep at his friend's hotel. He stayed with me, and I'm not sure how to handle the emotions his actions are causing.

"You should go to the hotel," I try again, hating how tense my body is waiting for his response.

"Not happening. But you're telling me they couldn't let a pizza through?"

I shrug as he nods with his head to the seats we had vacated not that long ago. Once we're settled, he holds up questionable nachos and a shriveled up hot dog.

"Pick your poison."

My eyes dart between the two choices, and finally, I point to the nachos.

"Good choice," he acknowledges as he hands them over with a bottle of water.

Reaching down to grab the bag he'd placed beside him, he upends it on the table in front of us. Chips, candy bars, cookies, Pop-Tarts, and trail mix tumble out onto the table.

"Not exactly the dinner I wanted to offer you, but beggars can't be choosers, I guess."

Nudging his shoulder, I attempt to lighten his mood. He's pouting over snacks, and I'm not sure why I find it so endearing. "I was planning to have granola bars, remember? This is like a four-course meal."

"I'm claiming a re-do. This is not what you're going to remember as our first date."

41

I choke on my water so hard it flies out of my nose. Chuckling, he holds a napkin to my face like I'm a toddler.

"Presumptuous much? We never discussed a date," I say when I've semi-composed myself.

Now it's Colton's turn to blush, and I have the irresistible urge to run my fingers through his gorgeous, dirty blond hair. Luckily, he recovers quickly before I do something stupid.

"Are you seeing anyone, Winnie?"

He's so blunt that he constantly catches me off guard. I don't have time to school my expression.

"Newly single?" he guesses.

"Ah, yeah. Sort of. I moved out three days ago."

"What happened? If you don't mind me asking?"

Am I imagining it, or did he tense up just now?

As I try to come up with an excuse, I can't help but replay all the information he's given me about his family. I'll probably never see him again, so I guess I have nothing to lose.

"I was at work and I got a notification on my phone. For the nights I watch Wes, I have a baby monitor in my living room. And it was strange because no one was supposed to be home, so I logged on thinking someone had broken into my apartment."

This time, I feel Colton tense beside me, but he keeps his gaze neutral as he waits for me to continue.

"Ah, it wasn't an intruder. Travis was hooking up with my best friend on the sofa. I took a screenshot, sent it to them, and moved out that afternoon."

"Jesus. What the hell kind of friend does that?" His face is adorable even when he's angry, I realize.

"It doesn't matter. Both relationships were probably over a long time ago, anyway." I shrug my shoulders, but can't quite look at him.

"You're very calm about all of this," he observes.

"I'm focused on moving on."

"But something like that has to sting."

Sadness threatens to creep into my heart, but I force it down.

"I should have known better, Colton. There are very few people in this world who haven't let me down in some way. It's made me who I am, and I'm okay with that."

The sincerity in his expression is almost enough to make me believe in a happily ever after. "I'm sorry they hurt you, Winnie. But mostly, I'm sorry you don't have more people in your life to count on. Not everyone's like that, you know? Someday you'll find the people you were meant to be with. Don't lump us all in with those who hurt you because you might miss out on the best parts of life."

I don't miss how he slipped himself into that sentence, and I have to wonder if he even realizes it. He doesn't give me long to process any of it though, because once again, he's full steam ahead and dragging me with him.

"Have you ever speed dated?"

Thankfully, I had no water in my mouth this time, or I would have repeated my less than ladylike snort. "No. I … ah, I've never had much time to date, and now I'm getting ready for law school."

"Sexy and smart," he says, clutching his chest. "Would it scare you if I told you I like that you don't have time for dating? Well," he scowls, "I like that you don't have time to date anyone else. But, Winnie, we have twelve hours."

"And?" My voice sounds skeptical, but my insides are a flutter of anticipation.

"I want to speed date you."

Wrapping my arms around my waist, I angle my body away from him. *Danger. Danger. Danger,* rings out in my head out of habit, but I tamp it down with a forceful shove. Maybe it's his smile, his swagger, the way he always seems to be memorizing my face, but I want this time with him. If nothing else, it will give me fodder for fantasies for the foreseeable future because men like him don't exist in my world.

"For fun. Twelve hours. Twelve dates. Whatever we can come up with. What do you say?" he prods again.

"I'm still not sleeping with you." *Jesus.* I can't even say that with a straight face.

"Fair enough." He returns my goofy grin. "Is that a yes?"

Tossing my hands in the air, I do something I never do. I throw caution to the wind, and hope for the best. No to-do lists. No pros versus cons. I simply jump in headfirst, somehow knowing Colton won't let me fall. "Sure! Why not? Our first date starts now, though. Tell me about your nickname."

"First date. Get to know you? Is this how you want to spend our first hour?"

"Yes. It most definitely is." I don't even try to keep the excitement out of my voice this time.

"Okay, then. Dig in." He points to my nachos, takes a bite of the vending machine hotdog, and tries to choke it down. "My brothers all take after my dad in some way. Preston has his need to protect. Easton got his temper. Halton got his artistic ability. Ash ..." He grows quiet, and a flash of sadness takes over his entire body. "Ash has his sense of duty, I think." Shaking his head, he forces a smile as he stares through me. "Me? I got his sense of humor. My family has been through some shit the last few years. Heavy, sad, sometimes scary shit, and I feel an overwhelming need to bring levity to them all. My dad loved practical jokes. Really loved them. When he passed, I took over, trying to make everyone laugh. I'm not irresponsible. I'm not trying to stay young forever, but I am selfish. I don't want a family until I know I can give them my everything. So, my brothers think my love of life, my need to make them laugh, and my refusal to settle down yet as Peter Pan. It doesn't bother me that much, so it's not worth trying to correct them."

"But that also means they don't really understand you."

His head tilts to the side, and he pinches the back of his neck with his free hand. He's done that a few times, and I'm noticing it's his unconscious way of dealing with discomfort. "Maybe," he finally acknowledges. "But my brothers have been through a lot. They've dealt with some pretty intense things alone in a misguided attempt to protect us all. We all get that from my dad, too. However, when the time comes, I know they'll realize I'm not living in Neverland."

"Do you think you're trying to do the same thing by not letting them in? By pretending to be the happy-go-lucky brother?"

Colton leans back as he regards me, slowly nodding with his lips turned down.

"Maybe, Winnie. I never thought of it like that, but I'm also happy with my life the way it is for now, so maybe they have a point. I don't think I'm pretending to be happy. Right now, I have nothing to hold me back. I like to have fun, so why not drag them all into it with me?"

"Well, I don't think you're a lost boy, Colton. Not from the way you describe it. Someday you'll find the thing or the person worth settling down for."

He holds my gaze for an uncomfortably long time. I'm not prone to fidgeting, but suddenly the invisible lint on my pants is easier to stare at, and I glance away. When I steel my nerve to sneak a peek in his direction, I find smoldering eyes focused entirely on me. I've never understood how someone could smolder, but Colton Montgomery is a prime example.

"When I find the woman worth growing up for, I promise you, I'll be all the man she needs."

His words make me shiver. In the quiet of the deserted airport terminal, his words feel as though he's speaking them not just to me, but about me. It's a ridiculous notion, and I'm not prone to childish fantasies, but for the briefest of moments, I can envision him as my future. Shaking my head, I pop another nacho into my mouth and don't miss the heat that fills his gaze as he watches my lips move.

Holy freaking intense.

"Ah, so what kind of pranks do you do?"

His face transforms, and I can suddenly picture him as a little boy. Dirt on his hands, grass stains on his knees, and always, always causing trouble. The vision is adorable, but the man is breathtaking.

"Anything with glitter. Nothing pisses off grown men quite like glitter. That shit gets everywhere. And when you pour it by the gallon into swimming pools, car filters, and water guns?" He howls with laughter. "I swear, they piss glitter for days."

I'm laughing with him as I envision grown men I've never seen covered in sparkly colors.

"Do your brothers look like you?" I ask when my side hurts from laughing.

"We're all slightly different versions of our dad, so yeah." The laughter dies with each passing word. I open my mouth to apologize for saying something wrong, but he cuts me off. "So, law school? That's what you were studying when I rudely interrupted you earlier?"

"Yeah. I wasn't as prepared as I should have been the first time I took the LSAT. I want to do better."

"One-sixty is pretty good, isn't it?"

"It is, but I want one-seventy. I can get one-seventy. I know I can."

Colton tilts his head, studying me in a way that makes my skin feverish. "Wow. Impressive. What kind of law?"

"Women's rights," I mumble. "Family law, I think."

Surprise crosses his face, but he recovers quickly. "Have you always wanted to be a lawyer or is this, ah, new?"

"I thought I would be a therapist." I laugh, but it's humorless, and I shrug my shoulders to ease some of the tension that settled there when I wasn't paying attention. "After everything my mom has gone through with my dad, I realized I wanted to help people, but in a different way. My psychology degree didn't exactly prepare me for law school, though, so I've been taking a few classes to get ready."

"Does your mom need an attorney?"

The way he asks, I get the feeling he would have one at my doorstep if I said the word. It's an odd feeling to get from a stranger, but peering into his intense gaze, I know I'm right.

"Not right now, but my dad is always doing stupid shit. He threatened to sue her for custody of Wes not that long ago. He would never win, but it scared us both."

"You're an incredible woman, Winnie." His words hold a conviction that brooks no room for argument.

He's going to make a great partner someday. The thought of him with a wife and kids makes my stomach clench, and I have to get myself under control.

It doesn't help that my body preens under his praise, so I force myself to avert my gaze. Thankfully, we're interrupted by my phone buzzing in my lap. Glancing down, I see my mom's face and I fumble with my phone, attempting to answer it quickly.

"Hi, Mom. Everything okay?"

Her face comes into view, and I frown. She looks exhausted. "Sorry, hunny. Wes is missing you. You know how much he likes his routine."

"Shit. His song."

She smiles, but it's forced. "Yeah. You have a minute to sing to him?"

"Of course." Colton's leg presses into mine, and I realize with a start that I'm about to completely embarrass myself in front of the hottest man I've ever met in my life. Internally I cringe, but there's not much I wouldn't do for Wes.

As I stand, I feel Colton studying me. Taking a few steps, I prop the phone up on the windowsill and move into the frame just as Weston's pudgy, little face appears.

"Bubba! I miss you, buddy." Warmth fills my chest for this little guy. "Ready for na-nights?"

"We-We!" He does his best jazz hands, and I plaster on a smile as I sing the Violent Femmes, "Blister In The Sun".

Colton's bark of laughter adds to the soundtrack of my humiliation, but staring into the happy face of my baby brother, I force myself to continue. When I hit the chorus, I reach to the ceiling, doing my best impression of a tree in the wind, and as the tempo picks up, I shake my jazz hands like my life depends on it. When the song winds down to a whisper, I lower my voice but continue the same dance routine I've done nearly every night since he was born. Weston follows along as best he can while his eyelids become heavy.

After a few minutes of whispering the chorus, his eyes remain closed, and I know he's out. The screen pans to my mom, and she whispers a thank you. I do the same and blow her a kiss.

I take a few deep breaths before I garner enough courage to face Colton. When I do, his face is an unreadable mask.

"You sing your baby brother to sleep with a song about masturbation?" Humor laces every syllable.

"That's never been proven," I say haughtily. "Even Gordon Gano hasn't confirmed it, and someone asked him point-blank in an interview."

Colton stands with a smirk on his handsome face and closes the space between us in just a few strides. "Is that so?" he queries when he's close enough to touch.

"Yes," I reply, defiantly raising my chin in a huff.

"Baby, I haven't listened to that song since I was a teenager, but I can promise you, it'll now be the soundtrack to my late-night fantasies for an entirely new reason." His voice is low, gravelly, and it hits every nerve in my female anatomy.

This man is sexy, and I'm playing with fire, but I've never been one to back down either. I'm used to taking care of myself so I can hold my own in this battle of sexy innuendo.

"Big hands, Colton. They may blister in the sun, but can they light the inferno between the sheets?"

He growls. His eyes blaze with a carnal need I've never experienced in real life, and I take an involuntary step back.

"Abso-fucking-lutely."

The way he drawls the word fucking has a squeak sneaking out of the back of my throat. *Maybe he won this round after all.* My gaze follows his as he glances at his watch. A predatory grin on his face.

"My turn."

Gulp.

CHAPTER 6

COLTON

"*M*y turn," I tell her. "Date number two. I think we should continue the *get to know you* phase with some games."

Winnie's throat works past the second vocal gulp in a matter of minutes, and when she speaks, her voice trembles with nerves that she valiantly attempts to tamp down. "What kind of games?"

I grin. Drop my gaze to her lips, and my grin grows impossibly larger.

"My brother had a lot of luck winning over his wife playing Never Have I Ever."

Her hands fly to her luscious hips, and I clench my jaw to keep from groaning. Jesus, what I wouldn't do to give those hips a squeeze. Hard. Realizing that I'm literally glaring at her midsection, I tug on my collar again and refocus my gaze.

"Was he sixteen when they met?" she asks sarcastically.

That fucking mouth.

I shake my head. "Are you scared, Winnie?" Something tells me she won't back down from a challenge.

"Pfft. As if. This is a drinking game, though. Unless you

bribed an attendant for mini bottles of liquor when I was in the bathroom, we're out of luck."

"We can always modify the rules, Win." My tone is smooth confidence, yet I feel anything but suave around her. I'm on edge and insecure. Not two emotions I'm used to. I also can't seem to keep the distance between us, and my feet move of their own accord in her direction. "The first one to raise their hand for ten never have I evers loses, and has to choose truth or dare."

Her smile is tentative as she shakes her head. Keeping her gaze averted, she whispers, "I'm going to regret this, aren't I?"

Oh, baby, but it will feel so good.

"I'll never make you do anything you don't want to." It's important to me that she realizes I'm not like the other men in her life. "Are you ready, Winnie?"

She nods, and I hold her gaze. "Never have I ever been kissed so good in an airport that I forgot my name."

She narrows her eyes, but raises her hand.

"Never have I ever had sex on an airplane." She smirks, confident in the question, but her eyes go comically round when I don't raise my hand. "Bullshit. You're telling me you've had sex on a plane before?"

I nod slowly, never allowing her to break eye contact as that information sinks in.

"How is that even possible? You're like a giant. How would you even fit?" She stops mid-sentence and holds her hand up to stop me from speaking. "Never mind. I don't want to know details."

"I don't always fly commercial, Win. My turn." Her pupils dilating is my only indication that I'm ruffling her. "Are you ready, sweetheart?"

With her face in flames, she nods.

"Never have I ever been arrested."

Winnie huffs as she raises her hand.

This is almost too easy.

~

"*I*'m pretty sure you tricked me," Winnie complains.

"Sweetheart," I coo, "there was no trickery involved. I won fair and square."

She stands across from me with her hands fisted at her hips. Ample hips that squish in slightly where her fists press against her sides. Winnie is a gorgeous woman. Beautiful in a way that's real. Curves in all the right places with enough on her bones to grab hold of without fearing you'll break her. I've always hated that about the women I've dated in the past—predominantly models with bones protruding that make you think they're fragile, even if they're vipers. I have a feeling I could grab hold of Winnie and lose myself in her completely.

Her cream-colored sweater is cropped just above the high-waisted jeans she's wearing, allowing a hint of skin to show when she moves. She isn't waif-like, but her tummy is flat and smooth, and my gaze flits to that barest glimpse of skin whenever it appears.

Winnie crosses her arms over her chest, and that fucking sweater rises just a fraction more.

"Fine. Dare."

"You're choosing dare?" My tone reflects my shock.

Her chin raises defiantly, and my jaw ticks. The effort of not pinning her to the wall is nearly unbearable.

"I am," she says matter-of-factly.

As my gaze scans her head to toe, I rub my chin with my thumb and forefinger. I'm fucking delighted when the faintest blush reappears across her cheeks.

"How about if we save the rewards for the end?"

"Fine," she huffs out and marches over to her bag. Leaning down, she pulls out a notebook and pen.

When I step closer, I see she's making a winner and a loser column. She likes to keep score.

Game on, baby.

"What's next?"

"It's your hour. Your turn to choose."

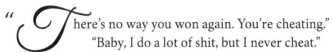

"There's no way you won again. You're cheating."

"Baby, I do a lot of shit, but I never cheat."

Her eyes narrow in frustration. She wasn't lying when she said she's competitive.

"Dance off," she nearly shouts.

The bark of laughter that falls from my lips has her face frowning and turning all shades of red.

"You're sexy as hell when you're pissed off."

"Dance. Off," she repeats.

Having tossed my suit coat hours ago, I slowly roll up the sleeves of my dress shirt.

"You're on. Name your terms."

"We choose a song for the other person, and you have to dance to whatever plays."

"What determines the winner?"

"Sexiest dance wins." The way her eyes shimmer, I know she's about to play dirty. I fucking love dirty.

"Game. On. Sweetheart. Play my song."

The arch of her perfectly sculpted eyebrow raises a fraction. I know I laid down the gauntlet and I cannot wait for this to play out. She points a long finger to the other side of the aisle, so I take my time walking away from her and wait for the song to play.

Bump. Bump. Bump, comes out clearly through her phone's speakers. I know immediately what song it is. As "Build Me Up Buttercup" by The Foundations starts, I throw my head back and laugh while I sway my shoulders to the beat. Lowering my gaze, I focus on one thing, and one thing only. The sexiest woman I've ever met in my life, Winnie.

I spin in place, kicking a foot out at the end as I let the old-timey music filter through my soul. I pull out all the moves as I stalk toward Winnie, sitting alone in her chair. Clutching my chest, I act out the words, then go all in. Her eyes grow large as I charge forward at full speed and drop to my knees. Shock registers on her face as I slide across the floor, landing at her feet, and rip my shirt open. Buttons fly everywhere as she laughs. Knowing I made her this happy makes those caveman tendencies spring to life again, and I'd swear I was the king of the goddamn world right now.

Slowly, I place my hands on either side of her legs. My thighs burn with effort as I crawl inch by inch up her body until I'm standing, bent over her. My lips are mere inches from hers. The scent of her weaves its way through my conscious, and I know I'm branded by her.

"I need you, darling," I sing, taking liberties with the lyrics, but my voice is strained with the effort of not breaching the distance between us.

I want her lips on me more than I can remember wanting anything in a very long time.

"Wh-What do you do for work, Pan? Do you moonlight as an exotic dancer? There's no way you should have been able to make that song sexy."

Grinning, I give into temptation. Ever so slowly, I lean in and press my lips to her cheek. When she gasps, I linger a few more seconds before whispering in her ear, "I can make anything sexy if I'm staring at you, darlin'."

Eventually, I stand to my full height and cross my arms over my chest. I don't miss the way her gaze lingers on my tight undershirt that's straining over my muscles because every fucking inch of me is wound tight. No one has ever gotten under my skin like this, but she's there, planted firmly. Somewhere in the back of my mind, I know I'll never be the same after this night.

"I have a feeling everything you do is sexy," she grumbles.

"Right back atcha, baby. My turn." I curl my pointer finger

at her, indicating it's time for her to stand. Pulling my phone from my pocket, I smile wickedly, already knowing what I want her to dance to.

Boom. Crash. Boom. Crash.

The dark, dangerous, rhythmic beat of the bass and snare drums echo in the otherwise quiet space. Winnie's eyes flash with warning. She recognizes the song and I blink innocently. "Closer" by Nine Inch Nails. Her gaze flits all around, searching the empty space, and lingers on the camera above us. I'm about to tell her she doesn't have to go through with it when her face transforms. She's gorgeous in every moment, but when she sets her mind to something, she's downright mesmerizing.

I'm in fucking trouble. The crass, raunchy lyrics pick up, and her body flows toward me as if she were made from the song itself. Her legs and hips move in time to the beat. Heel-toe. Heel-toe. Heel-toe. One. Two. Three. Four. Until she's maneuvered herself between my legs. Her long arms glide up her side to the curve of her breast, and I swallow my response. Winnie grins. She knows she's winning this battle.

Her hips sway from side to side, and each movement hits the inside of my thighs. I shift in my seat to make room for the erection that's reaching for her. When she turns in place and bends over, my hands fly to her hips, and I thank my lucky stars when she doesn't swat them away. Instead, she lowers herself, hovering just inches above my cock. She's not touching me, but I can feel the heat radiating off her and it sends shock waves of pleasure rippling through my body.

If I can get this worked up just by being close to her, what the fuck will happen when I make her mine? I realize my mind has already made a decision where Winnie is concerned. Now I need to get her on board.

Shamelessly, my hips lift off the seat, aching for contact, and I don't even care that this is probably being recorded by some poor security guard in an office close by. Winnie tosses her hair over her shoulder, searching for my face. When our eyes meet, I lose all control.

"Turn around, Win."

Her mouth parts, but she follows my command. She knows what I want to do to her; the song sings it for me in the dirtiest of ways. But not here. Not now.

As she spins in place, I don't remove my hands. I can't. I may never be able to let her go. My fingers squeeze her hips, and they feel as delicious as I thought they would. Fingertips knead into her flesh as I inch forward. Or maybe she leans down, but our faces draw closer. Her gaze flicks to my mouth as my tongue runs across my dry bottom lip, but it doesn't help. I'm parched, and her mouth is the only liquid I need.

My heart is pounding wildly because she opens her mouth like she's going to say something. She's so close I can taste her breath. She's the sweetest thing I've ever touched.

Please don't pull away, I silently plead. There's an inferno raging inside of me. She'll either put it out or we'll combust from the sheer chemistry of us together as one. I'm not sure which I want more.

"One …" My voice is harsh and needy as I search her eyes for any sign that she's about to bolt. I don't even care that I'm about to beg this woman for a kiss. "One kiss, Win. Just one little—"

I don't get to finish that sentence because she catapults herself toward me. Lips and teeth smashing against one another. I was right. Explosive. My body goes up in flames as I taste her for the first time. I need this woman more than the air we share. It takes less than a second to recover and fully take over this kiss. If one is all I'll get today, I'll make sure she never forgets it.

Hooking my fingers into the belt loops of her jeans, I pull her down onto my lap. If I had any less self control, I would have come right then, but I focus on her lips that taste like cherry cola. While my brain fights over the taste of her, my

57

body works on autopilot. I deftly slip a hand into her curls and groan when I realize they're as soft as I imagined.

Closing my fingers around a fistful of them, I angle her face to the left while plundering my tongue deep into her mouth. I swallow her sexy moan and feel myself get painfully hard against her.

She's a feisty kisser, fighting for control, but there's no way I'm giving that up. I won't survive her if I do. Instead, I grip her cheeks with both hands. Our tongues are at war in an erotic dance that tastes like forever and promises I've never made before.

Winnie's hands grip my hair tightly, and it adds to the full body sensation that is all Winnie. Desire courses through my veins in a way I didn't know existed and couldn't put into words if I tried.

I lick, nip, and suck on her bottom lip until she grinds down on me, completely lost in the kiss. She's lost in me, and I want to fucking roar with gratitude. I have enough self-awareness not to let this go too far, but Jesus Christ. Knowing how easily we get lost in each other is like a drug I never want to give up.

Every nerve ending in my body is keyed up. Electric. A rumble starts deep in my chest, and I know no other kiss will ever compare. The sound brings Win back to the present, and her eyelids flutter open. Her eyes are more teal than gray right now, but they're dazed, foggy, and I'm thankful she's as affected by this kiss as I am.

I know she's about to pull away, so I lean in for a gentle peck. Lips to lips. Soft but firm. She blinks in rapid succession, confusion, fear, and lust flitting across her expression. I can't bear to think she regrets the best kiss of my damn life, so I pull her head into my chest.

"That was, ah, fucking incredible, CC," I admit, forcing air into my lungs.

Winnie mumbles, and I realize I have a death grip on her head, pressing her to me. Relaxing my hold, she inhales deeply.

She releases a small sigh on an exhale, and my chest puffs up with pride. She can sniff all she wants. I'm certainly memorizing everything about her, from the way she smells to the way she feels and sounds. Even as I catalog her to memory, I know I won't be letting her go.

When my brain works again, I answer her question. "No lap dances in my day job. I work for my family's company. A lot of boring business meetings, planning, and putting out fires multiple times a day."

"Yeah? Well, if that doesn't work out for you, I think you could have a future in performing. Did you call me CC now?"

Brushing the curls back from her face, I wait until she raises her gaze to mine. When she does, my throat goes impossibly dry. I could fall for this girl.

"Only for you, baby. These hips don't move like that for anyone but you. And yes, my CC, I did. You taste like cherry cola, and it's my new favorite flavor."

She very indelicately rolls her eyes, but I keep quiet because her fingers are tracing the outline of my torn shirt and I grind my teeth to keep from saying something stupid. Something like, "I need to fuck you like an animal."

"You ruined your shirt."

I shrug because I don't give a fuck about the custom Armani. "I'll replace it. The memory is more than worth it."

Winnie pulls away and slides off my lap. She appears shy, embarrassed, and I can't have that. I'm standing before she can get lost in that head of hers.

"I would ruin a thousand shirts if it meant I got to see you do that again, sweetheart. You're my new favorite memory."

She blushes, but at least she's smiling.

"This," she says waving her hands frantically, "is so …"

"Unlike you?"

Her head whips up to find my proud expression waiting for her. "Yeah. I don't tend to be the fun one. I-I'm a planner. I'm the one who makes sure everyone has a ride home at the end of the night."

"You take care of everyone."

"Yeah. It helps me feel safe, I think."

"You like control, and that's an admirable way to live, baby. But sometimes? Sometimes it's okay to give up control to someone you know you can trust. It makes living a hell of a lot more interesting."

"I trust you?" Her words are a breath above a whisper and asked as a question, like she's only now realizing she's comfortable with me.

"And trust doesn't come easy to you?"

She shakes her head.

"Well, baby, I'm fucking ecstatic that I'm the one you put your trust in."

She nods. A fake smile is plastered to her face, and I can tell she needs a few minutes alone.

"I'm going to grab my carry-on and go change. I'll be right back, okay?"

"Mhm. Okay."

"I think it's my turn now. Why don't you pick a movie on Netflix, and we'll just chill for a bit?"

"Sure. Sounds good."

I walk toward the restroom, glancing at her frowning face over my shoulder. I may have gotten my kiss, but if I want more with this girl, I need to find a way past her emotional armor. I pause mid-stride.

Is that what I want with her? More? The possibility of more? Scrubbing a hand over my face, I sigh as a frown forms on me, too.

We're both lost in thought when I return, and we start the movie in silence, but I'd bet money neither of us is paying it any attention.

*C*olton: Do you believe in love at first sight?

Lochlan: Shite, it's four in the fucking morning.

Lochlan: Why are you up and not resting that pretty boy face in my hotel?

Lochlan: (Eye roll emoji) I don't bloody know, mate. I guess anything is possible. Why? Are you wankered?

Colton: You're more American than British at this point, arsehole. Use words I don't have to look up. Wankered? No, I'm not wasted. I'm asking because you'll give me less shit than my brothers. Don't make me regret this.

Lochlan: Can't help it, MAN. This is what happens when you wake me in the middle of the fecking night.

Lochlan: Who is this girl that has you staying up all night in a dirty airport?

Colton: Winnie. We're speed dating.

Colton: Well, we were until she fell asleep on me watching a movie.

Lochlan: If you're being a wanker while she sleeps, we cannot be friends anymore.

Colton: Fuck off. You're no longer my best friend.

What an asshole. In fact … let's make it official.

Colton: You're officially listed as Cack on my phone.

Cack: You're calling me a shite, mate? Seriously? What kind of voodoo magic does this girl have?

Colton: Picture sent.

As soon as I send the picture, I wish I could take it back. Winnie is asleep on my chest, but you can only see the side of her face. Her curls are a wild mess framing her delicate features. I hate I shared this moment with anyone.

She's mine.

Cack: You're good and well fucked.

Cack: My dad married Nova's mom after three days. He still contends that she was the love of his life. Anything's possible.

Cack: My advice is to see where it goes. Don't do your normal Pan shite if you like her. You're more than you let people see.

Colton: Fine. I'll change your name back.

Lochlan: Thanks, mate. Good luck.

Colton: There's room in the villa if you change your mind. Punta Mita? A wedding? How can you turn it down?

Lochlan: You know how I feel about weddings. And unlike you, I don't have a bunch of brothers to lean on. I actually have to work for a living.

Colton: You've always got the Westbrooks.

Lochlan: Appreciate that. Get some sleep. Keep me posted on the girl.

Colton: Winnie.

Lochlan: Right. You're fucked. Have fun with that, Pan.

Colton: (Middle finger emoji)

Lochlan: (Kissing face emoji)

Winnie shifts, and her head slides lower down my chest. Inching my ass forward, I position myself so she's comfortable. After a few moments, her head falls fully into my lap, and I absently rub my hand through her hair.

I'm staring at the side of her face as our speed dates flash before my eyes and I spend the rest of the night wondering what it all means.

CHAPTER 7

WINNIE

$\mathcal{I}$ wake with a start, pain piercing my neck with a cramp. It takes half a second to realize I'm lying on someone, but I'll remember his scent for the rest of my life. Pulling back, I find Colton smiling at me.

"Morning, baby." The low, sexy timbre of his sleepy voice causes a shiver to run up my spine. No one should sound that sexy at this hour. And hello! Baby?

"Er, morning? What time is it?"

"Eight forty-five. Flight boards in about half an hour."

I'm suddenly wide awake and aware of the people all around us. I'm also painfully aware of a wet spot on Colton's shorts where my face was. *Geez. I had to drool on the man?*

Straightening my spine, I push back fully into my own seat. "Ah, sorry. I never sleep that soundly."

"You'll never hear me complain, sweetheart."

Colton might be the most verbally affectionate person I've ever met in my life, and I'm utterly incapable of knowing what the hell to do with him. Focusing on his face, I notice dark circles under his eyes and guilt washes over me.

"You look tired. Did you sleep at all?" My forehead wrinkles with worry as I search his eyes.

His face softens with his smile, but his eyes sparkle with mischief. "Always taking care of everyone." He says it with a hint of awe, in reverence, and it plays out across his features. It's unnerving to have someone notice me like this. Really see me. And I get the impression Colton is taking in all of me.

"Excuse me?"

I glance up as a woman in an American Airlines uniform approaches us.

"Joanna, right?" Colton smiles warmly at the woman.

"Ah, yes. That's right. Mr. We—"

"Colton, please." He sits forward, placing a hand on my leg to keep me still. It's not a possessive grip, it's one that says, *I'll just be a minute, but I'm still paying attention to you.* That is not a Peter Pan move. It's a Prince Charming move, and it unnerves me.

"Colton." She nods, glances my way, then nervously returns to him. Whatever she wants to say, she obviously is uncomfortable having an audience.

Squeezing his hand, I place it back on the armrest between us, and Colton's worry lines appear around his eyes. They're gone in a flash, though, so I'm guessing they don't appear often. Is he Peter Pan or not? Geez, I'm spending way too much time worrying about someone I'll never see again once we land.

"I'm just going to run to the ladies' room. I'll be right back."

Colton reaches for my hand. So much for the no touching rule. Although honestly, I don't even care.

I nod with a smile. "I'll be right back."

"Okay, sweetheart."

Grabbing the handle of my carry-on, I bolt for the closest bathroom. I can only imagine what I look like.

When I reach the restroom, I'm thankful it's mostly empty. I quickly pee and change into a light summer dress because Lanie warned me it would be hot as hell when we arrive and getting through customs and security can take a while.

Once I've made myself as presentable as I can, I glance at

my reflection one more time, attempting to view myself as Colton sees me. I know I'm pretty, full enough to be considered plus size, even though a size twelve or fourteen is actually average. Twirling in the mirror, I smile at my reflection. Even with day's old makeup, I like what I see. Sure, I could starve myself into a size eight, but for what? To be miserable? No thanks. I'll have my cake and eat it, too.

Having the attention of a man like Colton Montgomery is addictive, but I'm not naïve enough to think it would ever go anywhere. We obviously live in different worlds. I'm a fun distraction for a few hours. And he's ... well, he's unexpected.

"You're my new favorite memory."

My heart nearly explodes, remembering his words. Well, Mr. Montgomery, you're my new favorite memory, too!

After making sure I have all my belongings, I casually stride back toward Colton and beam with pride at the heat that registers in his eyes. His nostrils flare, and I add a little bounce to my step. He's leaning back in his seat with both arms spread wide across the back row of chairs. He appears relaxed, but I see his jaw tick and I bat my eyelashes at him. I have a feeling Colton is an eternal flirt, and for once, I welcome it.

He's out of his seat before I reach him, pulling me to his side. "I didn't know you were changing."

"Is that a problem, Mr. Montgomery?"

He flinches, and I wonder if calling him Mr. Montgomery reminds him of his father. I'm about to apologize when we're interrupted again.

"All set. We'll make an announcement when you board," his friend, Joanna, announces.

"Thank you, Joanna. I let Tilly know to expect your call. I'm glad you decided to take me up on my offer." His smile and demeanor are genuine, relaxed, honest.

"Well, after Googling you, I think I'd be a fool not to. My family is over the moon that I'll be home more often." She smiles at him like he's responsible for everything shiny and happy.

"That's wonderful," he replies warmly. "I'm happy I could help." Watching this interaction, I think she might be right.

"You're a good man, Colton. It will be an honor to work for you."

Colton leans in and gives the small, older woman a hug. She simply beams at him, and I wonder if he has this effect on everyone or just women. "Well, Tilly is my brother's sister-in-law. She'll have no problem giving you the low-down on how we run things. She tends to do things her own way." He chuckles. "We'll all be happy to have you on our team."

"Thank you. I should get back to work. It's my last day, after all."

He nods and his smile causes a reaction deep in my core I'm not accustomed to. "We'll see you on board?"

"Absolutely," she replies, pulling away and giving me a grateful smile. "He's a keeper."

I have no reply for that, but Colton laughs.

Leaning in, he whispers, "I paid her to say that." We stand side by side, watching her walk back to the gate.

"Somehow, I doubt that. She had a little hero worship on her face."

"It's nothing. A passenger was giving her a hard time on my last flight. I offered her a job with my family's company. I had overheard her mention she wanted to slow down, and it just happened we had a position open up recently. It's no big deal."

I turn my body to get a good look at him. "Seems like a big deal to me. You must do pretty well for yourself if you can just go around offering jobs to strangers. That was a really nice thing you did, Colton."

He shrugs off my compliment, and his nickname bothers me. Pan? Obviously, the people in his life are not paying attention to the things that matter. Colton just might be more Robin

Hood than Peter Pan, and that knowledge makes me like him much more than I should.

"Come on, baby. Let's get some coffee."

"You call me baby a lot," I mutter more to myself than to him, but because he's so in tune with me, he heard it.

He stops short and turns to look at me. "Do I?" he asks with a tilt of his head. It reminds me of a puppy who just heard the word treat.

"You do." I raise an eyebrow, so curious to see how he'll respond to being called out. I'm not prepared for him to step into my personal space and tuck a wayward curl behind my ear, though.

"Is that a problem, sweetheart?"

"Baby? Sweetheart? You're very demonstrative."

His gaze narrows in on my lips, and my body heats from within remembering what he did to my lips a few hours ago. One little kiss sent my body, mind, and soul reeling into an orbit I didn't recognize as my own. I'm finding it hard to make eye contact, but it's impossible to tear my gaze away from this man. He has a hold on me that should be frightening, but all I want is for him to set my world on fire again and again.

Colton drops his face closer to mine and his voice to just above a whisper. "I am. I was. And I always will be, Winnie. Get used to it."

"Get used to it?" I croak. "Our time's almost up."

He straightens, and I see the smirk appear on his handsome, chiseled face. "We'll see, baby. We'll see. Coffee. Now. Are you hungry?"

Damn him. The command in his voice does ridiculous things to me. It makes me desperate to obey. "I'm always hungry." Thank God my voice sounds semi-normal, even if my insides crash like waves in a tropical storm.

"Fucking hell," he says, taking my free hand in his and dragging me behind him. "I love that answer. Let's feed you."

"You don't have to look so upset, CC." Colton has the gall to laugh. "I told you, I had already purchased the seat next to me before I met you. It would have remained empty, and I would be a damn fool if I didn't fill it with your sexy self."

How do I explain to him I don't like feeling indebted to anyone? Certainly not him. I wave my hand dismissively while I work through this in my head. "It's fine."

He smirks. "You've been fine for almost an hour."

My lips curl into a smile, and I angle my body toward him. "You're impossible to stay mad at, you know that?"

Colton leans into my space, something he's becoming very comfortable with. "It's my superpower."

Laughter escapes as I shake my head. "I appreciate the upgrade, Colton. Really, I do. It's just ... hmm, I don't know."

"You don't like owing anyone. You do everything yourself. You don't know how to handle someone being on your side."

It's like he has a front-row seat to all my hang-ups.

"It's just been my mom and me for as long as I can remember. She worked hard to give me everything I ever needed or wanted, but I learned early in life not to count on anyone. She did the best she could, but she had to miss out on so many things to provide for us. One day I just stopped asking and learned to do everything myself."

"Is that why she tries to be the fun one now?"

My fingers twist in my lap as I formulate a response, but Colton gently places his warm palm over them, and my body calms with the contact.

"She's always been free spirited, but she made sure I was her priority. I think now that I'm grown, she worries that she never taught me how to have fun."

"You know, it's admirable to be self-sufficient, but occasionally, you have to take chances, too. Life is too short to always play it safe, Win."

He punctuates each word with his penetrating gaze, and my body hears, *Take a chance, Winnie. Take a chance on me.* I shake away the thought because it's ridiculous.

"Champagne?" Startled by Joanna's interruption, I yank my hand free from Colton's grasp.

"S-Sure. Thank you." I take the glass she hands me, then pass one to Colton. His caramel eyes twinkle, and it makes my chest ache.

When Colton smiles, he looks like my best decision and my worst heartache all rolled into one devilishly handsome face.

"To new beginnings," he cheers.

"To open, honest, and sometimes raw conversations with strangers."

His smile morphs into something sexily dangerous. "We're not strangers now, are we, CC?"

Gah! How can he drop his voice like that and set fire to all my lady parts? It's terribly unfair.

"No, Mr. Montgomery. I suppose we're not."

Something I can't decipher crosses his face as he unlocks the tray in front of me. "So, Win. About that. I—"

Ding.

"Hello, this is your captain speaking. Please take your seats and buckle up. There's a thunderstorm ahead of us. We'll be flying above it, but there will be some turbulence ahead. We'll halt the beverage service until we reach a smoother cruising altitude."

The plane shakes as it hits a pocket of air, sending Colton's champagne flying all down the front of me.

"Fuck. Sorry, baby. I—"

"Here you go, honey." Joanna hands me a paper towel on her way by.

"It's okay," I shriek as the plane rocks again.

Standing suddenly, Colton reaches into the overhead bin

and produces a T-shirt before anyone has a chance to yell at him.

My knuckles are turning white on the armrests, and it takes me a minute to realize he's slipping it over my head.

"Colton?"

"Baby, I fucking love that dress, but if you don't put this on, I'm going to be fighting a hard-on the rest of this flight."

Embarrassment and shock have me forcing my arms through the shirt quickly. As my head ducks into the soft, gray material, I realize he's taking care of me. Again. I catch sight of myself as the material floats into place. My thin summer dress is entirely see-through now that it's wet.

"Oh," is all I can think to say as my head pokes through his shirt that smells unfairly sexy.

"When you decide to show me that lacy pink bra, I want it to be your choice. Not because I'm a klutz who spilled a drink on you."

I should be upset by his presumptuous nature, but there's not a single part of me that is. On any other man, it would be cocky. On Colton Montgomery, it's hot as hell.

"We'll see, Colton. We'll see."

~

"I'll meet you on the other side of customs, okay?" Colton sounds slightly panicked. I know he's pissed off that we can't go through the checkpoints together, but he has some sort of international travel pass or something and I don't, so I had to wait in line with eight thousand other travelers.

"Okay. I'll be fine, Colton. Seriously, I'm a big girl. I've traveled by myself before." His concern is endearing, but you'd think he'll never see me again by his expression. "Honestly. I'll see you on the other side. Go," I shoo him, and he reluctantly leaves me in the queue.

Definitely not Peter Pan.

~

*I*t's two hours before I get my luggage and make my way through security. Lanie wasn't kidding that it could take a while. My heart sinks, knowing I didn't get to say good-bye to Colton. But my mind knows it's for the best. The more time I spent with him, the harder the inevitable end would be.

Dragging my suitcase, my head down, I smile sadly at Colton's T-shirt I'm wearing over my dress when my phone chimes with an incoming message.

It's about time. I've had no service this entire time, and I need to check in with Mom and Wes. Fishing my phone from my bag, I roll my eyes when I see Claire's name. My frenemy since kindergarten. I'm old enough now to realize we've had a toxic friendship at best. I debate just erasing the message, but I notice it's a video and curiosity wins out.

Claire: You lucky bitch! Just look at this hotness you get all to yourself for two weeks!

Claire: Video Loading.

Claire: You're not seriously still mad about what happened with Travis, are you?

Claire: Are you seriously that selfish?

The video finally loads. It's of a well-dressed man dancing. Or drunkenly swaying is a better word for it, I guess. He's surrounded by women, and the man to his left is yelling something about him getting any pussy he wants. "Use 'em and lose 'em," the pig shouts.

Why the hell is she sending this to me? I go to swipe the video away when the man in question stumbles into the camera and all the blood drains from my face. *Colton.*

"Mr. Westbrook," the faceless camera operator asks, "how do you feel about being labeled a pussy magnet? The Westbrook Heartbreaker? Do you like having a different woman every night?"

Loud, masculine laughter has me pulling up short. Straight ahead is a group of men. A lot of sexy, smiling men, and Colton is in the center of them all. His eyes dart back and forth.

He's searching for me.

That's when I recognize Lanie Cross standing beside him and reality hits me like a tsunami. Living in Vermont, I've heard the tales of the Westbrook billionaires Lanie brought home with her. I don't live in Burke Hollow, but a town that size doesn't acquire a family of billionaires without the entire state taking notice.

He isn't Colton Montgomery. He's Colton Westbrook. Brother-in-law to the woman who employed me for the next two weeks.

He lied.

I desperately need this job.

He lied.

To me.

Tears prick the back of my eyes. Blinking them away, I dart into the restroom to my right before he notices me.

This was all just a game?

Peter Pan.

Think, Winnie. You need this job. Having a vacation fling with Colton could jeopardize that, and that's obviously all he's interested in.

Law school. That's my priority, so even though it's a dick move, I can't risk getting caught up in Colton Westbrook.

I scroll my contacts with a heavy heart and pull up Lanie's name. I call her before I can get too caught up in how stupid I am for feeling so sad.

"Lyn!" She uses the name I go by at work. "How are you, chica? How was your flight? We're waiting for you near the Corona stand."

"Oh, oh really? That's so strange. I must have missed you. I-I didn't see anyone, so I just got in a taxi."

"Oh, no! That's going to cost you a fortune. I'm so sorry. All the guys are here and everyone's so excited. We must have gotten to talking, and I didn't pay close enough attention."

Lanie is seriously one of the kindest women I've ever met and I'm definitely going to hell for this. "I had kind of a rough flight. I might have just walked past you in my rush to get some fresh air."

"Ugh. One of the guys was on your flight. He was just telling us how bad it was. I'm so sorry. Well, listen. We'll be back at the villa soon, and you have tonight off. Like I said before, this really will be like a vacation for you. We only need you for a few nights, and the rest of the time is yours. I hope you'll be able to relax a little. Betty Anne told us you've been working yourself ragged."

Betty Anne. She's the mother of one of my mom's friends from the hospital. She's completely crazy, but not as nuts as Lanie's grandmother, GG, who insists on calling me Wendy. The two of them together are trouble.

"I actually have a ton of studying to do. Being able to do it in shorts instead of thermals will be vacation enough." I try to keep my tone light, but it's nearly impossible with this new ache crushing my chest.

Lanie laughs, and it's a sweet, gentle sound. "Okay, I'll get these animals rounded up, and I'll see you soon. Thanks again for doing this. I can't tell you how much of a help it is to have you here."

"It's my pleasure. I'll see you soon."

"Bye, chica." Lanie Cross has this way of truly making you feel like a friend, even when you're the hired help. It's crazy to think not that long ago, she was in my position.

"You guys go ahead. I need to find Winnie." Colton's voice carries over the quiet space, and I freeze. "She should have been out by now. Sir? Are there still passengers coming from flight 1918?"

"We're all clear back there," a heavily accented man replies.

"What the hell?"

I pace the small space. Why is he still waiting for me? There are like fifteen people there to greet him.

"Winnie? Are you in there?"

My eyes grow wide with alarm as a woman walks past me. I shake my head wildly and the woman pops her head back out the door.

"Sorry, it's empty. No one in here." She shuts the door and gives me a smile as she heads into the stall, tipping her head when I mouth a silent thank you.

I have no idea if I'm doing the right thing or not. I don't know how billionaires work, but I do know my only priorities are Weston and law school. The money I'll make working for Lanie will ease the financial burden of my first semester.

Weston and law school. That's what matters. That, and avoiding Colton Westbrook for the next two weeks.

God, give me strength.

As luck would have it, Lanie told the truth about my hours, and hiding out in my private villa made it much easier than I imagined.

CHAPTER 8

COLTON

"Where are you going now? We've barely seen you all week."

My shoulders slump at Halton's words. I was hoping to sneak out before anyone noticed I was gone.

"Ah, just for a run."

"Bullshit. Rodrigo said he's been driving you to scour neighboring pool clubs every day. Who are you searching for?"

I grip the back of my neck, and my brother smirks. It's a tell for the both of us, a nervous habit we picked up from our father. "Fine. There's this girl."

His eyebrows raise and a knowing smile shows off his sparkly white teeth that I want to knock out. "The girl from the airport?"

"How—"

He shrugs. "Loch told Rylan you gave up a hotel room to spend time with someone at the airport. We were shocked you didn't take her back to the room."

"Whatever, asshole. She's not that kind of girl."

"No, seems like she's the kind of girl to ghost you."

"Fuck you," I growl. My spine goes ramrod straight and my fists clench at my sides.

He holds up his hands at my harsh tone. "Colty, I was just teasing. Why are you so worked up about this girl?"

Roughly, I tug on the ends of my hair before raking my hand through it a few times. "I don't know, Halt. She … there was just something about her. Something … real. And I'm worried about her. We made a plan to meet at customs and she didn't show. Something isn't right and I don't know how to fix it."

"So, you're spending your vacation searching high and low for a woman you know nothing about?"

"That's just it. She doesn't feel like a stranger to me. She feels like … more."

His brows shoot to his hairline and his mouth gapes open.

"Just, never mind. Forget I said anything."

"Colt, if this—"

"Just leave it, okay?

He claps me on the back. "I know you don't want to hear this, but you're probably better off. You waited; she didn't show. You deserve better than that. There's a woman out there for you that will make you her whole life."

He means well, and he's probably right. *I'm not ready to settle down, anyway.* That's what I tell myself for the rest of the trip, and into the months that follow, but my heart knows it's a big fat lie.

~

One Year Later

"*W*hy are you on my sofa? Again," Halton grumbles, handing me a beer.

"My house isn't done yet."

"It's not done yet because you're dragging your feet picking out shit for it."

We all had houses built on the backside of GG's mountain.

76

It was part of our grand plan to save her ski lodge from the piece of shit Macomb a couple of years ago. They finished Ashton's first because it's the farthest up the mountain and outfitted like Fort fucking Knox. Slowly, all my brothers' and adopted family's homes went up. Some of us are here full time, like Easton and Ash, and some of us come and go.

Besides Ash, I'm the only one without a family, so we built mine last. I don't need my own space like Ash does.

"Whatever," I mutter. I don't tell him I haven't been able to pick out the furnishings because it feels like something is missing. *Or someone,* my conscience whispers darkly. I also don't admit the spicy scent of dinner cooking in the crockpot kicked me in the chest when I walked into his home.

"Rylan told me you were pissy because she couldn't go out for drinks with you tonight."

Guilt slaps me across the face. I was a little short with her earlier. "I'll apologize."

"You're right."

I roll my eyes. The last thing I need is a caveman lecture right now. "I was having a bad day. Everyone's busy every damn night."

"We're growing up, Colt. It might—"

"I don't need a lecture, Halt. I said I'd apologize."

He nods and turns on the TV. "Wanna talk about the Fenway deal?"

Fuck me.

"Nope."

"That's the third client to leave in as many months."

"Yeah, well, why don't you get on Ash and find out why the fuck Macomb is still free to mess with our shit? If he put him in jail where he belongs, we wouldn't be having this problem."

"You've been in Page Six a lot lately, too. You're making it too easy for him to get to you."

I stand abruptly, setting my now empty beer down with enough force to shake the table. "I know you all want to label me the fuck up, but I'm doing my damn job just as you're doing yours. I can't help it if Macomb is out to get us. Ash needs to fix this shit."

"Colt, all I'm saying is you're making yourself an easy target for him. Maybe just lay low for a while."

That's easy for him to say when he has Rylan at home. It's not that I begrudge my brothers' happiness, but once they got married, it's like they forgot all about me. I know, poor little rich boy. That's why I keep my complaints to myself.

"Yup."

Halton scowls. Thanks to being sickeningly happy with my best friend, he's less grumpy than he used to be, but he still has the attitude. "Where are you going?"

"I'm going to stay with Ash tonight." I hadn't planned to, but dealing with his pissy ass suddenly feels like the safer bet.

"You don't have to leave." Resting his forearms on his thighs, Halt sighs heavily. His hair is darker than mine, and his glasses give him a nerdy look, but our mannerisms are pretty similar.

"I know. Thanks. And I am moving on the house. But I, uh, was wondering if you'd make something for me."

This gets his attention, and he mutes the game. "What did you have in mind?"

Halton, grumpy as he is, is an amazing artist who has truly found himself with Rylan by his side. Pulling a folded piece of paper from my pocket, I hand it to him. I'd printed out the picture of Winnie months ago and finally know what I want to do with it.

"Can you do something with this?" I ask, handing it over.

The scowl lines deepen as he stares at the picture of Winnie I'd sent Loch so many months ago. "This is the girl?"

"Winnie." I nod.

"She left that much of an impression on you, huh?"

I don't tell him that I feel like a piece of me is missing because that's fucking ridiculous. You don't get feelings like that after twelve hours. *Liar.* Can you throat punch your own conscience?

"Yeah," I mutter. "She did." *And she left a fucking hole in my heart the size of Texas*, I want to yell.

"And you didn't sleep with her?"

My head jerks to the left at his words. "Why would that matter?"

"Just making sure you didn't scare her away with your micropenis."

What an asshole.

"No, dickhead. I didn't sleep with her. I barely even touched her. One little kiss is all I got." But it was enough to ruin me, I think. I haven't been able to even look at another woman since that kiss and it's really starting to piss me off.

I'm officially in the longest dry spell I've had since I started having sex and it's putting me on edge. I also don't admit to purchasing all the Bonne Bell cherry cola lip balm I could find or that my hand is working overtime thinking about a woman who ghosted me.

"What exactly did you want me to do with this?" he asks, staring at the picture again. When he brings it in for a closer inspection, I know he's staring at me. I'm watching Winnie in the picture, and the expression on my face haunts my dreams. It looks an awful lot like love.

"I-I don't know. The girls said I needed something to go above the fireplace in the family room. So maybe that?"

"You sure you want a constant reminder right in your face like that?"

No. No, I'm not. But since she occupies my every waking moment anyway, I might as well have a visual to go along with it.

"Yeah, I do," is what I tell him. "I may not know what happened, but she was a good girl, Halt. I'm sure of it. In just twelve hours, she made me think of possibilities. She was …

enchanting. Having a reminder of that feeling I had with her is exactly what I want."

His expression is neutral, but I can see his mind whirling.

"Also," I clear my throat, "I'm invoking a Westy."

Halton chokes on his beer, the smirk falling from his face. A Westy is something we made up as kids. Invoking a Westy swore the other person to secrecy. It was our childhood version of the bro-code.

"You don't want anyone to know about her?" he asks incredulously.

I shrug. "For what? She's gone. I know nothing about her except she meant more to me than I did to her. Why would I want to broadcast that?"

"You've always been a leap and be damned with the conse-quences kind of person, Colt. You go a hundred miles an hour and expect everyone to keep up with you. Maybe it scared her."

Like I hadn't already thought of that.

"Then she wasn't the girl for me, right?" I smile through the words, even though they feel like walking on shards of glass. "It's not a big deal, Halt. She's just a girl I spent a few hours with that left an impression I don't want to forget. No big deal."

"No big deal," he echoes.

"So, can you do something with it?"

He stares at the piece of paper in his hands for a long time. "Yeah." He glances up with sympathy I don't want. "Yeah, I can do something with it. I'm working with some colors right now. Give me a bit to work on it."

"No rush," I say, picking up my empty bottle. Carrying it to the kitchen, I spot Halton and Rylan's wedding photos on the counter. Love. Happiness. Contentment. They're overflowing with it all in every picture. My chest aches with that unfamiliar pang of longing that's becoming a daily habit.

I need to get out of here. Suddenly, the love my family has always exuded is suffocating. "I'll see you for brunch tomor-row," I call over my shoulder.

Getting drunk feels like a great fucking idea, so I head back down the mountain and grab some beer before crashing Ashton's solitude.

~

"What now?" Ash grumbles as he opens the door.

I hold up the case of beer. "Halt and Rylan are still in the honeymoon phase. I'm in the getting drunk phase. Care to join me?"

"If I say no, are you going to leave?"

"Nope." I smirk, pushing past him.

Ash shakes his head. "I have work to do."

"It'll still be there tomorrow. Besides, since you refuse to go after Macomb, you owe me."

"It's not that I'm refusing, Colt." His voice gets weaker the more he speaks. A few years ago, his mission with our brother, Loki, went south. He was beaten and tortured before they were rescued. His facial scars are fading, but they'll never go away. His voice is getting stronger, but it'll never be the same. It's his soul that seems to be irreparable, and that kills me.

"No. You're waiting for Pacen to magically appear and do it for you." I shrug my shoulders and head to his kitchen.

But not before I hear his whispered words. "She needs to do it for herself."

I don't push him on it because whatever happened between him and Pacen needs to be worked out in his own time. I just hope time doesn't bite us all in the ass while he figures it out. The beer makes a clinking sound as I set it on the counter, and just like I knew he would, Ash begrudgingly joins me a few minutes later.

I hand him a local IPA as my phone makes a series of dings that have me shaking with laughter before I even open the messages. *Perfect timing. I need a fucking laugh.* Entering my passcode, I open the texting app.

Lochlan: Dick. Did you send a bloody glitter bomb to my office?

Colton: Not just a glitter bomb. There were edible panties too!

Lochlan: I can't get rid of this shite, mate.

Lochlan: I just held a staff meeting looking like I came straight from a stripper pole.

I roar with laughter and show Ash my phone. He doesn't find it as funny as I do, but I see the smirk sneak onto his face.

Colton: You've been in such a bad mood lately. I thought you could use some brightening up.

Lochlan: This is war. You realize this, yes?

Colton: I look forward to it.

Colton: Send a selfie.

Lochlan: Not on your life.

Colton: You know I'll sweet talk your assistant into sending one. Why not cut out the middleman?

I can hear him grumbling about his incompetent assistant all the way from New York.

Lochlan: (Picture sent)

Ashton's peering over my shoulder as the picture of Lochlan scowling at his desk, sparkling like a fairy princess, loads. This time, it's both our laughter that fills the room. Which is exactly what I needed.

CHAPTER 9

COLTON

Present Day

"*Wha-wha, wha-wha-wha-wha.*"

It's never a good sign to be woken up by your oldest brother sounding like Charlie Brown's teacher.

I turn my head toward the sound, only mildly alarmed that I'm unable to open my eyes. Lifting my hands feels like a herculean effort, but I do it and stab numb fingers at my face until my fingertips land on my eyelids. Prying them open with both index fingers, I wince.

"Who blew sawdust into my eyeballs?" my voice croaks, followed by a groan.

What the fuck is wrong with me?

Something hard sails past my face, landing less than an inch away from my head. Rolling my neck to the left, I find an iPad.

"Why the hell are you throwing shit at me, Pres?"

He yells again, but it sounds like we're underwater, so I don't answer him. Before I know what's happening, he rips the covers from my body. Cool air glides over my skin, and I shiver. My dick takes notice, and I realize I must be nude.

Well, it's nothing he hasn't seen before. That'll teach him to bust into my house at this ungodly hour.

Halton sits on the edge of my bed. I hadn't even realized he was here. Someone definitely pissed in their Cheerios, though, because as he hands me a cup of coffee, anger radiates off him like an atomic bomb ready to go off.

"Get the fuck up, Colton." Preston's words are finally taking shape.

"What's your problem? Why are you breaking and entering this morning?"

"You don't remember? Jesus, Colton. Our family doesn't need press like this. We work our asses off to stay out of the tabloids, and you ruin that in one fucking night you can't remember?"

My head throbs as I scoot up in bed. Preston tosses a pair of shorts at me, so I lay them over my cock. Trying to get them over my legs right now is too much work.

"What are you talking about?"

Preston jabs an angry finger into the iPad, and the screen comes to life.

"How could you do this to us, Colton? I knew you could be selfish, but I never imagined you'd be destructive, too. After this little stunt, any chance we had at splitting The Westbrook Group into separate entities is gone. There's no way our board will vote in favor of us diversifying. You've essentially fucked every one of your brothers over. I hope a little pussy was worth it, you asshole."

"Do you have any idea what this is going to do to Mom?" Halt asks quietly.

Right on cue, "Stacy's Mom" by Fountains of Wayne, blares in the background. It's the ringtone I set for Sylvie Westbrook. She has always complained about how inappropriate it is. It drives her nuts, so obviously, I kept it.

"What the hell are you talking about?" I try to yell after the song fades, but my throat feels like the Sahara, and it comes out gravely and weaker than I intend.

Preston practically throws the iPad in my face.

"Preston, calm down. Beating the shit out of him won't help matters."

I stare between Halton and Pres. Whatever they think I've done must be big. Preston has never once threatened me.

Peering down at the tablet, I see TMZ is open, and my naked ass sits slumped over in between two girls I've never seen before in my life.

"This isn't real. I've never seen these girls before."

"Oh, yeah? Then why did we just escort them out of your condo with threats of a lawsuit?" Preston snarls.

My head snaps to his. "No way. I didn't even … I didn't even drink last night."

Preston gives an undignified huff, and Halton shakes his head.

"You party every night, Colton. You have no responsibility to anyone."

I know that's how it appears, but I rarely drink, and last night, I ordered a fucking root beer.

"This is bullshit, Pres. You can check my tab from The Loft; that's where I was last night. I was drinking fucking root beer, watching the Braves game."

"And you woke up hungover, naked, with two girls rifling through your kitchen." Preston sneers.

"I'm not hungover, you dipshit. I. Didn't. Fucking. Drink."

Memories of last night try to pierce my consciousness, but everything's fuzzy. "Was one of the girls a redhead?"

"So, you do remember?"

"No … I mean, sort of? She sat down and asked me to buy her a drink." Scratching my head, I try to remember if I actually did. "I think I bought her one, but told her I wasn't looking for company. I just wanted to catch the end of the game."

"You should have watched it at home," Halton mumbles.

85

Anger and sadness fill my chest. "I don't like watching the games by myself, and you two assholes were too busy."

"We have responsibilities, Colton. Families that depend on us. We can't just drop everything to have a fucking beer with you when you're feeling lonely." Preston turns to Halt. "I'm so done with the Peter Pan bullshit."

"What's that supposed to mean?" I growl.

"It means you need to grow the fuck up. You may have just ruined the opportunity that would allow Halton and East to run a branch of The WB the way they want to. That fucks up their plans, Colt. Do you even give a shit about anyone but yourself these days?"

I admit, I've been a little more carefree lately, but what does he expect? Every person I know and love is in a committed relationship that doesn't always include me.

"You know I do, Preston. None of this makes sense. I swear to you I wasn't drinking last night."

"So what? You're telling me they drugged you?"

I hadn't thought about it, but now that he's said it, I think he's on to something.

"Yes, actually. I think I might have been. You don't black out from root beer," I snarl.

My oldest brother narrows his eyes like he's contemplating his next move. Then he rakes a hand through his hair, spins in place, and lands a punch into the drywall next to the door.

"Get dressed. Emory will take a blood sample, but you've left me with no choice here, Colt. I have to put you on administrative leave, effective immediately. The media has already surrounded your building. Those girls gave a statement from your sofa, saying you forced them here, and until we can prove otherwise, you need to get out of town. Someone has already hired them an attorney and there's talk of a lawsuit. The chopper will be here in an hour, and Ash is expecting you. I'm sure the gossip columns will track you to Vermont, but no one is getting past Ashton's security. You're on lockdown until we can sort this shit out."

"But I didn't fucking do anything, Preston."

His expression softens but doesn't lessen the blow. "You put yourself in this position, Colt. Maybe not intentionally, but you know that you need to be aware of your surroundings as well as we do. We've literally been taught to watch out for those that will try to take us down since we were kids. You've racked up quite the reputation over the last few months. Now my hands are tied. It's my job to keep our ship afloat, and as CEO, the only option is to suspend you. As your brother, it's the last thing I want to do. As the CEO, it's my only choice."

"So ... what? You want me to go into hiding like I'm guilty?"

"I'll have Ash pull security footage from The Loft and start interviewing anyone that was there last night, but until we have concrete evidence, yes. You're to stay out of sight. We cannot handle another scandal right now, Colt. This will devastate Mom, too, so we need to get you out of here before she shows up."

I cringe, knowing she's probably just seen pictures of me naked as the day I was born. But the only thing that matters to me right now is that my brothers believe me. I may be the fuck up as of late, but I love them and this family with all that I am.

"Fine," I agree. "But I need to know something first." I wait until two sets of eyes, so similar to my own, find their way to me. Darting between them, I ask a question I both need and fear the answer to. "Do you believe me?"

Preston and Halt share a look that hits like a lead weight to my gut.

"Yeah, Colty. We believe you," Halton says softly. "But you make it really fucking hard sometimes."

≈

*T*he helicopter lands on the roof of my building, and I push forward against the wind that's trying to force me back. Climbing into the cockpit, I see Tony, our pilot, with a grim expression, but it's Halton that speaks.

"You're on administrative leave, Colt. This is a company chopper."

Realization hits like a punch to the nuts. I'm not insured by The WB right now. Cursing, I climb into the back and buckle in with Halton to my right.

Ashton and I got our pilot licenses over the last year and a half. It's been our way of bonding, I guess. I fly into Boston, though I won't admit that I'm spending way too much time aimlessly searching for Wendalyn-no-last-name, then head to Vermont, where we use a private company to get our hours in.

How the fuck did I not get her last name? The question eats away at me every damn day. Is the memory of her going to mess with my head for the rest of my life?

Blowing out a harsh breath, I close my eyes. Ems took a blood sample and flushed me with fluids, but I still feel shaky.

"Ash said it's a goddamn zoo at the gate." His voice is tinny through the headphones.

"Great."

Luckily, Ash had insisted on a security gate at the entrance to the private road leading to all our homes.

"Colt?"

With a fortifying breath, I turn to face my older brother.

"What's going on with you?"

"Wish to fuck I knew." Closing my eyes, I don't open them again until I hear Halton curse.

I glance out the window to where he's peering down. At least fifteen news vans crowd the mountain road near our private entrance with cameras pointed to the sky. We basically just announced my arrival.

CHAPTER 10

COLTON

"*R*eally got yaself in a pickle this time, didn't ya, Pan?"

"Jesus, GG. Can you let him walk in the door before you give him shit?" Ash scolds.

At least someone's on my side.

"Hey, GG." Even with the shitstorm happening around me, I can't bring myself to be mad at the crazy, old lady. She tells it like she sees it, and that's never going to change. "Yeah, I think it's pretty bad."

"Bad, Colt. Bad? It's a clusterfuck of epic proportions," my brother, Easton, barks from the kitchen.

Groaning, I drop my bag. "Is everyone here?"

"Unfortunately," Ash grumbles.

"Great. Let me have it," I say to no one in particular.

East takes a menacing step forward and tosses magazine after magazine on the coffee table between us. There are at least forty of them, and I recognize the last one that came out six or seven months ago declaring me the bad boy Westbrook. He throws another one down and it says the Westbrook player of uptown.

Interview after interview given by people who've never met

me. Finally, he tosses the latest edition. *US Magazine* with my naked ass front and center.

My jaw clenches when I realize he's not even allowing me to explain. He's already made up his mind.

"You come here every damn weekend and hang out with my kids. We left them in your care because we trusted you."

The past tense of his statement makes bile rise in my stomach, and a bitter, cold rage form in my heart.

"Easton," Ash's tone carries a warning East ignores.

"But it's not just your niece and nephew you've fucked over with your carelessness, Colton." My name sounds like daggers flying from his mouth. "We could have helped hundreds of families here. We could have made a real difference for this entire fucking state, and all you cared about was getting your dick wet?"

"East, we think they drugged him." Halton attempts to ease the tension, but East chooses a side just like Preston. And it's not mine.

"Do you have anything to say? Anything at all?" Easton yells, but I'm done. I've never felt more betrayed by my family than I do right now.

Turning to Ash, I try to control my tone. "Do you care which room I take?"

He closes his eyes and shakes his head. "Just not Sadie's. She'll be here tomorrow for a pizza and movie night."

Nodding, I hope he can see the appreciation in my expression, because I don't trust myself to say much else.

"That's it?" East bellows. "You're always going on about how our family needs to communicate, and you're just going to walk away? Preston and Emory had to change their plans to come here and help fix your shit, and you're going to walk away?" His rage heats the entire house.

I'm in front of him, toe to toe, before I can stop myself. "Why would I say anything when you've so obviously already made up your mind?" I hiss. "I've never given any of you a goddamn reason to think I'm incompetent, yet you've riddled me with the title of black sheep for years now. Why? Because I try to lighten the heavy fucking shit our family has been through over the years? Because I like to laugh and have a good time? Because I'm trying to be like dad?" That last part slips out and pisses me off even more.

Easton's eyes go wide just before regret flashes in them.

"Fuck you, Easton. Pres too. I've spent years trying to keep us together, and the second I need you, what happens? Y'all turn on me like I haven't had your backs my entire life. So, excuse me if I don't want to talk, East. Excuse me if I don't want to see any of you right now."

With that, I shove past him and take the stairs two at a time. Doors slam behind me, curses are shouted, but I block them all out and take refuge in Ashton's guest room until a gentle knock lands on my door.

"Come in," I yell from my prone position. I'm sprawled out on my back, arms crossed behind my head. It's a relaxed position, yet I'm anything but. My body is a tightwire, ready to snap.

"Hey," Rylan, my oldest friend and newest sister-in-law, says quietly as she enters the room. "Sorry I missed the welcome party." She glides across the room and climbs in beside me. We lay side by side, staring at the ceiling. "I'm sorry," she eventually whispers.

My neck cranes to look at her. When I see a tear slide down her cheek, I roll to my side just as Halton walks into the room, uninvited.

"Never thought I'd actually be okay with finding my wife in bed with my brother, but then again, I should have known marrying my brother's best friend that nothing would ever be normal."

Rylan chokes out a sob, and I cast a worried glance in his direction. Halton wears his concern like a coat of armor as tension settles in my spine. When she finally turns her gaze to mine, I scan her face in confusion. I know this girl. She's happy, sad, and fucking terrified all at once.

"I'm sorry," she repeats. "I haven't been a very good friend lately. You've always been there for me, and I know you're feeling neglected." Halton shuffles around to the other side of the bed and takes her hand. "W-We've been trying to have a baby, Colty. Unsuccessfully."

Understanding slices through my heart. My best friend has been suffering, and I've been the prick, worried about being left out of movie nights. Uncomfortably, my eyes shift to my brother, and he shrugs.

"You're my best friend, Colt, but th-this was something Hatty and I had to go through on our own."

Emotion clogs my throat, so I nod through the painful haze.

"But," she peeks up at Halton, and a smile spreads from her face to his, "we just made it through the first trimester."

Shock registers first. "You're … you're pregnant?"

Rylan nods while more tears slip down her cheeks. A genuine smile forms on my face as I hug her and punch Halton on the arm at the same time.

"Congrats. I'm so happy for you guys. I'm sorry I've been such a shit."

I examine how they stare at each other, and I'm overwhelmed with many warring emotions. Happiness, sadness, emptiness. I'm ecstatic for them, but know it's another step in the opposite direction for me.

When did I become such a selfish asshole?

"We wanted to tell you first because obviously, we want you to be his godfather." Rylan smirks.

"His? It's a boy?"

She nods emphatically. "We found out this morning."

Halton has been quieter than usual during this exchange.

"Are you sure you still want me in that role?" I ask, never breaking eye contact with my older brother.

Sighing, he pinches the back of his neck. "Of course we do," he grumbles. "This entire situation is fucked up, Colt, but I know it's not your fault. It's just put everyone under unbearable stress. We have to scramble to find a solution before the board shuts us down completely. And with you on leave—" He cuts off, but I know what he was going to say.

"You're down a man," I finish.

"Yeah."

"I'll still pull my weight through Tilly," I say, pissed off I didn't think of it earlier. "She's family, so she's invested, and she can handle it. She's been by my side for almost two years. I can still do my part. Well, if Preston and East don't murder me first."

"I was thinking the same thing," Halt mumbles, pulling his wife to his side.

I stand and walk to the sitting area of the room. Three in a bed and all. A shiver tears through me, recalling what the world already thinks about me.

Halton smirks, like he knows exactly what's running through my mind. "I don't think you slept with those girls," he finally answers. "Emory got your blood results a bit ago. She's running toxicology on them, but there was something in your system."

"Fuck." Ashton's curse causes us all to turn toward the door where he leans on the frame.

He's been through so much, but anger still flares in my gut.

"You know this was Macomb, right?"

Ash nods, his gaze trained on me but unseeing.

"Then why the fuck haven't you turned him in, Ash? What the hell are you waiting for?"

"Pacen," he says quietly, and my anger deflates. "Macomb is into more than you could ever imagine, and he put his own daughter in unthinkable situations. I want her to have the chance to take him down herself."

"It's been years, Ash. Maybe that's not what she wants," Halt says gently. "She made it pretty clear she wasn't coming

93

back. Is it possible you're wasting your time trying to find her?"

"It's my time," he hisses. "It's my life. It's my call."

"Maybe, but what about the rest of us? This is fucking with all our lives, Ash."

"I'll fix it."

"It shouldn't all fall to your feet," I tell him.

"Yeah, well, thanks to Dad it does." He slaps the doorframe and mumbles something about work.

We all know he's heading to the secret room none of us have ever entered. The one that's triple reinforced with steel and every biometric shield known to man. Ashton has turned dark over the years, and I worry we've lost him for good.

"He's still keeping someone's dark secrets," Rylan whispers. "And I think they're your dad's."

The lump in my throat threatens to suffocate me. Closing my eyes, I count to ten. When I open them, Halton is watching me closely. "What?"

"Do you want to see it?" he asks cautiously.

I don't need to ask what *it* is; it can only be one thing. I have to force that damn lump in my throat down.

"You finished?"

Rylan beams beside him. "She's beautiful. Are you going to tell me who it is?"

Shaking my head, I respond with the only truth I know. "She's just a ghost of what could have been. That's all." Her eyes widen with surprise, and damn, do I wish I could snap those words back, but they're out there now. "Let's go see it, huh?"

Rylan and Halt exchange a glance I no longer have the inside knowledge to read. The third wheel to their love story is not how I saw my life playing out, but I won't begrudge them their happiness, so I suck it up and head out the door.

∽

"We probably shouldn't stay long," Halton reasons as we enter my nearly finished home. "I know Pres is pissed off, but he's right about lying low. They aren't backing down with the lawsuits, and who knows what Macomb has planned next. You seem to be the target he's after right now, so we must take every precaution."

"That slimy little shit is going to get what's comin' to him. You just wait and see," GG's voice calls from the foyer.

"Jesus, GG. What are you doing in here?"

"I'm waterin' the plants. Who do you think does it in all these houses you boys built?"

"Ah, I have plants?" I ask, a little shellshocked. The last time I was in this house, the contractors had just started hanging sheetrock. Now it's fully furnished and has plants?

"Well, ya weren't telling us what ya wanted, and ya know how impatient Lexi is."

Easton's wife, Lexi, was a buyer for a large department store in another life, so it makes sense that she took over decorating all the homes.

"Yeah," I mutter, flipping on a light as I make my way through the home. It's stunning. And empty. It doesn't feel or smell like a home. It's a house. That uncomfortable feeling in my gut takes center stage until I find the mantel in the family room. Resting on the edge is what I assume to be a large canvas wrapped in brown paper.

My hands shake as I reach for it. Halton is by my side seconds later.

"It's heavier than it looks," he explains.

"GG? You still here?" Lanie's voice rings out. Lanie is GG's other granddaughter and wife to my adoptive brother, Dex. Really, she's the OG of our new extended family. If it weren't for her, none of us would have found our way to Vermont, and three of my brothers wouldn't have found their other halves.

"In the family room," GG barks just as Halton helps me rip open the paper, revealing Winnie inch by inch.

My breath seizes in my lungs, and I actually feel faint. Halton's artistry has exploded all over the canvas. Winnie is larger than life, staring right at me, and I don't know where to look first. My gaze darts all over the artwork, but it's her eyes that have me blinking away feelings of forever.

Halton has her sitting in a field of lilies, leaning against a weeping willow tree. Her curly hair falls over her face exactly as it did so many times in real life. Her lips, plump and slightly pouty, seem so real. I swear I can smell cherry cola on them.

"You … it's her," I choke out.

"Well, Jesus Mary. You did meet Wendy after all."

GG's words make me dizzy, and the world tunnels around me for a beat too long.

"What did you say?" I croak.

"Holy crap. That's Lyn. Why do you have a portrait of Lyn in your family room, Colt?"

My mouth is so dry I can't speak. Between the sand on my tongue and the sudden need to vomit, I'm unable to speak. Finally, Halton does it for me.

"What do you mean? Who is Wendy? Who's Lyn?"

"That's Wendy," GG says.

At the same time, Lanie says, "That's the girl that babysat for us at your wedding. That's Lyn."

Time stands still as I gape from one person to the next.

"Wendalyn," I croak. "Winnie. You …" I point between GG and Lanie. "You know her?"

GG cackles, but Lanie's eyes are wide with shock as she nods her head.

"Where is she?" I demand. There's a fire burning hot in my gut, and I don't know if it's anger, fear, or something else, but my entire body buzzes with it.

GG lays a hand on my forearm as I pace. "Colton." The fact

that GG used my given name has dread settling in. "I told ya you weren't ready for her yet, but I think you might be now."

"Ah," Lanie's voice is small and shaky. "Colt. I don't know what's going on, but Lyn—"

"Winnie," I interrupt.

"O-kay. Winnie. She isn't the same."

"Lanie's right, Pan. Wendy's been through more than any one person ought to go through in the last year. Her light's been dimmed by circumstance, and it might not be yer time yet."

I hear their words, but I only have one question. "Where. Is. She?"

CHAPTER 11

WINNIE

"*H*ave a good night at work, sweetie. I saw you playing with Weston today. He ran hard. I'm sure it'll be a better night than the last few," my landlord and mother's oldest friend, Beth, informs me with a warm smile.

Tears, always so close to the surface these days, threaten the back of my eyes.

"Thanks, Beth. I-I don't know what we'd do without you." I choke out the words as she pulls me into a motherly hug.

"Oh, sweetie. Don't go leaking out your eyeballs again. I loved your mother. She was one of a kind. Things won't always be this hard. My mother's convinced good things are just around the corner for you."

My tears dry as a giggle works its way into my throat. "Betty-Anne is trouble with a capital T."

"You should have seen her when I was a kid," Beth says conspiratorially. "But even I'll admit, she and Rosa together are a formidable force. Go to work, Winnie. We'll be fine tonight."

"I'm saving. I'm saving to have him tested. To get us some help."

Kind eyes find mine in the dim light. "I know you are, sweetheart. I also know it isn't fair how life plays out sometimes. You and Wes are family. You're always welcome here. I just wish I had more room for you than a dusty, old studio above the garage."

More than once since my mother's passing, Beth has tried to find ways to give us more space than she has.

"It's perfect. And exactly what I can afford. We don't need anything else. I promise. Because of you, we're good."

Beth is one of the few people who know I spent my entire life savings caring for my mother, and even that wasn't enough. In the end, ALS suffocated her in her own body, and I had a front-row seat.

"Okay, dear. You're going to be late."

Grabbing my purse off the small table, I give her a grateful nod. "He did pretty good today. We didn't have any episodes, so I'm really hoping he'll sleep through the night."

"I can handle it."

"And if …" I swallow bile. "If Jason comes by—"

"If Jason shows his face here again, David will pull out his shotgun. Then we'll call the police."

Thank God for Beth and her husband, Dave.

"He may be your father, Winnie, but he's no man. You remember that. He can threaten all he wants. There isn't a judge on the planet that will hand Weston over to him. Go to work. Take deep breaths and know you're not alone."

I nod erratically as I reach for the door. Words are too painful. Life is too painful.

∼

J arrive at the hospital with a few minutes to spare, so I rush to the restroom before my shift starts. I'm thankful to Beth for getting me the position. Under normal circumstances, I would love to be a family liaison, but the nightshift is taking its toll. Caring for Weston is a full-time job, and the lack of sleep is causing my body to break down.

It's not like I have any other choice.

Staring in the mirror, I no longer recognize myself. Dark circles line my eyes, and even the most expensive concealer couldn't hide it, so I stopped trying. I'm lucky if I run a brush through my hair most days.

At twenty-eight years old, I could easily pass for forty. Sighing, I straighten my shoulders and head to my office.

Please let it be a quiet night. When families don't need me, I've been able to use the hospital resources to research Weston's symptoms. The staff pediatrician has been wonderful, and we're both fairly certain that he has some sort of sensory issue, if not fully on the spectrum, but without testing for a diagnosis, it's impossible to get him any help.

The four thousand dollars it will cost to have him evaluated at a private facility might as well be four million dollars. Maxing out all of our credit cards in my mother's final days was not my wisest decision, but it was the only one I could make.

Wouldn't you do whatever you could to give life to the one person who's always been your rock?

On days like today, the ones where I struggle to breathe, to see any light in my darkening tunnel, I allow my mind to drift back to the one time I truly felt wanted. The one man who saw me when I couldn't. Colton Westbrook.

He may be a player, but he gave me a memory I hold close to my heart when I need to find peace.

I put my head down and walk toward my office with a heavy sigh. I could make this journey blindfolded, and that's pretty much how I've been living.

Rounding the corner, I see a stack of files hanging outside of my door. I drop my purse in an empty desk drawer with a sigh too heavy for my soul and take the file from the top.

Lily Anders, room 332.

Heading that way, I scan her chart. She's a new mom, my age, and in good health. These are the easy jobs.

I knock on her door, and she smiles as I enter. She's a pretty girl with an easy smile. The little bundle of pink resting comfortably in her arms wraps the new mother in a happy glow.

"Hi, Lily. I'm Lyn Darling. I'm the family liaison, and I just wanted to see how you're both doing."

"Hi, come on in." Her voice is tired, but her smile is genuine. "We're doing really well. If my husband and I could decide on a name, we'd be even better."

I smile even when it hurts. I love this part of my job, so I push on. When I glance over the top of the blanket, Lily shifts her arms so I can peek at the baby. My gaze lingers on the sweet rosy cheeks when another knock comes from the doorway.

"Dad, you guys made it!" Lily exclaims. It takes me a second to release my gaze from the bundle of pink, and when I lift my head to greet her visitor, my stomach plummets.

"Winnie?"

My eyes blink too quickly as the color drains from my face. All my childish dreams once hung on this man's word.

"Dad? How do you know Lyn?" Lily asks.

Fear and sadness cover Dennis Tilman's face. It's then that I notice an older woman standing at his side wearing a confused expression, and the young boy standing between them, completely oblivious.

"Dad, do I get to hold my niece yet?" the little boy asks.

"Y-You left us for another family?" My voice wavers with no filter and my heart races wildly.

"Winnie, it wasn't like that. I, I didn't know how to keep you. You weren't mine," my former stepfather explains.

Heartache I thought was long buried rushes to the surface.

"Emily, this is Winnie. Mara's daughter."

Understanding replaces confusion on the woman's face.

Lily's daughter chooses that moment to test her lungs on a

cry that echoes in the room. I mentally shake my head, nearly stomping my foot, trying to gain control of my words.

"I thought about reaching out to Mara, but I—"

I raise my hand to stop him. There's no explanation or excuse he can give that would repair my seventeen-year-old heart. My biological father had never wanted me, but Dennis raised me, then decided I wasn't worth staying either. I won't be the receptacle for his guilt.

"There's nothing you can say, Dennis. This is the story of my life, right?" I swallow hard when my voice sounds slightly hysterical. "I'm just the girl no one wants to keep."

"Winnie," he tries again, and maybe it's unfair, but he deserves to hurt, too.

"And no worries about calling my mom. She's dead."

I stare just long enough for the shock to register, then force my way out of the room. I'm rushing down the hallway, trying to catch my breath, but it's no use. By the time I reach my office door, I'm hyperventilating, and tears threaten to break my composure.

A choked sob escapes as soon as I cross the threshold. I get a hand over my mouth, but not in time. I'm suddenly acutely aware that I'm not alone in my office. *His* scent hits my senses first. Then strong hands grasp my elbows to keep me upright. I shake my head to remove the curls from my eyes, but my body zings to life and heat shoots up my arms from this stranger's touch. My blood heats like a live wire, sending a familiar awareness to every inch of my body.

"Winnie." The low, gravely baritone has me sucking in air only to choke when it gets lodged in my chest.

I didn't think this night could get any worse, but I should know better by now. Things can always get worse.

I lift my gaze with a heavy heart to find a concerned Colton. He's also shooting daggers with a hard stare that has me shriveling in his grasp, and once again, I have to find the courage to walk away from him. My life is not my own anymore, and with Jason digging around Weston, I can't take any chances.

"Mr. Westbrook. It's lovely to see you again," I whisper, willing whatever strength I have left to surface. "If you'll excuse me, I have to get to work."

His jaw clenches and his gaze narrows in on mine. "You know who I am?" His voice is low and controlled, but the vein throbbing in his neck gives away his calm façade.

"I do. I-I have work to do."

He grasps my elbow and leads the way. "Funny thing about that, Winnie, or is it Lyn? Not Wendy, I remember that much. I'm your new volunteer."

My feet forget how to work, and I trip over myself. His hand is unforgiving though, and he holds me upright.

"Did you know who I was in the airport?" he almost hisses.

My shoulders slump. I'm so tired. Too tired to fight this beast of a beautiful man. "Not until we landed in Mexico," I finally admit. This has him pausing mid-step to stare at me. For the first time, I notice he's in costume. Not just any costume either. He's dressed as Peter Pan.

I must be delirious.

"Peter? I thought you were more of a Robin Hood."

Colton almost smirks. Almost.

"I read the children bedtime stories tonight. I-I had a hard time getting in here unnoticed, so we thought a disguise would work. My brothers took it a bit too far," he mutters.

"I'm sorry, you what?"

He shakes his head and drags me around my desk, gently nudging me into the seat, but he doesn't give me much space.

"I have so many questions for you, Winnie. Too many. But first, what the fuck is going on with you? Are you sick? I know this is a dick thing to say, but you look like hell. When's the last time you slept or ate?"

I'm too tired to find my indignation at his shitty comments.

Instead, I cast my eyes downward. "What do you want, Mr. Westbrook? I have work to do and no energy to waste."

"That. That's what I want. Why do you look like you've lost your puppy and your best friend? Why do you look like you haven't slept in months or eaten for longer than that? I know it's not my place, but fuck, Winnie. Why did you ghost me?"

The hurt is written on his face. I can hear it in his tone. And I hate myself because I know I'm about to do it again. If the tabloids hold even a sliver of truth, he'll be back out partying in no time. I've tried not to look, but his face is plastered all over social media and in magazines at every check-out counter. He has a bevy of women at his disposal, so whatever game he's playing with me for his own amusement is going to stop.

"I'm not interested in belonging to your harem, Mr. Westbrook. Whatever it is you've done to be assigned to me, I'm sure it can be resolved quickly. Just give me your supervisor's name, or whatever court-ordered form you need filled out, and I'll get it to the right people."

"What I did? You think someone is forcing me to be here?" he growls. "Did you learn nothing about me in Miami? Nothing at all?"

"I learned what I always learn, Mr. Westbrook. People show you what they want you to see."

"I'm here because I wanted to see you, Winnie," he yells, causing me to flinch.

Knock. Knock.

"Come in." I yell, then immediately wish I hadn't.

Dennis stands chagrined, and my stomach attempts a revolt. How much shit can a girl take in one lifetime?

"Do you have a minute, Winnie? I'd like to know what happened to your mom."

"Fuck." It slips past my defenses. So much for professionalism.

"Now's not a good time," Colton spits.

"I'm sorry," I say to them both. "I-I'm not feeling well. You'll have to excuse me."

Grabbing my purse, I do the only thing I can do. I run straight to the nurse's station. "Ginny, I'm so sorry. I must have caught a stomach bug," I tell her, reaching for a hospital mask. "I don't think I can keep anything down. I'm going to head home."

"Oh, dear. Are you all right? What can I do for you?" Ginny is another friend of my mother's, and I appreciate her concern.

"I'm okay, thank you, though. I'll call tomorrow. I'm sure I'll be fine by my shift."

Sensing eyes on me, I glance over my shoulder just in time to see Colton make a beeline for me. Rounding the nurses' station, I use the employee key card to slip into a locked side door.

My hands shake as I enter the parking garage. My chest aches with emotions that try to drown me. I really can't afford the night off, but I also know I cannot see Colton or Dennis again without losing myself completely in dreams that will never come true.

I can't hide from them forever, but sometimes a girl just needs to bow her head and let the tears come. There are times to be strong, and there are times you can only be strong after you've completely fallen apart. I need to break, and then I'll rebuild.

CHAPTER 12

COLTON

$\mathcal{I}$ take the steps to GG's lodge two at a time, painfully aware of the camera crews jumping into action all around me.

The lodge is open to the public now, but I cut across the foyer and head for her private dwelling. A large door on the other side of the parlor leads to her small apartment. Crossing the room, I knock on her door and wait. Then wait some more.

"GG!" I holler. "Open up."

"Well, Pan, you sure know how to make an entrance," she cackles from behind.

Turning in place, I find her walking toward me with a sheet of cookies. My brother, Halton, must be here baking. A pang of guilt tries to break free at the thought I'm causing him to stress bake, but that worry will have to wait its turn.

"Where does Winnie live?"

Sadness falls to the old woman's face, and my gut churns. "Colton," she sighs.

It's never a good sign when she uses your real name. In fact, before tonight, I don't ever remember her using my real name.

"Move outta the way. Come sit with me. We need to talk before you go flying off to save her."

"Save her? Save her from what?" There's a tremor to my words, and I clear my throat even as my hands shake. I've only ever felt fear like this a few times, but it's a sensation you never forget.

GG glances up at me, her face weathered with wrinkles, but still glows with a youthfulness she shouldn't be able to pull off. She shrugs her shoulders before they droop forward again. "Herself, Pan. And circumstances. That gal of yours has lost everything. Been beaten down with no one to lift her up for a long time. But now? Now she's truly alone, and even the almighty Pan might not be enough to fix her."

Adrenaline shoots through my system. It's a warning, an accusation. Fear. "What does that mean, GG?" I ask on a shaky breath. "Do you know where she is?"

GG sets the tray down on the coffee table and perches on the edge of the sofa. "I do, Colt, but sit down."

The scent of cinnamon and sugar wafts past my nose, but it doesn't bring comfort. It makes my stomach sour.

My fists clench and flex multiple times, but I do as she asks. My knee bounces with nerves as I wait for her to speak.

"Wendy—"

"Winnie," I interrupt. "She doesn't like being called Wendy."

A smirk pulls at the corner of GG's lip. "And you like Pan?"

A harsh breath escapes on a sigh, and I shake my head with laughter that's not funny. "No, GG. I've never been much of a Pan fan." My chest is tight as I force myself to remain calm. "I … I really need to talk with her, GG. Do you know where she lives?"

She nods and hands me a cookie, but my nose wrinkles and she sets it down. "So, I take it the hospital visit didn't go well for ya?"

An angry chuckle escapes before my words. "You could say that."

"Yet ya still want to pursue her at this late hour?"

Glancing at my watch, I cringe. It's almost nine p.m.

"I'm gonna give ya the cliff notes, Pan, 'cause it's not my story to tell. But Wendy's got a different life now, and before you go playing white knight, there are some things you ought to know. First, her mother passed away. Wendy was her sole caregiver, but that girl saw things no child should ever see. Now, she's a single parent to her brother, and he's ... well, he needs some help. She needs someone she can count on, but with a child in the picture, you can't go messin' in her life unless you're prepared to be there for the long haul. It ain't fair to her, or that little boy. Ya hear me?"

Razors slice my throat, but I nod in understanding. "Sh-She's all alone," I mutter.

"More alone than anyone I've ever known. We try, ya know. But she doesn't let many folks in. Betty-Anne's daughter helps with the boy and gives them a place to stay that she can afford. But I'll guarantee you, she's never been so low, so you need to really stop and think about what you want from her, Pan. Is she worth growing up for? Or are ya gonna stay a Lost Boy?"

My gaze is on her, but it's unfocused. We talked about a lot of things that night at the airport. Enough for me to know that her mom and brother were her whole life. While I've been out living, she's been struggling to survive and still losing everything.

"So, whatcha gonna do, Pan?"

"I-I don't know, GG."

But that's a lie. I knew it the second I laid eyes on CC again. The moment I touched her, my body knew what my heart desired. When Winnie focused those clear gray eyes on mine, I had the overwhelming urge to fix her. To hold her. To love her.

"Do you, ah, do you believe in love at first sight, GG?"

She crosses her arms with a knowing smile. "Oh, Pan. I wouldn't have married my Benny after a couple of months if I didn't, would I?"

"No, I guess not." Even as fear grips my every sense, a small smile forms on my lips.

"It's not gonna be an easy road, Pan. You're in for the fight of yer life. Think ya can handle that?"

"GG, if Winnie gives me a chance, I have a feeling I'd burn this world to the ground before I let her go again."

Her bushy brows raise with skepticism. Her small, knowing smile grows broader on her thin lips. By the time I leave GG's lodge with a handful of cookies and armed with information, I'm ready to battle my way to the car through at least a dozen camera crews.

Fucking hell.

Thankfully, I parked behind the garage, where they don't have access. Sprinting behind the old, converted barn, I find Halton leaning against my car. It's late April, but there's snow on the ground, and he's standing here in a sweatshirt. I really shouldn't say anything since I'm the one in tights, but I know he has to be freezing his balls off.

"What the hell, Halt? It's fucking cold out here. Why are you just standing there like that?"

Pointing in the direction of the lodge, he shakes his head. "Preston's going to be pissed. You can't just come and go like this until we get the vultures to back off."

I know he's right, but it was an emergency, and I tell him so. "Yeah, well, I had to talk to GG."

"I know. Rylan was eavesdropping, but don't tell her I told you." He tosses me his keys and nods his head at the black SUV with tinted windows. "I'm not putting on your fucking costume," he barks, "but if we leave at the same time, they won't be able to tell who we are. I'll take your car to Ashton's and walk home from there. Keep the SUV for a while. Unless someone sees you get in it, they'll assume it's me. It should buy you a couple of days, anyway."

My body propels forward, and I wrap him in a Westbrook special. "Thanks, Halt. I … you know I'm sorry about every-thing. I really didn't do it. I'm not the fuck up everyone thinks I am."

"I know. We'll figure it out," he promises, then heads to my car. "You really going after the girl dressed like that?"

Glancing down, I frown. "Nah, I'm just going to drive around for a bit. I'll go see her tomorrow."

He chuckles, then gives me the finger. "Good luck with that, Colty. You ready?"

"Yeah, and thanks for this," I say, holding up his keys, but he's already climbing into my car.

I follow him around the barn, and at the end of the lodge's driveway, he turns right to head around to the backside of the mountain. I take a left and head toward town, already knowing my destination.

Forty-eight Hill Street is a small, craftsman-style cottage set back from the narrow road. And when I say small, I mean there may be two bedrooms at most. It's white with black shutters and matching window boxes. The never-ending snow in this part of the country has kept any flowers from blooming yet, but they're full of Easter decorations, and it gives the place an almost cheerful appearance even when everything around it is still dead from the long winter.

I hope she's happy here.

Putting the car in reverse, I back up until the detached garage comes into view and that foreign frown forms yet again. If the house is small, the garage is downright miniature, and it sets off all kinds of protective feelings I'm not sure what to do with.

GG told me she and her brother live in an apartment above the garage, but there's no way this is the right place. It's a one-car garage and the apartment above it can't have more than a single room.

My forehead wrinkles, and I find myself pulling on my bottom lip as I watch the buildings from the darkness of the truck. Rolling my neck, it cracks, easing some of the tension building there, so I roll it to the other side then have to brush the hair out of my eyes. *I really need to get a haircut.*

Tapping my ring fingers on the steering wheel in time to the music playing over the speakers, I debate what to do. I know I can't go see her right now, but I can't bring myself to leave either.

"What are you doing in there, Winnie Darling?"

GG had also given me her last name. I like it more than I should. Winnie's sarcastic smile pops into my mind just as Nine Inch Nails comes on my playlist like a sign.

My chest constricts when I turn back to face her place and unease settles deep in my bones as Winnie walks down a sketchy looking staircase on the side of the garage. She's holding a garbage bag in one hand and hanging onto the railing with the other.

Fuck it. I'm here, and there she is. I exit my car and lean against it as I wait for her to return from wherever she's dropping the trash. After a couple of minutes, I pace. After five minutes, I huff. Closing in on the ten-minute mark, I let impatience get the better of me. Pushing off of the car, I stomp through the slush to find her.

CHAPTER 13

WINNIE

The door handle rattles as I slip inside of the cold shed. I take a minute to dump the trash in the proper bin, place the baby monitor on the workstation in the corner, then sit on the stool against the wall.

Pulling tissues from my jacket pocket, I don't know where the tears stop or the blood starts, but I put the wad of balled up tissue paper to my forehead.

Who makes children's toy trains out of solid wood, anyway?

Poor Weston.

A sob escapes, and I welcome it. In here, I can let go. In here, I hide. In here, I survive.

"Why did you leave me, Mom? Why?" Snot rolls down my lip, and I use the back of my sleeve to wipe it away. "You," I choke on a painful cry. "You were the only one I could count on. I-I'm failing everyone. Wh-Who do I turn to now?"

My body shakes uncontrollably. I don't even know if it's from crying or the cold, but it doesn't matter. This is my safe space. Tomorrow I'll be strong. Tomorrow I'll do better for Wes.

Encircling my left wrist with my right hand, I turn it back and forth. I'm not sure when the habit started, but I've rubbed the skin raw there so many times the skin is leathered with thin scars. Over and over I twist as my mind runs rampant with my next steps. Plans to save money. Ways to help Wes. Always Wes. He's the one bright spot in my life.

"You weren't supposed to die, Mom," I yell with a hoarse voice. "We had a plan. We had this all figured out. Now what am I supposed to do?"

The metallic taste of blood mixes with my tears and reminds me of the cut on my eyebrow. "God, Mom. What do I—"

The shed door wrenches open and Colton barrels through, scanning the small space. Tension flows from his body and his jerky movements cause my cried plea to freeze on my tongue.

"Winnie? What the hell happened to you? Are you okay?" He's frantic, but I'm too confused to move. "Baby, talk to me. What's going on? Why? Holy shit. Why are you bleeding?"

He spins in place, searching every crevice for something. He moves so fast I have whiplash and have to hang onto the stool to keep my balance.

"Winnie?" he barks. "Talk to me, sweetheart. What happened?"

My mouth moves, but no words come. I feel my eyes blinking rapidly, but it only makes my vision blur more.

"Jesus Christ, Winnie."

My head sways as he tears at his coat. In slow motion, or an out-of-body experience, I watch as he lifts his kelly green spandex shirt over his head. Next comes his undershirt, and before I can figure out his next move, he's pressing it to my forehead as he replaces his Peter Pan costume.

"Baby? Is Weston here? GG said he lives with you? Is he okay?"

He's asking about Weston?

"Oh God. What time is it?" I finally find my voice.

"It's a few minutes after nine. What happened? Why do you have a cut on your face?"

I shake my head, but it makes me feel nauseous. "H-He didn't mean to hurt me. It was an accident."

"He?" Colton growls as his face contorts into rage fueled by emotions I can't understand. His body radiates with it as he glances from me to the door behind him. "Someone did this to you? On purpose?"

"No. Yes. I mean, no, he didn't mean it. I swear. You don't understand. You don't understand him. No one understands him." I sob because that's the most truthful thing I've said in months.

"No. One. Gets. To. Put. Their. Hands. On. You." His words are staccato. Held together by a quickly slipping control.

No, he doesn't understand. Open your mouth, Winnie. Say something.

But I'm frozen. I'm frozen in the vortex of Colton Westbrook as he glares at me with thinly veiled hate. Yet, somehow I know it's not me he's angry with.

Oh, shit. He thinks it's—

"Stay here," he commands. If this were any other situation, I'd be scared to disobey him, but as he bolts from the shed, every protective instinct I have takes hold and I rush out after him.

Colton's strides are no match for mine, though, and he's halfway up the stairs before I reach him.

"Colton," I gasp. "Please. Please don't."

But it's too late. Colton rips open the door, nearly tearing it from the old, wooden frame, and then it comes. The scream. The sounds of skin hitting skin.

I bound up the stairs as fast as my body allows.

At the top, I push Colton out of the way and enter our small home. I drop to my knees in front of Weston, holding his hands at his sides. Holding his little body to mine. I rock and sing and cry. It's the only pattern I know some days. Rock. Sing. Cry as Weston writhes beneath me, attempting to free his hands. Little hands that want to connect so badly with something.

Anything. Usually his head. I don't understand it. I hate it. I hate it more than anything, but I know it will pass. I just have to hold him. Rock him. Sing to him. And cry.

Long moments, or short hours, I'm not sure. Eventually, his body goes limp. His fingers doing their dance, searching for his trains. Ring fingers, pointer fingers, middle fingers. Over and over again until I fill his tiny grasp with a blue toy train that cut my forehead open earlier, and a little white helicopter with a painted-on smile in his other hand.

At almost three years old, Weston's words, when he chooses to use them, always threaten to rip my heart from my chest.

"Momma. Momma," he whispers, running the back of his knuckles over my face.

"Shhh. Wes. Shh. It's okay, buddy. It's okay. It was an accident. I'm okay."

When his eyes dart around our home as they always do when he's nervous, I know the instant he notices Colton and my heart breaks all over again. I'm not surprised he stayed for the show, but it'll only be a matter of minutes before he runs away as fast as he can.

"Thupahero?" Weston asks with wonder.

It takes every ounce of strength I have, but I turn to face Colton, fully expecting to give him an out. What I see stalls the breath in my lungs.

Colton smirks at my little brother with kind eyes and a gentle demeanor. He crosses the room slowly and kneels down beside me.

"Do you like superheroes, little man?"

Weston nods with a smile that could rival Christmas morning.

Colton grins, easy and loving as he rests back on his heels. "Then I guess I'm your superhero, buddy."

"Thupa. Thupa fly?" My little brother is full of wide-eyed wonder, and I'm struggling to breathe.

My mouth is moving, but once again, I've forgotten how to

speak. Colton reaches over and closes my mouth. The gesture is so innocent yet so familiar tears spring to the backs of my eyes.

"I can't fly, buddy. But I can fix things." He's speaking to my brother, but his gaze never leaves mine. "Right now, I'm going to fix up Winnie here. Is that okay?"

Weston whimpers.

"I know, buddy. It's okay."

I need to put a stop to this insanity. But Wes is attempting to talk. To a stranger. I don't know if it's the superhero angle, or if he's as smitten as I was the first time I met him, but I can't take my eyes off the two of them. Wes doesn't do strangers. He took stranger danger to new heights, and it never left him.

Weston holds up his train, then covers his ears.

"The train came, and we weren't ready for it," I explain. "Loud noises scare him."

"A train came, and you don't like the noise?" he repeats to Wes, who shakes his head, but doesn't say anything.

When his little lip trembles, I know we've pushed him too much. "Wes? Buddy? How about if I let you watch a show while I help Mr. Westbrook out?"

Wes is a kid that needs a routine. I've known that for a while, and this is surely going to make tomorrow miserable, but I don't have much of a choice. Moving through our home, my body suddenly feels too heavy to hold myself up. I need to get Colton out of here.

"Well, that's not happening."

My head whips to Colton, and I blink away the sudden wooziness. "What's not happening?"

"I'm not leaving you here, Winnie. Not with that cut on your head, and not with your front door like that." He points to the open door, and I cringe. My front door hangs by one hinge, and I can tell it won't shut properly just by looking at it.

How am I going to afford to fix that?

117

"I'll take care of it in the morning," Colton whispers. "But for tonight, you can't stay here."

"Where would you like me to go, Colton?"

A sad smile plays across perfectly white teeth. "At least I'm back to Colton."

"I-I have to stay here." My words croak painfully in my throat, but something feels off. I don't feel right, and he senses it.

"Winnie? Win? What's wrong, baby? What's … hey? Winnie?"

"You should go," I force out. "Please go."

A strong arm wraps around my waist, and I have no choice but to sway into him. I feel like I'm drowning with no water in sight.

"I'm not going anywhere, sweetheart. Ever."

My shoulders shake with unshed tears. "Everyone leaves eventually, Colton. Everyone. Please go. I'm just going to go to bed. Wes, come here, buddy. It's bedtime."

At least, I think that's what I say. The words slur together, and it's hard to hear over Colton's shushing, but I'm so tired. So very tired. I feel my feet leave the ground, then Wes curls into my side. Somewhere I hear Colton speaking, but my body is succumbing to sleep.

"What?" someone barks. I wish I could open my eyes.

"I need Emory. Now. Forty-eight Hill Street. Please hurry."

CHAPTER 14

COLTON

"*D*id she take anything? Any drugs? Prescription pills?" Emory asks, entering the room.

"Of course not," I bark, affronted.

"Colton, are you sure? How well do you know this girl?"

"I know," I say through clenched teeth.

"It's important, Colt. Do you know that for sure?" she pushes.

Fuck. No. But I do. I can't explain it, but I know.

"Of course she didn't take nothin', Ems. His Wendy walks the straight and narrow." GG's voice surprises me. I wasn't expecting her, but I'm thankful for the backup.

She enters the room followed by her blue-haired partner in crime, Betty-Anne, and another woman I don't know.

"This is Betty-Anne's daughter, Beth. She owns the house and knows Wendy better n' anyone."

"Wendy?" Emory asks with a knowing smirk as she sits down beside Winnie.

"It's Winnie," I clarify.

"Only GG calls her Wendy. It drives her nuts," Beth says cautiously. "Is-Is she okay? Where's Wes?" Her voice rises with panic as she searches the small space. Lifting my arm, Weston peeks his little head out from under me, and she gasps. "Hey, Wessy. Ya got a new friend?"

"Thupahero," he whispers, and my chest expands ten sizes.

"Beth?" Emory interrupts. "You're sure she hasn't taken anything?"

"I'm just," Winnie mumbles.

"Oh yes. Not Winnie. Her life is Weston. She would never do anything to jeopardize that. Especially not with you know who pulling his parental rights crap."

My body tenses. Instinctively, I know Winnie is fighting battles in every corner of her life, alone.

"Okay, do you know what her schedule is? Any medical issues? Changes in her diet recently?" Emory asks as she numbs the area around the cut on Winnie's head.

"Are you a doctor?" Beth asks nervously.

"I am a doctor, but I'll be honest, I'm a heart surgeon. These Westbrook boys are making me regret my decision, though. I think I'd be more helpful to everyone if I was a general practitioner."

Beth wrings her hands, and I push myself up to a sitting position, taking Weston with me and placing him into my lap. She pales while watching me.

"Beth? We're all on Winnie's side. I just want to help her. I would appreciate anything you can do to assist Emory. From the small bit GG's told me, I don't want to take her to the emergency room unless we have to."

"God, no. That could be a disaster." Beth stresses each word. "Honestly, I've been telling her for weeks she's been showing signs of exhaustion. I saw it a few times in the hospital. Doctors working too many hours, nurses pulling doubles. I've been so terribly worried about her, but she can't slow down. She doesn't have a lot of options."

"Are you a nurse?" Emory asks as she deftly places stitches in my girl.

My heart races with worry that Winnie doesn't even flinch.

"I was. I worked with her mom, and I retired last year."

"Shouldn't that wake her up? Shouldn't she be awake? Why wouldn't that wake her up?" I ask impatiently.

Emory uses tiny scissors to cut a black thread, then places them back in her medical bag. I watch as she leans in to listen to Winnie's heart and lungs. Presses on her fingernails and runs her hands all over Winnie's body, presumably searching for other injuries.

"She is awake, Colton. Sort of. She's mumbling answers when I prompt her," Emory explains.

"What happened to the door?" Preston grumbles.

Shit.

"I, ah …"

"Thupa." Weston grins.

"Thanks, buddy," I groan.

"I found Winnie in the shed, crying, and bleeding. She said H-E did it," I spell out and roll my eyes toward Weston, hoping they get the hint without upsetting him again. "I didn't know who H-E was, so I took off ready to kill the son of a b-bobcat that hurt her."

Preston narrows his gaze on me, obviously still pissed off and not ready to cut me any slack. But he came when I needed him. That's something I've always had. Glancing around Winnie's small, one-room home, I wonder who she can call when shit hits the fan. The truth hits me like a linebacker.

"She's more alone than anyone ever ought to be." GG's words from earlier have me clutching my chest as if in pain.

"You gonna be okay there, Pan?" GG asks knowingly.

"Yeah. I—"

"So, who is she?" Preston barks. "This girl? This kid? Who are they?"

"Mine." One word and I feel it with every ounce of my soul. "She … they're mine."

Preston scoffs and rolls his gaze toward the ceiling. "Don't you think you've caused enough drama for a while? What is

121

this? A public relations stunt? I don't think having an insta-family will make anyone forget you were caught with your pants down with two women who are making waves about consent. You can't Peter Pan your way out of this one, Colton. Neverland is catching up to you."

His words cut deep, but they don't hit their mark. It's Weston that they affect. With every raised word Preston threw at me, the little boy in my lap grew more and more agitated. Beth and I are the only ones who seem to notice. She takes two steps forward, cutting an irritated glance in Preston's direction before she's by our side.

"He isn't a cuddler, Colton. Affection happens on his terms, and his terms only. Even with Winnie. This," she swipes her hand between Weston and me, "is very unusual. He likes you," she whispers.

"He's upset," I murmur.

"Noises bother him."

His hands were covering his ears earlier.

Instinctively, I wrap my arms around his little body and rock the way I'd seen Winnie do it. I can't remember what she was singing to him, but I do remember her song at the airport. So as my family stares at me in shock, I quietly sing the Violent Femmes song, "Blister In The Sun".

"For the love of God, Colton. You couldn't think of anything else?" Preston scolds.

"Get. Out." I sound calm, but my words are deadly.

"What?"

"You're upsetting him. Get. Out."

"You want me to leave?" he asks incredulously.

"You obviously are not here to support us, so yes. Get out. I won't say it again."

"This isn't how we do things," Preston hisses. "We stick together."

"Yeah, that's good advice, Pres. I suggest you go home and figure out if that works both ways."

Dropping my gaze to Weston, I continue singing as Preston storms out of the building and down the stairs.

"Is he, is he on the spectrum, Colton?" Emory asks patiently.

"I don't even know what that means," I admit.

"Autistic," Emory corrects.

"No," Beth answers for me. "The pediatrician doesn't think so, but there are so many variables. Winnie isn't sure. She hasn't been able to afford the testing he needs yet."

"Something's wrong with him?" My throat is dry, and my stomach clenches with worry.

"No," Winnie mumbles behind me. "He's perfect. Where is he? I-I'll take him."

She's disheveled and confused, but mad as hell.

"That's a trigger for her, Colton. There is absolutely nothing wrong with him. We just don't know how to help him," Beth explains.

"Stop talking about him like he isn't here. Stop, please," Winnie cries as her eyelids grow heavy again.

"What the hell, Emory?"

"I agree with Beth. I think Winnie is experiencing full-blown exhaustion. It can manifest in several ways, from hallucinations to a practically functional sleep-walk." Emory rounds the twin-size bed we're all crammed around and crouches down beside me. "Do you have any idea the amount of stress and lack of sleep it would take for someone to reach this level of exhaustion?"

I swallow the fear attempting to creep into my words. "What does she need?"

"Sleep. Honestly, most of the time, being hospitalized for exhaustion is an excuse for celebrities to detox, but this is one of those rare cases of someone actually needing it."

"No," Winnie attempts to sit up.

Beth places a hand on her shoulder to keep her in place. "She's Weston's sole caretaker, and her father is trying to get

123

custody. H-He's an alcoholic and in no way fit to parent, but he wants the money she gets from the state for raising him."

"Mother fucker," I hiss.

Emory scolds me with a silent expression while making eyes at Weston.

"Sleep." I nod. "What else does she need?"

"She's a little dehydrated, but nothing that requires IV fluids. She needs rest, Colt. And probably someone to talk to. She might have a slight concussion, but head injuries always need to be monitored."

I nod, a plan already formulating in my head. "Beth, could you help me pack up some of their stuff?"

She glances from me to Winnie and back again. Her concern is apparent. "Where are you taking her?"

"Home. I swear to you, I'm only going to take care of them."

GG, who has been uncharacteristically quiet, steps forward with a bag I recognize from the airport. "She'll be in good hands, Beth."

"B-But what about Weston?"

The little boy wraps his arms tighter around my middle, and my heart explodes with love. For the second time in my life, I believe in love at first sight.

"I'm going to take care of him, too," I promise. "GG will give you a code to get in the gate on our side of the mountain. My house is number ten on Brookside Trail. You're welcome to come check on them at any time."

Winnie mutters something behind us, but she's fast asleep when I turn. I know my life will never be the same as I watch her. She's worth growing up for, and I don't even know her. But then I see it. My T-shirt I placed on her in the airplane. It's folded neatly, sitting on an egg crate next to the bed.

She's thought of me. Tears form in the corner of my eyes as I draw Weston closer. It's the only sign I need. Winnie and Wes are my future.

CHAPTER 15

WINNIE

*W*eston's giggles wake me from the deepest sleep I've had in a long time. My eyelids flutter open, expecting him to be at my side, but nothing is familiar.

Glancing down, I don't recognize the bed. My clothes. This room. *Oh my God. Where are we?*

I scramble from the luxurious sheets I'm tangled in and face three doors. I tear at the first and find a bathroom. The second is an enormous walk-in closet that assaults me with a scent my body recognizes. *Colton.* I run to the third door and exit the room, following my brother's peals of laughter and feel a pain so visceral in my chest I think I might have a heart attack.

Rounding the corner, I forget how to breathe. People mill about, but the only one making noise is Weston. A woman who looks eerily like Lanie Cross with shorter hair stands with a little girl on her hip. A man I recognize as Colton's brother, Easton, crosses behind her, carrying a large bin overhead. GG and Beth sit sipping tea on the sofa, and sitting side by side on the ottoman with their heads tilted to the left at identical angles are Colton and my baby brother.

I can't see what they're watching, but I can hear the telltale song of his favorite train. A loud whistle comes through the sound system, and that's when I realize Weston didn't freak out or cover his ears. My gaze frantically searches his body for signs of discomfort, and then I register bright blue headphones on his head. They look like ones a pilot would wear, but it's the fact that he nuzzles his face into Colton's side that has tears spilling from my eyes.

"Colton?" The Lanie look-alike calls his attention to my presence.

Everyone in the room slowly turns toward me. Once again, he's rendered me speechless and dumbstruck. I can't move. Tears just cascade down my face until I feel faint.

"Why are you here? I mean, why am I here? Why are we here?" I fumble with my words, each one tripping over the next, trying to catch up to the chaos in my head.

Colton leans down, gently lifts the headphones from Weston's ears, and whispers so only the two of them can hear. Jealousy curls low in my belly. I've spent every waking minute getting close to my baby brother, and he comes in and has him wrapped around his little finger in no time.

Wes turns to face me. Delight and joy radiate off him, and I hate myself for never being able to bring those emotions out in him. He jumps off the ottoman and runs to my side. He slips his little hand into my palm and tugs until my feet move, and he drags me toward the other side of the house. No one stops us, and he's so excited that I follow.

Glancing over my shoulder, I find Colton watching me with apprehension. But it's his cheeks blushing the slightest shade of pink that has me concerned.

Weston pulls me through what I assume is Colton's home until we reach a door that has a giant W on it.

Blood rushes in my ears as he turns the knob and pushes through the door. Easton stands in the center of the room, erecting what can only be described as a small train city. The tracks weave effortlessly around the bed that is three sizes bigger than the one we have at home, along the wall, and back through tunnels, mountains, and tiny wooden buildings.

"What the hell?" I gasp, finding Weston's name in wooden letters on the far wall.

Easton turns at my words, placing his hands on his hips, and shaking his head. "I told him he was going overboard."

"What are you doing?" I choke out.

Weston releases my hand and runs to the train depot that houses a large box full of trains. Filling his hands with as many as he can hold, he places them on the round table. Carefully, he puts each one on the track.

"What's going on?" I repeat.

"Win? We need to talk." Colton's voice covers my fears like a warm blanket, but I quickly shake it off. If there's one thing I've learned in this life, it's that you can't count on anyone. Especially not someone like Colton Westbrook.

"You think?" I scoff. "What the hell is going on? How could you do this to him? He's too little to understand that he can't keep any of this stuff. Don't you ever think of anyone but yourself?" I'm shrieking, and drawing an audience, but I can't find it in myself to care. "Did any of you stop to think about how this would seem to him? He's three years old. Three!" I run out of steam. The effort of holding in tears overwhelms me.

"Winnie, stop," Colton commands, and I hate how my body responds to his tone. "My entire family has misjudged me my entire life, and I've let them. But not you. You may not understand it yet, but you know me. Not the Peter Pan version, the real one. Me. And I have done nothing but think of you and Weston for the past two days."

My shocked expression tells him I had no idea I'd slept an entire day away. *What the hell, Winnie? What will the judge say?* Sweat forms on my upper lip, and with no couth whatsoever, I reach up to wipe it away with trembling hands.

"Stop, Winnie."

"Stop telling me what to do," I roar.

When Wes whimpers, I take a shaky breath and attempt to give him a comforting smile.

"Yes, you slept for almost twenty-four hours because you needed it. The only people that know about that are here, in this house right now. Plus, my brother, Preston, and his wife because she's a doctor, and I wanted to make sure you were okay. Your dad, the judge, even your work, has no idea. They think you have the stomach bug."

As Colton speaks, I'm painfully aware that he must know my entire life story, and shame wracks my body. Goosebumps break out across my arms, and I find myself twisting the skin around my left wrist again.

Colton crosses the room until we're face-to-face. He reaches down and stops the assault on my wrist with one hand. He raises his other hand to cup my cheek. "You're not alone, Winnie. I'm here to help."

Mucus gurgles in the back of my throat when I attempt to speak, and once again, he cuts me off.

"My family has always called me Pan because they think I can never grow up. The world thinks I'm the black sheep, a playboy, reckless. And none of that has mattered since the moment I found you at that airport. I left Neverland that day, Winnie, and I'm never going back. I don't care what anyone thinks of me but you. I'm going to help you through this. I'm going to be right here for you."

Pieces of a conversation come to me, and I finally understand what this is. I mentally slap myself for believing, even for a second, that his words were true.

"A PR stunt. An insta-family. You need me to fix your reputation," I surmise.

Tilting his head the same way Weston does, he studies me. "That's what my brother thinks, yes. But that's not the truth."

Pulling away, I walk toward Wes. "Of course it is. Why else

128

would we be here? Why on earth would you be going to all this trouble if there wasn't something in it for you?"

Out of the corner of my eye, I see Easton back out of the way.

"You're right. There is something in it for me. But it's not what you think."

Rolling my eyes, I lower myself to the ground, mentally preparing for the meltdown pulling Weston from this room will create.

"Winnie," Colton rumbles, and I feel his words all the way to my toes.

Why the hell do I like it so much when he bosses me around?

"Look at me, CC." His tone leaves no room for debate, and as messed up as it is, I want to listen to him. I want to believe in him even though I know in my heart it can only lead to disaster.

With a heavy breath, I lift my gaze. My body heats under his intense focus. "I know you've probably seen all kinds of shit about me in the press."

The way he's examining my every move is too much, so I refocus my gaze on Weston.

"Winnie," he snaps, causing me to jump. "None of it's true. None of it. As far as I'm concerned, my last night as a single man was January twenty-first of last year."

January twenty-first? My head snaps to his as the date registers. Miami. The airport.

"What are you saying, Colton?"

"I'm saying I want you and Wes to move in here. Live with me. Let me help you get permanent custody, and then I want you to marry me."

Easton is the one who chokes this time, spraying water all over the floor. Wes finds this hilarious, and his shoulders shake with a belly laugh as Easton attempts to wipe up the mess.

"Dude, you can't be serious. You don't even know her. It's one thing to move them into your home that you're never in, though Preston is going to rip you a new one over this, too, but marriage? You've always jumped into the deep end then learned how to swim. You make a decision and it's full steam ahead, but you're talking about people's lives here, Colt. You're being careless. Especially with The WB having the issues it is. What will it look like to our board of directors when this all blows up?"

"Shut up, Beast," the Lanie lookalike growls, entering the room with a little girl still attached to her hip. "I'm Lexi, by the way. You'd think these jackasses would have had some etiquette lessons with all their money, but just ignore them."

As soon as she says her name, I remember GG talking about her other granddaughter, Lexi. My arms instinctually wrap around Weston in case I need to run. I'm beginning to think they're all insane.

"Everyone get out here," GG calls from the hallway. "Stop crowdin' her."

Lexi crouches in front of Weston and me. "Hey, buddy. Do you want to come play with me and AJ in the other room? Beth is there, too."

Wes glances from me to the little girl in Lexi's arms and then to Colton. He slightly nods his head with a warm smile, and Weston beams. It's like Colton just poured salt all over my busted-up heart. It makes me hate him a little.

Moisture dampens my eyelashes, and I blink to keep them at bay as Wes hoards as many toy trains as he can carry. "Leave those here, buddy. They aren't ours. We have to leave them here."

"Go ahead and take them, Wes. They are yours, forever. I won't take them from you."

It's one thing to tell me what to do, but this asshole does not get to mess with my kid. Weston, sensing I'm about to correct him, scatters from the room with all the adults scurrying behind him. I stomp across the room, anger making my hands twitch with the need to break something.

"How dare you?" I seethe when I'm inches from his body. "You do not get to tell him what to do. You do not get to undermine my authority with him. Is this some kind of sick joke to you? This is my life, Colton. My fucked up, exhausting, thoroughly chaotic life. You don't get to go messing around in it on a whim, you arrogant, self-obsessed, prima donna playboy."

He takes a step forward, forcing me back. Then another, and another, until my back is against the wall and I'm breathing hard.

"One more time, Win. Everyone else in this fucking world can misjudge me. You cannot."

"Why? Why does it matter what I think about you?"

"It matters," he rumbles, "because you're the only one in my life that I need to impress."

"Why?"

"Because from the second I saw you, I was invested. The way you read with such intensity. The way you pushed when I pulled. The way your eyes sparkle, and your competitive nature. You got under my skin in a way I haven't been able to give up, even when you ghosted me. It matters because, despite what you say, you need my help, and I need you."

"To fix your reputation."

His finger hooks under my chin, and my lip quivers as he raises my face within inches of his. "To fix me, Winnie. I don't give a shit about my reputation. I need you because I think you're the missing part of me."

"Y-You don't know me."

He grins, and my knees buckle. If the wall wasn't holding me up right now, I would certainly fall. "That's the best part about me, baby. I dive into the deep end and learn as I go."

"That's not how I work."

"We'll figure it out together."

"You're crazy." Shaking my head, I try to clear my thoughts. I can't think when he's this close. *Too close*. My body bends to his will so easily it's terrifying. And heady. I need to keep my wits about me. "You can't just move strangers into your home."

"Why not?"

"Colton, be serious. You don't know me. I don't know you. And I have Weston to think about. He's the only thing that matters to me. I know what it feels like to have a dad walk out on you. I've had the displeasure of it happening twice. I can't have him getting attached to you, and then have you bail when it's not fun anymore. I won't do that to him. Plus, you don't know me!" I wail. "You don't know what kind of mess I have on my plate."

Colton reaches for my hand with graceful speed, clasping it to his chest. "I know your mother passed away. That you were her only caretaker, and that it was a horrific way to die. That it caused you unbearable pain. I know you're concerned about Weston and his struggles, but I can already tell he's an incredible kid. I know he calls you mom, and you both love and hate it."

"How—"

"I see it in your expression when he calls you mommy. You are his mother now for all intents and purposes, but I see the guilt you carry for accepting that honor. I know your father is a piece of shit more interested in money than Weston's care. I know the big, shitty pieces of your life, and I know I can help make them better. I also know that you'll need to fill me in on all the details that made these big events so painful whenever you're ready. So don't tell me I don't know you, CC, because I do. And I'm still here. I want you and Weston. I want it all."

Gah! What the hell?

"I'm sorry, Colton. But you're insane. You know about me, that doesn't mean you know me. What did you think was going to happen here? I was going to wake up, look around, and think, hey! I just hit the jackpot! Score! Let's live happily ever after? This isn't a fairytale, Mr. Westbrook. My sad excuse for a life will not clean up your reputation. I won't allow you to use us that way. I appreciate you taking care of me when I was ill, but if you think I'm just going to move in with you because you said so, you really don't know me at all."

I huff past him and turn in circles in the hallway. This house is like a freaking maze. Finally getting my bearings, I find everyone in the family room talking to the sheriff, who looks anything but pleased to be here.

CHAPTER 16

COLTON

*P*ushing my hands deep into the pockets of my jeans, I roll back onto my heels and let out an exasperated sigh.

"Well, that didn't go like I thought it would," I tell the silver train that seems to watch me from his perch on the roundtable. "You're scary little fuckers, you know that, right?" Raking a hand through my hair, I puff out my chest and leave the toys alone.

I've got my work cut out for me with Winnie, but even the thought of her makes me smile. Fucking East. Is what I'm doing impulsive? Possibly, but I know it's right. I feel it deep in my bones and I'll be damned if I let anyone ruin it. I just need to figure out how to get through to my girl.

"Wendalyn Darling? I'm here for a welfare check for one Weston Darling." The low, unfamiliar baritone makes me pick up my pace until I stand at Winnie's side.

"Sheriff," I acknowledge, thrusting my hand out and introducing myself. "I'm Colton Westbrook. What can I help you with?" I've positioned myself between him and Winnie. Acting as a shield, I cross my arms over my chest, and relief hits me when I feel Easton's similar stance to my right.

GG crowds us all, and we form a protective wall around Winnie and Wes.

"Mr. Westbrook, I'm here for a wellness check on a minor. A witness saw Ms. Darling being escorted out of their home. The witness was concerned she was incapacitated, and now I'm here to fill out a report for the court."

"Was this concerned citizen Jason Darling?" The sheriff's eye twitches, and I have my answer.

"I'm not at liberty to say."

"Anderson! Aren't welfare checks supposed to be conducted with a social worker present?" Lexi inquires, and I throw her a grateful nod.

"Come on, Lex. You know how things work around here."

"I do because my cousin was almost killed doing one of these welfare checks on her own."

Everyone in Burke Hollow remembers when Lanie was attacked years ago, and it's enough to make the sheriff back off.

"Ms. Darling, would you prefer to do this with a social worker present?" Sheriff Anderson asks.

"I don't—"

"We'll wait for the social worker and our attorney," I interrupt.

"Colton!" Winnie's eyes are wide with fear, and I fucking hate it. Reaching for her, I drag her into my side.

"Mr. Westbrook, can I ask how you're involved here?"

"It's my family," I growl.

His shocked expression silences everyone else in the room. "I-I didn't realize."

"Now you do. We were in the process of moving into our home now that it's finally finished, and Winnie hit her head on a cabinet door hard enough to require stitches. So yes, I helped her to the car, then I carried Wes and all their stuff, too. What kind of man wouldn't help his fiancée to the car? I think your source," I spit the word, "needs to do some fact-checking next time."

"Colton, please." Winnie's fragile voice is like nails on a chalkboard. I'd rather have her yelling at me, throwing snark, sass, anything but scared.

I lean down and press my lips to the side of her head. It's a gesture that feels so damn right that my chest actually aches with the need to fix the entire fucking world just for her. "Shh, baby. Everything's going to be okay. I promise you."

"What do you need for this wellness check, Anderson?" Lexi snaps. She can be a real bitch when she needs to be, and right now, I couldn't love her more.

"Well, shit, Lex." I notice for the first time that Sheriff Anderson is about our age, so he's probably known Lexi his entire life. With a heavy sigh, he pulls papers out of his jacket pocket. "I need to observe Weston and Winnie in their home environment. I need to do a home check to ensure his safety."

"That's it?" she asks with arms crossed over her chest.

Glancing around the room at my family, pride swells in my chest. They're all standing at attention. Soldiers ready to fight a battle they weren't prepared for but march full steam ahead because I need them.

"That's it."

"Tsk. Tsk. Andy. You wait 'til I tell yer mama," GG scolds.

"I'm just doin my job, GG." I swear to God all I heard was aww, shucks come out of this man's mouth. GG can literally bring grown men to their knees.

"Well, you git to it then. My boys got work to do so that little boy can sleep in his new bed tonight."

"Yes, ma'am. Wendalyn? May I proceed?"

"It's Winnie. Um ..." Her teeth sink into her bottom lip, and I can feel her fear. Someday she'll understand we all have her back.

"We won't let anything happen to either of you, Win."

If looks could kill, I'd be a dead man. I know I just forced her hand about moving in with me, but I have faith. This will be good for us all.

here isn't much I hate more than the silent treatment. The silent treatment from Winnie, though? Hot damn, that's enough to make me glitter bomb my own house just to get a reaction out of her.

By the grace of God, the home inspection was painless and over relatively quickly. Sheriff Anderson didn't understand Weston's headphones, but it was none of his business as far as I was concerned, and thankfully, he let it go.

Winnie has paced, huffed, cursed, paced, slammed a door and then quickly apologized to the wall, and paced again. None of it has been in my direction, but all of it is because of me. I showed her where to put her stuff, and when I tried to help, she smacked my hand away like I was caught in the cookie jar.

Now she's standing outside of Weston's room. Her bottom lip is caught between her teeth again and she's worrying that wrist of hers. I hate when she does that most of all. Her skin is red and irritated, like she has no idea how rough she is on herself.

I'm standing at the end of the hall, but I can't watch the pain and indecision any longer. I'm in front of her in four long strides.

"Tell me what's wrong." I have no idea why I keep barking orders at her. I'm not this dominating asshole, but something came over me when I saw her in the hospital the other night, and for the life of me, I haven't been able to control it since.

Her jaw sets tight, and her nostrils flare in anger. Her body is wound so tight, I almost expect her to stomp her foot just to release some of the tension. Instead, she speaks through clenched teeth. "Everything, Colton. Everything is wrong. We don't belong here. It's going to end up hurting Weston in the end, and you gave me no choice in any of it."

"We have a lot of ground to cover. But I mean here." I point to Weston's room. "What about this, Weston's room specifically, is bothering you?"

Her body deflates as she drops her gaze, like the weight of life is literally dragging her to the floor.

"Baby, please let me help."

"Don't baby me. Just don't. You don't know me or how hard you're making my life."

"We'll talk about all of this as soon as Wes is asleep. But please, help me break things down and I'll fix them one at a time. What about his room is bothering you?"

"He's never had his own room before," she whispers so softly I almost miss it.

Bending my knees so we're eye to eye, I wait for her to continue.

"Wh-What if he needs me? What if he wakes up in the middle of the night and can't calm himself down? I've always been within reach. If not me, then my mom or Beth. I-I'm already failing him in so many ways. I don't want this to be another."

Winnie's lip quivers until she juts out her chin, stubbornly sucking in tears I want to lick away.

"Can I show you something?"

She doesn't even glance up, but she nods, and I open Weston's door. Taking her hand to keep it from rubbing her wrist raw, I drag her into the room.

"East installed the best baby monitors he could find. He has the same one at his house for his twins. You'll be able to see and hear him from your phone. There's also a monitor in the kitchen and your bedroom. You can even check on him from work if you want to. My brother, Ash, set it up so it can't be hacked. It's all fully secure. And, CC?"

Her hand trembles in mine, but she glances up, and I want nothing more than to rid the fear from her eyes.

"He slept in here last night, even before all the train stuff, and he did great. Beth and I left the door open. We put on the

139

sounds of the ocean on my phone, and I slept in the hall, right outside of his door, just in case. But if you're more comfortable in here, we can get another bed tomorrow."

She shakes her head no, but the tears fall free. "I usually sleep with him or on a blowup bed next to him."

"Jesus, baby. No wonder exhaustion hit you like it did."

"Momma." Weston plops down on the bed with a grin. He's wearing his new superhero pjs, and I can't wait for him to see his surprise in the morning.

"Nice jammies, buddy." She smiles through a shaky voice.

"Thupahero," Wes replies proudly, pointing at the giant star on his chest.

"They're great, Wes. Did you say thank you?"

Weston jumps to the foot of his bed, and I run to the side, scared shitless that he'll fall.

"Hey, no jumping on the bed, okay?"

He nods with a "Thupa," thrown in as he hugs me.

Winnie shudders beside me and covers her mouth as a strangled sound attempts to escape. Squaring her shoulders, she pulls herself together and steps between Wes and me.

"Bedtime, buddy. Are you so excited about sleeping in this awesome room tonight?" she stresses the word tonight.

I want to correct her, but I know better than to push my luck, so I bite my tongue.

Weston nods his head with the brightest smile I've seen from him yet. He leans in, and she tentatively wraps her arms around him. When her shoulders bounce, I know she's holding in tears again.

As I watch them, my first thought is, *Are hugs really that rare for him?* It's followed closely by, *How much does she hold inside?*

I say my goodnights and allow them privacy to do their routine. Standing outside of the door, I smile as she sings about blisters and the sun. By the time Winnie emerges, I've slid down the wall and am sitting on the floor.

"You're not sleeping there again. Are you?" she gasps.

"No, sweetheart. I was just waiting for you. You ready to talk?"

"This won't be a talk, Colton. This is a war you started, but I'll win it one battle at a time."

I try to keep my smirk in check and fail miserably. While Wes slept, she was lying in there with him, planning her attack. "Game on, baby. I'm playing for keeps."

CHAPTER 17

WINNIE

*C*olton told me to make myself comfortable in the family room while he changed, but I'm too keyed up to sit. Pacing the room, I've had plenty of time to take in its beauty. He built the entire home into the side of a mountain, and they used every opportunity to bring the outdoors in.

The walls are a warm shade of green, and it has dark, exposed beams everywhere. The furniture is oversized and comfortable. It's all positioned to highlight the floor-to-ceiling windows showcasing the natural beauty all around.

It's cozy, and it causes me to pause and really take everything in. It's not at all what I would have expected the Westbrook playboy to live in. Granted, this is like a vacation home or something, but still, he must have had some input.

Everything is impeccable. From the long, linen drapes to the coordinating throw pillows. The only thing off is the giant package sitting on the mantel. With the rest of the home fully decorated, it's odd that this piece sits unhung.

"Okay, Win. I'm ready for battle."

I take three long breaths to calm my racing heart before facing him. Gathering my courage, I slowly turn and all I can do is blink.

Blink.

Blink.

He's so absurd, a shriek of laughter falls from my lips. I can't contain it or control it. I laugh so hard my stomach cramps and I'm tempted to lean over on my knees to catch my breath.

"What?" I seriously can't stop laughing. "What are you wearing?"

He shrugs with a warm grin plastered on his face. Not an ounce of embarrassment to be found. "I can't be a thupahero without the right gear."

I can't tell if it's my heart or my ovaries, but one of them just exploded for sure.

"You bought matching superhero onesies for you and my brother? When? Was I out for a night or a week? How did you get all this done in twenty-four hours?"

"Anything can happen for the right price, baby. And there isn't a price I wouldn't pay to make things right for you."

I really wish he wouldn't say stuff like that.

He stands, legs spread as wide as his grin in a man-sized onesie complete with the attached cape and a Captain America shield in his left hand. He holds something up in his other hand, but I'm thoroughly confused.

"I know you're ready for a fight, Win, so I brought you some gear, too. Not sure if Thor can beat Captain America, but it comes with a hammer for you to beat on me with." He smirks, but seems unsure for the first time since I met him.

"You dressed up to … to fight with me?"

"Oh, I don't want to fight with you, CC. But I will fight for you. You want the truth?"

Gulp.

"Yes. Always."

"I was kind of hoping gearing up in my thupahero gear might take the edge off your anger. Did it work?"

Hope tugs at my chest, but hope is dangerous, so I force it away.

"It's not easy to be mad at a sexy man in spandex."

"Hey! I'll have you know this is one hundred percent fleece. It's super soft. Wanna feel?"

My eyes attempt to bug out of my skull, and I shake my head so fast he roars with laughter.

"Colton …"

I'm not sure what I want to say to him, but we have to put an end to this before Wes really gets hurt.

"I know, Win. I know. We need to talk." He holds up the Thor pajamas that actually look like they might be my size. "Do you want to prepare for battle first?"

"Why are you doing this?"

"This specifically?" He holds up the pajamas again, and my eye roll has him dropping them into the chair beside him. "I'm trying to show you I'm not going anywhere. I want to help you."

"But why? Why me? Why now? What do you want from me?" My words sound small. I feel weak. Wounded. Broken.

With graceful steps, he crosses the room until he's standing right in front of me. "What do I want from you, CC?"

An ocean full of tears fills my eyes, but I keep them in check as I nod my chin stubbornly.

"That's easy, baby. Just you. I'll only ever ask one thing of you, and if you can do that, I get you. And Weston."

"Are you insane? You can't just claim people you don't know."

"You keep saying that, but you've been embedded in my soul since the day I met you."

I huff out my disbelief and try to turn from him, but he catches my elbow.

"I haven't been able to think of anyone but you since the day you left. I promise you that."

145

He's so earnest, I almost believe him. He's like the sun, though. I can't look directly at him and still form a coherent thought, so I drop my gaze. I land on a pile of gossip magazines when I do, and I'm instantly reminded that I'm being played here.

"You're so full of shit, Colton. I've seen the pictures. The articles. You may remember me, but I've been the furthest thing from your mind." Reaching down, I grab a handful of glossy magazine covers, lift them, and smash them into his chest.

He reacts as quickly as I do and catches my wrist in his grasp, holding it tightly to his chest as the magazines flutter to the floor. The dominating tone is back when he speaks, and I shiver while silently cursing myself.

"I will only ever ask one thing of you, Winnie. The only thing I want from you."

"What's that?" I ask, full of insolent aggression.

"Your trust. Your trust in me. The image those photographs portray is not me. It's not true. I'm not a Lost Boy, unwilling to grow up. I'm just a man who was waiting for the one worth changing for. I'm just a man who's been waiting for you."

He must see the disbelief in my eyes, even as my heart pinches with the need to believe him, because he releases me and walks away. I open my mouth to protest, hating the sudden distance, but he stops a few feet behind me. When I turn, he's staring up at the package on the mantel.

"This might scare the shit out of you." He chuckles.

Of all the emotions this man drags out of me, somehow, I know fear is nowhere near registering for me.

Colton reaches up and carefully pulls down the covered package with great care. I'm shocked he can move it so easily. He sets it on the floor with a thunk, and I know it must be heavy. Then he takes half a step back. It has to be five feet tall and almost as wide.

"You, Winnie Darling, are the only one who's been on my mind." He leans forward and pulls the sheet away.

My knees buckle, and I slowly lower to the sofa. My gaze is unblinking. Shocked. Amazed. Confused. My mouth opens, but no words come out as I stare at a portrait of me in a white, gauzy gown. My hair cascades over my right shoulder as I peer down over the left. A shadow covers my body in the portrait, and the more I stare at it, the more I recognize it as the shadow of a man. It has a very distinct Peter Pan vibe, with a unique twist. A stranger may not make the connection, but once I see it, there's no unseeing it.

Whoever did this created a fairytale version of me as Wendy, with Colton's Peter Pan shadow watching over me.

"Who? When? How did you do this?" I gasp after an eternity.

To Colton's credit, he stands back and gives me time to take it all in. Noticing something in the corner of the portrait, I stand to get a closer inspection. There's an outline of an airplane in the background. Without thinking, I reach out and run my finger over it. Wendalyn is faded, almost as if the artist wasn't sure if they should include it or not, on the body of the plane.

Colton's warm breath caresses my hair as he speaks. He's so close I can feel his heat.

"I couldn't let you go, CC. I needed something to remind me you were real. Halton made this for me."

"He's incredibly talented."

"He is. Turn around, Winnie."

My spine tingles at his command, but I have an over-whelming urge to obey. Slowly, I turn in place. He makes no move to give me space, so I'm cocooned between him and the portrait.

"I know this has been a giant clusterfuck, but I see you. I feel you. We can take this as slow as you need, but I have never wanted anything more in my entire life than I want your trust."

He could have asked for a million dollars and that would

have been easier than what he's asking for. Trust? I don't think I can.

"I don't think I know how to trust anyone anymore, Colton. You could ask me to harness the moon and it might be easier."

Sadness washes over his face as tears glisten in his honey-colored irises. So sweet. So clear. And seemingly so honest. I'm not sure I've ever faced a more open expression in all my life, and he sucks the air straight from my lungs.

"Everyone needs a rock, Winnie. Someone to trust. A partner in this cruel world. All I'm asking for is a chance to be that for you. A chance to teach you to trust in me. We have a world of insecurities and realities to face, starting with getting Weston the help he needs, and I want to do all of it with you. Figure it all out, with you, for you, because of you."

"Wes, he's—"

Colton places a finger over my lips to silence me. "Emory spoke to Dr. Welch. Before you set that fire in your eyes free, she didn't speak to him specifically about Wes. She said that would be a breach of patient confidentiality or some bullshit. But she spoke in generalities and found out the best center for testing is just outside of Boston. The Claymar Center. Weston has an appointment next month."

"Next month?" I gasp. I know about the Claymar Center. I've been saving, but there's no way I can have the money in four weeks. My body shakes, and he once again steps into my space.

"It's all taken care of, CC. I'm taking you there myself. I'm paying for it. We're going to figure this out."

It's too much. It's all too much, as he wraps his arms around my shoulders and pulls me in close. His body envelopes mine as he comforts me. Tears turn to sobs, yet he doesn't pull away. If anything, he holds me tighter.

"You can't do this stuff, Colton. You just can't. I have to take care of it. I have to do it for Wes. For my mom."

"Don't you see, Win?" he whispers as he rests his chin on my head. "You are doing it. By allowing me to help you, you are taking care of him. If you keep giving all of yourself, eventually you'll have nothing left to give. We're not meant to be solitary creatures, CC. Life's too hard to do it all yourself. Let me take some of the burden. Let me carry some weight of your sadness because doing it alone is crushing you, and I can't stand to see you like this."

"I have nothing to offer you, Colton. We're essentially a charity case for you, and I honestly don't know if my ego will allow me to live with that."

Long fingers make their way under my chin, and he once again lifts my face to his. We're separated by barely a breath, and when he speaks, the air he expels is like a million tiny butterfly kisses coating my skin in a safety net.

"You changed me with one little kiss, Winnie Darling. My world was off kilter before that kiss, and you set me straight. I haven't been the same since, and holding you in my arms like this? I know I'll never be again. You make me a better person just by being in my sphere. If you can do all that after just one kiss, I know you have more to offer me than my money could buy in a lifetime."

"You keep talking about forever and lifetimes. This isn't make believe, Colton." I pull back to stare him in the eye. "Love at first sight doesn't account for real world problems, and stress, and the messiness that life creates. I don't know if love lasts forever, but I do know that it takes time to develop. I don't believe in love at first sight, or happily ever afters. That's not the world I come from."

He regards me as he holds me tight in his grasp. Against his hard body, I feel every ridge and plane of sculpted muscle beneath my fingertips. I also feel the other worldly rod between his legs as it presses into my belly, and my core clenches with a need I've only ever read about.

As if his mind has just had the same thought, he pulls his hips back and shrugs without a hint of remorse. "Sorry. I can't

149

control that when you're around. When I said there hasn't been anyone since I met you, I mean there has been *no one* since I met you."

When it dawns on me what he means, I'm left speechless again. Is he seriously saying he hasn't had sex in a year and a half? I don't believe it for a second. His raised brow interrupts my thoughts.

"Trust, Winnie. I'm asking you to trust me as we right your world."

Trust. The one thing that keeps me safe. By only trusting myself, I ensure I won't get hurt. How can he possibly expect me to give that up?

Slowly, I pull away, and I catch sight of the giant star in the center of his chest. My very own thupahero.

Visions of Weston crying at the park because he wants to play with other kids but doesn't know how punch me in the gut. Weston at a birthday party, clinging to my leg, crying, begging to go home.

Weston.

I stare up at Colton, who waits patiently for me to work through my inner turmoil, and I have my answer. He wants to help Weston. He says he wants me. All I need to do is trust him. Or try to.

Fighting all the demons of my past, I put my faith in the man standing before me.

"I don't know how to trust, Colton. I don't know if I'll ever be able to fully with anyone. But, if you promise me that no matter what happens, you'll always be kind to Wes, I'll try. With you, I'll try."

I swear the heavens open up and cover him in sunshine, because the smile he flashes my way causes that sliver of hope in my chest to burst free.

If this life with Colton doesn't destroy me, I just might find myself again.

Colton wraps me in another giant hug and lifts me clear off

the floor as he spins us in a circle. "We'll take things slow, CC. But I'm telling you right now, once I decide something, I never back down. I am going to marry you someday."

Nervous laughter falls from my lips, but I feel freer than I've felt in a long time. The dark shadow that follows me is no match for the light Colton exudes.

He finally sets me on my feet, and I think he'll lean in to kiss me. I don't realize how much I actually want that until his lips land on my cheek.

Please don't ruin me! my inner voice screams and fear pounds on my chest cavity. Then he smiles, and I'm forced to smile back.

"Slow, remember?" I remind him.

"We'll go at whatever speed you want, CC. But I want a redo of our first date. Soon. Okay?"

I giggle. Actually giggle. It's a foreign feeling, but not entirely unpleasant. "Okay, Mr. Westbrook. I'll accept a redo."

"Colton," he growls. The sound is addicting, and I'm going to make it my mission to hear it every chance I get. "Colty. Colt. Mine. Any of those are acceptable. The only time I want you to call me Mr. Westbrook is after you say I do. Got it?"

Wide-eyed, infuriatingly turned on, and uselessly confused, I nod.

"Good. Welcome to the chaos, baby."

CHAPTER 18

COLTON

*W*innie has slowly gotten comfortable in our home over the last two weeks. She's gone to work, having Beth come over every time to stay with Weston, but the circles under her eyes have finally disappeared, so I don't push it. Weston is adjusting remarkably well to our living situation, and I'm pretty sure I'm one of his favorites. I rank right after that toy helicopter he carries around.

They say a parent's love is unparalleled, and that scares the shit out of me, because I love this kid so much already. I can't imagine not having him in my life. Since I'm on leave from The WB, I've had time to observe him. He definitely does better in his own environment, and I now understand why Winnie gets so upset when someone asks what's wrong with him. There's nothing wrong with him. He's perfection in a tiny, train-obsessed package. I think he just takes in the world differently than most of us.

Knock. Knock.

"I got it." Winnie and Wes sit on the family room floor with train tracks spread out all around them.

I make it to the foyer before Preston lets himself in. My oldest brother has always done whatever he wants.

I've banned my entire family from showing up unannounced. I want Weston to get comfortable here before we traumatize him with the Westbrooks' chaos.

"Preston," I say in warning. "What's up?"

We haven't spoken since I moved Winnie into my home. He left a bunch of messages about me hiding out at Ashton's and that it's in the best interest of the family to stay out of sight.

I ignored them all.

He walks toward me, tension still visible in his shoulders, but he wraps me in a hug anyway. It's the Westbrook way.

"What's up, Pres?" I repeat.

"Ash got the video feed from the bar. I'm sorry I was a jackass, but the girls are still moving forward with a civil suit. We need to talk."

Fear grips my chest when I find Winnie watching us, but if I've learned anything from my brothers, it's that nothing good comes from keeping secrets.

Rubbing a hand over my face, I open my arm to lead him into the family room.

"I have one rule," I say, reality setting in when I see Wes staring at us with worried eyes.

Preston notices him, too, and he checks his inner asshole at the door. With a warm smile, he waves and turns to me. "What's that?"

"Wes doesn't like loud noises. If you can't keep your temper in check, you'll need to leave."

Preston isn't really an asshole. He took over as head of our family when our father passed away, and the strain of that responsibility must be massive, but he needs to learn I'm not the baby brother playing practical jokes to get noticed anymore.

Maybe it's my fault for allowing these assumptions to carry on as long as I have, but staring at Winnie and Wes, it stops now.

"Uh," Winnie interrupts, "I can take Wes to the library or

154

something." She's already moving to his side, but I catch her arm.

"I'd like you to stay. I'm not keeping things from you. Not now, not ever."

"Shit," Preston curses under his breath, and I shoot him a glare.

"Watch it, Pres." My tone is even, but my words cut through the air like a sword.

Winnie slips from my grasp and scoops up Wes. "It's okay. I've been wanting to go. It's a safe space for us."

I nod as she carries him from the room, hating that they need a safe space.

"What are you doing, Colt?" Preston's words are heavy. He doesn't sound like a pissed off bear anymore, but concern is etched in every syllable.

"Securing my forever," I admit without a hint of shame.

"And you're so sure she's it? Someone you knew for twelve hours. Did you at least get her to sign something? An NDA? Maybe a prenup if the time comes?"

My blood goes cold. "You have some nerve, Preston," I hiss through clenched teeth. "How did the prenup work out with you and Ems? Oh, that's right. You refused one. What about for East? Halton?"

"They were different. They're not—" He stops when I step into his space.

"They're not what? The screw up? Is that what you were going to say?" My voice raises a fraction, and I ball my hands into fists to get myself under control. "When have I ever done anything irreparable to our family, Preston? When have the gossip columns ever gotten it right? When did I become the punching bag for everyone else's insecurities?"

"Colton. We're in the shit here with this lawsuit. Halton and East's futures with The WB depend on this merger."

"And I've done my part to make this company a success. This clusterfuck is not my doing, Preston, and you know it.

Macomb is waging a war against me, and Ashton isn't doing a damn thing about it. What happened to the Westbrook way? Taking care of our own? Why am I the only one who doesn't get the support I need when someone is taking shot after shot at me?"

"The Westbrook Group needs—"

"The Westbrook Group. The Westbrook Group … what about me, Preston? Your brother. What about—"

I'm cut off by a high-pitched scream I know in my bones is Weston. I take off at a dead run toward his room. Sounds of shouting have me barreling in the other direction to the front door.

Yanking it open so hard I'd be surprised if it's still on its hinges, I find my worst nightmare. Winnie stands at the bottom of the stairs, clutching Weston to her chest as paparazzi surround her.

The world blurs around me as I barrel down the stairs, pushing and shoving reporters until I reach her. Panic clutches my chest when I see her face. The photographers close in, shoving cameras in every angle. Weston is crying and scratching at Winnie like he's trying to climb inside of her to hide. A protective rage overtakes my body as I take him from her arms. Blood trickles down her collarbone from his tiny fingers.

I'm going to kill these fuckers.

"Is this your son, Colton?" one of them yells.

"Are you hiding the mother away for a reason?" another asks, pressing a microphone into Winnie's face.

"What's your name?"

"How long have you been together?"

"Are you claiming the child?"

"Did you plan the pregnancy?"

"Did she trap you?"

Holding Weston to my chest with one arm, and Winnie in the other, I use my foot to shove the man in front of me out of the way. The action has more bulbs flashing, and people yelling, then Preston is at my side. He leans down and picks up Winnie just as Ashton comes flying around the corner on a four-wheeler.

Preston forces his way through the crowd with Winnie, and I follow in his wake, cradling Weston. Out of the corner of my eye, I see Ash face the crowd with a gun in his hand. Since the attack that scarred his face, paparazzi have become his worst nightmare, but he willingly puts himself in front of them so we can escape to the safety of our home.

"Put the cameras down and your hands up. You're trespassing, and we're pressing charges," Ashton grunts.

I slam the front door closed and pick up my speed to follow Preston. The little body in my arms is trembling so hard his chin bobs against my chest. My little guy is frozen in fear and his body shuts down. I know he peed all down the front of me, and it makes me hate myself even more for not protecting him.

Preston places Winnie on the sofa. "Are you okay here?" he asks. "I'm going to help Ashton before this sets off another PR nightmare we can't get out of."

"Because you're protecting The WB?" I spit.

"I'm protecting our family, Colton. And yes, a big part of that is The WB."

"Get out," I bark.

Weston curls his little face into the crook of my neck.

"I'll make this really easy for you, Preston. I quit. You'll have my resignation by morning."

"You can't quit your family, Colton," Preston exclaims as he stalks to the front door.

"You can when your family gave up on you a long time ago. I quit, Preston. This is my family, right here. Until you can support me and my family like you do everyone else, you're not welcome here. None of you are."

My brother's shoulders slump. "I'm doing the best I can, Colt. I'm doing what I think is right."

Shouting erupts outside, and Preston actually looks torn, but eventually, he heads outside to help Ash.

That's fine. Everything I need is right in front of me, shell-shocked and sad.

"Winnie, I'm so sorry, baby. I-I didn't think they'd go past the gate." My hand moves up and down Weston's back in a gentle rhythm as his body slowly releases tension.

She doesn't speak, so I sit down beside her with Wes clinging to my chest. His terrified little face is tear stained, and my brain misfires trying to figure out how to make those assholes pay.

"Why would they do that? He's just a baby. They knew they were scaring him, and they kept going. They surrounded me and wouldn't let me move." Her whispered words have me wrapping an arm around her and pulling her into my side.

"It will never happen again, Win. I swear to God, it will never happen again."

Time speeds on around us, but we don't move. My tiny family sits huddled together on the sofa as we process the events of the day. Wes falls asleep on me, but I make no move to clean either of us up. Right now, I need to hold them and know we're safe.

I don't know how long we sit in the silence as red and blue lights flash through the windows, followed by angry voices, and car doors slamming before it finally goes silent again.

The front door creaks open, and I know I'll have to have it repaired. Leaning against the sofa cushion, I turn my head to see my entire family file in one by one.

I guess the ban is over.

CHAPTER 19

WINNIE

"*W*innie?"

I lift my head to find Lexi crouching down in front of me. The house is full of Westbrooks. Whispered conversations all meld together as they attempt to keep the peace.

I blink, bringing Lexi into focus.

"Winnie?" she tries again. "Come with me, huh?"

The gentle hum of the room slowly fades away.

"Actually, I need to go help Colton," I tell her.

"Colty has Wes in his bathroom. They're getting cleaned up. I want to get those scratches cleaned out, though, so they don't get infected." She points to my chest, so I glance down. Streaks of red seep through the cotton of my shirt.

Pulling at the collar, I peer down at my chest. Weston's tiny fingernails really did some damage. My heart splinters, having physical proof of his fear.

Silently, I stand. "I'll shower. It'll be fine." I walk on dead legs toward the master bedroom where I've been staying at Colton's command.

"I'll bring in some antibacterial cream and bandages. Emory is also here if you need help."

"Thank you," I reply numbly.

My heartbeat whooshes in my ears as I climb the stairs. I don't even know how to process everything that happened today, but I could feel Colton's anger, his fear, his concern. As fucked up as everything that happened today was, he was there to protect us. He was there for me.

When he told me Wes had an accident, I wasn't surprised. I almost pissed myself, too. The body's reaction to fear can be visceral. What shocked me was when he refused to give up Weston and opted to give him a bath himself. I'm not sure he's ever given a toddler a bath before, but not a single person around me questioned it, and the expression on Colton's face told me he needed to do it. He feels responsible for us being attacked at his home.

My immediate reaction was anger at Colton for putting us in this position, but I knew that wasn't fair once I was safely back inside of his home. He didn't hesitate to put himself between us and the danger.

I'm so confused. My body moves on autopilot through his house, and it isn't until I'm standing in the master bathroom that I realize the shower's running. My gaze darts to the glass enclosure, and the bits of my heart shattered by broken promises tremble with the effort of healing. Like pieces of a magnetic puzzle, they wiggle and sway, trying to become one.

Colton stands in black boxer briefs under the rainfall shower with Weston's little head resting on his shoulder. Rocking back and forth, Colton gently sings. I recognize the melody, but it takes me a minute to place the song. He's singing "We're Going to Be Friends" by The White Stripes.

As if he senses me standing there, he turns and gives me a sad smile. Water cascades down his chiseled face, but I see the tears. Closing his eyes, he raises his face to the spray, and when he opens them again, he's put a mask in place. He's hurting. For us.

Walking toward the shower, it never occurs to me that I'm

staring at a mostly naked Colton Westbrook … until it does, and nerves have me stumbling over the shower mat. Embarrassed, my gaze darts around the room.

"I wasn't sure what the etiquette was for showering with a tiny human," he admits, glancing down at the underwear clinging to his body.

Against my will, my eyes drift to his, and a smile tugs at my lips.

"He's going to have quite the musical repertoire by the time he gets to school." It's all I can think to say, and Colton chuckles softly. Hearing my voice, Wes turns to me, but clings more tightly to Colton's shoulders.

"I—" Panic floods Colton's face.

"It's okay," I tell him, and actually mean it. "It's good that he feels safe with you."

"I was going to put him in the bathtub, but he didn't want me to put him down."

My gaze lowers, and I lean in to run a hand down Weston's back.

"You like the shower, don't you, buddy?"

Wes smiles and cuts his hand through the water to splash me. His tinkle of laughter eases some of the ache, some of the pain sitting just beneath the surface.

"Jesus, Winnie." Colton reaches over, sloshing more water my way as he runs his pointer finger along the collar of my shirt. He slowly pulls it down. Not enough to flash him, but enough so he can see the deep cuts that look like I was in a fight with a tiger. Before I can respond, he lowers his mouth and places a gentle kiss on my collarbone. And then another. And another. When he pulls away, I'm nearly panting. There was nothing sexual about his kisses. They were meant to heal, to soothe, but they ignited a fire deep in my core that I don't know how to control. "I'm so sorry, baby. I'm so, so sorry." His voice cracks, and Wes glances up in concern.

I watch in shock as Wes leans in and kisses Colton's chest. "Thupa. Bedda? Thupa otay?"

"Yeah, Wes. I'm okay. Thank you, little man."

Wes smiles, and with a full belly laugh that can only come from a toddler, we begin to heal.

~

I'm sitting on the edge of Colton's bed long after he and Wes left me to shower. The sounds coming from the family room have slowly risen, but it's happy. Joyful even. There's an energy that comes with a big family, and I can feel it even behind the closed door of Colton's room.

If I'm being honest with myself, I'm afraid to join the party. As a little girl, I dreamed of brothers and sisters. A father. A family. But now that I'm presented with it, truthfully, I'm terrified.

A knock at my door makes me jump, and my hand takes purchase at my heart in an attempt to calm the racing organ.

"Come in?" It's not my house, so it comes out as more of a question than a statement. I'm not sure if I'm supposed to let people in or push them away right now.

GG pokes her head in the door. When she finds me sitting on the edge of the bed, she pushes it open and enters with a regal looking woman behind her.

"Wendy, this is Sylvie. Colton's mom. She wanted to check on ya. You've had quite a time of it lately."

I watch in silent horror as Sylvie glides across the room and gracefully stands before me.

Her smile matches Colton's, and my shoulders relax a fraction.

"It's so nice to meet the girl who has captured my Colton's heart."

"Oh, I, yeah, I don't know. Um …"

Sylvie laughs, and even that sounds elegant. With no warning, she pulls me into a hug, and I immediately know where Colton gets it from. She's warm and loving, and I'm so overwhelmed I pull away for fear I'll sob, and snot will end up on her shoulder.

"I hear my other boys have been giving him a hard time again."

I glance over my shoulder to find GG sitting in the armchair. "She's talkin' to you, not me," she cackles. The sound could raise the dead.

Sylvie places a soft hand over my wrist, and I realize I'm wearing the skin there raw again. She pats it a couple of times and then sits next to me.

"They'll come around, sweetheart. They always do. All my boys are stubborn. They get it from their father." She smirks, and it's impossible not to see the similarities between her and all her boys. "They each got a piece of their father in their own ways. Colton got my husband's impulsive nature, but don't mistake impulsive for indecisive. He and his father had the uncanny ability to make a decision at the drop of a hat and know, in their hearts, it was the right one. My other sons? Well, they're more like me in that way. We think everything to death. They've never understood that about Colton, but I recognized it right away. Do you know his father told me he was going to marry me after three dates?"

My mouth hangs open, and GG cackles again. She's uncharacteristically quiet otherwise, and it's unnerving.

"What I'm trying to tell you is, just because something happens quickly doesn't mean it's wrong."

"But aren't you upset Colton moved strangers into his home?" I can't help but ask the question. It's been bothering me for days. What must his family think of me?

"Why would I? I admit, I was surprised, but not concerned or upset. I always knew when Colton fell in love, he'd fall hard, fast, and forever."

"Oh, no. You're mistaken. We're not even dating."

She pats my leg and smiles. "Oh, Winnie. I know my son. He's never looked at anyone the way he does you. And Wes? That child is already a part of him."

I swallow feelings and questions and so many emotions I'm surprised I don't choke.

"It's okay to go slow. And I commend you for putting your brother first. You're a remarkable woman, Winnie. Your mother would be very proud. But I also see so much of myself in you."

I snort. I actually snort because we couldn't be more different.

"I'll tell you my story someday, but I wasn't always a Westbrook." She winks, and I gape at her. "Once upon a time, I was the girl from the wrong side of the tracks who thought she had to do everything herself. Clinton, that was my husband, he had to work hard to get through my walls, but when I realized he was a man of his word and I let him in? He changed me, Winnie. He opened my eyes to partnership. What a real relationship should be. When he broke down my barriers, I finally found myself. Colt is just like his father. If you can find it in your heart to let him in, I think you'll find an army of people ready and willing to join your battles. Sometimes trusting others feels like an impossible feat, but nothing is as hard as trusting yourself after being knocked down so many times. Find a way to trust yourself again, and I think you'll find my son on the other side waiting for you."

"How? You don't even know me. How can you be so sure? What if I'm not the one for Colton?"

"I know enough," she says cryptically, then nods in GG's direction. "Plus, I'm in the habit of trusting my boys and their decisions. Colton loves you, honey. The mess with our company will sort itself out. But I have a feeling he's shown you who he is. Trust yourself enough to make your own judgments. Now, let's get you out of here and something to eat before Colton comes looking for you, okay?"

They lead me to the family room where people mill about. Enough food to feed a stadium is on every available surface. Colton sits on the floor, leaning against the sofa with Wes at his side. My little brother runs a train up and down Colton's leg as he feeds him bites of pasta.

I sit on the sofa just off to the side, and when I sink into the cushion, Colton turns to me, content but full of concern. "How are you doing?"

"I think I just got a pep talk from your mom."

His brow shoots up to his hairline, but Lexi places a plate of food in my lap. He nods to her appreciatively.

"They'll be leaving soon," he whispers. "They just needed to make sure you were okay."

"Why?" It slips from my lips, and I feel the heat rushing to my cheeks.

"Because you're mine, which means you're theirs," he murmurs, leaning in to place a kiss on my open palm. "I'm so sorry about today, CC."

"It wasn't your fault." It really wasn't, but no part of me wants to have this conversation in front of his family. It feels too personal. Too intimate. Too … much.

Someone clears their throat, and we both glance up. Preston looms over us, and my throat goes dry. Colton shifts his weight and lifts both him and Wes to the sofa beside me with a hand on my knee.

"Winnie?" Preston hums.

A sound rumbles deep in Colton's chest, and Preston lifts his hands with a smirk identical to Colton's.

"I owe you an apology," Preston continues. "I don't think you've gotten a very good impression of me since you've been here. I'm not usually this …"

"Much of an asshat?" Colton supplies helpfully.

"I was going to say surly. But yes. Unfortunately, you've seen the worst side of me, and for that, I apologize. It has nothing to do with you specifically. It's the situation we're in and that I'm unable to fix it."

Staring at him, I find a kindred spirit. Someone who feels the weight of the world on his shoulders but carries it alone.

"There's no need to apologize," I tell him, feeling more confident with each passing minute.

"Yes, there is," Colton and Preston exclaim in unison.

"Anyway," Preston smiles, "I will do better. But, Colt? I don't accept your resignation. We'll figure it out. We always do."

"We do when you talk to us, Pres. We're stronger together. We've always known that. We need to be a united front. Always."

"I know."

"Well, I think it's time we get movin' along," GG says, standing. "Let these kids get some rest."

Slowly, people leave. Ash is the last to go.

"I'm sorry about today," he grunts with a grainy texture to his voice that sounds painful. "I'm installing more security tomorrow. It won't happen again."

"It wasn't your fault, Ash," Colton lectures. "Macomb is after me, and I'm willing to bet he's behind this, too. It's time, Ash. Whatever you're waiting for with him? Is it more important than your family?"

Ashton grumbles words I can't make out and leans into Colton for a hug. "I'll take care of it."

"Thank you," Colt says, hugging him back so tightly it feels more like wrestling, and I almost laugh.

"You'll need to get Tilly out here soon, though. One of the assholes was live streaming everything. The entire world is going to know about them by morning." Ashton's words have my chest squeezing tight.

"Fu—" Colton growls but stops when Wes wiggles on his chest.

"There will be a lot of interest in you for a bit, Winnie. But we'll always protect you." When Ash bends down to hug me, his whispered words sit heavy on my heart. "Colt is a good man, Winnie. You can trust him, and us."

It's like every Westbrook within a ten-mile radius knows my kryptonite. The one thing that could destroy me, and they're all asking me to hand it over to the man before me. For the life of me, I can't figure out why it's a bad idea anymore, though.

We're silent as Ashton lets himself out, and I clasp my shaking hands in my lap. "What does he mean there will be an interest in me?" My words are stilted and much higher than my regular tone. It scares me that I'm not in control here, and my body betrays me.

Colton pulls me farther into his side so my face rests on his chest. With a free hand, he slowly smooths my hair down my back. "Our family will always draw attention, Win. It comes with the territory of having a bank account like ours. But there's also someone determined to hurt us, and he assumes I'm the weak link, so he's coming after me. You've been drawn into that now. The public doesn't care if what they print in the gossip magazines is true. They're looking for clickbait. They live for it. They never once stop to think about how damaging those stories can be. The reason I'm even here right now is because someone came after me, drugged me, and posted false stories anywhere they could. Now, they're going to print that I have a love child or some other bullshit. That will make people crazy to find out who has tamed the playboy."

I lift my gaze to find Colton watching me. His barely controlled rage at the situation vanishes when he sees my expression. "We will protect you, Winnie. I'll protect you both, no matter the cost."

≈

$\mathcal{T}$he Town Cryer

GG: Colton Westbrook has found happiness with the lovely Wendalyn Darling.

GG: I'm sure a wedding will follow soon enough.

Betty-Anne: They look smitten.

Lexi: GG! WTH?!?! There must be a family code of conduct or something!

GG: Quit your belly-achin.

GG: The public needs to know.

Easton: GG. (hand to forehead emoji)

867 unread messages.

CHAPTER 20

COLTON

"*A*re you sure you'll be okay with him?" Winnie asks, worrying that damn wrist again. I'm tempted to buy her some sort of bracelet just so she won't rub the skin raw, but I'm afraid it would make it worse. I'll need to ask Rylan about it.

"CC," I coo, "I've been watching East's twins for a while now. If I can handle two at the same time, I can handle Wes. Plus, his son, Julian, is slightly insane. I've got this, I promise."

She nods frantically with a frown forming a small V between her eyes.

Stepping closer, I bend my knees to make sure she sees me. "I promise you, he's in good hands."

It's the first time she's leaving Weston with me, and I can tell it's hard on her. Ever since the assholes cornered her and Wes outside of our house, she seems to have put a little more trust in me, but it's still a work in progress.

The tabloids exploded with theories and false information. The WB Group ended up putting out a statement, asking for privacy, but that never works. The tiny mountain town we call home has been better at keeping her safe than any statement we could give. Burke Hollow takes care of their own almost as well as the Westbrooks. They've run off more reporters in the past couple of weeks than an army of security ever could have.

"I know trusting someone doesn't come easy to you, baby. But I promise on my life I'll take good care of him."

"I know you will," she finally relents, releasing her wrist.

I move without thinking and take the battered hand in my grasp. Lifting it to my lips, I gently kiss the skin that's smoothed over like a scar.

"Have you always done this?" I ask, nodding toward her wrist.

Embarrassed, she tries to pull it away.

"I'm not judging, Win. I'm trying to understand. I only want to help."

She glances down at our feet, and I can see her fingers twitching on her right hand. If I wasn't holding her left hand in mine, I have no doubt she'd be worrying her wrist again.

"I guess it's like a nervous habit. I've done it since I was a kid, but it's probably gotten worse since I lost my mom. I don't even realize I'm doing it. I've actually rubbed the skin raw a few times, but was so lost in life I didn't notice until I started to feel it scab over." She peeks up at me with red cheeks. "You must think I'm insane."

Releasing her wrist, I cup both of her cheeks in my hands. Glancing back and forth between her eyes, emotions well in my chest. "I think you're incredible. Patient. Kind. I think you've been through a lot and it's your way of handling stress because you've never had someone to help carry the burden. Someday, I hope you'll understand that I want to be that person. I want to be your partner. The one to hold your hand when life is overwhelming."

She swallows, then licks her lips. My gaze darts to the tip of her tongue, and I want that cherry cola taste so bad my body hums with need.

The sound of train tracks crashing has me pulling away. Three weeks ago, the sound would have sent me running, but now I walk to the other side of the room where Wes has dumped out the bucket of tracks, searching for a piece.

Winnie stands beside me, watching him. Without putting too much thought into it, I wrap my arm around her shoulder and pull her into my side. My heart nearly explodes when she rests her head against me. I swear I heard a tiny sigh and I know I'm home.

"I hate that you're still working the night shift, Win."

Glancing down, I watch her lips curl into a hint of a smile. "I have to work, Colton. I have bills. A future to plan for."

It guts me that she hasn't included me in that future yet. "What if we hire you at the Lodge?"

She shakes her head. "I need the job at the hospital. It has benefits, and I can't afford to be without insurance with Weston."

"I'll put you both on my insurance. Or I'll pay for you to have your own." Her widened gaze tells me I'm screwing this all up. Turning her in my arms, I hold her close, thankful she no longer pulls away immediately. "I meant it when I said I'm going to marry you, CC."

Winnie rolls her eyes and turns to Wes. "Hey, buddy. You be good for Colton, okay?"

Wes nods, but otherwise doesn't acknowledge her.

Before she can get away, I pull her in for a hug.

"Do you always try to fix everything?"

"When I can. But I'm not fixing things because I think you're incapable. I want to fix things because it's easy for me to do, and I want what's best for you. I want to be what's best for you."

Winnie smooths down her hair while regarding Weston and me. She fidgets when she's antsy or worried. "What are you going to do for dinner?"

"Oh, we have big plans, don't we, buddy?" Wes is singularly focused when placing trains on his tracks.

"Yeah?" Winnie flashes a dimpled grin my way, and I want

to kiss her senseless. Keeping my hands to myself is becoming harder by the day.

"Oh yeah. We're going to McDonald's." I sense her hesitation and feel her concern like a wet blanket. "I know how to use car seats. We'll sit in the back of the restaurant where it's quieter, and I'll bring his headphones. We're good, Win. And he's excited about going."

When her eyes fill with tears, I feel as if I was just sucker punched. "It may not seem like much, but going to McDonald's is a big treat for him. I can't really afford to take him out very often."

Fucking hell. If only she knew I'd buy the place if either of them asked. She turns and reaches for her purse. I grab a box of tissues and go to hand them to her, but she's pulling out her wallet, and I stand there, confused.

When she tries to hand me a five-dollar bill and five ones, I narrow my eyes. Placing my hands on my hips, I let out a long sigh and get ready for our next battle. Money.

"What is that?" I ask, working hard to keep my voice calm.

"He'll probably want a Happy Meal. This should be enough to cover it. I-I don't have any more cash, but if you think it'll be more, I'll stop at the ATM on my way home." She tries to shove the money at me, but I keep my hands firmly on my hips.

"You're cute."

She gasps with an open jaw.

"Do you have any idea how much money I have, CC?"

"Well, I mean, I guess I have an idea, but that's not the point. You can't keep paying our way for everything. It's my job to take care of Wes and all his needs. It's why I work so many hours. I have to provide a good life for him. It's my responsibility."

"And someday, you'll allow it to be our responsibility. Until then, I will keep paying for everything because you're mine. You and Wes are my family, and I can only hope I'll be yours."

Now it's time for the fight. Reaching around her, I grab my

wallet from the side table and pull out a credit card with her name. Handing it to her, I watch her face turn beet red.

"Why is my name on your credit card, Colton? I didn't ask for that." If this were a cartoon, steam would be shooting from her ears.

"I know you didn't, but I need you to take it in case of emergency. My brothers would have gone about this high handedly and just put cash into your account. In fact, I'm pretty sure Preston did just that a couple of times, but I know how important your independence is to you, so I'm hoping we can do it this way." When she stares at me unblinking, I continue, "There's no limit on this card, Win. I'd like you to use it for anything and everything you or Wes need, but if that's a hard no for you right now, at least take it in case of emergency. If you only carry ten dollars with you, it would make me feel better knowing you have options."

"I'm not taking your money, Colton. We're already living here, rent free. You won't even let me pay for groceries. I'm … Jesus, Colton. You can't keep doing this. I can't get used to you doing it, either. What happens when this ends? I have to support myself and Wes."

Anger and fear flood my veins, and the possessive animal she brings out in me roars as I pull her to me. Face-to-face. Our bodies pressed together. My tone commands her to listen. I've never been like this with anyone before, but I can't control it around Winnie Darling.

"This? You mean you and me? There is no end date for me, Winnie. I don't know how to make you understand that, but I would marry you tomorrow just to tie you to me in every way if you let me. As for supporting yourself? I'll never tell you what to do. If you want to work, I'll fully support you, but I'd rather you go back to law school and do something you love."

She gasps and goes pale, but I push on.

"I will not betray your trust by depositing cash into your account, even though everything in me wants to do it. Ash already tried, but I told him not to. I didn't want to push you that way. But for Wes? Halton already started a trust for him, just like he does with every other child that enters this family."

Tears fall from her fragile gray eyes and slide down her face as she shakes her head like she can make what I'm saying untrue.

"It's all done, Winnie. If you decide you don't want me, it will kill me, but I won't walk away from Wes. Once a trust is in place, it's there for him, no matter what." Gurgled words get stuck in her throat, so I continue, "I want to give you the world, too, Winnie, but I don't want to scare you off. I need you to take this card, though, for me. It gives me peace of mind. So, if nothing else, take it for me. Use it, don't use it. That's up to you, but please take it. For me."

I can tell by her expression she's going to fight me, so I cross a line I haven't stepped over with her yet. Lifting my hand, I run the black, metal card down her neck and keep going to her cleavage. Allowing the backs of my fingers to brush along her skin, I slip the card below her shirt.

She gasps, and her chest rises and falls in time with my racing heart. I feel like a fourteen year old about to cop a feel for the first time. I don't, but it takes every ounce of self-control I possess not to dip my lips to her skin.

Slowly, I remove my hand and growl like an enchanted beast when she leans into my touch. I don't even think she means to do it. Her body reacts to me when her mind stops overthinking everything, and that makes me happier than I have any right being.

"I want to kiss you, Winnie." My voice is rough, my lips parched, and the only thing that can quench my thirst is her.

Her mouth opens, then closes again. She grasps her wrist, then lifts her gaze to meet mine and nods ever so slowly, and I pounce. I take her bottom lip in my mouth and suck, savoring that goddamn flavor that I'm growing addicted to. Cherry cola and Winnie Darling. It's a heady mix, and my body comes alive as my tongue prods and pushes until she grants me access. A silky moan slips from the back of her throat, and I swallow it like the greedy, greedy man I am. My hands take purchase in her curls, holding her to me, molding her body to mine. I tilt her head so I can kiss along her jaw up to her earlobe.

"I want you, Winnie Darling. More than I've ever wanted anything in my life, but I'm not going anywhere. I'll wait however long you need. I'm going to prove to you that you're it for me."

"I-I," she pants. I'm about to take her lips again, when I feel little hands curl around my leg, and I pull back so quickly she stumbles forward.

Glancing down, I find Wes smiling up at me. My gaze drifts back and forth between these two people who have righted my world. Made me grow up. Make me want things I didn't know I was ready for, but know without a doubt, I'll do whatever it takes to keep them.

Bending down, I scoop Wes up in my arms. I've learned he actually does like to snuggle, but it has to be on his terms. He isn't the kid you can just pick up and kiss his cheeks. Sometimes it's hard not to pull him into my lap to hold him, but he's very good at letting me know when it's okay.

"He's not like this with anyone, Colton. He doesn't warm up to people. He rarely even lets me cuddle him." The hurt in her voice breaks my heart. "I hope you know how much that means to me, but …" She swallows hard, and out of the corner of my eye, I see her hands moving. Her chin trembles. She's fighting so hard to keep emotions in, and I don't know how to get her to trust me enough to share them.

"Winnie? I won't hurt either of you. I promise."

She lunges and wraps her arms around my middle. The three of us stand there in an embrace that feels like the most powerful drug. I kiss the top of her head, and Wes leans down to do it, too. Feeling him, she lifts her face to his, and her tears finally spring free.

"Wub you."

Winnie chokes on a sob but forces her words out through a cloud of emotion. "I love you, too, Wessy."

"We're going to be okay, Win."

She stares at me, and I can see her brain working, taking in everything I've said. Eventually, she nods in silence and pulls away. Slipping her hand into her shirt, she pulls out the credit card.

"I'll hang onto this, but I won't use it, Colton."

So fucking stubborn.

"Okay. Thank you."

"I have to get ready for work. Are you going to dinner soon?"

"Yup. I figured I'd get him to use the potty, then pack up whatever he needs and go. I think Rylan is going to meet us there."

An emotion I can't read flashes across her face, but it's gone too quickly for me to decipher what it means. Winnie pats Weston's hand, then my arm, and turns to head toward her room.

I'm in a battle of wills with this woman, but there will only be one winner. Me.

CHAPTER 21

WINNIE

I'm standing in my office that I share with the other family liaison coordinators with my back to the door when a voice I never wanted to hear again calls out as shrill as ever.

"Knock, knock."

My hands ball into fists as I turn to find my frenemy standing in the doorway, all fake smiles to match her fake tits.

"Claire." Her name hisses through my teeth.

"Oh, come on. You're not still mad at me, are you?" She juts out her bottom lip in a pout that makes me want to throw something.

"You slept with my boyfriend. That's not something you just *get over*. What do you want?"

Claire is a pediatric nurse, which always baffled me. She's terrible with kids. Wes especially. How she's able to keep her job is beyond me.

"I switched shifts with someone so I could have the weekend off." She waltzes into my office like she belongs there. "I went by your place yesterday, but it looked empty. Did you move?"

Of course she would peek in the windows. It suddenly

occurs to me why she's here. Claire hates nothing more than being left out of things, and the way this town gossips, she has to know I'm staying with Colton.

"That's not really any of your concern, Claire. If you'll excuse me, I have work to do."

She scoffs, but doesn't move out of my way. "Come on, Win. I broke up with Travis for you. What else do you want?"

"I don't know, maybe not to sleep with him in the first place?" I feel my body tensing and I grasp my wrist, but Colton's worried face comes to mind, and I release it.

"I made a mistake. I'm sorry. Really, I am. I miss you, Winnie."

This is Claire's MO. We've gone around this toxic frenemy rollercoaster way too many times, and I've finally hit my limit. Maybe Colton is giving me some confidence back, or maybe I'm finally not so exhausted that I can see her for who she really is. A user. I'd bet money she isn't here for me. This has to do with my sudden connection to the Westbrooks.

"You're two years too late for an apology, Claire. If you cared about me at all, you would have been around when my mom was sick. What's this really about?"

"I do miss you," she huffs. "I just thought maybe we could go out. Catch up. Maybe we could double date sometime?"

And there it is.

"You're not using me to get to the Westbrooks." Grabbing the files I need, I push past her.

"You still think you're so much better than me," she hisses, her true colors finally showing. "It's only a matter of time before he gets tired of you. You know that, right? I mean, what could you possibly have to offer him? Travis said you were shit in bed, so that's not it." She steps closer, and I can smell the stench of her cheap perfume. "How long do you think he's going to put up with your little shit freaking out in public? That can't be good for their image. Enjoy it while you can, Winnie. No one sticks around you for long, and you know it."

A direct hit. She knows me well enough to know my deepest insecurities, and she's bitchy enough to use them against me. When I don't reply, she knows she won. With a toss of her bleach blonde hair, she smirks and walks out of my office.

My body moves on autopilot through the rest of my shift, but my mind plays tug-of-war between Claire's vicious words and Colton begging me to trust him. Claire has done nothing but hurt me since we were teenagers. Colton has been nothing but patient and kind.

By the time I pull into his driveway well before dawn, I've made my mind up. I'm going to give this man a chance. I need to give us a chance and pray to God he doesn't destroy me. Something tells me I would never recover from Colton Westbrook.

Entering Colton's home, I can't ignore the sense of relief that washes over me. Within these walls, my body relaxes in a way it hasn't in years. It scares the crap out of me. In my experience, if something seems too good to be true, it usually is.

"No one sticks around you for long." Claire's words rattle around my head like a bad hangover I can't shake, but they evaporate when I stop short at the kitchen island.

There, lined up like tiny toy soldiers heading to war, are six mini hero figurines from the new Marvel movie I know came in Weston's Happy Meal. But I also know that only one toy comes per meal. Everyone knows that. So, the only reason he would have all six is if Colton made it happen.

I know it's true in my heart without even thinking about it. I still haven't processed what he said about a trust for Wes. Or what that entails really, but somehow, staring at these six little, plastic heroes, I believe Colton Westbrook would truly do anything for us.

My heart beats rapidly in my chest as I tiptoe through the house to Weston's room. I won't be able to sleep until I check on him. I can see light spilling out from Colton's open bedroom door. My gaze is glued to his space, so I completely miss him sprawled out on the hallway floor.

My toe catches on his foot, and my head whips down to the floor as my body propels forward with ungraceful speed. One minute I'm falling through the air, and the next I land on top of Colton with a loud oomph.

"Oh my God, I'm so sorry," I whisper.

He brushes some hair out of my face and smiles. Up close, I can see the sleep in his expression. He was sleeping on his back in the hallway right outside of Weston's door. I can't swallow the uncomfortable lump in my throat, and I can't get my body to move, either.

Laying here, with my legs straddling Colton's muscular body, I feel safe.

"I'm not," he murmurs.

"Why are you sleeping out here?" I ask, but make no effort to move. In fact, Colton wraps his arms around my back and holds me closer to him.

He shrugs, an embarrassed grin gracing his beautiful face, bathed in the soft glow coming from the light at the end of the hall. "Wes rolled to the bottom of his bed, and I couldn't see him as well in the monitor. I wanted to make sure I could hear him. I didn't actually intend to fall asleep out here. Or let you catch me sleeping out here anyway," he grumbles.

I can't help it. I smile. A big, toothy, happy, carefree smile.

"Why are there six superheroes on the island?"

Colton's smirk has my gaze catching on his lips for a little too long. When I finally lift my face to meet his heated stare, wetness pools between my legs. I've never once in my life had a reaction like this to a man. Sex has always been just that, sex. Not that I'll ever admit it to him, but I don't think I've ever even had an orgasm. Not for lack of trying. I always just assumed I was broken. But the reaction Colton stirs just by staring has me rethinking all kinds of possibilities.

"He wanted them," he admits sheepishly.

"He wanted them, so … what? You just bought them? I'm sure he wants a lot of things. That doesn't mean you have to go out and buy them. Wanting things makes you work harder."

"Oh, Winnie. I know that's true." The spark in his eye has me melting into him a little more. He's made it no secret he wants me, and I can feel just how much growing between my legs. He shifts his body, and I slip farther down. "But to answer your question, I tried. They wouldn't sell me the damn toys, so we bought six Happy Meals. There are some burgers and nuggets in the fridge if you're hungry." He chuckles.

"Colton!"

"CC." His voice drips with sex, and it does something to me.

Without giving myself time to talk my way out of it, I climb up his body until we're face-to-face, and I kiss him. Hard. Here, on the hallway floor, another piece of my carefully constructed wall breaks free.

Within seconds, his hands are in my hair, around my waist, on my chin. He's all-consuming, and every nerve ending I own is on high alert, waiting for their turn.

"Baby," he growls.

I moan.

We move together as one in a kiss that's more like a dance of wills. He takes and takes and takes, but somehow it feels as if it's my idea. The longer we kiss, the more my body zings with an awareness that feels out of control. But I know better. Colton is in full control here. In every aspect of our lives. Like a puppet master, he calls the shots and makes me feel like I have a say. It's dangerous and exhilarating. I've never wanted to give up control in any part of my life, but right here, right now? I want nothing more than for Colton Westbrook to own me.

"If you want me to stop, say so now," he warns.

My mind briefly fills with all the things I should worry about, but one nip of his teeth on my neck and I bend to his will.

"I, I don't want you to stop," I gasp.

Colton pulls back just enough to stare into my eyes. Whatever he's searching for, I hope he finds it, because if he stops, I think I might truly combust.

After what feels like an eternity, he pulls my face to him. We're nose to nose. "You're mine, Winnie Darling. Now," he kisses my cheek, "and forever." He bites down on the sensitive skin at the juncture where my neck and shoulder meet, and I whimper my consent.

"Yes."

His fist tightens in my hair, shooting sparks of arousal throughout my entire body. "Say it again," he grunts.

"Yes. I-I'm yours."

In one fluid motion, he lifts us both off the floor. Adrenaline must be coursing through his veins, because that was no easy feat. Once we're standing, he takes both of my hands in his. His penetrating gaze sends a shiver down my spine.

"Are you sure about this, Winnie? If we do this now, I don't think I can ever let you go."

I gulp, and it sounds far louder than normal in the eerie silence of night. But when I study Colton's face, all I can find is love. Love for me, love for Wes. Love for a life he envisions with us. I decide right here that I will give him everything I can. Including myself, and eventually my trust.

"I'm sure, Colton."

He scans my face one last time, then drags me behind him to his room. Once inside, he closes the door and smiles. I feel like prey, and as he stalks forward, I can only move back in tandem until my legs hit the edge of the bed.

I had a few one-night stands in college, and then there was Travis. Ugh. I hate that my mind doesn't stop for even a second, but the way Colton is watching my every reaction has me on edge. I've never felt the connection I have with Colton with any other guy, and that's kind of depressing, considering I lived with Travis.

"Winnie."

His harsh command has my brain pausing mid freak out.

"Are you having second thoughts?"

"No. No, why?" I shake my head, trying to unscramble the four thousand thoughts vying for my attention.

"In here, Winnie, it's only you and me." He reaches down and turns up the volume on the baby monitor. "I don't want you thinking about anything else. Your fears," his hand slips to the buttons on my shirt, "are mine to worry about now." He undoes the top button, and then another, and I swear his eyes glow with lust. "All I want you to do is feel. Not think, not worry, not obsess about getting everything on your list done. We will, together, but in here, you're mine. And I'm yours. Can you do that for me, baby?"

Shit. Shit. Shit. I honestly don't know if I can.

His hands slide up my stomach, over the soft skin of my ribs, to the sides of my breasts. My breath catches as he slips my shirt off my shoulders and down my arms.

"I asked you a question, Winnie."

There goes that audible gulp again. I'm like a frog. That's super sexy.

"Winnie," he snaps, and my brain freezes. "We're going to have to work on your ability to stay in the here and now, I see." He's grinning as he trails hot kisses over the cups of my bra. The heat from his mouth has my nipples pebbling against the cotton. "But we'll get there, and you'll be using every ounce of energy not to scream my name and wake up our little guy down the hall."

God, how I want that. I've read about it. A lot. But that's not how sex is for me. As Colton reaches for the waistband of my skirt, panic begins to set in. The way Colton reads my body, my reactions, I know he'll never allow a faked orgasm. I'm biting my lower lip and tension fills my muscles.

"Tell me what you like, Winnie. How do you make yourself come?"

I've never had anyone be so blunt before and it throws me.

I'm unsure how to answer. Do I tell him the truth? Do I make something up? I know what they say in my romance novels, but is that something a man like Colton expects?

"Colton," I whisper.

He freezes and glances up at me.

"I-I need to tell you something."

His eyes go wide, and he straightens immediately. "Are you a virgin, Winnie?"

"What?" I croak. "No. I'm not a virgin."

Relief washes over his expression, and he leans in to kiss my neck again. When he does this, he short circuits my brain and he knows it.

"Then what is troubling that beautiful mind of yours?" His whispered breath against my skin leaves goosebumps in his wake.

"Nothing. Never mind. I'm good."

Colton steps back and searches my eyes. He won't settle for anything but the truth, I can tell by the way he watches me. Like he's memorizing everything he can. Heat floods my cheeks, and I have to glance away. How do I tell a man like Colton that sex is just meh, and not to take it personally?

"Not good enough, sweetheart." He crosses his arms, still fully clothed, I realize while I stand in a bra that's not even cute and a stretchy skirt I got on clearance at Target. "I'm doing everything I can to earn your trust, but I can only do that if you're honest with me. What got in your head just now?"

There's no way I can look at him and say this, so I slowly sit on the edge of the bed, still staring at the floor, while I gather my courage. "You asked how I make myself come." My muttered words seem amplified in my ears, and I cringe.

"Okay," he drawls, and I hear the smile I can't bring myself to view. "Did that embarrass you?"

"Not really." *Oh, sweet baby Jesus. Am I really going to explain this to him?* "I liked it … I think." Daring a peek, I lift my gaze and find him watching me with intent.

"Do you not want to tell me? Because I can have just as much fun figuring it out on my own."

What it must be like to have his confidence, geez!

"Have you been with a lot of women?" I blurt.

It's his turn to cringe. "More than is polite to mention, probably."

"And they've all been ... er, satisfied?"

"Are you afraid I won't live up to expectation, Winnie?" He smirks, but his gaze flashes a dangerous warning to my vagina. *Run, pussy, run. I'm going to destroy you and watch how much you like it.*

Holy Moses! What's wrong with me?

"Gah. No, I—" I what? *What am I doing?* Dropping my head into my hands, I attempt to shut him out so I can collect myself. But I already know him better than that. His enormous hands land on mine and pull them away a second later.

"Talk to me, Win. What are you worried about?"

"I just don't want you to spend too much time worrying about if I'm, ya know, happy."

"I'll always worry about your happiness, Winnie. But specifically, are you talking about an orgasm?"

With a sigh that weighs a thousand tons, I nod. "Yeah, I can't orgasm, Colton. It's not anything to do with you. It's a *me* issue."

He's quiet for a moment, so I chance a peek in his direction. I swear the way he watches me he must have a roadmap of my entire body by now.

185

CHAPTER 22

COLTON

I am one thousand percent sure I misheard her.

"It's a *you* issue?" I repeat for clarification. "Did a doctor tell you this?"

"God, no. It's just how it is. I've tried, believe me. I just can't." Her voice wobbles, so I clasp her hand in mine.

"Game on, Winnie Darling."

"What?" she cries. "What are you talking about?"

"Your issue, as you call it, is now my life's goal. Lay down, Winnie." The low timbre of my voice drops an octave on her name. I don't move as she follows my directive, but I get my fill of the view. She's fucking gorgeous. Smooth and soft everywhere. Her body is perfection. A beautiful, real woman, and I love every inch of her delectable body.

I don't know who the fuck-faces are that couldn't get her off, but I won't stop until I've succeeded. When she peers up at me, an idea forms and I hold up one finger.

"Stay right there, Win. I'll be right back."

I sprint from the room to the master closet and pull down a heavy box. Carrying it with me, I take my time walking back so I can calm the fucking rod between my legs down. When I enter the room, her face floods with relief, and I never break eye contact as I move closer and set the box down beside her.

"What's that?" Nerves have found their way back into her tone, so I don't hold out on her.

"This might freak you out, but let me explain," I say in warning.

Opening the flap of the cardboard box, I upend it next to her. Dildos, vibrators, sex toys of every flavor, size, and shape come tumbling out.

"Oh shit," she mumbles. "I-Is this? What is this?" She's holding up anal beads, but I take them from her and place them back in a pile. "You've used all this?"

"No. It's all brand new," I state calmly because I'm ninety-nine percent sure she's about ready to run.

"So ... what? You have it lying around for when it's needed?"

Laughter escapes my chest. It's deep, and full, and uncontrollable. "No, Winnie. During sex, I rarely use toys. I kind of feel like that's something you do in a committed relationship. I've never committed to anyone. Until now."

"You bought this for me?" she squeaks.

So innocent.

"No. But I figured maybe something would help you relax. All of these were gag gifts. I thought I would get to host Rylan's bachelorette party, but she and Halton nixed that idea before it ever got off the ground."

I watch as her shoulders relax a little, and I smile.

"There's no rush here, baby. But if you think for one minute I won't love every second of proving you and your *issue* wrong? You have another thing coming."

"And if I can't?"

"Then we'll keep trying." Leaning down, I cage her in with my arms and lick a line down her center. "Again and again until we get it right. I'll spend hours savoring you until I get you there. Is that okay with you?"

She squirms below me, her chest rising and falling in rapid succession.

"In here, Winnie, it's just you and me. The second your mind wanders to anything else, you shut it down. Focus on me." I hook my fingers into her waistband and slowly tug it down. "And how I make you feel." I exhale deeply, so my warm breath hits her center, and she gasps. "Understand?"

"Yes."

My lip twitches, and I smirk against her skin. "Get comfortable, CC. We're going to be here a while."

That's the only warning I give her as I yank her pink cotton panties down her thighs. A rumble forms in my chest at the landing strip of pale blonde hair neatly cropped. Just waiting for my tongue.

"Fuck me, Winnie. It's like a roadmap pointing me right where I need to be." Her skin pinks from her cheeks and creeps down her neck toward her chest. "I think you like my dirty talk, don't you?"

Taking a thigh in each hand, I spread her legs wide. I waste no time dropping between them and running my nose up her center. The scent of her arousal has me gyrating into the bed like a horny teenager about to pop his load for the first time.

"Ah." Winnie tries to wiggle free, but I clamp down on her thighs to hold her in place.

"Stay. Feel." I'm so fucking ready to taste her that I'm incapable of forming sentences. Slowly, I move my palms up and down her legs in gentle caresses meant to relax her. With glassy eyes, her gaze follows my hands until they reach the apex of her thighs.

I never break eye contact as I inch my thumbs closer to her slit. When they finally find her entrance, she holds her breath. With great effort, I move the pads of my thumbs slowly up and down her opening, coating them with her wetness.

When I can't take another minute, I spread her open and drop my tongue into her for a taste. "Jesus Christ, CC. You're so fucking sweet. And so fucking mine." A beast was just set free, and I lick her with abandon.

In and out, and up and down, I'm a wild animal drinking in all of her. Inching higher, I use my thumbs to coax her clit. When the tiny nub responds, I suck it into my mouth and flick it relentlessly with my tongue.

To my goddamn delight, Winnie moans, and writhes beneath me, but I can tell it's not everything she needs. I wasn't lying when I said I would stay here forever. "I could lick your pussy for hours," I whisper against her slick skin. "And I will, if that's what it takes."

Winnie groans as I slip a finger in her.

"Oh, baby." I sink another finger in and twist. "You're going to feel so fucking good around my cock."

"I, I want …" She's gasping. It feels good, but she's still not there.

"What do you need, baby? Tell me. I'll give you whatever you need." As my tongue attacks her clit, I curl my fingers inside of her.

"I want to see. I want to see you."

A wicked smile mars my face while I give her clit a light nibble, and she bucks against my face. "You want to see me, baby?"

"Yes."

Placing an open mouth kiss against her pussy, I reach down and shuck my pants. I have to pull away to take off my shirt, but her hungry gaze roaming over my body is worth it.

"You want to see all of me, Winnie Darling?"

She catches her bottom lip between her teeth and nods. I pull my boxer briefs down and kick them away from my legs with one swift move. My cock springs free, and my hand automatically gives it a squeeze.

Her eyes bulge in her head as I run my fist up and down my shaft. She squirms while I rub over the head and back down.

"Is this what you want?" I ask, moving between her legs again, still stroking myself.

Her gaze never leaves my cock, and it twitches in my hand. Her body glistens as the first rays of sunlight filter in through the open blinds.

"Open your pussy for me," I demand.

She hesitates for only a moment before reaching down and spreading her lips.

Fuck me. I jerk my cock harder. "Show me how you touch yourself, Winnie."

Her face flames red, but she follows my order. Licking her middle finger, she lowers it to her clit and begins to rub with frantic swipes.

"You like it fast, sweetheart."

She doesn't answer. Her gaze is flying between her open legs and my cock. Leaning over her, I dig through the pile of vibrators until I find the one I'm searching for. A clit stimulator that uses air pressure.

I shred the box, getting it open, and pray to God the battery has some charge to it.

Her hand pauses, and I shake my head. "Keep going, CC. I didn't tell you to stop."

My cock bobs as I step away from the bed. I know she's watching me, and the head of my dick weeps with need. Turning on the device, I flash a devilish smile to Winnie, who pauses and swallows hard.

"Have you ever used one of these?"

"No."

"Have you used a vibrator before?"

She glances away, embarrassed, but I reach up and turn her to face me. "Winnie? I'm going to have my tongue, fingers, and dick inside of every part of you and I'm going to fucking love it. There's no reason to be shy. I'm going to tongue your ass and your pussy. I'm going to fuck you into next week and I'm going to describe it all. In detail. So, when I ask you a question, you answer me. Got it?"

"Uh, huh." Her wide eyes dart around the room. "I've used a vibrator, but not like that."

"That's my girl," I growl. "First time for everything, sweetheart."

She licks her lips, and my cock responds. With tentative fingers, she reaches out and grabs my shaft. I clench my jaw and lock my knees to keep from thrusting into her waiting palm. Winnie glances up at me with a tentative expression through long, dark lashes and my composure slips.

"You're the most beautiful woman I've ever seen." Using both hands, I cup her face and kiss her with every feeling coursing through my veins. Lust, need, desire, love. Mostly it's love, and it doesn't even scare me. If anything, it makes me want her even more. "I need you to be mine, Winnie. In every way."

"Okay. I am," she moans as I slip my hand between her legs and press the vibrator to her swollen nub. Keeping the toy in place, I lean over her so we're eye to eye.

"I need to see your eyes, baby. I want to know what feels good, and I want nothing more than to be the one to please you."

"Oh God." She pants and her hips buck, causing my cock to bounce against her leg.

I press the button, and the intensity of the vibrations picks up. I search her face for reactions. There's surprise and delight. Fear and passion. Her face scrunches up. Her body bucks. Her shoulders shake, and I watch it all.

"I can't, Colt. It's too much. It ... God. It, it hurts," she cries.

I drop the toy to the bed and bring her lips to mine. "Are you okay?" I ask over her swollen lips.

"Yeah. I want you, Colton. I need you, please."

Without hesitating, I notch my cock at her opening.

"Condom," she rasps, panic filling her face.

Holy shit. I almost slipped inside of her without ever thinking of a condom. I've always wrapped that fucker up. What does it say about her that I want nothing more than to be bare? Blinking away the fantasy, I sit up to grab a condom out of the nightstand.

Once it's rolled on, I move back between her legs and take the toy in my hand. "I'm going to turn it on low, okay? I won't turn it up as high this time."

She bites her lip, but nods in agreement.

"Did it feel good, though?" I ask as I open her up again with my thumb and place the vibrator on her clit.

"Yes. It was just too much."

"Okay, I'll keep it low." Turning it back on, I move it until I see her eyes gloss over again, and then slowly, I move into position. With my cock at her entrance, I wait for her to give me the okay. When she nods again, I ease in, and I immediately see stars.

I've had plenty of sex in my life, and with just my tip buried inside of my girl, I know nothing will ever compare. She's tight, though, so fucking tight. I ease in and out, allowing her wetness to coat my cock. After a few pumps, she lifts her hips and impales herself on me.

I forget how to breathe, and I stay fully seated in her. The vibrations from the toy coursing through her body. It only ratchets up the sensations of being squeezed by her trembling walls.

"Colton," she moans, and I clasp a hand over her mouth. Her eyes go wide with panic as she stares at the door. I hold still inside of her while we wait to see if any noise comes from the hall. When all stays silent, I move. In and out. I rock into her as slowly as my body allows, and I feel her pussy clenching with each thrust.

"That's it, baby. Clench down on me. Fuuuck. You feel so good."

My teeth find her neck, and I bite down. Not enough to

mark, but enough to add another sensation and keep her in the here and now.

As my thrusts pick up speed, so does the vibrator. Sweat covers both our bodies, and Winnie's head rolls from side to side.

"I can't, Colt. I—"

"Shh. I've got you. Just feel, Winnie. Feel my cock and how your pussy clenches and sucks it back in like it doesn't want me to leave. Feel how I twitch and shake with every spasm of your body. Feel how connected we are. How in sync we are. Feel me, Winnie. Feel what you mean to me."

With every passing word, my thrusts become more frantic. I lift her legs over my shoulders so I can get even deeper, and tears spring to her eyes. "Are you okay?"

"Yes. Yes. Yes," she chants, and something in me snaps.

I pound into her with unrelenting speed.

"Too much. Colt. Too, too much," she whines.

Tossing the vibrator to the floor, I press on her lower stomach with the palm of my hand and nearly come when it puts more pressure on my dick.

Winnie's eyes roll to the back of her head, and her legs shake around my ears. Her moans are music to my ears, and I press a little harder. The effort nearly makes me black out.

"Come for me, Winnie. Give it the fuck up. Give it to me. Give me all your orgasms. Now and forever," I growl, and she explodes around me.

Electricity shoots through every limb, lighting me up from the inside out as her chest rises off the bed. I watch as wave after wave racks her body. She writhes below me, and I keep up a steady rhythm, riding out every last second of her orgasm.

"Yes, Winnie. Thank fuck, yes," I roar as her wild spasms turn to slight tremors. Two more deep thrusts and my spine catches fire. Pushing as far as I can inside of her, I cling to her body as she milks an orgasm from the depths of my soul. Spurt after spurt shoots into her and all I can think about is making her mine. Marking her and doing this for the rest of my life.

When I can form a coherent thought, I realize I'm crushing her. Lifting up to my forearms, I see her dazed expression. She blinks slowly as I kiss the tip of her nose. Her cheek. Her jaw. And finally, her lips. When I pull away, she's fast asleep with me buried so deep inside of her I can't breathe, but my cock tries to harden again at the sight of her.

With one final gentle kiss to her lips, I ease out of her and rush to the bathroom. Tossing the condom, I grab a warm cloth and clean her up. I'm only mildly concerned that she doesn't even flinch.

I fucked her senseless, and I couldn't be prouder of myself.

I'm tossing the washcloth in the hamper when she rolls in her sleep, incoherently babbling, but content. I know Wes will be up soon, and I'll get him so she can sleep. Wes and I need some more boy time, but for now, I climb back into bed and pull her limp body to mine.

Warmth fills my chest. A love I've never known filling every pore. I realize with a start that this is happiness. This is my life, and I'm more content than I've ever been.

Winnie and Wes are my life. My entire life, and it's time to make that permanent. On a heavy sigh, I allow myself to succumb to a few more minutes of sleep.

CHAPTER 23

WINNIE

*B*aby babble wakes me from a delicious dream. Raising my arms above my head, my body tenses, realizing I'm not alone in bed. Slowly, I crack one eye open and I'm suddenly aware that I'm not in my own room either.

Colton leans over me to lower the volume on the baby monitor. His smattering of golden chest hair scrapes my nipples as he moves, and they're suddenly standing at attention, begging to be touched. He doesn't miss the reaction either. Moving slowly, he leans down and captures one between his teeth. With a flick of his tongue, my body arches off the bed.

Weston sings merrily as I hear the telltale sounds of wooden trains hitting the tracks. I know we don't have much time before he calls for me, but Colton continues his leisurely assault on my left, then right nipple.

Sensing we're about to be interrupted, he pulls away, and my body tries to follow his heat. Hovering over me, he clasps the sides of my face in his hands.

"Morning, beautiful." His voice is raspy with sleep, and it's quite possibly the sexiest thing I've ever heard.

"Morning," I croak like a bullfrog, trying not to breathe my morning breath stank on him.

"This is the happiest I've ever been at six in the morning," he confesses.

My heart nearly explodes.

"I want to wake up like this every morning, Win. Is that okay with you?"

"Like, like this?" I ask, waving my hand between him and me.

God, his sexy smirk could make me do anything.

"Yes, Winnie. Just like this." He punctuates his words by thrusting his hard cock against my belly. "In my bed. Beside you. In you. Whatever you're willing to give."

"Oh," I gasp. I'm not sure I'll ever get over his blunt, dirty talk.

"I want to move my stuff back into the master bedroom. I want you to be mine in every way. Please say yes, CC."

His words cause that strange flutter in my chest, but fear is also creeping in. "For how long, Colton? I know we haven't talked about it, but you don't even live here. You're going back to North Carolina. I live here."

Weston's singing picks up as he babbles to his trains, and we both glance at the monitor. Colton's wistful gaze could make anyone's ovaries explode. Slowly, he turns to face me.

"I'm going back to Waverley-Cay today, but that's not my home anymore. My home, Winnie Darling, is wherever you and Wes are. I'll be in Waverley-Cay for two days to pack up some stuff, get Tilly up to date on a few things at the office, and then I'll be back. Preston and I will look at property here to renovate for new offices as soon as I get home. Do you want to come with me to North Carolina?"

My breath hitches in my throat. His home is wherever I am? He's coming back? "You're going to stay here? In Vermont? I can't go, I have to work. I have Weston's appointment on Friday in Boston. I can't just uproot him to—"

Colton places a finger over my lips to silence my word vomiting. "We, Winnie. We have Weston's appointment on Friday. I'll be back for that. We're facing all the big things together from now on. If you'll let me. We're an *us*, Winnie, and that means we're in this together."

Geez, how can this man make me cry so much?

He leans down and kisses my lips gently, but chastely, before pushing off the bed and pulling on some boxers. "I'll get our little guy and we'll start breakfast. I don't leave for about an hour, so take some time for yourself. I'll call you when the food's ready."

"You cook?"

He pauses in the doorway to flash a brilliant smile. "I can be very domestic for the right lady, Winnie. Lucky you." He winks, and my entire body blushes.

"Okay, then," I mutter to an empty room long after he's left. I watch him enter Weston's room on the monitor. Even through a six-inch screen, I can see the love he has for my little brother. I realize with a start that he's wearing a similar expression to the one he uses with me.

"No one sticks around you for long." Claire's words enter my consciousness, but for some reason, they don't have the same barbed edge as they normally do.

Glancing back down at the screen as Colton lifts Wes into his arms, I finally see the possibilities of a future.

$\approx$

*W*es runs up and down the hallway leading from the family room to the foyer. Over and over again he runs to the door, wags his arms like he's an airplane, then flies back to me on the sofa. It takes a few minutes to realize he's searching for Colton.

"Hey, Wes?"

Turning in place, he smiles at me, and my heart melts. He's

like a different kid here, and guilt threatens to eat me alive. I couldn't make him this happy or at ease on my own.

"Are you looking for Colton?" His eyes light up like the Fourth of July as he runs to the door again. "Hey, buddy. Colton had to go away for a couple of days, remember? He'll be back on Thursday."

"Coto. Lub Coto."

"You love Colton?" I ask through a lump in my throat.

"Yup," he replies happily. "Yup, lub Coto."

"Th-That's good, Wes. He loves you, too."

With bright silver blue eyes, he nods. "Yup. Yup. Yup." A second later, I've lost him to a train table in the corner of the family room that showed up at some point during my last shift.

A knock at the front door has us both freezing in place, and before I can react, I hear the door open, followed by a masculine voice.

"Winnie? It's just me, Halton. I wasn't sure if knocking would freak you out. Is it okay if I come in?"

Jumping from the sofa, I stare down at my sweatpants and disheveled T-shirt. With no time to change, I do my best to make myself presentable as I walk toward the hall. Peering around the corner, I find him standing in the doorway, tucking a package under his arm.

"Oh, yeah. Of course, come in. Come in. Sorry. I wasn't expecting anyone."

Halton chuckles as he pushes the door open to allow his wife, Rylan, to enter ahead of him.

"One thing you should know about the Westbrooks is you can always count on company. Especially if someone knows you're home alone." Rylan smirks. "It's how they do things."

Rylan is a beautiful woman with dark chestnut hair and bright green eyes that exude kindness.

"Oh, did Colton ask you to stop by?"

"No, but we wanted to check in. And Halton had something for Wes."

"I hope that's okay," he adds quietly. "When I drew you and Colt, I didn't know about Wes. We don't like to leave anyone out." He holds up a smaller canvas wrapped in brown paper. "Is it okay if I give it to him?"

My hand drifts to my wrist, but I control my movements even as my heart tries to escape my chest.

"You made something. For him?"

Halton pinches the back of his neck. It's a move I've seen Colton do, too.

"They really are very similar." Rylan laughs, obviously noticing the same thing.

Halton chuckles but removes his hand. "Yeah, ah, I don't like to leave anyone out. Is that okay?"

He seems so unsure, and I feel like a jerk. "Oh my gosh. Sorry, of course. Come in. I feel weird inviting you into your brother's home. Ah, I'm not really a very good hostess, I guess."

"Winnie, Colton wants you to feel at home here. You host or don't host, whatever works for you. No one in this family will ever judge you for that," Rylan exclaims.

"You've known them a long time?" I hate that I sound insecure, but I don't trust easily, and I've never had many female friends.

She smiles, grabs my hand, and leads me into the family room. Once we're seated on the sofa, we position ourselves so we can chat, but also watch as Halton lowers himself to the floor next to Wes.

I'm about to help Wes with introductions when Halton whispers something to him, and I watch in shock as he elicits a belly laugh from my little brother.

"He comes off gruff, but he's really good with kids."

Turning my gaze to Rylan, I see the love in her eyes as she watches Halton at the train table, and I relax into the cushions.

"But yes. I've been friends with Colton since I was six years old, and Halton almost as long." I nod as I take in her words, and she keeps going. "I know you've been through a lot, but I've never met better men than the Westbrooks. I hope you'll give Colty a chance to show you that. I've never seen him like this with anyone. He watches you like he's loved you his entire life, and I think if you give him the chance, he just might prove that."

I'm saved from answering when Halton's phone chimes loudly in his pocket, and Wes backs into the corner with his hands over his ears.

Halton's panicked eyes search for me. "I'm so sorry. When I was in the studio, I had the volume up. I forgot to silence it."

Rushing to Weston's side, I talk in hushed tones.

"It's okay, Wessy. It was just Halton's phone. Look." I point to Halton, and Weston's harried gaze follows.

"Jesus," Halton mutters. "I'm so sorry."

"It's okay," I assure him while making eye contact with Wes. "It just startled him. Noises he isn't expecting seem to bother him the most. Right, buddy? But we're okay, see?" I give Wes a smile I hope he returns.

It takes a minute, but when he relaxes, he holds up his helicopter to Halton. An olive branch of sorts, and I'm not sure if my heart can take the sweetness of the moment.

Halton holds out his palm, and Wes places it there, then snatches it back quickly.

"He tried to share." Halton laughs. "I'm not great at sharing either, buddy."

I know I should use this as a teaching moment, but little Wes slides out of the corner and takes a seat next to Halton, and I let it go. Within minutes, Wes is back to playing, and Halton pulls the wrapped package closer.

"I've got something for you, buddy. Do you like presents?"

Weston's eyes shine with hope. He hasn't had many presents in his short life. Really, he's had more in the last couple of weeks than he's ever had in his life.

"Yup. Yup." He bobs his head happily.

Halton chuckles and sets the package on the floor between

them. "I thought we could hang this in your room, you know, if you like it?"

Wes twirls in a circle around it, too excited to sit.

"Want me to help you open it?" Halton asks gently.

"Yup." Wes doesn't even hesitate as his fingers dance with excitement.

Halton tears open the paper with a kind smile, revealing a portrait of Wes standing on a platform next to his favorite train. Halton has drawn Wes as the conductor, and my little brother beams with a happiness I rarely see from him.

"Wessy!" Wes screeches, pointing at the portrait. He runs off toward his room, and we all stand there confused until he comes barreling back into the room with a conductor's hat I've never seen.

"Where the heck did that come from?" I ask, confused.

"Coto. Coto lubs."

Colton. I'm going to have to have a discussion with him about spoiling Wes, but seeing his happy face, I can't bring myself to be mad right now.

"It's not worth the fight," Rylan says beside me. "The Westbrooks love gifts, and Colton has finally found someone worthy of his love. Let him shower you with it. I have a feeling you both could use it."

I don't know what to say as I stare at Halton's gift. It's so thoughtful and beautiful.

"Thank you, Halton. For this. It's … he's never had so many people pay this much attention to him. It really means a lot."

"You're family now, Winnie." He says it as if it's a reality that I have to get used to, but before I can think about it too much, he pulls his phone from his pocket and curses under his breath.

"Shit." His eyes go wild when we hear a knock at the door.

"Another family member?" I smirk, but the smile fades when I see Halton's face.

"Stay here, okay? Let me handle whoever's at the door."

Panic fills my body, and Rylan takes me by the elbow and leads me to the floor beside Wes.

"Hattie?" Rylan's tone carries all the warning bells going off inside of my head. I don't even have room to process the nickname she's using.

"Just stay here, okay? All of you." With purposeful strides, he crosses the room.

Hushed, angry voices filter down the hall, but I can't make out what's being said or who is at the door. What feels like an eternity later, Halton returns with an envelope in his hand, his face a stony mask.

Rylan pats my arm and meets him in the center of the room. "What's going on, Hattie?"

His gaze cuts to me, and a fear I've only ever felt once in my life freezes me to my spot.

"We'll take care of this, Winnie. I promise you. Colton, none of us will let him get away with this." His voice is lethal, but it does nothing to calm my nerves.

"Take care of what?" I whisper, terrified of what he'll say.

"You've been served," he bites out. "By your father."

My world threatens to crumble beneath me, and my vision blurs.

"S-Served for wh-what? What d-does that m-mean?" I stammer.

"He's suing you for custody of Weston."

He could have stabbed me in the chest, and it would have hurt less. My head is shaking wildly as I try to comprehend his words.

"He ... No, he can't even take care of himself. How's he going to care for a child with special needs? How?" My voice breaks, and Wes lays his head in my lap. My body shakes with fear. I can't stop the trembling or the way my tears fall.

All I want right now is Colton. And he's not here. He's not here when I need him. I know that's not fair, but it's a stark reminder that I need to do this myself. Relying on others only leads to heartache.

Rylan and Halton sit beside me, offering comfort, but neither are sure what to do.

"Would a court really take him from me?" My whispered words relay my deepest fear. "He's an alcoholic. He's abusive. He—"

"Hey," Halton wraps a strong arm around my shoulders, "I said we would figure this out. You're not alone anymore, Winnie. You have the entire Westbrook family behind you now. Our name carries a lot of weight, and we'll hire the best attorneys money can buy."

"But he's his father." Words keep tumbling from my mouth. The effort of holding in my fears tearing me apart.

"And you're his family. You give him stability, and you can give him something your father will never be able to."

"Wh-What's that?"

Halton waits until I lift my gaze to his. His waiting smirk makes my heart clench with the need for Colton. A need I don't want, but is there trying to suffocate me, anyway.

"The Westbrooks," he says without a hint of sarcasm. "You have us, Winnie."

"I don't even know how to explain you, though. How is that going to help in front of a judge? Just because I have rich friends, that can't outweigh parental rights, can it?"

"It would if you were one of us," Rylan chimes in without an ounce of irony.

"What?"

"I know Colton wants to marry you. He texts me every day asking what kind of ring he should get you. Maybe it's time to throw caution to the wind and say I do."

I gape at her like she's lost her mind. I'm physically incapable of forming words, and before I know what's happening, Easton and Lexi enter the family room, each carrying a toddler on their hip, followed by Preston and GG.

"What's the plan?" Preston asks, hanging his suit coat over the back of a chair.

"What?" It falls from my lips in a whisper.

"No one messes with our family, Winnie." This time it's Easton who makes the declaration. "Until Colt can get home, we're staying by your side. We won't let some asshole threaten you like this. Weston is ours. End of story."

I'm not sure I've blinked in a full five minutes. My hands shake at my sides, and most shocking of all, Weston is making the rounds, learning how to fist bump with all these Colton look-alikes.

"This isn't real life," I mutter.

"Oh, Wendy. This is life, all right. You've just been missing out while Pan found his way back to ya."

Ashton enters the room at full speed, sliding to a stop next to Preston.

"Your entry needs some work, bro." East pats him on the back, hands him a little boy, and walks toward the kitchen. "Who's hungry?" He opens the fridge as I stand in a haze. "Looks like it's a taco night."

I stand slack jawed as he empties contents from the fridge.

Lexi crosses the room to stand in front of me. She's so stinking tall she has to bend over to get in my line of sight. "Are you okay?"

"I, uh …" Unable to form a sentence, I shake my head no.

"They can be overwhelming, but they say what they mean, Winnie. It took me a long time to come around to their all-in way of family-ing, but I've never once regretted letting them in. Trust takes time. It's earned. I know that better than most, but try, Winnie. We're all here for you because Colton loves you, so we do, too."

My blinking becomes erratic as I fight off tears and she drags me in for a hug. "I'm not a hugger, but look what these assholes did to me? I get needing to be tough, Winnie. We all have stories to tell, but for now, just do your best to let us in."

"I'll try," I mutter against her shoulder.

She pulls away and smiles. "Okay, then. Welcome to the chaos, Winnie."

"I heard that," Easton calls from the kitchen.

Lexi rolls her eyes, then steps back and places her little girl on the floor next to Weston. I watch in shock as he stares at her, then smiles. Without saying a word, he hands her his helicopter. He gave her his prized possession. I'm floored by the intrinsic trust he just placed in a new friend.

My nerves are frayed. My emotions are all over the place. I feel more fragile than I've ever been, and something else I don't want to admit is what's really turning me inside out. I feel loved. And for the first time in my life, I feel safe.

I don't know how to handle any of this. As if sensing my impending meltdown, Preston stands guard at my side.

"Normally, I'd like to mess with my little brother, but if you don't take his call soon, he might burn the entire city of Waverley-Cay to the ground."

I turn to him so fast I'm dizzy.

Preston places a hand on my elbow to steady me, and smirks. With a mischievous grin, he shrugs. "He's been calling my phone on repeat for five minutes. I don't think I can make him wait any longer. He's calling for you, though. Want to take it in his office?"

My gaze snaps to Weston. I want to talk to Colton so badly my body buzzes with need, but I'm not sure I can leave Wes. What if he loses control? What if he can't handle all the people?

Preston is abnormally good at reading people, and he wastes no time putting my fears to bed.

"We all have children, Winnie. Wes is a part of our family now, and we'll always take care of him. Emory will be here any minute. She's a doctor. Between all of us, we can handle anything that comes up. But I promise to come get you if we can't. Trust us."

"Everyone keeps saying that." It slips from my lips like a

sullen teenager. I open my mouth to apologize, but he shakes his head.

"We're a lot to take in. I don't know your story, Winnie, but we all have skeletons in our closet that make us who we are. Sometimes it takes a village to finally bury them once and for all. Trust is earned, even in families. Just give us a chance to earn it and I promise you, we'll protect your trust with everything we have."

My gaze darts between Wes and Easton's little girl, Ada James, then back to Preston just as the phone in his hands lights up. Again.

"Okay. If he … if he has any trouble, please just yell and I'll be right back."

"You have my word. We'll take good care of him. Go talk to my brother before he has an aneurysm."

"Thank you, Preston." I glance around the room full of Westbrooks. "For everything."

He smiles, but I can see the burden he carries as the eldest brother, and I feel my trust in this family growing a little stronger.

CHAPTER 24

COLTON

"It's about fucking time," I bellow as the screen turns from black to a soft glow surrounding Winnie. "Thank fuck. I'm sorry, baby. I thought you were Preston, but I'm glad it's you. I'm so sorry I wasn't there. Fucking hell, why wasn't I there?" My voice cracks, communicating my anguish more than words.

I watch as she lowers herself into a chair, and my heart explodes as she breaks down.

"Shh, CC. Shh. It's okay. It's going to be okay, I promise."

"He's the father, Colton. Child services warned me when I took custody that this could happen if I didn't get his rights revoked. I couldn't afford to do it. I— But … what if he takes Wes? He's all I have left, Colton. He's all I have left of my mom. I can't lose him."

"Goddamn it," I bark. "Get this fucking plane in the air now."

Winnie's face comes into focus, and I can tell she's trying to make sense of my surroundings.

"I'm coming home. I'll be there as soon as I can. I should never have fucking left." I'm so pissed at myself. I can barely contain my rage. "He won't take him from us, Winnie. This is about money. Nothing else."

"How can you be so sure? I don't have money to give him. He'll take me to court, and then what? What if he wins?" she sobs.

"That won't happen. Weston isn't what he wants." Dark thoughts cloud my mind, but I leave no room for doubt in my tone.

"How do you know?" she asks cautiously.

"Call it a feeling." A feeling I wish I didn't have, but I know in my bones he's looking for a payout. "We've dealt with scum like this before. We'll preemptively take steps to ensure we're seen as the safest, most stable family for Weston. Then we'll wait for your father to play his hand. He's after something, Winnie. Mark my words, it isn't Wes."

I sound more confident than I feel, but it seems to put her at ease, at least a little.

"I'm sure my brothers are all there by now. Are you feeling overwhelmed? Is Wes? I can tell them to leave. Maybe just Ry can stay with you?"

"They're teaching Wes to fist bump." Emotion muddies her words and a hiccup escapes. She's slightly dazed, possibly confused by this information, but there's also a spark of awe in her tone.

A slow, satisfied smile creeps across my face. My brothers and I may argue, but family first is something we never back away from. "Yeah?"

She nods emphatically, almost like she doesn't trust herself to speak. "Yeah, and he gave Ada James his helicopter."

I can't hide my shock this time. That helicopter is his pride and joy. Little AJ is a miracle worker. I watch Winnie's face closely for any signs that this is troubling her, but I find none.

"You always see me," she whispers.

"I do. I pay attention because it's important. You're important, and I don't want to miss any signs that I'm screwing this up."

Her gaze leaves the screen, lost in her head, and I give her a minute to collect her thoughts. But a minute turns into two and I start to worry. "Winnie?"

She shakes her head, and I smile.

"What? I'm sorry."

"I'll be home in less than four hours. I'm going to fix this, but now more than ever, I need you to trust me, okay?"

"I do, Colton. I trust you. I'll stumble sometimes, but I do trust you."

Pride swells in my chest. There's strength behind her words and I know she means them.

"I just ... I'm not used to feeling so weak, so inept. I've always been the fixer."

Watching her expression change, I see how hard that was for her to admit.

"Having your trust is the most beautiful thing I've ever heard, Win. You make me the happiest man on earth, but you're far from inept or weak. I'm not trying to fix you, CC. Just your situation. You're perfect in every way, and I have no doubt you would do all of this on your own if you had to. I'm just speeding things up because I can, and I want to. Try to change your mindset here, sweetheart, because I've never met a stronger, more courageous woman in all my life." I study her face, letting my words sink in. She's so beautiful it hurts not to be near her. "Let our family take care of you until I get home, but don't let them boss you around. They mean well, but they can be a lot."

The worry eases around her gray eyes, and laughter slips from her beautiful lips. "I've never met a family quite like yours, Colton."

"Ours, baby. Our family. I'll be home soon," I promise. If I can't get this damn plane in the air in the next five minutes, I'll tear this place apart.

"Okay." The bravado she had before is gone, and I see her trying to stay in her safe zone.

"Deep breaths. In and out. They all love you as much as I do. I'll be home soon."

Her eyes go wide. I know what I just said, and by her expression, she does, too. However, the first time I tell her I love her will not be over FaceTime.

"Ah, I should go check on Wes," she says shakily.

I agree so I don't slip and say what I really want to say. "I'll be home soon."

When the screen goes black, I lean back in my seat. Winnie Darling is about to become mine for real.

~

My flight was uneventful, but there was no way I could sit in a car for two hours to get home from the airport in Burlington. I feel weary as the helicopter lands next to Ashton's house in the open field. I have a plan in place. *Will Winnie go for it?* I've never felt more nervous or more sure of anything in my life. I'm not about to back down from a fight now, so with shaking legs, I jump out of the back and jog to a waiting Ash.

"She's okay," he croaks. "Scared, but okay."

I wrap him in a hug. He hands me the keys to a four-wheeler when he pushes me off him. Our homes are not that far apart, but he knows I'll want the quickest way down the mountain to where Winnie waits in our home.

"Thanks, Ash. Is everyone still there?"

"Rylan and Pres, I think. He sent everyone else home about an hour ago."

I nod, and throw my leg over the four wheeler. Turning the key, I rev the engine, then take off as fast as I can get it to go. Minutes later, I spin into the driveway with pebbles shooting out from the back tires and run to the front door.

The house is quiet except for a song I could sing in my sleep. The theme song for Weston's favorite train filters through the house, and I find them all on the sofa.

Sensing me, Winnie glances over her shoulder, and I rush to her side.

Weston squeals with delight, and I scoop him up off the sofa. "Dada," he yells happily, and we all freeze as tears well in my eyes and I have no desire to stop them.

"Me?" I choke out.

"Dada," he sings again, and rubs his nose on my chest.

My worried gaze darts to Winnie, who's as shocked as I am.

"What do I do?" I whisper yell.

"I-I," Winnie stumbles as she shakes her head, clearly at a loss, too.

"Are ya in for good, Pan?" GG's voice carries loudly from the kitchen.

"Yes," I say adamantly.

"Then let it be. Don't worry 'bout it so much. If your willin' to be that boy's daddy, just love on him, and let things play out naturally. If you're not comfortable, then ya repeat your name when he says it. Keep it simple, Pan."

My gaze cuts to Winnie, who shrugs.

"I don't know what the right thing to do is," she admits.

Wes wiggles in my arms, and I set him down. He's immediately absorbed in his show again, and Winnie and I gape at each other until we both laugh.

"That's not the welcome home I was expecting, but I'd be lying if I said I didn't love every second of it."

Winnie's shocked gasp makes my chest fill with a possessive need to make sure she always knows she's wanted.

"We'll get out of your way." Rylan grins between us.

"Thanks, Ryguy."

"That stupid nickname," she grumbles, but pulls me in for a hug before turning to do the same to Winnie.

I grab hold of Winnie's hand as we walk Rylan and GG out.

213

Closing the door behind them, I remember Preston. "Ash said Preston was here. Did he leave?"

"Oh, no. He's in your office. I hope that's okay?" The uncertainty of her words cuts deep.

"CC? This is your home, too. If you're okay with something, then so am I. Why don't you get Wes ready for bed while I check on Pres, and then we can talk?"

Winnie's shoulders sag, like the events of the day are physically weighing on her, and it makes me hate her father even more.

"Hey." I catch her arm and turn her toward me. Cradling her face in both hands, I lower my lips to hers. The kiss is gentle, but firm. My lips hover over hers as I speak. "I won't let anything hurt you or Wes. That includes your asshole of a father. We'll do everything in our power to fix this."

She shudders under my touch. "But, what if—"

I cut her off with another kiss, then pull back a couple of inches. Our breaths mingle as I stare into the misty gray depths of her eyes. "There is no other outcome, CC. I won't allow it. You and Wes are my family now, and I'll fight 'til my last breath to keep you happy and safe." Even as I speak, my plan solidifies in my heart.

This right here, with Winnie in my arms, is where I'll spend the rest of my life. Love at first sight, last sight, she's all I see in this world. For the first time in my life, I have a purpose. I have a reason to be the man my father raised me to be, and I'll be damned if I let some jackhole screw this up for me.

"Go get Wes ready. I'll check on Pres and then come find you both."

She nods, her chest rising and falling in an uneven tempo. I like that I affect her like this because she sure as hell knocked me on my ass. She turns to Wes, and I head to my office.

I find Preston sitting behind my desk with steepled fingers. A folder sits in his lap, and dread fills my soul.

"What's going on?" I ask, swallowing an unease that's attempting to claw its way out.

"Are you going to marry her?"

Immediately my defenses rise. Crossing my arms across my chest, I prepare for battle.

"If she'll have me." My tone is clipped, but he remains impassive, unreadable.

"You haven't known her long, Colt."

"Did that stop you? Or East? Jesus, Preston. Halton was the only one of our brothers who knew his wife longer than a few months before they married. Did you give them shit? Or is it because I'm the screw up of the family?" My teeth grind and every muscle in my body tenses as I wait for his reply.

The asshole just stares at me for so long my eyes go dry from refusing to blink first, but I hold my ground. I'm not the imbecile he obviously takes me for. Preston's lips twitch at the corner, and we both break out in a grin.

On a heavy sigh, I sink into the chair opposite him. "What's going on, Pres? If that's some bullshit prenup or something equally offensive, you'd better leave now before I'm forced to knock you out."

His laugh is unexpected. The rich, deep sound reminds me of our father. "Let's clear one thing up. I'm an asshole sometimes."

My brow rises skeptically, but I let him continue.

"I think because I had to take over The WB at such a young age after Dad died, I forget that there are all these rights of passage that most people go through. I missed out on a lot of that, but I wouldn't change it for the world. What I'm saying is, I'm sorry for jumping to conclusions with those girls, and for not having your back at first."

All the fight leaves my body. Preston gave up so much when our father died. He's had the pressure of being the head of our family since he was just a kid himself. He took over so the rest of us could have the normalcy of growing up, making mistakes, and learning from them.

"You've had a lot of pressure on you, Pres. You were never allowed to make mistakes like we were. There was too much riding on it, I get that. I do. I'm sorry I never thanked you for that."

"I'm not looking for thanks, Colt. I'm just explaining why I acted like an ass." He smirks, and I know that was painful for him to admit.

Leaning forward, I place my forearms on my thighs. I lift my head with clasped hands, eyes pleading with my brother. I realize at this moment that I need his help. I need his guidance, and I want his respect more than anything.

"I think I've loved her since the moment I saw her in the airport, Pres. This lawsuit? Her father trying to get custody of Wes? It scares the shit out of me. I need …" My head drops while I collect my thoughts. When I lift it again, I see all the compassion of an older brother, a father figure, and a friend all rolled into one. "I need your help. I don't want to screw this up. They mean too much to me."

A heartfelt smile spreads across his face and it's like staring at an older version of myself. Preston drops his gaze to the folder in his lap, and without speaking, opens it up and lays it on my desk.

I glance at it, then back at him. "You're forgiven." I chuckle. Pulling the folder closer, I flip through the pages. He's already pulled a preliminary report on Winnie's father. The last page shows an order for Envision Securities to start a full-on investigation into the man.

I'm suddenly overcome with emotion. "Thanks, Pres. Honestly."

"No thanks necessary. It's what we do, right?"

"Take care of our own," we say in unison.

"Yeah, but—"

Preston cuts me off. "You're going to need all the help you

can get. Something tells me getting Winnie to marry you will be harder than anything her father throws at you."

I laugh because he's right. Glancing over my shoulder at the door, I shake my head. "She doesn't trust easily. She's used to everyone leaving her."

"Then I guess it's time you showed her she's worth sticking around for."

Standing, he watches me closely as he rounds the desk, and I stand, too. When he draws me in for a hug, I accept the embrace.

"For what it's worth," he says, pulling away and clapping me on the back, "I think you're good for each other. You'll balance each other out. She needs some fun in her life, and you ... well, I think you were just waiting for the one who could ground you. I see her doing that already. As for her father? We've got this."

"Thanks, Pres."

We walk together through the quiet house, and I can feel him glancing around as we go, so I'm not surprised when he says, "This place is really starting to feel like a home."

He's right. It is. It's my family home, and no one will mess with my family, not if I have anything to say about it.

Closing the door behind Preston, I go in search of Winnie. It's time to make them my family for real.

~

*F*amily Chat
        Preston: Colton, why the fuck are there 4000 plastic donkeys holding sticks in my front yard?
    Dexter: Priceless.
    Halton: Pictures or it didn't happen.
    Preston: What the hell are people going to say?
    Colton: It's not 4000...only 2000 (crying laughing emoji)
    Preston: WHY???

Sylvie: I think it's a reminder to remove the stick from your ass every once in a while, son.

Preston: ...

Halton: ...

Dexter: ...

Ashton: ...

Colton: EPIC (laughing emoji, laughing emoji, laughing emoji)

CHAPTER 25

WINNIE

"*H*ow do you feel?" Colton's hushed words startle me out of my daze, and I blink feverishly.

"Ah, it's a lot." Glancing down at the twenty pages of notes in my lap, I close my eyes and rub my temples. "It's a lot," I repeat. I slump forward in the seat of Colton's SUV, and his strong hand lands on my back, rubbing in soothing circles.

"It is."

Wes laughs in the backseat, and we both turn to him. Buckled into his car seat with a pair of headphones Colton had specially made for him, he watches the small screen hanging from the ceiling. Another luxury I could never give him myself, but I can't deny it made our trip to Boston much easier.

"I thought Dr. Hamilton was very thorough, and she gave us so much great advice. Most importantly, she gave us a starting point."

As he speaks, my gaze drifts over the harried notes in my lap, each page with a different header.

-Sensory Processing Disorder.

-Neurodevelopmental disorder: look this up. What does it mean?

-Different from autism, but can present with similar charac-teristics.

-Vision: he has trouble tracking. Vision therapy is recommended.

-Speech delay: auditory over-stimulation, multiple ear infections. Confident he'll catch up with therapy.

-He lives in a state of fight or flight. Sensory therapy is suggested and tools to minimize triggers.

It's the last one that makes me tear up. How must it feel to live in a constant state of fight or flight? Regular stimuli that I deal with daily are magnified to an intolerable level for him, and I had no idea. Guilt makes my stomach turn like acid.

Colton leans over and places his palm on top of my notes. "There's no way you could have known this, CC. But now we do, and we can take steps to help him. She even said, with the right therapies, he could outgrow or learn to tolerate most of these."

Fear grabs my throat like a vice, and my words break on a sob. "C-Colton. There's no way my insurance will pay for this stuff. I had a hard enough time getting them to pay for amoxicillin when he had his tenth ear infection. Maybe … maybe if I take on more hours? But then I'd have to find a babysitter and I don't know that I'd make enough for it to even be worth it. Beth will help, but what about when she goes to—"

My notes go flying as Colton hauls me over the center console and into his lap. The horn blares as my ass rests on it, and he pulls me into him. My jaw nearly comes unhinged in shock as he grabs the sides of my face and draws me closer.

"Wendalyn," he rasps. "I know you think you have to do everything yourself. I know you use your independence to ward off heartbreak. If you don't trust anyone, they can't let you down, right? I'm learning all your defense mechanisms, baby, and I'm not here to dismantle them. But I will help reinforce that you're worth more than any dollar amount in my bank account. You're worthy of love. You don't have to prove how strong you are. I see it in everything you do. I'll never take away your independence, but you need to let me in. Trust me when I say I'm here for the long haul. The good and the bad.

I'm going to stand by you through everything if you'll only let me. I know that every other male in your life has let you down, betrayed your trust in the most brutal of ways, but I'm not them. I will mess up. But I'll never leave. I'm here for you and for Wes."

I'm sitting in an expensive SUV on Colton's lap with my legs draped across the center console and he just put Band-Aids over every insecurity I've ever had. Slowly, day by day, this man beneath me is healing my broken heart and building a fortress around us that feels safer than anything I've ever experienced.

"Please don't hurt me, Colton." My breathy words bleed every emotion I'm holding in.

Dragging my face closer, his lips ghost over mine. He makes me a promise with a single word. "Never." Before I can respond, his mouth claims mine. It's a brutal kiss of clashing teeth and intense promises. It's a kiss that tells me I'm his, and a kiss that instills hope.

"Yayaya. Lub Coto. Lub Coto, too," Wes screeches, clapping his hands wildly.

Laughter mixes with tears as it flies out of me. Unfortunately, so does snot, and I'm too close to Colton for it to go anywhere but on him. I'm completely mortified as he grabs a napkin from somewhere beside me and wipes his neck.

"Oh my God." I can feel my face flushing red. "I'm so—"

He cuts me off with another kiss, and I feel his body shake with laughter. "I'm here for it all, baby. Snot rockets and everything."

Mortified, I slap a hand on his chest and push myself off of him. I'm scrambling to drag myself back into my own seat when my hand hits the horn again and I slip. I reach back to catch myself and my palm lands right on his crotch.

Without missing a beat, he slips a hand under my ass and guides me back to my seat effortlessly. "Save that for later, CC." The devilish grin he graces me with has my insides curling with need as he starts the engine and pulls out into traffic.

I'm not sure if I had an orgasm with him or not. It wasn't the totally blissed out feeling I read about, but it was intense. I felt something. More than I had ever felt, even from my own hand. It was a full body experience that knocked me out for a solid eight hours and I'm more than ready for a repeat performance, if that's what sex with Colton Westbrook is always like.

"Winnie?" His voice makes me jump in my seat. *Jesus.* I was completely lost in my head. Thinking about sex. *Who am I?* My face turns scarlet as I clear my throat.

"Sorry. What?"

Something sounding like an avalanche rumbles in Colton's chest and he takes my hand in his. "What were you thinking about just now?"

"Nothing," I blurt much too quickly.

"Ah ha." He leans in, checking on Wes in the rearview before dropping his voice to just above a whisper. "Were you thinking about my head between your legs, CC? Your clit between my teeth?"

"Gah, I," I draw out the word so long I run out of air.

"Or maybe my cock when it first enters you?"

"Holy shit." I just went from red faced to all out inferno.

Tearing my hand from his, I play with the vents in front of me, forcing air onto my overheated body, and Colton laughs. The sound vibrates with warmth throughout the entire SUV, and Wes laughs along with him, no doubt just delighted to hear the happy sound coming from a man he's already attached to.

"Winnie?"

I freeze in place. My nerves that had been firing on all cylinders calm at his commanding tone. *How the heck does he do that to me?* More importantly, do I like it? Goosebumps form on my arms. It's like a race and my insides are all raising their hands to say, *Yes! Yes, we like it!*

"Ah, huh?"

Colton's eyes gleam with dirty thoughts. "I said, I have a surprise for you tonight. But only if you're comfortable with it."

Colton Westbrook is a cyclone and I'm caught in his wake. I can't keep up with him if I tried. He's superhuman in the way he jumps from one problem to the next with a smile on his face. It's addicting. It's infuriating. It's all consuming. And the worst thing of all is I think I like it.

"What surprise?" I finally force out.

"Tilly came into town. I have to go over some proposals with her, then I thought she could spend some time with us, and if you and Wes are comfortable with her, she offered to babysit after we put Wes to bed so I can take you out on a real date."

My body responds to his words like a threat. My spine stiffens. Sweat forms on my upper lip, and my hands clench together so tightly they turn white. Somewhere in my head, I know this is not a normal response, but I can't seem to control it.

"Hey, CC. Look at me."

Pulling at the collar of my shirt, I turn toward him. *Why is it so hot in here?* Staring into kind eyes with the ring of blue that reminds me of a summer sky, the breath I didn't realize I was holding comes out in a whoosh.

"Sorry."

"No. Don't apologize. Listen to me. I understand you more than you know. I get that you've had to rely on yourself for a long time, and me throwing all these people at you is hard. But please know that everyone in my life is there for a reason. I would never put you or Wes at risk. Tilly is my assistant, but she's also family, okay? She's Preston's sister-in-law, and she grew up helping raise their youngest sister. She's great with kids, but if you're not comfortable after meeting her, we'll stay in. It's no big deal. Can you agree to meet with her though? See for yourself before you decide?"

Ugh. Why am I such an asshole?

Releasing my hands from the death grip I have on them, I'm nodding before my brain can even catch up. "Yeah, of course. And if we leave after he's in bed, it will probably be fine." *I hope.*

Colton leans over the console and kisses my forehead. "That's my girl. We're almost at the hotel. Loch is waiting for us."

"Your friend? The one who works at the hotel? I'm confused. I thought he worked at a hotel in Miami?"

His smirk tells me I'm missing something big. "I may have omitted one small detail about Lochlan."

"Ah, what's that?" Why am I suddenly nervous again?

"He doesn't work at the hotels. He owns them. All over the world, actually."

Oh my God. Of course he does. Billionaires would be friends with other billionaires. My gaze drops to my outfit, and I close my eyes to center myself. I have as much self confidence as the next girl, but I don't fit in this world.

"CC? I know what you're thinking, and you can forget it. You're perfect. You look perfect. If you wore a burlap sack, you would still be the most beautiful woman in the room."

I don't have time to respond because he pulls up to a valet and my attention goes to the window. Having grown up in Vermont, Boston always felt like my city, but I've never spent much time in the Beacon Hill area. Glancing up at the towering building with ornate details and gargoyles on the roof, I'm in awe that someone I know could own something like this.

A bellhop rushes to the car and opens my door, but I don't move.

Colton chuckles. "It's okay, CC. Just be yourself. I promise you, you'll still have better manners than a lot of the socialites they're used to in places like this."

"How do you always know what I'm thinking?" Once the words are out, a smile spreads from ear to ear. Colton Westbrook has a hold on me, whether I like it or not.

Leaning in close, he whispers words just for me. "Because I know you, CC. I'm so invested in you that I pay attention to every detail. And that will never change. You're it for me, sweetheart." If my eyes get any bigger, I'm pretty sure they'll fall right out of my head. "Go ahead. Get Wes out of his car seat while I help with the bags."

In a Colton-induced haze, I follow his orders. Wes is abnormally quiet as I hoist him up onto my hip, but as soon as Colton rounds the car, he babbles with happy sounds and arms outstretched. The man before me doesn't hesitate as he reaches for Wes and easily cradles him in one arm.

When he lays his head on Colton's chest, singing away happily, something unlocks in my chest. It's a feeling I can't name, but I know it's big and scary as hell.

"Ready?" he asks, taking my hand in his and leading me into the fanciest hotel I've ever been in. Crystal chandeliers hang from the ceiling, twinkling and shining like the biggest diamonds.

"Why does it smell so good in here?" I whisper.

"Loch infuses all his hotels with a signature Blaine scent he spent an excessive amount of money curating. He also won't tell anyone what's in it. He says it's proprietary, but I'm not sure even he knows. It's pretty incredible though, right? Calming? He spent hours with control groups testing it."

"That's ... wow."

"There he is. Huh. And there goes Tilly. What the hell?" he says under his breath as he leads us through the lobby to a man crouched down, picking up a pile of papers scattered on the floor around him.

CHAPTER 26

COLTON

*W*hy did Tilly just have a faceoff with Lochlan Blaine? I wasn't even aware that they knew each other. He's my best friend, but she's family, and it has me taking fast strides toward him with Winnie in tow.

"Loch. What was that about? I didn't realize you knew Tilly."

"Tilly?" he asks, genuinely surprised.

"Yeah, the girl that just stormed out of here looking like she wanted to smack you." Winnie tugs on my hand, and I lower my voice. "She's Preston's sister-in-law and my assistant."

"Huh."

"That's all you have to say? What was that about?"

A lecherous grin spreads across his face, and I'm worried I'll have to fight my best friend. "We literally bumped into each other. I was looking down at my phone, and she was … well, I'm not sure what she was doing. We've been running into each other a lot lately." He says it almost to himself, and it has me more curious than angry.

"You've been running into each other? Where?"

"Weddings. Three in a row, actually." Loch's eyes dance with mirth as he speaks, and it sets off alarm bells.

"Stay away from her, Loch. She's family. You know what that means."

"Yeah, yeah. You take care of your own. I just … Never mind. Doesn't matter." His phone dings in his hand and the oddest expression crosses his face as he pockets it. "Now, who do we have here?" he asks, dropping his gaze to Weston before turning to my girl. "And you must be Winnie. I've heard so much about you."

"Y-You have?"

"Oh, yes. I've been hearing about you since Miami."

"Loch," I say in warning. "That's enough. It's good to see you, man." Leaning in, I give him an awkward chest bump instead of a hug because one hand holds Winnie's and the other holds Wes.

He laughs, and everyone in a twenty-foot radius takes notice. That's what I've always loved about this guy. He can be an ass for sure, but he loves hard, laughs loud, and is as loyal as they come.

"You too. It's about time we were in the same city." Turning to Winnie, he extends a hand. "I'm Lochlan. Welcome to The Beacon Bryer Hotel."

Winnie graciously accepts his handshake with a practiced confidence I've grown to love about her. "It's nice to meet you, Lochlan. This place is …" She glances around in awe. "It's beautiful."

"Thank you, Winnie. It's been in my family for about seventy-five years. We just completed a renovation to bring it into this century, though," he says with a million-dollar grin.

"This is Weston."

Lochlan holds out a fist, and I beam with pride when Wes fist bumps him.

"Nice to meet you, mate."

Wes holds up his little helicopter, and Loch smiles. "I have a real one of those on the roof. Maybe you'll get to see it sometime."

Unsure of how Winnie would feel about that, I change the subject. "Is everything all set?"

"Everything arrived about an hour ago. It's all set up in your suite. Come on, I'll walk you there. The front desk knows to bring your bags up."

In the elevator, curiosity gets the best of me. "When you say you've run into Tilly, what does that mean exactly? You didn't … you know. Did you?"

"Tilly." He shakes his head with a faraway look in his eyes. "No wonder."

The doors slide open, and Loch gestures for us to exit.

"No wonder what?" I push.

"I was told her name was Abby at every wedding we've attended." He chuckles.

This is news to me and confusing as hell. "Surely, you're mistaken."

"Oh no. Not this time, mate. I'll never forget our last introduction."

Fuck. He slept with her. I can tell by his tone. "If you were an asshole, Loch, seriously?"

"I wasn't," he mutters. "She didn't give me a chance. But I'm sure I'll be seeing Miss Tilly again sooner than she'd like."

"Loch," I growl as he pushes open a door at the end of the hall.

Winnie gasps beside me as she enters the suite, and I pause to look around. The place is truly stunning. Loch outdid himself with the renovations.

"I promise you there's nothing to worry about."

I glare at him, but see nothing other than sincerity in his eyes. "Fine. Please don't make me kick your ass."

"Ass. Ass. Ass," Wes repeats merrily, and I cringe.

Lochlan's silky laughter fills the room. "You've got your hands full. Don't worry, I have nothing sinister planned. I'll get out of your hair, though. I left everything exactly as you requested."

I release Winnie and clap Loch on the back, drawing him in so I can whisper a warning. "Don't fuck around with Tilly. I may kick your ass, but Preston will kill you."

He pulls back so we're face-to-face. "No worries. I have no intention of hurting her."

"I know. But I still had to say it." I grin.

"Jackass. Text me if you need anything. Winnie, it was a sincere pleasure. I hope you enjoy your stay."

"Thank you," she murmurs, still taking in her surroundings.

I watch as he lets himself out, and I set Wes down on the floor. Somehow our bags beat us here, and I grab the one I know has his trains. Dragging it into the suite with him following behind, I unzip it and help him set up the tracks on the floor.

"There you go, buddy."

He does his little happy dance and plops down onto the floor. Laying on his side, he watches the wheels go back and forth over and over again. Convinced he's settled, I turn to find Winnie watching us.

"Hey, you."

"Hey you," she repeats.

"I have some work to do. Why don't you order room service for you and Wes, then I'll bring Tilly back to meet you both?" I watch her intently.

"Yeah, okay." Her hand goes to her wrist, and I move to her with a sadness I can't explain. "What's the matter?"

Her gaze sweeps around the room before landing on me. "It's stupid." She laughs uncomfortably.

"Nothing you say or do is stupid. Just tell me."

She lifts her gaze to the ceiling, then drops her face to her hands.

Slowly, I lean in and pull them away. "Whatever it is, you can always come to me."

She shakes her head, and I see the insecurity I despise creeping in. "It's just, I'm twenty-eight years old and I've never ordered room service before. I have no idea how much to tip them or if you're supposed to tip them. This," she gestures around the room with her hand, "is so much more than I've ever experienced."

Reaching into my pocket, I pull out my wallet, grab a twenty-dollar bill, and place it in her palm. "This will cover it, and anything you order will be charged to the room. Get whatever you want, and get used to this, CC. You're in my world now and you deserve nothing but the best."

"What if I don't fit here?"

I pull her into my chest. This insecure Winnie isn't something I'm used to. "You fit with me, Winnie. Wherever I am, you fit."

She slips her hand into my pocket, and I instantly go hard until I realize she just slipped my twenty back to me. "I have my own money. Not much, but enough to cover a tip," she whispers. This is part of her stubborn independence. Her need to take care of herself.

I let it go. For now.

"Okay. Anything else before I find Tilly?"

"No. We'll be okay."

"I'll only be a couple of hours. Make yourself at home. If you need anything, text me or call the front desk and they'll bring you whatever you ask for."

She nods and nibbles on her fingernails, so I place a kiss on her head. When she pulls away, I turn to kiss Wes on the head, too.

"I'll be back soon, buddy." His little lip quivers, and it's enough to make me cancel every plan I have for the rest of my life. "I promise. I'll be back soon. I just have to work for a little bit, okay?"

Winnie swoops in to distract him. "Go ahead. We're fine."

A war breaks out in my heart, but eventually, I nod because words would hurt too much right now. Damn that kid. He could break me wide open with that sad expression. When I reach the front door, he's back to giggling with Winnie and the pain eases slightly. Ripping open the door, I hope Tilly is ready to get to work because this will be the fastest meeting we've ever had.

Colton: Meet me in the conference room on the second floor in five?

Tilly: Already here.

Colton: On my way.

Tilly: (thumbs up emoji)

⁓

*T*enter the conference room with a sense of unease I don't like. Tilly lifts her head and offers a smile. It always surprises me how much she looks like her sister, but with darker skin and dark brown hair that's so shiny light seems to reflect off of it like glass.

"Hey, Till. How are you?"

"Good, boss. We've got a lot of ground to cover, though. I've put your minions on the tasks that can be handled without you, and taken over in your place where I can, but …"

"Some of it I need to handle, even if I am on *probation*," I fill in.

"Ah, yeah. About that. Any idea how long this will last? I mean, I don't mind, but I'm kind of burning the candle at both ends here."

That's what I always like about Tilly. Where Emory is quiet and reserved, Tilly is outspoken and daring but just as sweet. She's the epitome of sunshiny happiness. It's why we get along so well. She's the female version of me, but taking in her appearance now, I can see she's exhausted. I owe her an apology.

"I'm sorry, Till. I didn't take into consideration that you've been pulling double duty. I'll talk to Preston and get a timeline going. Until then, we'll bring on an assistant for you."

"Ugh. That's just another person to train."

I smirk. Tilly has grown so much in the two years she's been with me. Both she and her sister, Eli, did internships with us. It only took Eli one summer to realize she wanted nothing to do with the business world, but Tilly has shone in her role here.

"Well, we both know you won't be my assistant forever, no matter how much I beg."

She ducks her head down so I can't see her face.

"This will make the transition easier when you leave me. How's your side business going? Ready to tell me what it is yet?"

"No way. If I tell any of you, you'll just stick your big noses in to help, and it's important to me that I build this on my own."

I could easily dig around and find out what she's up to, but I trust her as much as I trust Loch. And that brings me to my next question.

"Does this side business have anything to do with the murderous glances you were shooting at my friend, Lochlan, downstairs earlier?"

Tilly's head snaps up so fast I'm surprised her eyes aren't rolling. "That's ... Did he? Never mind." Her lips seal shut in a thin line. "I met him at a wedding and that's all I want to say about it."

My gaze lingers on her, but she stares right back. After a few minutes, I realize she won't back down, and I give in. "Okay, but if he did anything to upset you, let me know and I'll handle it."

"I'm good," she replies curtly. After shuffling the stacks of paper on the table, she places them in front of me and we get to work.

CHAPTER 27

WINNIE

"*W*es? Want a snack, buddy?"

Lifting his head, he glances at the door, then lays back down on his side, *zooming* his train back and forth. He's been there for almost two hours. I pulled him away to eat a late lunch, but he barely touched anything. I have a sinking feeling he's waiting for his friend, Colton.

I still don't know what to make of him calling Colton dada. He hasn't done it again, but it doesn't mean he isn't thinking it.

A click echoes through the suite, and Weston bolts upright and runs to the door before I can even get off the floor.

"Hey, little man! Did you miss me?" Colton's voice rings out just as he rounds the corner with Weston in his arms.

I stand in the center of the room at a complete loss.

"Hung-ee, hung-ee, Coto."

"You're hungry?" Colton asks, glancing around the room.

Shit.

"I ordered room service, but he refused to eat." It comes out in a defensive rush.

"Okay. Want to try again, Wes?"

He nods happily, and Colton carries him over to the table.

Lifting the silver tray, he finds his mostly untouched mac and cheese.

Colton sticks his finger right in the center. "It's still kind of warm. Good enough." Sitting down, he grabs two spoons. After handing one to Wes, they both dig into the lukewarm pasta. For every spoonful Wes drops, Colton follows behind making train sounds.

Feeling displaced, I clean up the mess we made with all the trains when there's a knock at the door.

"That's Tilly," Colton informs me. "Can you let her in?"

"Ah, yeah. Yup. Sure."

My bare feet make a plopping sound on the cold marble floor of the foyer. I still can't believe a hotel room even has a foyer, but before I let myself get sidetracked, I open the door to find a beautiful woman on the other side. *Oh.* Her hair is long and silky in the deepest shade of brown that matches her eyes. There's no mistaking the resemblance to Emory, but it's a shock seeing their contrasting coloring.

Tilly grins and raises her eyebrows. I realize I've been standing here staring at her like a lunatic. "Geez. I'm sorry. You must be Tilly? Come in."

"I am. It's so nice to finally meet you, Winnie. Colton has talked about you nonstop for so long. I feel like I already know you."

She's the second person to say that. My chin lifts as the knowledge of Colton thinking about me boosts my confidence at a time when I desperately need it.

"That's ... really nice," I settle on. "Come on in. Colton is getting Wes to eat."

"Just so you know, I'm CPR certified, if that makes you feel any better about me babysitting. I also helped raise my youngest sister and babysat throughout high school. I'm great with kids." She talks so fast my head is spinning, but her smile is infectious. She has a personality that is impossible to dislike.

"Thanks, Tilly. I appreciate that. And it's not that I don't trust you, it's just ..."

She lays a gentle hand on my arm. "He's struggling a little right now. Colton told me the basics. I'll follow whatever directions you have for me."

Her kindness causes tears to form at the corner of my eyes. "Thank you, again. Really, it's just a *me* issue, I think. I've only ever left him with Beth."

"And me," Colton chimes in.

"Coto, Coto. Lub Coto," Weston sings.

"And Colton," I acknowledge.

"Till, this is Wes. Wes, this is my good friend, Tilly."

Wes eyes her suspiciously. I'm turning to apologize when I see her stick her tongue out at him and cross her eyes. He busts out in a belly laugh so hard he sprays mac and cheese into the air.

"Well, I guess this will work out after all," I say, a little bewildered.

Tilly winks. "I told you I'm good with kids." Walking closer to Wes, she bends down, so she's at eye level with him. "When you're done eating, can you show me your trains? I heard you have some pretty epic ones." She keeps her tone soft and faces him head-on so she doesn't startle him.

It makes me realize Colton did more than listen at the doctor's office. He committed the information to memory and relayed all the important pieces to Tilly. I can see it in the way she moves around him, careful to never walk behind him. It's part of the visual tracking that Wes struggles with and why groups can be difficult.

My gaze shifts to Colton and I melt. Once again, he's watching my every reaction, ready to step in, lend a hand, and sometimes just hold me. A rush of heat fills my body, and I feel lightheaded. This man is a master at breaking down my defenses, and I'm not sure I have anything left to hold back.

Please don't crush me, Colton. The words go 'round and

'round my head, but as he stalks toward me, everything else fades. I have no fears when he's this close. Never in my life have I had the sense of calm that I do when I'm with him. *Is this what love feels like? Is that what this is?*

"What do you think? Did she pass the test? Can I have you tonight?" Colton's words cut into my inner musings, and I blink a few times to clear my head. *Love?* Did I really just have that thought? Could I be in love with Colton Westbrook?

Turning my attention back to Wes and Tilly, I smile at the silly clapping game they're playing before returning my attention back to Colton. "I haven't been on a date in a really long time."

His lips dart down and capture mine. He keeps it brief, but it's enough to have my head spinning. "Then I guess it's time I fixed that. In that bedroom over there," he points to my right, "are a couple of boxes I had Tilly arrange for you. Pick out whatever you're most comfortable in and get dressed. I'll get Wes ready for bed and come get you when it's time to tuck him in."

Wow. That's a lot of information to unpack. "You bought me clothes?"

"And shoes. Before you even think about not accepting them, you should know I will do this a lot. As much as I can. You, Winnie Darling, are the kind of woman that should be spoiled, and I'm the man lucky enough to do it. Don't fight me on this." His tone deepens, and it feels like a command, a plea, and a promise. "You won't win."

"Fine," I say, lifting my chin. "I'll accept the clothes. Tonight. Only if you promise me we can discuss all future gifts another time."

He chuckles darkly. "Are you always this stubborn about receiving presents?"

"I don't know. I don't get many of them," I confess.

He pulls me impossibly closer. Our thighs press together, and I feel his heartbeat racing erratically against my breasts.

"That is going to change. Go get ready." And with that, he releases me.

I gasp for air, like breaking the surface of the ocean. I can't get my footing. He throws me so far off balance I don't know which way is up, and I think he likes it that way.

"Get ready," I mumble absently.

He smirks, then walks away like he knows he just fried my brain. Jesus. If this is what life is like with him, I'll never survive it.

The last thing I hear before I close the bedroom door is Weston's peals of laughter as Colton chases him around the suite. And just like that, another stitch in my armor comes undone.

∽

"Winnie?" Colton asks, cracking open the door. "Hey, you're not dressed. Do they not fit?" The concern in his voice causes a riot in my chest.

"Ah, no. Everything's perfect. I …" My cheeks puff out as I sigh loudly. "They're all really expensive, Colton. What if I spill something on them?"

Nibbling on my nails seems to be my new go to nervous habit since I'm consciously avoiding my wrist wrangling. I have a cuticle between my teeth as Colton crosses the room, never taking his eyes off me.

"If you spill something and it ruins whatever you choose to wear, I'll buy you another one."

"That's what I was afraid of," I mumble.

"Winnie, please don't let money be an issue between us. I have it. You don't. End of story. If I have my way, what's mine will be yours soon enough. But I also know my brothers have all gone through this with their significant others."

My head spins at this news. "None of the girls were rich on their own?"

"No. My adopted brother Trevor's wife, Julia, probably had a good amount squirreled away. But Lexi? Sloane? Emory? Lanie? It took my brothers a while to convince them to get over the billionaire titles, and I'm pretty sure Lexi probably tried to shove a few gifts up Easton's ass." He chuckles. "She's feisty like that. Looks are always deceiving, Winnie. They each had hardships and moments of crises that they had to get through in their own time. We have enough hurdles already. Please don't make money one of them."

It's hard to breathe when my stomach is in knots, but staring into his eyes, listening to his words, I nod. "I'll try." It's barely a whisper, but he pulls me into the safety of his arms, and I wish I could bottle the comfort it brings.

Colton rests his chin on top of my head. "Which outfit did you pick?"

"The black sheath dress. Is that okay?"

His chest rumbles as he speaks. "Fuck yes. Go say goodnight to Wes and then get dressed. I'm going to take a quick shower."

"Okay." I try to pull away, but he holds me still while his lips ghost over my skin before landing on my mouth. This isn't a kiss for public consumption. This is a kiss that fucks me with his tongue, and promises sweet, sweet torture to come. He owns every inch of me while he tastes, nips, and sucks. He devours me until I'm breathless.

"My CC," he groans. "Mine. Tonight, I'll make you mine."

Yes! my body screams as electricity shoots through my veins. What he doesn't understand is he's already burrowed deeper into my heart than anyone else has ever been.

Peeling my body from his, I mumble incoherently as I walk backwards toward the door. Colton watches me leave, his expression hiding nothing. When he takes a step forward, a squeak escapes my throat, so I turn and run from the room with his laughter trailing me down the hall.

CHAPTER 28

COLTON

*T*ucked away in a semiprivate corner of the bustling The Hungry I, a Beacon Hill longtime staple, I see nothing but Winnie. Just a glimpse of her takes my breath away. But tonight? Tonight, she could make angels curse, and turn devils into saints for a chance to be near her.

"Is everything okay?" she whispers while leaning over the table.

The dress I chose has a squared neckline that cuts just low enough to tease what's below the tight fabric that does nothing to hide her pebbled nipples.

"This might be the best night of my life," I answer honestly.

She rolls her eyes, but I rise to the challenge. "It's better than every prank I've ever pulled on Preston. Better than when I got my driver's license. Better than graduating from college with a higher GPA than Easton. Being with you is better than any multi-million dollar deal I've closed. Tonight is the first of many *bests* I'll have with you, Winnie Darling. You look stunning."

"So you've said," she muses teasingly, but her skin flushes a lovely shade of red.

She lifts her wine to those plump, red lips, and I wonder

what they would taste like right now. Cherry cola, wine, and something uniquely her? My dick twitches against my zipper at the thought.

"And I'll keep saying it." I can't keep my gaze from lingering on her lips as I speak. "I hope you don't love that dress too much, though?"

"Oh no. Why?" she asks, frantically yet discreetly checking herself. "Did I spill wine on it?"

Leaning across the table, I still her hands that are skimming her lap, searching for a spill. "No, CC. I hope you don't love it because I'm going to enjoy ripping it from your body as soon as we're alone."

She sucks in a gasp, but my expression says it all. I'm not fucking around. I want her in the worst way and I'm already regretting this five-course meal.

"Are ve ready to order?" Jean-Paul, our waiter, asks with a thick French accent I'm inclined to believe is fake.

Winnie's eyes go wide as she stares at me and shakes her head. Regretfully, I let go of her hand and turn to Jean-Paul. "We're going to need a few minutes," I explain, with my gaze fixed on Winnie.

"Very vell." He tops off our wine glasses and slinks away into the darkness.

"I don't know what any of this is," Winnie hisses, "and I can't understand what he's saying." She tries to keep a straight face, but we both break out in laughter. "Do you think his accent is real?"

"Definitely not." I chuckle. "He sounds like he's failed one too many acting classes." Opening my menu, my laughter erupts anew. Everything is in French, at a French restaurant. Go figure. Placing it back on the table, I smirk at my girl. "Are you feeling adventurous tonight, sweetheart?"

She narrows her eyes, but doesn't back down. This is the Winnie I met at the airport. The strong, independent woman who didn't fall for my shit and I fucking love it.

"What did you have in mind, Mr. Westbrook?"

Seductress. And she doesn't even know it.

"We'll leave it up to the chef. Russian roulette style."

"Will we have to draw our weapons?"

"No, but I'll poke you with something thick and hard later."

"Oh, you did not just say that." She's sputtering her words through laughter. A sound I don't hear nearly enough.

"I can pull out my inner teenage self when the need arises. And if it makes you laugh like that? I'll always rise to the occasion." I waggle my eyebrows and glance down at my crotch.

Winnie nearly chokes on her wine, but the smile on her face makes her outshine the sparkling diamond I have in my pocket.

"Thank you for this." Her gaze darts around the dimly lit restaurant.

Unable to keep my hands to myself, I lean across the small, bistro-style table and clasp her hand in mine. "It's my pleasure, CC. Sincerely, I mean it when I say this is the best night of my life. And I hope it just keeps getting better."

I stare as her slim neck works to swallow the emotion she's trying not to show. I know she's holding back with me. Not fully trusting my intentions, but after tonight, I hope to put the rest of her worries to bed. Forever.

"H-Have you been here before?" Nervously, she brings her wineglass to her lips, transfixing me as I answer.

"Yes, actually. It's one of the last outings we all had together before my father passed away."

Her quick intake of air has her chest heaving. "I'm so sorry."

I smile sadly, remembering that night we took over the entire top floor. "Don't be. It's a wonderful memory."

"Will you tell me about it?"

My palm sweats in her hand. It's not that I don't like talking about it, but it won't set the tone I'm looking for. Still, if I want her to trust me and my plan, I can't hold anything back. "My dad decided he wanted to hit up all the baseball stadiums on the East Coast before Preston went back to college. We'd just come from a Red Sox game, so we really weren't dressed appropriately. But one of the things my dad did well was cater to my mom. She's a romantic. She didn't care about fancy, though. It was more about the experience, and this was a place they hadn't been to, but heard about often. Sadly, it'll be closing soon, so I wanted to make one more memory here before it does."

Winnie's eyes mist, but she holds back the tears.

"You're always so strong for everyone else, CC. You don't have to be with me. I'll always catch you."

She blinks nervously. "You really mean that, don't you?"

"With all my heart." Her free hand fiddles with her silverware, but I see her mind working.

"You said one of the things your dad did well? What else did he do?"

Warmth shows in my smile as I gaze at her. "He chose love every day, and he went full steam ahead with every decision he ever made. He always knew exactly what he wanted, and he made it happen. When he started The Westbrook Group, his family had cut him off for marrying my mom. Everyone he grew up with shut him out and made no secret of their skepticism that he could make it work."

"But he did."

My gaze finds hers, and my heart pounds in my chest. "He did. He always followed through. Even if it seemed like a rash decision to everyone else, he always had a plan. He never backed down from a challenge."

"You're like him." It isn't a question, but it feels like progress.

"I am. We all are in different ways, and we've all carried him with us after he passed. Preston and Ash write in journals. Easton builds things. Halton draws. Though my dad didn't do it much as we got older, he was always doodling on his desk calendar."

"And you?" She's staring at me like I'm a puzzle to solve. But there's no solving me yet. She's my missing piece and I know I won't be complete until she's mine.

"Practical jokes. Quick decisions. After he died, things were really heavy in my family for a long time. My brothers may not remember it, but my dad had the best sense of humor. He was constantly jumping around corners, scaring the shit out of my mom. He loved to make people laugh." I drift off as I hear his laughter for the first time in years, making my spine tingle. "Anyway," I surreptitiously take a glance around, half expecting to see a ghost, "he was a great man."

"So are you, Colton. You've shown Wes an example of what a good man is. Even though he's so young, I hope he'll always remember that."

I've hit my breaking point with her. "You say that as though I won't always be around." My voice is husky but calm even as my insides quiver in fear of her response.

Her hands shake visibly as she sets down her glass. I wonder briefly if she's nervous since she always seems to hold something in her free hand. "Colton." Her tone makes my jaw flex.

"Winnie."

On a heavy sigh, she tugs her hand free. "I don't know what you expect of me, Colton. This has all happened so fast, and what happens when you go back to your real life? What if my dad actually gets custody of Wes? What if—"

"What if I make you both mine permanently?"

She splutters, but no words actually form. Her chest heaves as she glances between my eyes, but I'm deadly serious.

"I don't plan to go anywhere. Ever, Winnie. I think I've known that since the second you took my breath away at Logan International Airport."

Shaking her head, she finds her words. "You mean Miami."

"No, I mean Logan. I first saw you in Boston and you scared the hell out of me. I ran away like a child. But when I saw you again in Miami, I knew it was time to man up. Something in my gut told me you were worth growing up for before I ever said hello. Call it love at first sight. Call it kismet. Call it whatever you need to make that pretty little head of yours understand. I love you, Winnie Darling. I love Weston. And that will never change."

I've heard some men say they were nervous before proposing. That their hands shake, or their pits sweat. I have nothing but certainty as I stand, then drop to one knee in front of her. Winnie's gaze goes wild as she frantically searches the small space. Reaching into my pocket, I pull out the ring. Her entire body trembles as she gives in to the tears.

"You can't be serious, Colton? It's been weeks."

"I don't need any more time. I want to marry you. I want to make a life with you and Wes. I want you to be my family. Someday, I want to make a bigger family with you, but I want you to go to law school first because I want you to have everything. I won't pressure you to get married tomorrow, although I would really fucking love that. And I should probably tell you now, I want a big wedding. I want to see you float down the aisle knowing I'm the one you chose." When she doesn't speak, I pull out the card I didn't want to use. "And an engagement will put us firmly ahead of your father in the eyes of the court."

"Are you asking me for Wes?" Her voice shakes and is barely audible, but I hear her fear.

"No, Winnie. I'm not. He's just a bonus. It may have moved up our timeline a bit, but I was always going to ask you to marry me. I think that's why I got spooked in Boston when I first saw you. My heart knew what took my brain a little longer to figure out."

"I'm not sure I'll be good at it."

Standing, I take the seat next to her, aware that we're drawing stares from neighboring tables but not giving a fuck. I need to be closer to her. "Not good at what, sweetheart?"

"Family-ing. I've never had one. It was always just me and my mom." New tears fall down her cheeks and it tears me to shreds. Yanking her from her chair, I pull her into my lap so I can hold her.

"That's the best part, CC. There were no rules about what makes up a family in my house growing up. Family is exactly what you make of it. It sounds like you and your mom were the perfect family, and I want to be part of that, just like I want you to be a part of my crazy, ever-expanding chaos."

"*This* is crazy, Colton."

"I love you, Winnie. With my whole heart."

"I'm scared." We've been in our own little bubble this whole time, but I'm becoming aware that chatter around us has quieted. She glances around and flushes, noticing it, too. She attempts to stand, but I hold her still.

"Do you trust me?"

She pulls back to search my eyes. Nose to nose, I know I could stare into her gray depths for the rest of my life and die a happy man. "I think I trust you more than anyone I've ever trusted in my life. But that terrifies me. You could ruin me, Colton."

Grasping her chin, I let the emotion show in my eyes. "I will never do that. I'll mess up. Probably a lot, but I'll always, always be by your side. Please, baby. Trust me to catch you." She opens her mouth, but I hush her with a kiss. "Please say yes, CC."

I don't release her lips, so her response is mumbled, but I'm pretty sure she just said yes, and my chest nearly explodes with a happiness I was sure didn't exist. And before her, it didn't.

"Is that a yes?" I beg when I finally release her face.

She nods, sending tears splattering to my chest. "Yes. It's a yes."

I'm standing before she gets the s out. Clutching her to my chest, I spin her in a small circle. "She said yes," I shout much too loudly for the intimate atmosphere, but applause and cheers ring out just as the chef exits the kitchen.

I place Winnie on her feet as he approaches.

"This is very fitting," he says with a sad smile. "We had a

proposal on opening night many years ago. It sends us off with good luck on our last. Have you ordered yet?"

"No, sorry. We got a little sidetracked," I explain.

"Very good. Very good. Let me prepare something special, just for you."

"That would be amazing. Thank you." Reaching out, I shake his hand. "I need to put my ring on my girl now." The chef grins and leaves me to it with a dramatic bow.

Sitting Winnie in her chair, I crouch down in front of her. I open the box and pull out the delicate band of pave diamonds with a single round solitaire. It's two karats, but not ostentatious. I had the jeweler intertwine a small ring of diamonds around the center stone with all three of our birthstones.

I slip it on her finger, and she gets a good look at it for the first time. "The center stone signifies our love. The outer ring has our birthstones, signifying us. Our family. I thought Wes should be part of it."

"I-I don't know what to say, Colton. It's the most beautiful thing I've ever seen."

"Then you know how I feel every time I look at you. We have a lot to figure out. Weston's therapies. Your piece of shit father. But I'll be there for it all, Winnie. I promise you. For better or worse, you're mine. And I'm yours."

"You're mine," she murmurs as a waiter places the first course in front of us.

A cork pops next to me. Someone pours champagne, and I have the overwhelming feeling that my life is just beginning.

CHAPTER 29

WINNIE

"Do you want to get a drink?" Colton hasn't let go of my hand since we finished dessert.

We're walking hand in hand down a cobblestone street in the Beacon Hill area of Boston. You can feel the history in each building we pass, but I can't help worrying about Weston. "This has been the most amazing night, and I don't want to ruin it."

"But," he pulls me to his side and kisses my head, "you're worried about our little guy."

"I'm sure Tilly could handle it, but I don't want him to be frightened. There's been so much change for him, and he's always needed a routine."

"Sweetheart?" He stops so suddenly I trip on the uneven sidewalk. He catches me before I make it very far. "I told you I'd always catch you."

"I didn't think you meant it literally." A giggle escapes and I have to think about how many glasses of wine I've had.

"I mean it in every way. But I was going to say that I'm not complaining about going home early. The sooner I get you home, the sooner I can strip you naked and lick every inch of your body."

Embarrassed, I glance around, hoping no one heard his dirty words.

Colton's amused. I see it in the way his eyes sparkle under the streetlight. He steps forward so we're pressed together and leans down. When his lips caress my ear, an involuntary shiver courses through my body.

"I'm going to lick you until your sweet pussy drenches my face."

My chest aches with the breath caught there.

"But I won't stop there, CC. I'm going to lick and lap until I've had my fill, and you're begging for me to fuck you."

"I never beg." Jesus, I can't even control my own voice. He will have me begging, but my pride won't let me admit it. Yet.

"I'll be happy to be your first then," he promises darkly, and I feel a small flood in my panties. "Tell me, CC. If I stuck my hand up your dress right now, would you be wet?" His hand skims the hem that hits mid-thigh, teasing the skin just beneath it. His hot breath in my ear only heightens my arousal.

"Soaked." My voice cracks, and I'm not sure my legs will hold me up much longer.

The deep rumble of a growl is the only warning I get as he cups the back of my head and pulls me into a bruising kiss. It's the most out of control I've ever seen him. The kiss is fiery, demanding, greedy. He probes my lips, sweeping his tongue around my mouth, savoring the taste that's simply us. It feels reckless yet controlled, and this is what he does to me. He makes me want to give up control in the most base manner. What's worse is I think I need to.

"You will beg." His words ghost over my lips. It's a tug-of-war. The push and pull is fraught with sexual tension. The delicious kind you read about in sexy books but never fully experience in real life.

Holy shit. I'm living out a romance novel with Colton Westbrook.

"Never. In fact …" I pull back from his embrace. Miraculously, my legs remember how to move, and I strut down the street. Albeit a little wobbly from that kiss. "I think tonight you're going to be the one to beg."

He catches up to me in two long strides. "Don't you know, Darling? I've been programmed to beg for you since our first meeting."

Gah! Swoon.

Colton surveys our surroundings. Finding us relatively alone, he takes my hand and rubs small circles on the inside of my wrist as we walk. "The first thing I'm going to do is rip that dress down the middle."

Absentmindedly, I tug on the fabric near my thighs. It's much thicker than he thinks. There's no way.

"Don't ever doubt me, CC. Once it's off, I'm going to suck on your nipples through that sheer bra I know you have on."

Affronted, I ask, "How do you know that?"

"I chose it myself."

Mother effer. The deep timbre of his voice has my insides quivering.

"I'm going to suck, bite, and tease your nipples until you're writhing beneath me."

Fuck me. How many blocks away is our hotel?

"Writhing I can do," I pant.

"And do it well. But when I'm ready, I'll hold you down at your hip with my hand as I kiss my way down your center and back up, over and over again. I'll get close to where you need me, but stay just out of reach."

"That's mean," I whine, knowing there's no way I'll be able to hold myself together. This walk alone is the best foreplay I've ever had in my life.

"It's all part of the experience, Winnie. I'm not satisfied with your last orgasm. I'll need to up my game."

"You. My. What? Colton, I passed out."

"Not good enough. I want you seeing stars and praying to every deity you can come up with. Then I'll make you come."

I gulp. Not metaphorically. I literally gulp, and it sounds like someone is strangling a cat. He never stops his rhythmic circles on my wrist. It's both calming and erotic. I hate it as much as I love it.

"Do you want my tongue on your clit, or my fingers? Fast or slow? Up and down or in slow, torturous circles." His fingers move in time to his words.

"I, ah. I. Do I have to choose?" I go for sultry, but it comes out squeaky as a mouse.

"Greedy tonight, CC? I approve. I'll start with my tongue because I can't wait to taste you. Do you know how sweet your come is?" I shake my head. "You can taste it on me tonight, then. And when I feel your belly quiver, I'll insert my fingers. I'll curl them until I find that spot deep in your core that'll have your entire body trembling."

"Colton." It's all I can say. I'm speechless. I want to shout from the rooftops, 'I'm ready to beg.'

"We're here. Prepare yourself. It's going to be a long night with my fiancée."

"Oh God."

Dragging me into the hotel, he whispers, "That's not good enough. I'll have you calling my name like a prayer before this night is over."

We step onto the elevator, and the second the doors close, he walks me into the corner and turns me around, so my back is to his front. He's blocking me with his body as he reaches around and cups my breasts. "I might even fuck these." When he pinches my nipples between his thumb and forefinger, I gasp. "But right now, you need to go talk to Tilly." He pulls away just as the door slides open and I have to grasp the handlebar of the elevator, so I don't fall over. Glancing up, I see him watching me with a dark expression. "The sooner you walk her out, the sooner my face can get between your legs."

I nod because I've lost the ability to speak. Entering our

suite, we find Tilly watching Bravo on the TV. When I don't say anything, Colton chuckles. "Was everything okay?"

"Oh, he was great. Not a peep out of him. He's a great kid."

"Thanks, Tilly. I know this is out of your scope of duties for The WB, but I really appreciate it."

"I didn't do it as your employee, Colton. I did it as family, and you're welcome." She makes eye contact with me and smirks. I can't even imagine what I look like. "I'll just get out of your way. Have a good night."

"Thanks. You too."

When the suite door clicks shut, Colton is on me. His hands in my hair, on my ass, my back. He's all consuming. "You have two minutes to check in on Wes and then I want you in our room."

"Okay. Yup." Shucking off my heels, I speed walk to Weston's room. Peeking in, I find him fast asleep with his helicopter in one hand and a stuffed train in the other. He's so peaceful when he sleeps. I take a minute to scan his room. Colton had guardrails placed on each side of the bed, and my chest bursts with an unfamiliar feeling. After kissing Wes gently on the head, I back out of the room, closing the door as softly as possible.

I take slow, calming breaths while I walk to our room. Stepping over the threshold, I'm confused when I don't see Colton. Then he pushes off the wall beside me and shuts the door, much less quietly than I did Weston's.

Colton holds a phone in his hand, and when he presses a button, "Closer" by Nine Inch Nails plays on a speaker by the bed.

Holy mother of pearl. He's going to do all the wicked, wicked things my airport dance promised.

"The monitor's on," he assures me, pointing to the small screen we brought with us. It's the last words he says before he scoops me up and tosses me on the bed with such force I bounce. Before I've even stopped moving, he's grabbing the hem of my dress. I watch in shock as he pulls something silver out of his back pocket. By the time I realize he has scissors, it's too late. A quick snip between my legs and he tosses them to the floor. Using both hands, he rips the dress up my center. "The dress was a thicker material than I thought, but I never go back on my word."

"Colton! Do you know how much this dress cost? I cannot believe you just did that."

True to his word, his tongue laps at my nipple. "I'll buy you a hundred of them if I can do this again." He uses his teeth to tug on my hardened peak, and my back arches off the bed. "Writhing so soon, fiancée?"

With great effort, I force myself to form a sentence. "Less talking." Okay, so maybe not a complete sentence, but he gets my gist.

He lowers his body to the bed, so his torso lies between my legs. It puts pressure on my clit, but there's no friction and I realize he's positioned himself this way on purpose as he goes to work on one breast, then the other.

"Are you ready to beg yet?"

"No," I say stubbornly, but my body screams at me to submit.

"That's my girl."

His girl. *His* girl. Two words that hold so much meaning in my trust deficient brain. Fuck yes, I want to be his.

Colton shifts his weight and his ass wiggles, so I know he's struggling, too. Maybe it's time to turn the tables. Can I, though? *Travis always said ...*

"With me," Colton growls, and nips my nipple harder than before. "Whatever you're thinking about right now, let it go. You're here. With me. In this moment, you think of nothing except what I'm doing to your body."

"How do you do that?" I pant, already knowing I don't have to explain my question. He might know me better than I do.

"I know when you're not giving me your body and mind,

Winnie. I read you. I know you. Stay with me." He uses the voice that commands me to obey, and I suddenly realize it's freeing. He isn't trying to control me. He's giving me the freedom to feel, live, experience. He's taking my worries so he can provide me with something much more significant. He's teaching me how to love.

"Okay."

He searches my eyes for half a second and he must be pleased with what he finds because, painfully slowly, he kisses down my body, and I remember every dirty vow he gave me on our walk home. He's fulfilling every promise he makes. He's teaching me to trust him.

Colton's tongue does magically, deliciously, scandalously dirty things to my body on his travel south. He tears my panties down my legs until they're pulled taut at my knees.

"I have to deviate from my plan," he explains as one long finger enters with a forceful thrust of his hand.

"Ahhh," I scream. Not from pain, but from shock.

His free hand covers my mouth. "Quiet. I will not be interrupted tonight until I'm satisfied with your orgasm."

Jesus. When he's satisfied? Travis never even knew I was faking it. Colton's hand drops to my breast, and he gives my nipple a rough pinch. It's a warning, I realize. He knew my brain had drifted again. *Holy fuck*. He really does know my body better than I do.

With slow, deliberate movements, he laps at my drenched pussy. My stomach tightens as his fingers work their magic and his other hand roams lower until it lands on my stomach. When he palms my very un-firm belly, I don't feel self-conscious. Surprisingly, I feel sexier than I've ever remembered feeling. He presses down, and the sensations his fingers cause inside of me become heightened.

"Holy shit." My back lifts off the bed until I'm propped up on my elbows, watching him.

He adds a third finger, and before I can object, his pinky

breaches my third hole. My very virgin ass clenches, and I feel him smirk against my clit. He sucks it into his mouth, and his firm tongue flicks back and forth at an alarming rate. He tongues me harder. Flicks faster. My breath is lost to the moment. I'm panting with a pleasure I'm not sure how to release. When all of his fingers move, and curl, and probe in tandem with his tongue, it's too much. Sensory overload has my head hitting the mattress hard and rolling left to right.

Colton growls against my slick folds and my body spasms. I'm afraid I'm having a seizure when my eyes roll to the back of my skull. "Col-Colton, please. Please. Please. Please."

"Please what?" His words vibrate against my sensitive flesh.

"Please fuck me," I yell, and immediately clamp my hand over my mouth.

"Are you on birth control?"

"What?"

"I want you bare, Winnie. Are. You. On. Birth Control?"

"Yes. Yes, please."

It's all too much. Tears form at the corner of my eyes just before he impales his thick shaft as deep as it will go inside of me. I cry out. I writhe. I moan as every nerve in my body lights up.

Colton lifts my legs so my calves rest on his shoulders, and he grinds deeper. His fingers find my clit as he thrusts hard and deep, then slow and shallow. I can't keep up. He isn't setting a pace. Each thrust is different, sending me spiraling and stealing the air from my lungs.

"You're close, Winnie. I can feel your pussy quivering," he says through clenched teeth.

I can't speak. I can't even think. All I can do is feel as he takes over every one of my senses. He's everywhere.

His thrusts get impossibly deeper as he leans down to kiss me. He tastes like … he tastes like mint, champagne, and me. He rests his face against mine, his mouth to my ear. "See how good you taste, CC? I want to drink you in for the rest of my life, and even that won't be enough. I'll never get enough of you. I fucking love you, Winnie Darling." He growls the last words, punctuates them with a forceful thrust, and sends my body flying.

I can't see him. He sounds like he's underwater as he groans in my ear. All I can do is feel every spasm. Every flicker, twitch, and shiver as an orgasm overwhelms me.

White lights, mixed with blue sparkles, flash before my eyes. I'm not even sure if I'm breathing as wave after wave of pleasure wrecks me.

"Fuck, yes. Winnie. You're mine. You're fucking mine," Colton roars as his body goes stiff, and I feel every spurt of his release. "I love you," he murmurs when he collapses on top of me.

I'm in a daze. Or maybe I'm asleep. I'm definitely in a head-space I've never felt before. Colton whispers words of praise that I barely hear. That wasn't an orgasm. That was a head-to-toe experience that took me to the brink of pain before plea-sure worked its way into every crevice of my body. *Holy shit.* That's what I've been missing out on?

"That's what happens when you trust me, Win."

My eyes fly open to find Colton watching me with a lazy smile. "I'll trust you for the rest of my life, then."

"Fuck yes you will." He drops down for a chaste kiss. "You should probably pee or something. I guess we should have talked about that before now. Are you okay with everything?"

Am I? I scan my body to see every inch of me is flushed. My brain is slowly processing his words, but when I do, I smile. "Yeah, Colton. I'm more than okay."

He smiles a smile I realize he reserves just for me, and my heart nearly explodes. I sit up so we're face-to-face. He tilts his head, knowing I want to say something, but I don't know how. He waits patiently, encouraging me with eyes that hold the key to my heart.

It takes a few tries, but I finally get the words out. "Colton?

I-I love you." As soon as they're out, I know I've never felt anything truer.

He pounces and grasps the back of my neck, lowering me slowly to the bed with his forehead pressed to mine. "Nothing, and I mean nothing, has ever made me happier than those three little words."

Without warning, he enters me easily and with languid, unhurried movements, he gives me my second orgasm of the night.

∽

*T*he Town Cryer
GG: Another Westbrook finds love in our small town.

GG: Colton Westbrook is engaged to the enchanting Miss Wendalyn Darling.

Betty-Anne: It's about damn time.

Lexi: Jesus GG.

Julia: Get a filter, woman!

Preston: GG. Some self-restraint would serve us well right now.

GG: Pfft.

GG: (eye rolling emoji)

Lanie: Who taught her how to use emojis?

1,472 unread messages.

CHAPTER 30

WINNIE

"*L*et me see it," Lexi demands as we exit the car. She's sitting on our front porch, waiting for us.

"Hello, Lexi. Good to see you, too, Lexi," Colton teases. "You could have gone in, you know. How long have you been sitting here?"

Rolling her eyes dramatically, she walks down the steps. "Hello, Colton. Now let me see the ring. And I haven't been here long, but I needed a breather. Easton is going overboard baby proofing the house. I had to leave before I threw something at him when I couldn't get into the refrigerator. Then I got the text in the Town Cryer. It won't be long before everyone and their mother shows up, so I wanted to welcome Winnie to the family before the crazy arrives."

"Ah, what?" I ask, pausing with Wes half unbuckled.

"Colton texted Ash, who texted Easton, who texted family chat. Then GG put out a wedding announcement in the Town Cryer," Lexi explains, as if this is common knowledge.

"Shit," Colton curses. "I have to call Preston. We need to get ahead of this before your dad does something stupid. Lexi? Can you help Winnie?"

Lexi already has my hand in her grasp. "Yeah, yeah. Go do what you do. Oh. My. Lord. Are these your birthstones?"

I'm holding Weston awkwardly, but she isn't letting go of my hand. "Uh, yeah. Mine, Weston's, and Colton's. He said he wanted Wes involved so we would be ah, uh family."

"Stupid asshole." She sniffs. "Why do all these men have to think of everything?" She drops my hand and uses hers to wipe her tears. "Sorry. Since I started therapy, my freaking eye holes leak over the dumbest things. But this is, this is pretty great, so I guess it's okay." Lexi moves around me to grab Weston's bags out of the car. "The guys can get the rest," she tells me, slamming the door shut with her foot. "Come on. You've got maybe fifteen minutes before the chaos takes over."

"The what?"

"The Westbrooks are like a pack. They travel in groups. They celebrate in groups. It was kind of annoying at first, but you get used to it. Oh, and before I forget, you're coming to girls' night at Ari's tonight. We planned it while you were away, but you don't want to miss this."

"Oh. Lexi, I'm not really a girls' night kind of girl." Actually, remembering all the girlfriends I've ever had, I'd rather bleach my asshole than go to a girls' night.

"You and me both, but it's all family. They grow on you. You can't say no. Everyone is here and my cousin, Lanie, is impossible to say no to."

"But Wes has had a long few days—"

"And Colton will be happy to snuggle him all night if he has to."

Not taking no for an answer, Lexi marches up the porch steps and swings the front door wide open. I'm still standing near the car when she turns and sees me. Making a sweeping motion with her hands, she snaps me from my version of hell, and I follow in her wake.

"It'll be fun. I promise. It's like a rite of passage for all the

Westbrook women. As soon as we found out Colton had a ring made, your fate was sealed."

"Shit."

She pats me on the back. "Winnie? We're all down-to-earth, and I promise you'll have a good time," she says, with a gentleness in her voice, like she's speaking to a wounded animal. "I know you don't know much about us yet, but we've all taken different paths to get to where we are now, and none of them were easy. This is the first time in my life I can honestly say I have a group of girlfriends that would have my back in a heartbeat. And now we're your friends, too."

I try another angle, "I'll have to talk to Colton."

"Already done. Or will be by the time he comes out of his office, I guess. Rules for tonight: No makeup. Stretchy pants. And no bras because they were invented by the devil."

My gaze immediately drops to my chest. "Ah, Lexi, I'm not sure if you've noticed, but I'm a big girl. There's no way I can leave the house without a bra unless I'm trying to scare off the neighbors."

"Girl, all your neighbors are family now." She winks. "There's no scaring us off, no matter how hard you try. We'll have you shimmying your tatas before the night's over."

I can't tell if she's joking or not, and as I stare, slack jawed, I realize Lexi is a younger, slightly tamer version of GG. We're going to be GG'd for the rest of our lives.

"All right. I'm out of here before the cavalry arrives. I'll be back at seven p.m. with the golf cart to pick you up."

"But—"

"Just bring yourself, but remember the rules. Julia is a stickler for rules."

"Julia?" I mumble to myself. "Do I know who Julia is?"

"We'll draw you a family tree," Lexi yells from the foyer. "Julia is Trevor's wife. Trevor is one of the Westbrook adoptees. See you at seven!"

I plop down on the floor next to Wes, completely overwhelmed by a plethora of emotions. Panic. Dread. Excitement. Fear. Happiness. They're all swirling around my brain like a carnival ride that makes the strongest men puke. "Oh, Wes. What have we gotten ourselves into?"

I haven't even finished my sentence before there's a knock on the front door, followed immediately by a handful of voices. *The cavalry has arrived, I suppose.* Steeling myself and placing Weston's headphones on his smiling face, I turn to see the first round of Westbrooks. This is what it's like to be part of a large family.

As people pile in, dropping flowers, snacks, and champagne on every available surface, I feel my tiny bubble expanding. These people are genuinely happy to welcome Weston and me into their lives. I can see it on their faces, in their hushed voices around Wes, in every tight embrace that brings me closer to tears. This is what my life can be. I'm in awe of it, but I can't help the niggling sensation that someone, somewhere, will take it all away from me.

∾

I'm sprawled on my back on the sofa, physically and emotionally drained. The Westbrooks, true to Lexi's word, traveled in three groups to spread love, offer well wishes, and welcome us to the family.

"You okay over there?" Colton asks with a smirk.

"I've never been so tired in my life," I admit.

He crosses the room, lifts my legs, then sits, placing them in his lap. An involuntary moan escapes when he uses his knuckles to knead the arches of my feet.

"I would tell you to skip tonight with the girls, but Julia's here, and she terrifies me."

Anxiety fills my stomach with acid. "I don't know any of these people, Colton."

"I know. And I know this is your version of a nightmare,

but they'll take care of you. They'll make sure you have fun. I really lucked out in the sister-in-law department, and it's a bonus that they all get along so well."

I stopped caring a long time ago whether or not people liked me, but it's different with this group of women. What if I don't fit in? What if I'm the outlier that ruins this Brady Bunch vibe they all have going on?

"Stop," Colton commands. My nether regions respond to him like a Pavlovian response. "All the self-doubt invading your head, knock it off. Trust me, remember? I wouldn't feed you to the wolves. The only one that's going to eat you alive is me."

And now I need to change my panties.

Colton glances down at his watch. Lexi will be here in about thirty minutes. My insides quiver with need until he says the dreaded words, "We need to talk."

I immediately sit upright. I don't realize I'm wringing my wrist until Colton pulls my hand away. "Trust me," he repeats. "I spoke to Preston. We need to talk about your dad and our next steps. Pres spoke to our PR people, and they think we should move fast and intentionally."

"What does that mean? And what are PR people? I thought that was for celebrities."

He gives an impish grin, and my eyes close in embarrassment. The Westbrooks are celebrities in their own right. Obviously, they have PR people.

"It's going to put you out of your comfort zone temporarily. Next Steps, that's our in-house PR firm, thinks it's the best approach."

Sweat trickles down my spine, and I wipe my clammy hands on my legs. "What is it?"

"You'll never be alone in any of this. I'll be by your side every step of the way, CC. Remember that. Next Steps is putting together a press release now. Then they'll set up some interviews. One with a gossip rag, as upstanding a one as they can get, one with a lifestyle magazine, and two with celebrity bloggers. Each will take less than twenty minutes, and Tilly will be on hand to intervene if questions are out of line."

"I don't understand. Interviews with you?"

"Us, Winnie. And some photos. You, me, and Weston as a family. A united front. We'll also offer the first ever public photo of all the Westbrooks, blood, and by choice, together. That was actually Ashton's idea, and he's hidden from the public since his attack. Halton, who has severe social anxiety, signed off on it because we'll do the picture ahead of time. Just family and a photographer."

"Why would they open themselves up like that? It must be incredibly painful for them both."

"Part of it, I think, is Ashton's way of atoning for not stopping a nemesis when he had the chance, and Halton is learning to manage his anxiety. This will be a controlled environment, so he's happy to do it. It's what we do, Winnie. It's the only way we know. There's a threat to our family, so we come together. We build a fortress, so the threat can't reach us."

"But how will this help? Who's going to be interested in me?"

His eyes soften, and he cups my face. "Everyone is going to be interested, CC. They want to know the woman who took down the infamous playboy. I was always front facing in our family. What can I say? I liked the attention, and it kept it off my brothers." He smirks, but the way he says it tells me there's more to it. "Now that Ashton proved those women suing me were lying, the press is searching for their next big story."

"You let the world believe you were this obnoxious playboy to protect your brothers."

He shrugs. "It wasn't hurting anyone, but yes. I saw Halton's reactions growing up. He hid it well, but he was my big brother. I looked up to him in many ways, but he changed when we were in public. I could see physical pain in his glassy gaze, so I started acting up. Drawing the attention away from him as much as I could."

"And they had no idea," I whisper, taking his hand in mine.

"There was no need for them to."

Oh, Colton. How can your family misread you so drastically?

"Um, when would this happen?"

"Day after tomorrow. Then we'll file a countersuit to have Jason's parental rights stripped, and if you agree, we'll start the adoption process immediately."

My head spins and I feel lightheaded. "Wh-What adoption process?"

"For Wes. He'll legally be ours, and he'll be a Westbrook. Uh," he rubs a hand through his hair, "that's assuming you want to take my last name when we're married?"

"Adoption is forever."

His heavy sigh is full of frustration. "That's what I keep telling you, yes. Forever, Winnie."

My gaze drops to my hand and the unfamiliar weight on my left ring finger. My thumb spins the band nervously. "Okay. You can do that? Take away his rights?"

Colton's expression goes hard. He's as cold as I've ever seen him when he speaks. "I'll do whatever it takes to make you both mine, Winnie."

Without thinking, I rest my head on his shoulder. His arm wraps around my back and he holds me tight against his side. We sit in the quiet, watching Wes push his wooden trains back and forth. It's comfortable. But it's so much more than that. Colton has given us a home. A family. I've spent so many years fighting that I forgot what it feels like to be content and safe. He's brought me peace, I realize.

The knock at the door has me groaning uncomfortably.

"Winnie? You ready?" Lexi calls as she enters our home.

"We really should start locking that door," I grumble.

Colton chuckles, but pulls me to stand with him. Wrapping me in a hug, he kisses the top of my head. "It wouldn't matter, CC. They all have keys."

"Ready?" Lexi repeats as she enters the family room. "If we're late, Julia will have a meltdown."

She sounds delightful. Obviously, I don't say that, but my expression speaks volumes. "Yeah, I'm ready. How late will we be?"

"East is staying at the lodge with the kids and GG so he can drive us home whenever we're ready."

"I don't think that's necessary."

"Oh, it is," Colton and Lexi say at the same time.

"I'm not really a big drinker," I object as Lexi drags me to the door. "Hold on, I have to say good-bye to Wes."

"Bye, bye." He waves without lifting his head.

My shoulders droop as I watch him.

"Come on. It's a good thing that he's so comfortable with Colton," Lexi whispers. "Plus, all kids can be assholes sometimes. Mine always go to Easton first. It pisses me off, and I think they know it now, so they do it on purpose."

It is good. It stings, but it's good. I let Lexi drag me outside with a final wave to my boys.

～

"Tell me again who Ari is?" I plead as we walk up a driveway to a house similar to the one I share with Colton.

"Ari is Seth's wife." Lexi must know I'm going to ask about Seth, because she continues, "Seth is the latest adopted Lost Boy. He was a superspy with Loki and now runs a security firm with Loki and Ash."

She pushes the door open and ushers me inside, where the sound of a thousand voices echo off the walls. I freeze halfway into the house.

"It's fine. Wine night always makes them louder." Lexi gives me a gentle nudge, and I stumble forward. "We're here," her voice singsongs through the entryway, and the other voices lower to a hush.

I follow behind Lexi, and it's almost easy to hide behind her six-foot frame, but as we round the corner to the family room, she tugs me to her side. "Okay, line up for introductions."

My eyes go wide as all the women, dressed similarly in leggings, oversized sweatshirts, and true to her word, no bras, line up along the back window overlooking the mountain.

"You know me, and Lanie." Lexi points to Lanie, who looks almost exactly like her. "This is Julia, Trevor's wife. Then we have Emory, she belongs to Preston. Her sister, Sloane, is married to Loki but not here because she's a New York Times bestselling romance author on a deadline. This is Ari, our hostess. I already told you she's married to Seth. And you know Rylan, Colton's bff and Halton's wife."

I wave awkwardly at the lineup of beautiful women, each smiling warmly before they file over and wrap me in a giant embrace. Julia's last, and she stands a few feet away with her hands on her hips.

"I hear your little guy has SPD."

"Excuse Julia," Lanie whispers. "She has no filter."

Julia rolls her eyes but steps closer. "Well, he does, doesn't he?"

My defenses rise, prepared to defend Wes. "Yes, he does," I reply curtly.

A broad smile crosses her face. "No other diagnosis? He's not on the spectrum?"

Now I'm getting pissed, and it appears everyone else is holding their breath. "No." It comes out through clenched teeth, but her smile glows impossibly brighter. Her eyes literally twinkle as she bounces from foot to foot.

"Me too," she squeals. "I have SPD, too. They probably recommended a lot of the therapies I went through. I wanted you to know that he will be just fine, and I can't wait to meet him. Easton said he already has the headphones. That's the biggest obstacle right there!" She talks so fast, I can barely keep up.

"When did you find out that you had it?" I'm genuinely curious now.

"Oh, as a kid. But I did all my therapies when I was a little older than Weston. I'm still quirky, but once I learned coping mechanisms and went through various desensitization therapies, I was like a new person. If you have any questions at all, please ask. I'm actually so excited to meet him. Gah, I already said that, didn't I? Way to scare her off, Julia."

"Ah, Julia has a hard time keeping private thoughts private," Lexi offers. "The good part about that is you'll never have to guess where you stand with her."

"Anyway," Julia interrupts again, "I went to the same center you took Weston to. It's an amazing place, and it's one hundred percent worth the travel time and cost. He'll excel there." She launches herself at me then whispers, "You're also welcome to talk to my parents anytime. They could give you some insight or offer suggestions. Or really, just commiserate with you. They're amazing people and would be happy to sit down with you anytime."

"Oh, wow." I try to extricate myself, but she's surprisingly strong for such a little thing. Eventually, she pulls herself away. "That's really nice of you, Julia. Thank you. It's all so new. I'm still trying to wrap my head around it all."

"No worries! Give me your phone." I scan the room, but no one seems to think this is odd, so I reluctantly hand it over. A few minutes later, Julia's phone rings in her hand. "There. Now you have my number, and I have yours! We'll be besties in no time."

"All right, Jules. You've monopolized enough of her time," Ari chides, handing me an entire bottle of wine. "Don't ask me. Apparently, they don't believe in glasses."

"Cheers!" everyone calls out, raising their own bottles and bringing them to their lips.

We go through another round of congratulations before Lexi leads me to a sofa and everyone piles in around us.

"Welcome to the chaos." Emory smiles. She's quieter than the rest, but her eyes gleam with a happiness that's contagious.

"Thanks. I think." A small laugh escapes, and then the rapid-fire questions begin.

"What kind of wedding do you want?"

"Have you picked out a dress yet?"

"Colton says he wants to get married like yesterday."

"Have you picked a date?"

"How did he propose?"

"Whoa, ladies. Give her a break," Lexi cuts in. "Let's play a game."

Lanie's sitting on my other side and groans loudly. "Lex, come on. The last time you made us play a game, I ended up throwing up for six hours and Emory ended up naked in a hot tub."

"Not naked. Nearly naked. There's a difference." My gaze cuts to Emory in time to see her flush a deep shade of red.

Lexi lifts my hand holding the bottle of wine to my lips, and I take a long sip, allowing the pleasant warmth to fill my belly. "Fine. No games. Party poopers."

For the next hour, we make pleasant small talk. They ask me about Weston and my work. They each tell me about themselves, and I'm surprised to find they're all really normal, and down-to-earth. And best of all, they're sincerely making an effort to include me. I'm lost in my thoughts when Mase's "Feel So Good" comes on in surround sound.

Julia jumps up on the coffee table, singing loudly and off key. "This is my jam!"

I watch in horrified amusement as every single one of these ladies stands up and quite literally shakes their tatas. Already a little tipsy, Lanie leans down, takes my free hand, and tugs me to my feet. "Come on, chica. It's a dance par-tay!"

Glancing around at the chaos, I laugh. A real, heartfelt

giggle that takes over my entire body. After taking a giant swig of my nearly empty bottle of wine, I set it down with a shrug. Turning to Lexi, I wait until she makes eye contact and I shake my tatas for all their worth, which causes her to double over laughing. In no time, we're all falling to the floor with laughter as our common bond.

"I t-told you," Lexi gasps through a giggle-attack.

I don't remember a time when I've ever had so much fun with a group of near strangers. *Another gift Colton has given me.* It's a sobering thought. He gives so freely. What could I possibly offer him?

I don't get time to think about it for long because Julia hits a button on the remote in her hand and "Gimme More" by Britney Spears blasts much louder than before. "We're the Westbrooks, bitch," everyone in the room screams over the song's intro and before I know it, we're all bouncing around the room, singing at the top of our lungs.

CHAPTER 31

COLTON

"*H*ey, sleepyhead. Your friends are here for brunch. Did you forget you invited them over?" My tone is teasing, but I can't help messing with her a little.

Drunk Winnie is a blast. She came in so bubbly and care-free; I vow to make her that way every day of our lives, but without so much wine.

"Nooo," she groans, dragging a pillow over her head so I lay on my side next to her.

"They're all in the family room waiting for you."

She rips the pillow off her head. Her lips are still purple from her wine, and her eyes are bloodshot. I fucking love this girl more than should be legal. I can't keep the smile off my face if I tried.

"Are you serious?" Her voice cracks, so I reach over her for the bottle of water I placed next to her last night.

Holding it out to her, I chuckle when she sits up. The girls had some sort of makeover party, and Winnie's hair has no less than twelve elastics with small ponytails poking out of her head in every direction. "Oh, I'm serious, sweetheart. Do you remember inviting them over?"

She shakes her head and instantly regrets it. "Vaguely. Colt, I don't think I can cook without tossing my cookies."

I cradle her face and lean in for a gentle kiss. "It's a good thing you told me about it last night, then. All your friends are accompanied by their husbands, who made, bought, or begged for all the food. They're setting it up in the kitchen while the ladies lounge in the family room looking a hell of a lot like you do."

"At least I'm not alone," she grumbles.

"Come on, up we go." I pull away the blankets, and my dick responds like it was shot out of a rocket. She's naked except for a tiny scrap of material between her legs. "Fucking hell, you're gorgeous. I'm definitely taking you up on your request as soon as Weston is in bed tonight?"

"My request?" she asks, rubbing her temples as I grab her a bra because my brothers are here, a T-shirt, and her leggings from last night.

I allow my fingers to trail her skin just beside her breast as I slip the sports bra over her head. Then I do the same with the T-shirt. "Oh yes. You were very insistent on licking me like a lollipop last night, but I told you we had to wait until you were a little more sober."

"You turned me down?" I've shocked her.

"I did. And your resulting pout nearly broke me, but I know all about consent, my dear fiancée. And you could not give it with a clear head, so we'll revisit this tonight." I lean in to growl into her ear, "And then I'm going to fuck you fast and hard. Just like you begged for last night."

"Oh God. How do I not remember that?"

"By the looks of the empty bottle of wine you walked in with last night, I'd say the Malbec got the better of you."

After sliding her leggings up her smooth skin, I help her stand and pull them the rest of the way up before dragging her behind me.

"I rarely drink that much," she whispers.

"Yeah, well, girls' night is a special occasion. So, you're lucky it doesn't happen as often as they'd like."

We stop just behind the sofa, and I watch Winnie's reaction as she takes in all my sisters-in-law. Each with varying degrees of hairstyles and smudged makeup, except for Rylan. She dodged the wine hangover thanks to the growing baby in her belly.

Winnie slowly lifts a hand to her head and gasps.

"Oh, geez! We did makeovers."

"Shhh," comes a collective hiss.

"Winnie, get over here so I can lean on you," Julia barks.

Very slowly, Winnie makes her way around the sofa and sits next to Julia. As soon as her head leans back, Julia collapses, placing her head in Winnie's lap.

"It's official. You're family now," Lanie groans from the floor.

"I feel like I'm dying," Ari sobs from the corner chair.

"Well, on that note. You ladies rest. I'll go see how the food's coming along." My heart bursts with happiness as I survey the room. I knew they'd welcome Winnie with open arms, but seeing it in action is another thing entirely. She fits with me, even if she doesn't feel like it yet.

~

"How is she this morning?" Preston asks with a knowing smirk. His wife didn't fare much better on her first girls' night.

"She's a little green this morning," I say, chuckling. "But she doesn't look much worse than the others. So, how did Seth, Dex, and Trevor end up at the lodge with all the kids?"

"You sure Winnie is going to be okay with Wes being at the lodge with everyone?"

I thought about that, but Weston couldn't move fast enough when East showed up with Ada James in his arms. "I think so.

Trevor has learned a lot from Julia, and I told him what to watch for. You know, signs that Wes is in distress, and if that happens, he'll bring him straight home. He's really drawn to Ada. It's funny. I haven't seen him like that very often."

Easton looks up from the quiche he set on the counter with a prideful smile. "AJ is pretty amazing." He stands to his full height and crosses his arms. "You know a lot about Wes."

Suddenly my throat feels tight, and my eyes fill with emotion. "I love him, East. He's a great kid. I'd do anything for him."

East, Preston, and Halt all stare at me with expressions I can't place.

"He's your family," Halton explains.

"Yeah. He and Winnie mean the world to me."

Preston leans against the island. "This is going to be a tough battle, Colty. Are you prepared for that?"

Anger radiates from every limb. "I will kill for them, Pres. No one's going to take them from me. Why do you sound like you know something I don't?"

"Because that's my job as your big brother, and as The WB CEO." He sighs loudly and pinches the back of his neck, a sure sign something is off.

A fear I've never experienced squeezes my lungs, making it impossible to breathe.

"What is it?" Easton barks.

Thank God for his impatience.

My gaze darts around the room. Every one of my brothers is as tense as I am, and it brings me comfort. My army is ready to stand guard.

"Somehow, Jason Darling has hired Max Sterling as his attorney."

"Fuck," Halton curses. "How the hell is he affording that? Ash pulled his financials. I saw them yesterday. He doesn't have a penny to his name. He legit lives welfare check to welfare check."

My head is spinning. "Who is Max Sterling?"

All eyes turn toward me. "He's the number one family court attorney on the East Coast. He's … Jesus, Colton! He's known for taking on deadbeat dads and helping them not only get visitation but spinning it so they rarely even pay child support. More than once he's gotten them full custody," Preston explains.

"He's as sleazy as they come, Colt, but he's abnormally good at what he does," Halton says. His words are full of malice.

"How do you know all this?" Easton barks as he paces the length of the island.

Fear makes it impossible to move. "He can't get Weston, Pres. He just can't. Darling can never provide the resources to help him that we can."

"I know, Colty. I have our entire legal team working on it and Ash is surfing the dark web to find anything and everything he can on Darling."

Somehow, that makes me feel even worse. "Not to sound like a dick, but Ash hasn't exactly had my back with this whole Macomb thing, so forgive me if that doesn't bring me much peace."

"That has something to do with Pacen and his connection to her. But he's our brother and you know he would never do anything to hurt you," Halton says gently. "He proved those women drugged you and lied about the entire thing."

"Honestly, Halt? I don't know that, and if he'd done what's right, I never would have been in that position. I don't give a flying fuck about Pacen. We saw her on Block Island two summers ago. She made a choice, and it wasn't him, so whatever kind of relationship they had, it's over. It's time for him to choose. Her, or me."

No one says a word for a long time until Preston slams his fist down on the island. "Colt's right. We're not doing Ash any favors, letting him hide out in seclusion. Whatever hold Pacen has on him, he has to let it go. I'll talk to him."

"Thanks, Pres. I-I can't lose them. I've only just found them, but they're already my whole life."

"I know," he says, pulling me into a hug. "I know. Dad would be proud of you, Colty. I'm proud of you, too. I'm sorry if I didn't say that soon enough. Winnie and Wes are your family, which makes them our family. We'll do everything in our power to keep them both safe and with you. I'll make sure of it."

As he releases me, I nod. I'm too overwhelmed to speak. My heart aches with fear for my family and pride in my brothers.

"It's what we do," East cuts in. "We take care of our own."

"Welcome to the chaos," we say in unison.

"Now, let's get this food out there before our girls barf all over your family room."

"Jesus. Please tell me you got pictures when you picked them up last night?" I ask East.

A mischievous grin spreads across his face. "Oh, I got pictures and videos. They're going to make a great slide show at Christmas."

Howling laughter erupts from each of us, followed by a hiss from the ladies.

"Shut up, or I'll cut you," Julia whines, but it lacks her usual ball-buster enthusiasm.

"We better feed them." I chuckle.

"And take a few more pictures." Preston smirks with his phone pointed in their direction.

Yeah, this is exactly where I'm meant to be. With Winnie, Wes, and my brothers, we're an unbeatable team. I hope, anyway.

CHAPTER 32

WINNIE

"It doesn't mean he's won," one of our attorneys explains for the fourth time.

Colton, Preston, and I are sitting huddled together on one side of a conference table while an army of lawyers sits across from us, flipping papers, typing on computers, and most of them mumbling to themselves.

Preston showed up a month ago with a team of men and women he said would make this nightmare go away. I'd believed him at the time. A group of six people entered our home with plans, papers, a common goal. Make sure Weston stays with us. A month ago, I had a man who showed me day after day how much he loved me and a group of women who showed up time and time again to welcome me into the fold. I had a fiancé and friends. I was truly living in a fairytale.

I still have the fiancé, and the friends, but it's beginning to feel more like a nightmare I can't wake up from. Tears stream down my face, but I make no noise. I'm terrified if I let it out, I'll never be able to stop. Colton has an arm wrapped protectively around my shoulders, and Preston has a firm grasp on my left hand.

He gives it a squeeze before he speaks. "He may not have

won the war, but he sure as hell won a battle in there, Marc. What are you going to do to make sure that never happens again?" I've never heard Preston in business mode. He's more than a little scary.

"I know it feels that way, but the fact that Darling got supervised visitation is not unexpected, and we ensured that Colton would be the supervisor."

I'm sure that tidbit pissed off my father, but it doesn't offer any consolation. My entire body trembles like I'm going through withdrawals.

Colton kisses the side of my head and whispers, "I won't let anything happen to Wes, Winnie."

I can only nod. I'm in a daze, or maybe it's shock. All I can do is shiver like a leaf in the wind. Colton has made so many promises, and he has always delivered. I just have to remember that.

"Next steps?" Preston barks.

"Well, first we're going to find a way to admit the information your brother found without getting him arrested." This time it's one of the women lawyers. She dressed exactly as I always pictured myself in my daydreams of law school. A perfectly fitting navy suit over a light pink silky shirt. She has her hair pulled back in a professional, yet stylish updo.

Staring at her, I let go of the only dream I ever had for myself.

"We'll get you there someday," Colton whispers. He still misses nothing.

I shrug sadly, not trusting myself to speak yet.

"When does this visit have to happen?" Colton asks.

"They've given him two hours per week. We negotiated that it would happen on Monday mornings, ten a.m. to noon."

I don't bother lifting my gaze to see which lawyer is speaking. I choose to keep my head down and concentrate on my breathing.

"For how long?" Preston hisses.

"Until our next court date, which is one month from today."

"Four visits? That's unacceptable, Marc. We're not paying you six figures for this kind of fuck up." Preston squeezes my hand once more before he lets it go to stand. "Eight hours is not acceptable. Figure this out, and now. Cut down the hours, and I suggest you do it soon before I find other representation."

"I can assure you, Mr. Westbrook, we're going to work around the clock until we find a loophole. Once we do, we'll request an emergency intervention on your behalf." This time the woman's voice is strong, determined.

I think I would have been like that as a lawyer. I like to think I would have been, anyway.

"One week. You have one week to correct this. Do you understand?" Preston's voice is deadly. I'm glad he's on our side. With deliberate movements, he retakes the seat next to me.

"Yes, sir. Of course. We'll make it happen."

"You may go." It's no wonder Preston is CEO. All the brothers carry themselves with authority, but Preston has an aura that commands attention. I guess that's what happens when you take over a billion-dollar company in your early twenties.

I'm speechless.

"Thank you, Pres." Colton's words sound forced. I can see him simmering just beneath the surface when I glance over.

Preston leans forward to see around me. "No one is going to fuck with our family. I don't care who they are. I'm going to speak to Ashton now. When this asshole takes a shit, I want to know. There has to be something else we can nail him with. No offense, Win."

My head snaps to the left so fast my hair falls into my face. "What?"

"Even though I think your father is a piece of shit, he's still your father and I should have more restraint around you."

I laugh. I can't help it. Maybe I'm delirious, but it's funny to me that he, Preston Westbrook, is worried about my feelings. My laughter doesn't stop either, and Preston is wearing an expression of horror.

Colton stiffens at my side. "Sweetheart? Are you okay?"

Tears roll down my face. Tears of relief that they're here for me. Tears of fear, anxiety, and yes, tears of happiness. "Y-Yes," I choke out, trying to sober to the moment.

My gaze doesn't leave Preston's and a slow smirk crosses his face. "What's so funny, future sister-in-law?"

"I don't know. That you're both here, helping me fight? That you're worried about my feelings? All of it, I guess. But you should know, Jason Darling has never been my father. He walked away from me years ago and let me know every chance he got that I was a disappointment."

"Fucking, fucker," Colton curses behind me as Preston's eyes turn lethal.

"That's good to know, Winnie. Then I'll take extra joy in bringing him to his knees. I'll also be sure to let him know how far from a disappointment you are." He softens his tone when he peers over my head at Colton, then back to me. I can only imagine what his expression is saying right now. "I'm sorry that we got off on the wrong foot. But I am honored to have you in our family."

My laughter dies on the unexpected praise. "Th-Thank you, Preston. For everything."

He nods once, then addresses Colton, "You'll wear a wire and a camera when you meet with Darling. We're going to need everything you can get from him."

"The only thing that will keep me from ripping his face off is Weston. But I'll do what I can to figure out what the hell he wants."

"Good. I don't need to tell you what attacking the fucker would do to this case."

"No, Pres. You don't."

Preston holds his gaze steady as Colton stands. "GG has

family dinner set up. Mom's plane will arrive in about an hour. Let's get home so you can prepare Winnie for the full Westbrook experience."

I stand so quickly my chair scrapes across the floor when the backs of my legs hit it.

Colton chuckles. "It's okay, CC. Everyone already loves you."

"Everyone?" The word comes out like a squeaky wheel.

"Everyone," he assures.

Good lord. How many people can *everyone* be?

~

Standing outside of GG's ski lodge, the number of voices filtering out from the closed door answers my earlier question. Colton stands at my side with Wes on his hip. When I glance over, I see him checking Weston's headphones.

"They're loud now, Win. But they love Wes, and they'll do everything they can to keep him comfortable."

"I know." I think I do anyway, but I can't help feeling apprehensive. Wes hasn't had a meltdown in weeks, but this is like his version of hell. Fight or flight, the doctors had said, and my heart skips a beat.

"Maybe this wasn't a good idea."

"Baby. Julia has given everyone instructions, and she can be scary as … well, you know." He glances down at Weston, obviously proud for catching himself before he cursed. That one small gesture has my heart rate returning to an acceptable speed.

Well, until I hear Julia on the other side of the door. "They're here. You'd all better remember everything I told you, or I'll kick you right in the taint. I don't care who you are. Understood?"

My horrified expression has Colton chuckling. "Told ya." He goes to open the door, but Julia beats him to it.

She stands in sweatpants, two sizes too big, and a T-shirt that says *Nerds do it best*. She also has headphones on that are identical to Weston's. When he tears his head out of the crook of Colton's neck, that's the first thing he notices. His little hand reaches up to touch his, and she does the same thing, a giant grin on her face.

"Hey, little man. Nice gear," she says, pointing to her ears.

Weston doesn't respond, but gives her a toothy smile. This crazy lady will win him over by the time we leave. I can feel it.

She lurches forward, her movements always reminding me of a strange bobblehead, and wraps me in a hug. "We set up the tables to accommodate Wes, and all the toys in the lounge are placed so no one will walk behind him," she whispers before letting go.

"Thank you, Julia. Honestly, th-that means a lot."

She winks and drags me inside. The volume of voices is much lower than when we were outside, and as we enter the lounge, I realize they've all done it for Wes. The sheer number of children running around is a chaos all its own, but when I check on Wes, he looks excited and content in Colton's arms. His gaze darts from one little friend to the next until he lands on Ada James, and he shocks the nerves right out of me when he reaches for her.

Colton looks to me for guidance, and I glance around the room, expecting everyone to be staring at us. I'm shocked again when everyone smiles warmly, then goes back to their conversations.

Lexi is the first to approach with Ada James in her arms. "Julia gave strict instructions not to bombard you all at once, so we're taking turns saying hello. We want to make sure Wes feels comfortable—"

She's cut off when Wes tries to escape Colton's arms with an excited "Ad-de. Ad-de."

Lexi nods toward a train table and I have a feeling they

brought this in just for Wes. Gratitude so great I can't breathe spreads through my body as we follow her across the room.

Colton sets Wes down next to Ada James at the train table. Wes immediately walks to the little girl and hugs her in the awkward way toddlers have. Tears fill my eyes when he plants an open-mouthed kiss on her head.

Strong arms wrap around my middle, and Colton rests his chin on my shoulder. "He's going to be just fine, CC. Look at all the people who love him already." He sweeps his hand around the room, and my gaze follows.

Before the tears can fall, the Westbrooks approach one by one to greet us, offering words of encouragement. Promises that we're not in this alone. And something I've always found hard to come by, unconditional love.

CHAPTER 33

COLTON

"*I* think I'm going to be sick."

Turning to Winnie, I see she's a little green. I feel like I might hurl too, but I don't tell her that. I summon all the strength I have, so she'll have at least a little confidence in me when we leave.

"I know, baby. But it will be okay." Weston's on the floor next to us, so I pull her into a hug. "It's two hours, and I won't leave Weston's side for a minute." When she doesn't immediately return the embrace, I lift her face to mine. I love this woman more than I ever thought possible. The fact that someone is hurting her claws at my chest like a wild animal. "The girls will be here soon to start wedding plans." I smile like a kid on Christmas morning. "I can guarantee they'll keep you busy. Two hours will go by in a flash. I want you to have the wedding of your dreams, so please try to enjoy the process, okay?"

"I really don't have a clue about weddings, but I'll try. Will you call me as soon as it's over?" Her voice is small, and I hate that Darling does this to her.

"You know I will."

The doorbell rings with a soft, musical melody I had

installed last week. It's less jarring than the original, and thankfully, Wes is handling it well. I release Winnie and turn to the door with Wes hot on my heels just as it opens.

"Hello, hello," Lanie sings. "We come with wedding planners, swatches, dress designs, flower samples, and Halton made cake!" Lanie is truly one of the sweetest human beings on the planet, and I can't think of a better person to sit with Winnie. Lexi and Rylan follow behind her.

"Ry-guy! Look at you!" I walk toward my best friend in awe of her growing belly. I'm not sure how I would have handled this a few months ago, but seeing her now actually glowing with my nephew growing inside of her, all I feel is pure joy. I've never seen her happier, or Halton, for that matter.

"Yeah, I'm thinking this little bugger is going to take after the Westbrooks in the size department."

I chuckle because Rylan is a tiny little thing.

I'm not paying attention, so I miss Wes walk right by me to Lexi. I'm always astonished he can tell Lexi and Lanie apart.

"Ad-de? Ad-de?" he repeats, peering around her legs.

My little guy either has a serious crush, or he's found his Rylan. Knowing that he may have a best friend built into his new family gives me more determination than ever to make sure he stays with us.

"He's never had a friend he asked for or talked about," Winnie whispers. "He hasn't stopped talking about Ada James since he met her, though."

Lexi drops to the floor so she's eye level with him. "You're about to go on an adventure with Colton, but I'll bring Ada James over as soon as you get back if that's okay with Mommy?"

He doesn't wait for her to finish before he's barreling down the hall to Winnie. "Ad-de. Ad-de," he says merrily, clapping his hands in excitement.

"Okay, buddy. Ada James can come over and play when you and Colton get back. Sound good?"

A squeal of excitement leaves his little body as he does that happy toddler dance I love so much.

"We should get going," I say to Lanie, knowing she'll catch my hint and take over distracting Winnie.

"Don't forget to call me as soon as it's over." Winnie's panicked, and it shows in her trembling lip.

Turning, I bend forward to kiss her. "I've got this, baby. Trust me?"

She nods with fearful eyes. "I trust you." She gulps as I scoop Weston off the floor. She places a kiss on his cheek while he squirms, then she turns and hustles out of view.

I turn to the girls, but they're all on the move, hurrying past me to get to my girl.

"Don't worry. We'll take good care of her," Rylan says, patting my arm on her way by.

"Thanks, Ry-guy."

She smiles and rushes to meet the others.

"Just you and me, buddy. You ready?"

"Coto. Coto. Lub Coto," he sings. It's the best song I've ever heard.

~

*W*e enter the library fifteen minutes early. I'm hoping to get Wes settled before asshat arrives, but just my luck, he's already here, looming over the young librarian. This guy has creep written all over him. She visibly relaxes when she catches sight of me, but it sets off alarm bells in my gut.

Unconsciously, I pat the microphone tucked inside of the pocket of my button down, and adjust the glasses I don't need, but hold a tiny camera.

"Stop touching the microphone." Ash hisses. His response sounds like my conscience because of the tiny transmitter he placed inside of my ear.

"Sorry," I mutter under my breath and keep walking right past Darling. His time doesn't start for fifteen minutes, and I will get Wes settled first.

"Hey," he yells, causing Wes to cover his ears.

I mistakenly thought the library would be quiet enough for him not to need his headphones, but I can see asshat won't let that happen.

With quick strides, I go toe to toe with Darling. "Your time doesn't start for fifteen minutes. He needs time to acclimate, and you will not raise your voice like that again or we're out of here." Although I want to tear into this guy, I'll never do that in front of Wes.

He sneers at me, then Wes. "You do, and my attorney will make sure you're held in contempt."

"Do you even know what that means?" I snarl. "Never mind. I obviously have my answer. Fifteen minutes. Not a second sooner."

I storm off toward the children's section, and as soon as we sit on the floor, I pull his headphones out of the bag housing all his supplies. Kids sure need a lot of shit for a two-hour outing.

I put them on Weston's head, and he places an open-mouthed kiss on my nose. "Thanks, little man. Love you."

"Lub Coto. Lub Cot—" He breaks off when he sees the train table. I know Winnie brings him here a lot, but the train table is a new addition, thanks to East. By the time asshat strides into the section, Wes is fully immersed in his trains.

"What the fuck is wrong with him?" Darling spits.

I'm on my feet before he finishes. "What. Did. I. Tell. You?"

"Whatever. Answer the question. Are you turning him into a sissy fuck? Jesus Christ, you are."

"Curse one more time and we're leaving. That's not how you speak in front of a child."

"I'll speak, however the fuck I want to *my* son."

"The son you've never paid attention to before now? The son you've never paid a cent in child support for? That son?"

288

He pushes past me and grabs Weston's headphones, ripping them off his head so roughly the little boy's neck snaps back.

"Did you get that?" I hiss to Ash.

"Got it. Don't do anything stupid to fuck this up." But I'm already in front of Darling.

Wrenching the headphones free from his grasp, I gently place them back on Weston's head, then lift the crying little boy into my arms, where he promptly buries his face into my chest. I gently stroke his back while glaring at Darling.

"Nothing is wrong with him. He's perfect just the way he is."

"He's some kind of ret—"

"Don't you dare finish that sentence." My jaw tightens and I hear my molars grinding.

"Jesus, Colt. Keep him talking. Don't lose your shit," Ashton commands.

"Watch your ignorant mouth," I growl through clenched teeth. "I'll repeat. There is absolutely nothing wrong with Weston. If you use a derogatory word with him in the same room again, it'll be the last thing you do."

"Mayday. Mayday. Don't threaten him, Colt. Back it the fuck up." Ashton's panic comes through loud and clear, snapping me from my haze of hate for the man before me.

"Are you threatening me, boy?" When Darling gets into my face, I can smell the cheap liquor on his breath.

"Have you been drinking?" My rage is at an all-time high. "You're drunk. It's ten in the morning, and he's drunk," I bite out.

"Keep him there. I'm calling the sheriff for a breathalyzer now." Ashton works faster than I can think.

"Don't matter what I'm doin'. Once I get that little fucker, I'll have all the money I need and nannies to watch the little shit."

"What do you mean, you'll have all the money? From whom? Who exactly is paying for your lawyer, Darling?"

"Ah, ah. None of your fucking business."

Wes curls his little body even more. Just like he did with Winnie, he's trying to crawl inside of me, and I hate that he's hearing this.

"But if ya want to double it, it might encourage me to walk away."

"You don't want Weston. You want to hurt your daughter."

"Fuck that little tramp. All I care about is the money. I don't give a shit what happens to him, and she's the biggest waste of space I've ever seen in my life."

My fist curls into a ball and I'm ready to knock the asshole out when Preston clamps a hand on my shoulder. "That's enough. We're done here."

"The hell we are," Darling shouts, stumbling as he lurches forward to grab at Weston, but I'm too quick, and Preston is too pissed. He doesn't make it a foot before Preston is shoving him back. When he trips over the train table, screaming about suing us, an officer walks in, shaking his head.

"What have you got yourself into this time, Jason?" the officer asks.

"I'm here to see my son, and these two assholes assaulted me."

The terrified librarian escorts a family I hadn't noticed earlier to another section of the library just as Preston steps forward to introduce himself. "I'm Preston Westbrook. This is my brother, Colton, and his *stepson*, Weston."

We've never used words like *step* in our family and I can tell it bothered him to say it now. I know it was like nails on a chalkboard for me. *Family is family, however they fall.*

"We brought Wes here for a supervised visit. However, when we arrived, Mr. Darling was intoxicated and has been belligerent since we walked in. I'd like a breathalyzer done and submitted to the court." I'm always amazed by how quickly Preston can turn on the charm.

"It's nice to meet you, Mr. Westbrook. I'd like to thank you for everything you've been doing to revitalize this town. It means a lot to some very good people. I'm Officer Russel."

"You don't get to tell the officer how to handle me," Darling slurs as he pulls himself off the floor.

"No, he can't. But he is right, Darling. If you refuse the breathalyzer, I'll be forced to testify about the events I'm walking in on, and I promise you it won't be in your favor."

Darling squints his eyes as he pops a piece of gum into his mouth. This guy really is an idiot if he thinks that will save him now. "I'll take the damn test," he spits. "Makes no difference to me. I ain't drunk."

"Officer, would it be okay for me to leave with Wes now? This has been incredibly traumatic for him." I attempt to pull the little boy from my body so the officer can see his tear-stained face, but he wails and claws at me, trying to stay close. My heart breaks. Rage fills my veins. I want to kill Winnie's father.

The officer is young, about my age, and his face softens at the fear Wes expresses in his body language. "I believe that would be best. I'll file a report and make sure social services get a copy myself. My wife and I just adopted a little boy about his age, so I have some firsthand experience. Take him home and love all over him. He'll be just fine."

"Thank you," I say, stepping forward to shake his hand.

Turning to Preston, I find him with his arms folded over his broad chest and a murderous expression on his face. He doesn't take his gaze off Darling as he speaks. "I'll stay, Colt. Go do what you need to."

I nod, grab Weston's bag, and haul ass out of the old building. "Time to go home, buddy."

CHAPTER 34

WINNIE

"*T*his cake is ridiculous," Rylan groans next to me. "Can my husband bake or what?" We're sitting around the coffee table that now has books, swatches, and pictures spread all over it. We'd started with the cake tasting because, hello? Cake!

Colton and Wes haven't been far from my thoughts, but I'd be lying if I said I wasn't having at least a little bit of fun with these ladies. Each has their own distinct style, and watching them haggle over what is best for my wedding has me smiling most of the time.

"You don't have any idea what you might like?" Lexi asks again.

"No, sorry, Lexi. I've never really been one to sit around daydreaming. There was no point wasting time thinking about something I'd never be able to afford."

"I know exactly what you mean," Lanie chimes in. "I never had much growing up. My mother made sure of it. Then one bad night changed everything for me. I had completely given up on love and I knew I'd never get a happily ever after. I was content with that. Or so I thought."

"Right." Lexi smirks. "And then you ended up with the real-life version of Prince Charming."

I laugh right along with them because I've heard tales of Dexter Cross and his epic romantic side.

Lanie snorts. "It's funny because it's true."

When we compose ourselves, Lanie pulls out a three-ring binder. "Okay. I've got this. You've never daydreamed about your wedding, but now you can. So, I'm going to ask you a series of questions. I want you to answer them honestly and quickly. Your gut reaction. Got it?"

"Sure." *I can do this, right?*

A bright smile lights up her face. "Princess or sexy vixen?"

"Uh…"

"Answer quickly. Your first reaction, just blurt it out," Lexi orders.

"Princess." I glance around. Everyone's so invested in making this my day. It's a little overwhelming.

"Traditional or modern?"

"Traditional."

"Fancy night out or comfy night in?"

"Comfy night in."

"Flowers or balloons?"

"What?"

"Answer. Quick, quick." Rylan laughs.

"Gah. Flowers."

"Navy or black?"

"Navy. What does that have to do with a wedding?" I'm so confused, but I can't stop giggling either.

"You'll see," Lanie promises.

"Sit down dinner or buffet?"

"Sit down. Buffets gross me out. What if someone sneezes?"

"Roses or lilies?"

"Neither?" I ask. "I've always been more of a wildflower kind of girl."

Lanie's eyes glisten. "Wildflowers it is. I think we just

planned your wedding. We'll need to go dress shopping, obviously, but that's an experience in itself."

"What do you mean, we planned it?"

"Yup. Guys will wear navy suits. We'll decorate with wildflowers, have a sit-down dinner, and you liked the lemon cake best. I saw it on your face."

"And lemon is Colton's favorite," Rylan says through a giant bite of chocolate cake.

"It is?" I ask, turning toward her. "Shouldn't I know that?"

"Nah," Lexi says dismissively. "I married East one drunken night in Vegas that neither of us really remembers. I knew next to nothing about him except he was a giant ass. Cake flavors are just details you get to spend the rest of your life figuring out."

A car door slams, and I'm on my feet as panic sets in. "It's too early for them to be home. Why are they home?"

Lanie, who is closest to the window, looks outside. "False alarm. It's just GG. She doesn't like being left out of stuff."

Just then, all their phones chime with alerts. Lexi's the first to make eye contact, and I immediately know something's wrong.

The front door bursts open, and GG comes clink clacking down the hall. "No need to panic. I was touchin' with the ladies."

"Texting, GG. You were texting with the ladies," Lanie cuts in.

"What she said. Betty-Anne was next door at the historical society when the cruiser showed up."

"Cruiser?" I ask meekly, feeling faint.

"Your dad is a piece of work, that one, but Colton and that little boy of yours are just fine. They'll be home any minute. I got Betty-Anne to hold off on the Town Cryer until I could get over here to warn ya is all."

"Warn me about what?" Glancing around, I find all three women furiously scrolling their phones.

"Nothin' to worry about, but I think it's time we added you to the Cryer. My boys took care of it all. I was at Ashton's watching the live feed, ya know? They'll take it all to court."

"Take what?" I demand, but my knees shake, and I collapse onto the sofa.

Another car door slams, then another. My boys are home, and Colton is standing before me like a teenage fantasy a second later. When the fear holding me captive subsides, I reach for Wes, and say a silent prayer when he comes to me.

"He looks okay. Is he okay? What happened? Why are you home so early? What did he do?" One question bleeds into the next, but Colton doesn't get a chance to respond.

"Ad-de. Ad-de."

Lexi pockets her phone and walks to me. "How about if I take him to my house for a few hours? We even have walkie-talkies. I can keep one turned on so you can hear him playing the entire time. Julia has given us all a run down, Winnie. I'll treat Wes like he's my own."

I know before she says it that she will. "He's—"

"And if he has a hard time, I'll bring him right back," she interrupts, then whispers, "Please, let us try? I think Colton needs you right now."

My gaze snaps to Colton, and I notice how tight his jaw is for the first time. His hunched shoulders and clenched fists replace his gentle, carefree nature. He tries to smile, and I know it's for my benefit, but I think Lexi's right. He needs me. After everything he's given me, knowing I finally have some-thing to offer him has me nodding as I speak.

"Is that okay with you, Colton? If Lexi takes Wes to her house for a while?"

Colton glances from me to Wes, and his body relaxes a frac-tion. "Do you want to go to Ada James' house, Wes? Auntie Lexi will take you to play?"

His grin and happy clapping are answer enough. When he

leans forward in my arms to reach for Lexi, I know he feels at home here. With this family, our family, he's home.

All apprehension leaves my body as Lexi snuggles him into her side, and he lets her. She isn't the soft and gooey type of woman, but she's kind and warm with Weston, and he appears to love her. "Okay, kiddo. Looks like you're going to Ada's house."

Colton hands Lexi his bag, and when I turn, I see that the girls have placed all the wedding materials into neat piles. "We got a great start on this," Lanie says, tossing her long, blonde hair over her shoulder. "We'll come back this weekend and get the ball rolling."

"Okay." What else am I going to say?

"We'll make this the wedding of your dreams, Winnie. And we'll help you figure out your dreams to make it happen."

"Thank you. All of you."

They each lean in for a hug—because that's what Westbrooks do, they hug—and then Colton walks them all out. When the door shuts, I hurry to the window just in time to see Lexi place Wes into a car seat.

Colton pulls me into him from behind as we watch Lexi drive away. "I need you, CC. I need to be inside of you. I need to feel you from the inside and tame a rage I can't control in here," he declares, crushing a fist over his heart.

Turning in his arms, I find a storm happening in his eyes. "What happened, Colton? Why are you so upset?"

"He showed up drunk. He ripped Weston's headphones off with such force his little head snapped back before I could stop it. On my watch, he got hurt, and ever since I've had visions of what life would be like for him if Darling got him. I can't let that happen, Winnie. I won't let it happen. He's ours." His words are hoarse, and his body trembles under my touch.

"Colton, I just saw him. He's okay, though, baby. He's okay." Even as I offer words of comfort, fear bubbles over in my chest. "GG said an officer showed up? What happened next?"

A single tear falls down Colton's face. His love for Wes, for me. It's all expressed in that one droplet of salty water. "I promise I'll do better protecting him, CC. I will. Preston's there now, making sure a report is filed and Darling's blood alcohol level is reported to family services. There's no way he can get him after we submit the video."

"Is it legal to record him? Will we be able to use it?" My brain is flitting through every scenario.

"The library has security cameras all throughout and it's posted at every entrance that recording devices are in use. Ashton said that will cover us, too. He doesn't want Wes, CC. He's after money. I just don't know from who."

This man, always so strong and confident, feels broken somehow, so I comfort him the only way I know how. Reaching up, I grasp both sides of his face and pull him in for a kiss. The second our lips touch, Colton takes over.

"I need you. I need you." He sounds so vulnerable. Not at all like the confident man who's been strutting around in superhero onesies.

"You have me, Colton. I'm yours," I whisper beneath his touch.

His tongue pokes and caresses my lips before sweeping inside, tasting me as deeply as he can get, but it still doesn't feel like enough.

He growls at my words. "I hate that you have his last name, Winnie. We need to change that and change it fast. You're mine. You're a Westbrook, and I need to make that legal. I have to."

There's a desperation in his plea that scares me. But the fear of losing him is greater. "Okay."

He pulls back sharply, eyes narrowing on my face. "Okay?"

"Mm-hm. We can get married as soon as you want, Colton. I'm done holding back from you." As I say it, I know it's true. It may be fast. It may be wild and reckless. But it's a love that's both terrifying and exhilarating. It's a feeling I never want to be without.

A long, low growl rumbles in Colton's chest. "I need to fuck you now, fiancée. It won't be sweet or gentle. It'll be fast, hard, and raw. Then, when I recover, I'll do sweet, but right now, I'm going to be deep inside of you. You'll think it's too much, but you can take it." His fingers tease the hem of my shirt, and he lifts it over my head. "Right, Winnie? Can you take my hard cock fast and hard? Thrust after punishing thrust?"

Colton is coming undone. I can sense he's holding on by a thread, but I need to show him that I'll catch him, too. "I'll take every brutal inch you can give me, fiancé."

As the word fiancé leaves my lips, Colton's eyes glaze over. He lunges for me, but I slip out of his grasp and drop to my knees before him.

"No," he grinds out. "Not. Now." Harsh words show how much today's interaction affected him. "I can't be gentle, Winnie. I can't—"

Undoing the button of his jeans, I glance up through long lashes. "I don't want you to be gentle, Colton. I want you to take what you need and know that I'll catch you, too."

His eyes roll to the back of his head as I lower his pants and boxer briefs in one tug. His dick bounces free, and I can't hide my gasp of surprise. He's all smooth skin and hard planes, but his shaft is truly magnificent. There's a pulsing vein that runs along the underside. His hard, thick member juts up toward his stomach, and I lean forward to follow that vein with soft kisses.

"Fuck, Winnie."

My tongue swirls around his tip, and I get my first taste of precome. My pussy clamps down, hating the empty feeling there. Lifting up, I grasp him with one hand, guiding him into my wet and waiting mouth. I use the other hand to cup his balls before sliding it down over his perineum.

"Jesus," he pants. "I can't do this, Winnie."

I freeze for half a second, thinking he's rejecting me.

"I wasn't lying, CC. I need to fuck you. Hard." What he's really saying is, *I need control, Winnie. I need you to help me regain my self-control.*

Thank God. "I want you, too, Colton. Take what you need." I drop my mouth to him once more, pulling him in so deep he hits the back of my throat, and I swallow around him. A strangled cry escapes as he cups my chin with one hand, and the back of my head with the other.

"Are you sure?"

I nod without releasing him.

"Keep your mouth open wide," he orders, and I happily comply.

With barely contained thrusts that cause my eyes to pool with tears, he fucks my mouth, just as I asked him to. Drool and mucus drip down my chin, but he doesn't stop. Using his hand holding my chin, he collects it with his fingers, then leans down to tease my nipple with the wetness. When he folds over me, his cock slips down my throat. I can't breathe, but I can smell him. He overwhelms my senses. His masculine, woodsy scent that's all him and sex and love. When I don't think I can stand another second, he pulls out, leaving me gasping for breath. But if I thought he was going to give me a moment to collect myself, I was dead wrong.

His hands hook under my arms, and he lifts me to my feet. "Bedroom. Now." He's breathing heavily. His chest rises and falls as his nostrils flare.

Turning on my heel, I glance over my shoulder. "Yes, sir," I say cheekily, resulting in a hard smack to my ass, and then he comes after me. I make it to the stairs, but he's too fast and catches me halfway up.

"You never have to call me sir, Winnie. But I can be the master of your body if that's what you want."

Yes. Yes. And yes.

CHAPTER 35

COLTON

*C*atching Winnie on the stairs, I press her body to mine. My hard length nestled into the crook of her legging-clad ass. I have to calm down before I hurt her. I've never felt so out of control. She arches into me, shimmying up and down on my cock. If she keeps that up, I'm going to come all over her back, so with one hand, I hold her still, and my other hand slips into her panties.

"Colton." It's a wanton plea, and I'm more than willing to oblige.

"I love you, Winnie. So damn much I can't think straight." My nose nuzzles her ear as my teeth bear down on the sensitive skin just below.

"Today wasn't your fault, Colton. He's a narcissistic—" The hand holding her hip clamps over her mouth.

"It was my fault, CC," I whisper harshly. My rough words complimenting the rapid movement of my fingers across her clit. Back and forth, up and down. Harder. Softer. Faster. And then a slap. I've found that keeping her guessing is the quickest way to get her to release her mind, so I never keep a pattern for long. "I was so invested in having a pissing contest with him, I let Wes get too far away from me. It won't happen again. When

301

I told you to trust me, I … Fuck, Winnie. I'll earn it by being better."

Her chest heaves, but I don't stop. I quickly tug her pants down to her knees. My hand goes numb from the reckless assault on her clit. Winnie's legs quiver against mine, and she rests her head back against my shoulder. My hand lowers from her mouth to grip her neck. Not hard, but with enough pressure that I can feel her pulse point beneath my thumb. When she lets out a sinful moan, I insert three fingers into her pussy.

She's slick skin, and throaty moans of pleasure that have me rocking my dick against her back for the friction it's desperately seeking. Never taking the heel of my palm off her bundle of sensitive nerves, I finger fuck her with desperation. When I feel her clamp down on my hand, I know I have her. Curling my finger to that spot no one else has ever reached for her, I massage and caress. I pull every ounce of pleasure I can from her body. I'm rewarded with a burst of moisture that shoots from her pussy, coating my hand.

"Gah. Colt. Fuuck. Ahhhh," she screams louder than I've ever heard her, and it releases the beast inside.

I gently lower her to the stairs. "Hold on to the step above you."

Winnie is still a shivering mess of orgasmic bliss, but I press her legs together, tilt her hips to the sky, and plunge as deep into her center as this position will allow. She's so goddamn tight like this I think my head will explode. But it's the onslaught of her unexpected second orgasm that has my eyes rolling to the back of my head.

As soon as I'm buried to the hilt, her inner walls squeeze, quiver, and quake around me. "Fucking hell, Winnie. Yes."

Her back is slick with sweat. Her sounds are music to my ears, but in no way coherent. Groans, moans, and slapping skin exorcise the demons of today until I'm lost to every sensation except her. *My CC.*

Gripping her upper arms, I raise her back to my front as I

continue to plunge deep inside of her. "Mine. My family, Winnie." I pound into her with everything I am, and adrenaline has me nowhere near ready to come. Holding her arched back to me, I lift her right leg onto the step above us.

I hit new depths in this position, and she cries out, her body spent. I can feel it in her lagging muscles, but she lifts her arms up and hooks them around my neck. She's letting me know she's here with me. For me.

"I'm yours, Colton. Body and mind. Forever more. I trust you with my body, my heart, and my family." Her shaky words send me spiraling into a fit of pleasure I'll never be able to explain.

Silence fills the stairwell. Panting breaths and racing hearts are the only sounds we hear. My arms wrap around Winnie's middle when I feel her legs wobble. Turning her to me, I lean down and lift her in a fireman's hold. I intend to carry her to our bedroom when my foot slips in a puddle and we both look down.

"Oh my God. What is that? Did I pee?"

Oh, my dear Winnie. "I'm so glad I get to experience these firsts with you, sweetheart. That, my love, is our love. You squirted," I state plainly but feel pride racing straight to my semi hard cock.

"What? No." Her horrified expression has me laughing loudly and carefree. The fact that I can feel so much with her is exhilarating.

Climbing the steps, I smack her ass. Not hard, but enough to make a loud snapping sound. "Yes. And my new mission will be to see how many times I can make you do it. We're going to need to invest in a lot of towels, fiancée of mine."

Feeling her shake her head, I know she covered her face with her hands. I chuckle darkly before tossing her on the bed. "I'll be right back."

She stares at me confused, flushed, and a whole lot fuckable.

I race to our bathroom, grab a towel and the spray cleaner,

then quickly clean off the stairs in case Lexi comes back sooner than expected.

Back in our room, I toss the cleaner under the sink and the towel in the hamper, then stalk back toward my future.

"Are you okay?" she asks quietly.

"Yeah," I admit. "I'm disappointed in myself, though. I should have known better. I—" My throat closes, and I cough to force the words out. "The second he touched Weston, fear hit like a tsunami. I should have noticed his bloodshot eyes. The way he swayed when he was leaning on the desk. I should have seen it."

Winnie sits up in the bed and crawls under my arm, holding me tight.

"Is this how he was with you?" I'm not sure I want the answer, but I have to ask.

She shakes her head against my chest. "He was worse, Colton. At least Wes is a boy. In my father's eyes, that gives him some value. You said he wanted something. Did he ask you for money?"

"Not exactly. But I have one guess as to who put him up to this. And Ash will end it, or I'll do it myself."

Winnie lifts her gaze to mine, and I kiss her forehead. "Thank you, CC."

"Thank you? For what?" Her raised eyebrows furrow in confusion.

"For being here. For trusting me. For keeping me from doing something stupid. Until I had you by my side, I felt out of control. I'm not sure what I would have done to your father if I didn't have you to come home to."

Her eyes glisten, even as they droop with exhaustion. "It's new for me, too, Colton. Loving someone so much, it's a little scary."

I watch as she slowly blinks a few times until her eyes finally stay closed. I sit here, holding her to me while she naps.

"Yeah, sweetheart. Loving someone is scary. But not as scary as losing them."

She doesn't flinch as I scoot us up the bed so I can rest against the headboard.

Winnie quietly snores while I grab my phone and set the wheels in motion for our future.

Colton: Update?

Preston: Emergency hearing Wednesday morning at 8 a.m.

Preston: He took a swing at me and is in custody.

Easton: What did you do to instigate that?

Preston: I put some pressure on him to talk.

Colton: Did he?

My phone rings in my hand. Glancing down, I see it's Ashton, so I carefully lay Winnie down, and slip out of bed. In the hallway, I answer. "Ash."

"Colt. Darling had three large deposits into his account in the last month."

"From who?"

"I'm working on it."

"Ashton, if this is Macomb …"

"If it's him, I'll take care of it."

"You keep saying that, and I keep getting hurt."

"I'll take care of it. I have to go, but is Wes okay?"

I sigh heavily into the phone. "Yeah. He's with Lexi and East right now."

"Good. I'll be in touch."

"Thanks, Ash."

I glance down at my phone, but he's already disconnected. I want to throw it against the wall because something about this just doesn't feel right. Instead, I grab a pair of lounge pants and head down to my office.

Behind the large, industrial desk that I didn't choose, I scroll my phone for the group chat I need. When I find it, I smile. If they can't get this done, no one can.

Coordinators of Chaos (group chat)

Colton: How fast can you put together a wedding?

Mom: I'll be there tomorrow.

GG: That's the way, Pan.

Lanie: OMG!

Julia: You have discussed this with your betrothed, correct?

Colton: Of course.

Lexi: Hell yeah.

Ari: I'll handle decorations, and Halton will make the cake.

Emory: Preston and I'll handle the entertainment.

Julia: Mom, GG, and I will take care of the food.

Lexi: Lanie and I will take her dress shopping.

Lexi: What's our timeframe?

Colton: Five days.

Lanie: You want to get married on Saturday?

Colton: Yes. Tell me what we need to do.

Julia: Go see my dad. He'll help speed up the marriage license.

Colton: Good. What else?

Sloane: I'll write the vows!

Colton: No!

Julia: No way!

Lanie: Ah ...

Lexi: Jesus.

Emory: Ah, Sloane. We love your writing abilities, but not sure Winnie will want a five-pepper rating for her marriage vows.

Sloane: (rolling eye emoji) I can write something other than sex scenes in romance novels.

Colton: Thanks, Sloane. I think we'll take care of our own vows, though.

Sloane: Fine. Loki and I will be runners for the day. We'll handle all of the last-minute shit.

Colton: Love you all.

Now for the group that causes the chaos.

Colton: I'm getting married on Saturday.

Preston: …

Lochlan: Aye, mate. Another one bites the dust.

Easton: You always jump in headfirst.

Colton: Nothing has ever felt more right.

Halton: The girls are gathering at my house now.

Dexter: Prince Charming is at your disposal.

Trevor: You really shouldn't advertise that, Dex.

Lochlan: Will Tilly be there?

Preston: My Tilly? WTF, Lochlan? How do you know my sister-in-law?

Lochlan: Just asking, mate.

Preston: (I'm watching you GIF)

Lochlan: (laughing emoji)

Colton: Family court at 8 a.m. Wednesday morning.

Easton: We'll all be there.

Colton: Thanks.

Colton: I'm getting married!

Halton: Peter's all grown up.

Colton: (eye rolling emoji)

I turn off my phone then because the sheer number of messages flying back and forth between the coordinators of the Westbrook chaos will be in the thousands by dinner time.

I'm sitting at the kitchen island with a glass of wine when Winnie comes down the stairs looking rested and sexy as hell wrapped in a fluffy, white robe with messy hair I had fisted in my hands an hour ago.

"Hi," she says shyly, walking to me.

I open my arms and greedily take her in. "Hi. Lexi called. Wes and Ada James are having a blast. She's going to bring him home after dinner. She suggested a sleepover, but I thought it might be too much for his first time." I'm watching her eyes for any signs that I've overstepped. "Should I have asked you first?"

"No, you're right." She leans in, so I spread my legs, and she rests against me. "Remember how I told you I would mess up sometimes?"

I stiffen almost imperceptibly, but try to keep my nerves from showing. "Yeah."

"Having another parent making decisions will take some time, too, but I know you have his best interests at heart."

My body releases my shoulders in relief.

"I have to work tonight, anyway. Do you want me to call Beth to see if she can babysit?"

"No, why? I'll be here with him. And it's not babysitting when it's your own kid. Lexi likes to point that out every chance she gets."

She throws her head back and laughs. "Well, it's true."

"It is. And he is. I feel like he's mine."

Winnie cups my cheeks, searching my eyes. "I know you do, Colton. You have no idea how much that means to me."

"I hate that you're still working the night shift. You don't have—"

She cuts me off with a finger to my lips. "I need to work, Colton."

"It doesn't have to be at night. And I don't have to like it." I'm sulking, and she laughs while placing a sweet kiss on my lips. When she pulls away, it's my turn to tell some truths. "Did you mean it when you said you'd marry me soon?"

She's thoughtful, and I fear she's going to take it back, but then she nods. "I did."

"How soon?" My gaze is laser focused on hers.

A nervous laugh escapes as she rests her hands on my shoulders.

My hands land low on her hips, and I pull her in closer. I love holding her like this. "How's Saturday for you?"

Her eyes go wide, and I'm pretty sure she isn't breathing. "Th-This Saturday? How is that even possible?"

"Anything is possible when you're a Westbrook, Winnie.

Well, when you're a Westbrook or have sisters-in-law who know how to get shit done."

She closes her eyes and takes a deep breath, but she's smiling. "Colton. I don't know the first thing about planning a wedding. Let alone a Westbrook wedding."

"You can call it whatever you want, but it's our day. You could say you want a rodeo theme, and I'd make it happen."

"You're insane."

"I'm in love."

Her lips purse, but I see her trying to hold back the emotion.

"I texted the girls while you were sleeping. Whatever you want, they'll help make it happen. And if you don't know what you want, they'll help you figure it out. All you need to do is say yes."

She glances behind me. "That's five days from now, Colton."

"I know." I smirk. "I thought the girls would kill me if I gave them any less time."

Winnie tosses her hair back and laughs. It's happening more frequently now, and it makes my heart happy. She shrugs, resigned to my craziness. "Okay," she says. "We're getting married in five days."

Without warning, I pick her up and swing her around, kissing her hard. "Five days," I growl. "I can't wait."

When I set her down, her cheeks glow. "What are you doing to me, Mr. Westbrook?"

"Loving you for the rest of your life."

Her smile cuts me to my core. I'm the luckiest bastard on earth.

"I have to get ready for work."

"For now. We'll talk about it after we get married," I warn.

She places her hands on her hips. "I have to work, Colton. That won't change with my name."

"I know. But there are other plans we're going to make, too."

"Like what?"

"Like law school."

She pulls away and fidgets with the belt on her robe. "Sometimes dreams aren't meant to come true, Colton. I gave up on that one a long time ago."

Grabbing her arm, I pull her back to me. "You may have, but I didn't. After I lost you, I spent all that time imagining you in court. Every time I went to Boston, I walked around the court-houses hoping I'd run into you."

"What?" she gasps.

"I thought you were from Boston, so I made every excuse for almost two years to be in that city. When I first met you, I was in awe of you, Winnie. The way you spoke about school and how you would help people? That passion still lives inside of you, and I'm not ready to give up on it yet."

"Life is full of choices and responsibilities. I chose Wes. I'll never regret that, Colton. My dreams are on hold so I can give him everything he needs. I'm okay with that."

"I'm not. I've lived every dream I've ever had. It's your turn. We'll get Weston settled with us. Legally. Then we'll talk about our next steps."

She glances at her watch, and I know she's going to agree just so she can get ready for work, but I'm not willing to back down.

"Okay. We'll talk about it another time. I need to get ready so I'm not late."

"I know. I'll wait for Wes."

"Thank you. I-I love you."

If my smile gets any bigger, I think my face will split in two. "I love you, too, CC. Go before you're late."

My cheeks hurt by the time she's out of sight. I may approach life like a tornado, but she'll always be the eye of my storm.

*B*rothers

Halton: Colton, you troublemaking instigator.

Halton: Did you put liquid X-Lax into my vanilla again?

Halton: I fly that shit in from Mexico, dude. It's expensive.

Colton: (laughing emoji)

Halton: It's not funny. East has been shitting his brains out for two hours.

Colton: (laughing emoji)

Colton: You wanted to find out who was stealing your cookies from the cooling rack before they were finished, didn't you?

Halton: I ...

Halton: ...

Halton: Thanks

Preston: That's harsh, man.

Lochlan: Note to self. Never eat cookies around Colton.

Dexter: Easton is going to kill you if he ever gets off the shitter.

Colton: (Takes a bow GIF)

CHAPTER 36

*T*here's a chill in the air that only comes with a New England storm. The air smells crisp, like sheets hanging in the sun, but it's heavy and thick. My thumb rolls the engagement ring on my left hand as nerves get the better of me. Colton holds my right hand tightly in his. He's the picture of cool confidence, but I see his anxiety in his flared nostrils. I see it in the rigid line of his shoulders.

"We've got this, Winnie."

"Okay," I mumble. It's the best I can do.

We climb the steps to the courthouse, and familiar faces greet us, though I couldn't tell you any of their names.

"Miss Darling. Mr. Westbrook," one of the attorneys says in greeting.

Colton shakes hands with all of them, but never lets my hand go, so the most I can offer is a weird, left-handed wave.

"It seems opposing counsel has dropped their client, or at least put in paperwork to do so."

"What does that mean?" I can't let hope form yet.

"It means that our job just got a lot easier. We should head inside. We'll guide you through the process, but only speak up if the judge addresses you directly."

Colton and I nod and follow the team he and Preston assembled. Entering the courtroom, I do a double take when I see one side of the room is full. Every Westbrook adult is in attendance, and they're giving me varying versions of a thumbs-up. My hand clutches my heart, remembering how alone I was the first time I was here.

Colton's mom hurries to our side and wraps me in a maternal hug. "We've got you, sweetheart. Go kick some motherly ass."

I gasp, never in a million years expecting a curse word from Sylvie Westbrook.

"Are you okay?" Colton whispers.

"Uh huh."

"What's going on?" He glances around the room. When his gaze locks, I know he's found my father, but I honestly haven't even noticed him.

"The first time I was here, days after my mom died, I was by myself. These rows were all empty, and I'd never felt so alone in my life."

Colton turns his head to me with a soft smile that causes his eyes to crinkle at the corners. "Lexi likes to say we travel in packs." He peers over his shoulder. "We're stronger together, Winnie. So, however we travel, we travel with you now."

"All rise," a booming voice states, causing me to jump.

My heartbeat whooshes in my ears as people talk all around me. I focus on breathing. On my hand inside of Colton's. To the kind hand that lands on my shoulder from behind and gives me a squeeze.

Time stands still as the judge asks questions. Lawyers from both sides plead their case. A vision of Weston playing at home with his trains is the only thing that keeps me from falling apart.

There's a commotion to my left, and I blink to bring everything into focus. "What happened?" I whisper to Colton, who stares at me with concern.

"Your dad basically just told the judge he'd turn over parental rights to me for a million dollars," he hisses.

"He—"

"Is not very bright, and is probably drunk," Colton finishes.

Turning my attention to the judge, I catch just the tail end of her berating my father before having him removed from her courtroom. He curses, and fights against the officer, and when the door closes behind him, you could hear a pin drop.

"Miss Darling. Mr. Westbrook. Please approach the bench."

Colton leans into my ear. "It's okay, CC," he whispers and pulls me to standing.

My legs shake as we walk toward the judge, who sits impassively, not giving anything away.

"Miss Darling. You've been in my courtroom before."

I feel Colton's gaze on me. "Y-Yes, I have."

"How have you been?"

My head snaps up to find a kind smile. "Um, good?"

"Do you know why I remember you, Miss Darling?"

"No, your honor."

"In my line of work, I see a lot of unfortunate situations. Tragic, sad, sometimes mystifying," she says, glancing at the door my father just exited. "But every once in a while, someone comes through here with the heart of a giant. The kind of person you just know will make a difference in the world. You were what? Seventeen when you sat in the back of my courtroom, taking in everything you could learn? And then again, just a couple of years ago, when you stepped forward to take care of your brother. You're meant to do great things, Winnie Darling. I hope you know that."

I feel, not so much as see, Colton's smile next to me.

"And you, Mr. Westbrook. I've heard a lot about your family in recent years. Please tell me why you're here."

"Well, your honor, I'm here because I love Winnie and Weston, and I want to make them my family. I want to take care of them and support them, but I want to keep them with me most of all. I want to be Weston's father. Legally. I want to make sure he has the best care, the best education, the best life we can possibly give him. My family isn't what you'd consider traditional, your honor. Look around." Colton waves toward his family. "My family has been made by blood and by choice since before I was born.

"There have been stories about me in recent years, but like any gossip, there's rarely a speck of truth to it. Winnie and Wes came into my life and gave me meaning. They gave me direction. They gave me love. I can support them financially, but what they need more than anything is my love. I can do that, your honor. I can be the stay-at-home dad so Winnie can follow her dreams. I can pick up my life and move it to wherever they are because I have the means and the familial support to do that. I will uproot my entire life for them, because they're the most important pieces of me.

"With them, I fit. I'm here today because I want you to help us be the family we were meant to be. Winnie and Weston deserve to be Westbrooks, not because they need my name, my money, or my connections. They deserve to be Westbrooks because I've never known a better example of family than my own. They deserve to be part of that. I need them to be a part of that."

Colton blinks a few times and rolls his shoulders like he's coming out of a trance.

"Well, Mr. Westbrook, that was quite the impassioned plea." She leans forward and hands me a tissue for tears I didn't even realize were falling. "A stay-at-home dad, huh?" she says with a smirk. "That's a pretty tough job."

"I'll give them the world, your honor. If you'll help me."

She smiles. He smiles. The sick feeling in my stomach eases as she nods her head, reading something in front of her.

"There are steps you need to follow. I'm sure your army of attorneys over there has mentioned that."

"Yes, your honor," Colton replies for us.

"It doesn't happen overnight."

Colton and I glance nervously at each other.

"But, after what I've seen here today, I don't see any reason we can't begin the process."

"I'll be able to adopt Weston, and Winnie and I will be his legal guardians?" The hope blooming in his voice is like salve on an open wound.

"As I said, Mr. Westbrook, if you follow procedure, I don't see any reason you can't get your wish. And, Winnie?"

"Y-Yes, your honor?"

"I hope to see you back in my courtroom one day. Sitting at one of those tables, as an attorney." She says something to our team standing behind us, clicks her gavel, and I hear everyone rise.

What the hell just happened?

The Westbrooks surround us on every side. Hugs, kisses, and fist-bumps are shared. Preston barks orders to the lead attorney, and he's assured they're already filing the paperwork. It's a buzz of activity all around me, but I'm standing still.

"Do things always just happen for you?" I ask Colton, a little in awe of this man.

"When I decide I want something, yes."

"He's telling the truth," Halton says to my left. "Ever since he was a kid. He'd make a split-second decision and then see it through. Never once contemplating if there was a better way, or another option." He turns to Colton. "You've always known exactly what you've wanted, and you've gone for it. I'm proud of you, man."

Colton tackle hugs him, and I take in the true chaos that floats around this family shrouded in love and light. I should be ecstatic. I should be over the flipping moon. I just wish I could get rid of the lingering sense of dread that someone will take it all away from me and this fairytale we've been living in will become a nightmare I'll never get out of.

317

CHAPTER 37

COLTON

Waking up with Winnie in my arms is like a drug. I can't get enough of her.

"Are you smelling me again?" she asks groggily, her smile curling into my chest.

"Always, and in two days, you'll be Mrs. Westbrook."

She rolls over to stare up at me, and I see all her fears, hopes, and dreams in those gray eyes. With her hair splayed out on the crisp white sheets, she looks like an angel. My angel.

"Do you think I'll smell different after we get married?" Humor sparkles brightly in her gaze.

"I know you will," I state confidently.

"What? You're insane." She bats my chest playfully, but I capture her wrist and bring her palm to my lips.

Kissing the inside of her wrist, I wait for the gasp that always comes when I lick her pulse there. I curl a finger under her chin and pull her to me when I'm rewarded with the sound I love. "After we're married, you'll smell like mine." The way Winnie's expression softens when I use that commanding tone has me rock hard and desperate for her, but glancing at the clock, I know I'm already late. "Don't look at me like that, CC. I have a meeting to get to."

An evil grin shows her playful side. Airport Winnie is slowly resurfacing. "I can be quick."

Her hand slips beneath my boxer briefs, and I lift up onto my elbows. "Is that so? What if I can't be?"

"I can be very convincing," she whispers huskily as I feel her hot breath through the cotton of my boxers. When she mouths me through the material, my hips buck wildly. Winnie holds my thighs in place and lowers my boxers with her teeth.

"What happened to being quick?" I grind out and immediately regret it. Her lips curl around my tip with the suction of a fucking vacuum cleaner, and Winnie makes good on her word. I come down her throat with a grunt and a curse minutes later.

When I have my equilibrium back, I haul her up my body and roll her beneath me, but my gaze catches sight of the clock. Now I'm really fucking late, and Preston will kill me if I miss the appointments with the real estate agent he lined up.

"I don't have time to do what I want to do to you, sweetheart. But tonight? After Weston goes to bed, I'm going to taste you everywhere and drink you in until you're begging for mercy."

"I look forward to it. And, Colton," she quickly adds when I start to stand.

"Yeah?"

Something in her gaze has me lowering myself to her again. "In case I forget to tell you, I'm really excited about marrying you. I mean, I want to. I'm happy, too. You've given me something I never thought I'd ever be able to have."

"What's that, baby?"

"Trust. In love, in life. In you. You've given me something I thought was beyond repair. You've made me feel and believe. You've given me the fairytale, Colton."

It's like she harnessed the sun after a month-long night.

"Winnie Darling, soon to be Westbrook, you are by far the best part of me. And our fairytale is just beginning, sweetheart." Fuck the time. I capture her lips in a kiss that's equal parts desire, love, and hope. I kiss her until she's panting and writhing beneath me, and when I pull away, her lips are swollen and red and still taste like cherry fucking cola. "I think I have to quit my job." I keep a straight face as long as I can.

"What? What do you mean?"

"It's getting in the way of making love to my fiancée whenever I want."

Relief floods her face, and she laughs out loud. With a chaste kiss, I leave her panting on the bed and head to the shower just as we hear Wes through the monitor. I freeze in the doorway, torn. Mornings have become our time; I hate missing even one of them.

"Colton. It's okay. Go get ready. I've got Wes. It wasn't that long ago I was all he had. He'll manage without you for a couple of hours."

"Doesn't mean I have to like it," I grumble.

Her laughter follows her down the hall.

How the fuck did I get so lucky?

∼

The luck of the Irish my ass. Today has turned out to be one clusterfuck after another. I'm standing in the middle of an abandoned motel with a realtor who knows as much about real estate as I know about brain surgery.

"Do you know the specs on this one?" I bite out. My patience with this woman wore out somewhere in the last building. I'm a consummate professional, but Lindsey is on my last goddamn nerve. *Where the hell did Preston find this woman?*

"Specs?" she asks, smacking her gum.

Reaching into my pocket, I pull out my phone only to see that yet again, there's no service. Every building she's shown me today has been one disaster after another, and I'm about to fire her ass.

Pinching the bridge of my nose, I take a calming breath and

nearly lose my breakfast. The stench is worse than our frat house basement after a party. And we had some epic parties. "Miss Tannery."

"Lindsey, please, Colton." With pouty lips, she steps closer to me.

My gaze does an unwilling scan of her body, and I notice for the first time how she's dressed. Her attire is more suited for a skanky club than taking a businessman out searching for potential property, and I narrow my eyes as her intent becomes clear.

She mistakes the change in my demeanor for interest, and when she's close enough, she wraps her snake-like arms around my neck, attempting to pull me in for a kiss. My hand flies up just in time to block her face with my palm and push her away.

"What do you think you're doing?" I caution, but apparently, she's used all her brain cells to get her horrid shade of lipstick lined on her nasty lips, because she throws herself at me again. I'm so stunned I can't say anything for a moment. Never, not once in all my years at The WB, have I been propositioned in such a disgusting manner.

Miss Tannery shimmies her shoulders and with lightning speed grabs my hand and places it on her ass. My stomach rolls, and I gag before anger rules every action. With a gentle shove, I step back. The venom in my gaze should stop her, but she continues to reach for me.

"Colton. It doesn't have to mean anything. We can just have a little fun."

Her perfume is nauseating. I'd thought so in her shitty car, but now it's as if it's burned all my nose hairs and I can't get it off me.

"What doesn't have to mean anything?" I roar. "What the fuck are you doing?" Glancing around, I search for cameras. Someone is punking me. That has to be it. "Preston?" I scream. "This isn't funny. You've gone too far."

"It's just us here, Colton," she coos.

"Mr. Westbrook." I seethe.

"No one has to know." Her crooked smile has a hint of jealousy I didn't notice before, and a sickening feeling threatens the contents of my stomach.

"What agency are you from?"

"Let's not discuss that right now." I think her words are meant to sound seductive, but they ring in my ears like my worst nightmare.

Keeping my gaze averted, I force my voice to take on a menacing tone when my entire being is actually terrified. "What agency are you from?"

"You won't even look at me?" she screeches, and I know nothing good can come from this.

"Fuck this," I mutter. I don't care if I have to walk twenty miles back to town. This crazy bitch is not about to ruin the best thing that's ever happened to me.

"Where are you going?" She stomps her foot, and I can't believe I let myself get roped into this position again.

I should have known after the second building. Fuck me for giving her the benefit of the doubt. I need to get to Winnie. Talk to Preston. Get the fuck away from psycho realtor Barbie.

Blood rushes in my ears and I think I might be sick. Not again. This cannot happen again.

I've been walking on a dirt road for ten minutes when Lindsey's car goes speeding by, kicking up dust. She's followed by an oddly familiar black Toyota that I can't place. That's what happens in small towns. You unconsciously notice what kind of car everyone drives.

As they disappear into the distance, I pick up my pace. My phone says it's after five. I've been gone, out of contact all day. My meetings this morning with Preston ran late, and by the time I got to the address he gave me to meet Lindsey Tannery, it was Weston's nap time. I had hoped Winnie would be napping too, so I didn't call.

323

I should have called.

Now I'm hating myself. I don't even know if I'm going in the right direction. I haven't seen a house in miles. The dirt road drags on forever, lined with trees that offer no point of reference. This town isn't that big. Eventually, I have to get out of hell and find another person. Right?

I've been walking for almost forty minutes when my phone dings. *Thank Christ.*

Winnie: Hey... I just realized you call me CC and I don't have a nickname for you.

Winnie: Anyway, I got called in to cover an extra shift. Since I'm taking tomorrow and Saturday off for the wedding, I need the hours.

Winnie: I tried to call, but it went straight to voicemail.

Winnie: I hope everything's okay.

Winnie: Lexi is going to watch Weston until you get home.

Winnie: Colton? I'm getting nervous. Just let me know you're okay, I guess. Okay?

Winnie: I'm at work, but I have my phone. I'm really getting worried, though.

Fucking hell.

Colton: Hey, CC. I'm sorry. I was out viewing potential buildings and didn't have service.

Colton: The day was ...

What Colton? I can't tell her this over text. Pressing her name in my contacts, I call her, but it goes straight to voicemail.

Winnie: Hi! I'm so happy to hear from you. I was worried. I can't answer my phone right now. The doctor on call has a thing about personal calls.

Winnie: Are you okay?

Colton: Yeah. I'm good, baby.

Colton: I love you.

Winnie: I love you, too.

Winnie: I'll see you in the morning.

Welcome to the longest night of my freaking life.

Pulling up Preston's contact, I stab his number with so much force I almost knock the damn thing out of my hand. I don't even wait for him to say hello. As soon as I hear him pick up, I lay into him. "Where the fuck did you find Lindsey?"

"Colton?"

"She didn't know a goddamn thing about real estate. She was dressed like a prostitute, and she made a pass at me. More than a pass, Preston. She fucking threw herself at me in an abandoned motel somewhere outside of town and now I'm walking my goddamn ass down a dirt road trying to get home to Weston and I can't tell Winnie about this yet because she's at work. This isn't the kind of thing I tell my fiancée with trust issues over the phone, Preston."

By the time I'm done, I'm sweating, and my voice is hoarse.

"Colton? Calm down. I don't know what you're talking about. Lindsey hit on you? Where are you?"

"She tried to stick her tongue down my throat, Preston." I'm all out of fucks at this point. I'm waving my hands wildly because he doesn't seem to get how messed up this is.

"Gross. She's like seventy years old."

My body goes rigid, and ice fills my veins. "What did you just say?"

"Lindsey Tannery of Tannery and Associates. She must be seventy years old. Are you sure you didn't—"

"The woman who showed me around today, Preston. The woman who introduced herself as Lindsey Tannery was not seventy years old. She was maybe twenty-five, smelled like cheap perfume, and had as many brain cells as my left nut after I jack off. What the hell is going on?"

"Where are you?"

Glancing at my phone, I share my location with him.

"Preston ..."

"I'm on my way."

CHAPTER 38

WINNIE

"*I* hear congratulations are in order."

Like a shark circling its prey, my frenemy catches me off guard. "Claire. What do you want?"

I'm in the break room grabbing another cup of coffee. I'm not used to working doubles, and with one hour left in my sixteen-hour shift, dealing with Claire is not high on my priority list.

"I just came by to see how you're doing." Her voice is sickeningly sweet, causing the hairs on the back of my neck to stand on end. "Your fiancé is quite the man." She trips over the word fiancé like her tongue got stuck in glue.

"He is."

Keep it short and to the point, Winnie. She has no power over you anymore. I walk past her, and she catches my arm. "Are you sure you want to do this, sweetie? I mean, the way he gets around."

"You don't know anything about him," I hiss, taking a side-step so I'm in her space. I'm taller, and bigger than she is, something she's never let me live down, but right now, I use every inch of my body to intimidate her.

She doesn't back down. "I know enough," she says, brushing nonexistent lint off her scrubs. "I mean, anyone that parties like he does and gets caught by paparazzi is sure to make excellent husband material, right?" She laughs, and it sounds eerie so close. When she snaps her gum, I jump, and the small flinch gives her the courage to push me even more. "Aren't you worried you won't be enough for him? I mean, you've never been able to satisfy a man. That's why they always end up with me. First, there was poor Teddy in junior high. Then Travis. You weren't even enough for your own father. Winnie," she says my name so condescendingly I see red, "you didn't really think you could keep a man like Colton, did you?"

"I'm not doing this with you, Claire. Colton is a good man who loves me. Nothing you can do or say can change that."

I step around her, but her words hit harder than a punch to the gut. "Not even if he slept with me?"

Her sneer is straight off a villain when I glance over my shoulder. Because she is the villain in my story. In my life, she's always been the one trying to take me down. Hurt me because it makes her feel better about her own pathetic life. Well, not this time.

"Colton wouldn't be caught dead with you, Claire. That's a fact."

"Is that so?" She confidently waves a manilla envelope in the air and my world tilts on its axis.

"What is that?" I'm proud my voice sounds strong because I'm dying inside. Begging, pleading for it not to be what she's insinuating.

"You work, and work, and work, Winnie. For what? A shitty apartment, and an idiot brother? You've always thought you'd be the first one out of this town, riding out on your high horse. But look at you. You're no better than the rest of us. You've just gotten fatter, sadder, and more pathetic. I almost felt sorry for you when I heard the news. Winnie Darling marrying a West-brook? Are you knocked up? Is that why you're so fat? Is that how you trapped him? You may force his hand at marrying you, but he'll never be faithful because you'll never be enough. You've never been enough, have you?"

My hand twitches, and I realize it's the first time in my life I've ever wanted to seriously injure someone. Instead, I clench my fists at my sides because hitting her, although it would feel amazing, would probably land me in jail. I won't give her that satisfaction. I bite my tongue and wait for her to say what she came here to say.

"I'll hand it to you. You picked the sexiest Westbrook. The way he moves?" She pinches her fingers to her lips and kisses them. "Chef's kiss."

"What do you want, Claire?" My lip trembles against my will.

She sticks out a pouty lip. "Oh, dear. Did I hurt your feelings? We're friends, Winnie. I'm just here to warn you, is all. I wouldn't want you getting your heart broken again over someone who can't and won't stay faithful to you."

I stand completely still and say nothing because I know it will piss her off, and I'm right.

"Don't you want to see what I came to show you?" she hisses. "I will say Colton is probably the best fuck I've ever had."

My hand moves involuntarily to my chest. It's like she shot me through the heart. But it can't be true. It's not true. Colton wouldn't do that to me.

"He has a dirty mouth, that one. Did you really think you were the only one he was whispering filthy promises to at night, Winnie? He may have moved you into his house because an insta family is a great PR move, don't you think? But he'll never settle for you. If it's not me," she waves the file around again, "it'll just be someone else. And someone else after that. You're not special, Wendalyn. You've never been special." She spits the word special, then tosses the file on the small table.

She leaves me standing there, unblinking. Barely breathing.

And shaking so hard my legs give out the second she rounds the corner.

It's not true. It can't be true. Colton said to trust him. I have to trust him. My gaze zones in on the file like it's a living, breathing thing. I'm hyperventilating as I lift myself from the floor and my vision becomes blurry as tears threaten. *Trust him.* I move closer to the table, eyeing it as if it will jump out and bite me. *Trust him.* I collapse into the chair, my hand inches away from it. My fingers burn as they land on the tan card-stock. *Trust him.* I forget to breathe as my index finger flicks the cover open and I jump back in shock at the pictures staring up at me and all the trust in the world can't make up for this.

Trust is no longer in my vocabulary.

~

"Winnie? Honey? Are you sure this is what you want to do?" Beth asks, opening the door to my old apartment above her garage.

I don't know how long I sat in the break room, but eventually, Colton started calling and I gathered up my stuff and moved to my car. I drove around until I ended up at Beth's house and begged her to pick up Weston.

"Yes, please. Just take him to the library until you hear from me."

"What should I tell Colton?" Worry laces every word.

"Nothing. Tell him nothing. I'll be in touch with him soon."

My face is puffy, and my eyes are rimmed red, but I have no more tears to cry. Beth pats my cheek and watches me with concern.

"I'm okay, Beth. But we'll need to stay here for a while, if that's okay?"

"You know you're always welcome here, Winnie. I just hope you're not making a terrible mistake."

"It's too late for that, Beth. I'll be okay, though. Please, go get Wes."

She shakes her head sadly, but heads back down the stairs. Soon after, I hear her car pull out of the driveway. Her house is less than a ten-minute drive to Colton's, so I expect I'll hear from him soon. I take a shower to gather myself. When I exit, I have a missed text.

Colton: CC? Is everything okay? Beth just picked up Wes, but she didn't know why? Are you stuck at work?

Colton: Weston would have been fine here with me.

Colton: Talk to me, Winnie.

Colton: I'm running over to Ashton's house. I'll be back in an hour.

That's all the time I need. I dress quickly and head to Colton's home.

∾

*B*efore Colton can return, I race around the home I once shared with him, collecting the necessities. I know I'll have to see him eventually, but today is not that day.

I spin in circles with an armful of clothes because I have no plan. *Think, Winnie. You need a bag.* Yes, a bag. But not one of his. I can't take anything I didn't move in here with. Except maybe a few of Weston's trains. Surely, Colton would want him to have them. This is already going to wreck the little guy.

Fuck. Why did I ever let Colton Westbrook into our lives? We were fine before. We were just fine.

A sob breaks free because even I don't believe my lies right now, but I keep moving. Without thinking, I cut through the dining room on my way to grab Weston's belongings and I'm hit by a wall of emotion.

Our wedding. My wedding is laid out before me like a road map. The Westbrook women did the unthinkable. They pulled

331

together a dream wedding I never even knew I wanted in less than a week. A wedding I'll never get to have.

More tears have me tripping up the stairs. I'm manic in my movements, propelled forward by adrenaline. I just have to get my shit and get out. I can break down later, but I know I'll never recover once I do.

CHAPTER 39

COLTON

"You've never seen her before?"

"No. I've never seen her before, Ash. You know what this is."

"I need more information."

"Ashton," I scream, feeling the tension between us thicken. "You know he did this. You know he put her up to it and it's only a matter of time before it hurts me or someone I love, and I can promise you, if this comes back to hurt Winnie or Weston there will be no coming back for you and me."

"If Macomb is behind this, I will take care of it," he rasps.

"Like you've taken care of him before? Not good enough, Ash. I have a family now. Coming after me to hurt you in whatever fucked-up game you've got going on will not work for me anymore."

He moves like he's going to come at me, then backs off. "It's not a game, Colt. And I never meant for you to get hurt. You don't understand the damage he did to his own daughter. I need her to have the opportunity to bring him in."

"She's had years, Ashton. Years! And she hasn't done it. She doesn't want to. She doesn't want to see you either. She made that abundantly clear. You have to let this go and do what is right for our family," I roar.

"You don't think that's what I've been doing my entire life, Colton? I've given my life for this family. I never had a choice. I'm doing things the way they must be done."

"Why? Why are there still secrets, Ash? What the hell—"

An alarm sounds, and Ash turns to a wall of screens just in time to see GG walking up the steps. "Jesus," he mutters while pressing a button on his desk that unlocks his front door. Within seconds, we hear her calling out.

"Colton? Ya here? Get yer ass out here and talk to me."

"I'm serious, Ash. For our sake, end this."

He nods and follows me out of his office.

"There ya are. Now listen. Not sure what happened, but Wendy just burst through that front gate like her heart was shattered."

My glare turns on Ashton, but he doesn't flinch.

"What do you mean?" he asks GG instead.

"Well, I was walking up the path and saw her running around like a ticked off chicken, shoving bags into the back of her car like she'd robbed a bank."

Anxiety unfurls in my gut. "Where was she going?"

GG shrugs. "She took off before I could get to her."

Spinning in place, I take off for the door, but she stops me. "Colton."

I snap my gaze to her. This crazy, tarot card reading witch has some pearl of wisdom to impart on me. Knowing she's the driving force in all my brothers' happiness, I give her my full attention.

"Well, you're not a Lost Boy anymore, are ya, Pan?"

I glance at my watch, and she cackles in that way she has.

"No, GG. I'm not. I've never felt more found in all my life. I fit with Winnie and Wes. It's like I've been waiting for them for my entire life."

In my periphery, Ashton watches on. A touch of sadness crosses his scarred face.

"I thought so. But you need to remember that Wendy is still finding her way. She's spent her life lookin' after others. Takin' care of herself doesn't come naturally to her."

"I know that, GG. I'm trying to take care of her, but now I'm worried I've screwed up somehow."

"Oh, Pan. I think you're the only one of my boys to do it all right. I have a feelin' Wendy's gonna need a little push and a big reminder."

"A reminder? Of what?"

"That you're not going anywhere, Pan. She learned a long time ago if she didn't trust anyone, she wouldn't get hurt. She stopped letting people in and worked extra hard to do it all herself."

"She can't get hurt if she's only depending on herself," I mutter.

"Whatever's crawled up her ass today will work itself out."

"If I remind her I'm not going anywhere."

"You got it, Pan. Now go on. I'm not sayin' it's gonna be easy, but my money's on you."

"Thanks, GG." I give her a quick hug but can't bring myself to glance Ashton's way. I pause at the door when I hear GG turn on him, though.

"Now, it's your turn, Hero."

"M-Me?" he sputters.

"Yeah, you. Don't ya think it's time to come out of the dark? Your family doesn't need you the same way they did before. They just need *you*. All of you. Even the parts that are buried and hurtin'."

"I've got work to do, GG. Did you need anything else?" Ashton asks coldly.

"Nope. Not a thing." She steps into the hall and catches me eavesdropping.

"Did you just give him a nickname?"

"Pfft. Ashton's story is still being written. Don't you worry 'bout him, though. Love has a funny way of working out sometimes." And cryptic as ever, GG struts out the front door onto the pathway that connects all our homes.

There are no missed calls or messages when I check my phone. *Winnie! What have you done?* Jumping in my car, I head home to see if she left a note.

There, on my kitchen island, sits a pile of photographs and her ring. Rage is the first thing that comes to mind because I recognize the woman in them. It's the woman claiming to be Lindsey. I snap a picture and send it to my brothers.

Colton: Winnie's gone.

Colton: None of these are real. Who the fuck is this woman?

Preston: …

Ashton: Working on it.

Halton: Ry says her name is Claire.

Why do I know that name? Fucking Claire.

Colton: Claire Milford? The woman who slept with Winnie's live-in boyfriend?

Halton: Yes, and she's not sure?

Colton: Where the fuck do I find her?

New Message

Rylan: I think she lives in the townhomes on Railroad Street. She works at the hospital.

Scooping up the folder, I race back to my car. Ashton is standing beside it.

"What now, Ash?"

"If Macomb had anything to do with this, you have my word it'll be the last thing he ever does. Pacen or no Pacen." Whatever he's hiding, I can see it cuts deep.

"If I've lost Winnie …"

"Since when have you ever lost anything, Colty?" A smirk I haven't seen from him in years appears on his face. "You make choices and see them through. Rules, people, obstacles be damned. You're not about to let a little miscommunication ruin your happily ever after, are you?"

I gape at him. I've been bitching about the communication issue in this family for as long as I can remember, and the D-bag just reverse psyched me. Tossing him my keys, I hide my grin. "You'd better drive. I'm too keyed up. We might not make it down the mountain."

He catches them easily. "Railroad Street or Winnie first?"

"Railroad Street. I'm not getting Winnie back until I have the full story."

~

*F*inding Claire proved easier than either of us had imagined. As we drive down the street, we see her sitting on the front stoop in between Jason Darling's legs. When he leans down to kiss her, I almost vomit.

"What the ever living, what?" Ash mutters beside me.

"Pull over," I sigh. "This will be fast."

Ash reaches across the console and holds me in place. "Think before you swing."

"Got it."

Jason notices us first and scrambles drunkenly to his feet as we exit the car. When Claire sees me, she rolls her eyes.

"I suggest you get inside. Now," I growl.

"This is my house. You can't tell me what to do," she replies stubbornly.

I take a menacing step forward. "You, Claire, are a despicable excuse for a human being, and I will see to it that you get what's coming to you."

Ashton steps beside me, a silent warning to reel it in, but her eyes go wide when she sees him, and she backs up toward the door.

"Looking like a monster has its advantages," he mumbles.

"You don't—"

337

He holds a hand up to cut me off. "Not the time, Colt." He nods his head toward Jason and Claire.

"Unless you want me to bring the full force of my family down on you, your career, and your miserable excuse for a life, I suggest you get the fuck inside, Claire. Now."

She glances between Darling and me a few times before scurrying into the building like the rat she is.

All the rage I have built up inside of me unleashes as I lurch forward, pinning Darling to the door with my forearm at his throat. Staring into glassy eyes, I search for understanding. How could this man treat my Winnie like a piece of trash? But he's dead inside. Hollow eyes blink unseeing.

"Hey. I'm gonna, I'm gonna sue—"

I press a little harder into his throat to restrict his airway.

"Why did you go after Weston? Why did Claire give my fiancée those pictures?" I don't know how, but I just know they're related.

He grunts and kicks his legs, but I don't ease up.

"Answer the question."

Turning my gaze toward my brother, I see something I've never seen in him before. He's cold and calculating. This is what years of working for a secret government agency has turned my baby brother into, and I hate it.

"Whatever," Jason wheezes. "Some guy. Some guy was gonna give me a shit ton …" He wheezes again, and I let up a little so he can speak. "He was gonna give me a ton of money if I found a way to hurt you."

"Hurt him how?" Ash fumes.

"I ain't into killing no one. Nothing like that. Just get to him, ya know?"

"By hurting your children," I surmise. "You were going to hurt your children's chances at happiness for a quick buck."

"I've never been a father. No sweat off my back. Then that little cunt went and—"

My fist connects with his face, but I don't stop. I punch

until he's curled into a ball, sobbing and bloody. I punch until Ashton pulls me off him.

"I'll make them all pay for this," my brother vows. But I'm not counting on his promises anymore.

"I'll believe it when I see it," I huff, staring at the two of them. "How the hell have we gotten here, Ash? I'm not a fighter. The Westbrooks don't mess around in barroom brawls and fucked up fathers. What happened in our lives to put us on this path? Are we ever going to break free of it?"

Ash stands with his hands on his hips. He doesn't make eye contact as he speaks. "I'm working on it, Colt. I'm trying."

I let out an exasperated breath. "One day you're going to learn, Ash. You'll learn that this ride you're on? It won't stop until you let us in. Our family doesn't work this way, nor should it. When you're ready to let go of whatever hate you're holding onto, we'll be here to help you break free. Until then, I don't even know what to say to you anymore. I'll send East to pick you up."

He doesn't lift his gaze. I have a fiancée to bring home, so I leave him to clean up this mess.

CHAPTER 40

COLTON

"*O*pen the door, Winnie. I know you're in there. I can hear Weston."

Her front door snaps open with such force it bounces off the wall. I catch it before it swings back and knocks her to the ground. Winnie stands before me, all red-eyed and rage-filled to her tipping point with pain.

I step forward, and she stubbornly stands her ground, so I keep walking until she's forced to step back and let me in. "I can't do this with you right now, Colton. I'm trying to get Wes settled, and it hasn't been easy." Her chin trembles even as she juts it out in defiance.

"Bring him home, Winnie." I keep my voice calm, even though I want to scream at her for not trusting me.

"We are home. You need to leave. I left everything you'll need on your island." Winnie turns away from me, but I follow.

"I got it."

"Then what are you doing here? You can't seriously expect me to go back to your house? Sleep in your bed after … after what you did."

Peering over my shoulder, I see Wes playing with his trains. It's a small space, but he hasn't noticed me yet, so I crowd

341

Winnie into the small bathroom, positioning us so she can still see our little boy.

"Please don't do this, Colton. I need you to leave."

"When I found you again, Winnie, I asked you to do one thing for me. One. Thing. What did I ask you to do?" My voice is gravelly. It belays my fear, anger, and anxiety that this will be the one thing I can't fix.

"Trust you," she spits, vitriol coating every word.

"The one person in this world I needed to trust me, to believe in me, couldn't do it."

"I did trust you, Colton. And look what you did? H-How could you do that? Why would you do it?" Her shoulders sag and shake with silent sobs. "Why are you here, Colton? Was it a game to you? Find out if you can get the broken girl with trust issues to fall in love with you?"

"You know me better than that," I grind out through clenched teeth.

"Do I? Because I thought I did, but looking at you now, all I see is a stranger. I need you to leave. If you cared about me at all, you'd leave me alone."

"I'm not leaving until I get what I came for," I say evenly. Even though there's barely a foot of space between us, I haven't touched her yet.

"What, Colton? What did you come for? Why are you here?" Her face drops to her hands, and tears spill out through the cracks in her fingers.

"CC. I promised you if you trusted me, I would never leave you. I'm here because I keep my promises."

She shakes her head and won't look at me. "I saw the pictures. I saw them, and I know I'll never be able to trust you again. You said it yourself a relationship can't work without trust."

"I have enough trust for the both of us."

"Are you insane?" She's openly sobbing now. "Is this fun for you? Do you like seeing me cry? How badly you hurt me?"

Wes lifts his head at her raised voice. He squeals when he sees me and runs toward us. I back out of the bathroom to give us more space, scoop down to pick him up, and breathe him in deeply when he buries his little face in my neck.

I hold up the folder again, and she flinches like I hit her. "Look at these again, Winnie. Really look at them, and then tell me if you trust me."

"I've seen enough—"

"Look. At. Them. Winnie. Look at them and count my hands in the top one. The second one looks bad, but that's because Claire pretended to be my realtor and set me up. With your father's help. Unfortunately, the bottom picture is of me from over a year ago, but Ash proved those women drugged me. Someone just did a bad job photoshopping Claire's face onto all of them."

I see the fear in her eyes, but I'll never leave her.

"Are you hyperventilating? I don't know what to do about that. I'll call Em—"

She holds up a finger to silence me and sinks to the hard floor. I can only watch on in horror. The scene before me is too reminiscent of the first time I stepped foot in this place.

"I hate this, CC. I hate seeing you like this." I slowly, cautiously, lower myself to the floor beside her. I'm trying to position Wes on my side, but he seems to be part monkey as he wraps his little body around me like a vice. "Open the folder, CC."

A garbled cry bubbles in her throat, and I pull her into me. "Open it," I command.

In slow motion, she reaches down between us and lifts the cover. I notice the second she sees the third hand in the poorly photoshopped picture. She flips to the next, and finally the last with trembling fingers. Her hands cover her mouth as tears cascade down her splotchy, but still beautiful, face.

"Y-You came for me."

"For the both of you. I always will."

"You stayed." She sounds numb, and I'm second guessing my decision to have her open the folder.

I lean forward and lift her chin. "You're worth staying for, Winnie. You own me, sweetheart."

"But I didn't trust you." Her entire body quakes with her words and I can't take the space between us for another second. Shifting Wes to my side, I drag Winnie over so I can cradle her between my legs.

Not wanting to be left out, Wes climbs forward and sits in Winnie's lap. He's the engine, Winnie's the heart, and I'm the caboose. I'll always pick up the slack. With Wes curled up on Winnie, she rests her back to my front, and I place my chin on her head with a contented sigh.

"No, you didn't trust me. But you know what you did do, Winnie?" She shakes her head, and I feel her tears land on my hands around her waist. "You told me that trusting would be hard for you. You told me you'd make mistakes. I listened, so here I am. Calling you on your mistake. Proving to you that I'll never leave, and also saying I'm sorry."

"*You're* sorry? For what?" She turns her head to look at me, her ear resting on my chest, and I know she can hear my erratic heartbeat.

"For not forcing Ashton to do something about Macomb sooner. For putting myself in a position like that with Claire. For giving you any reason to doubt me."

She shakes her head, ready to argue with me, but I silence her with a gentle kiss. Weston laughs, and claps like it's the end of a Hallmark movie.

"I'll always do better for you, Winnie. I'll catch you when you fall. I'll be the man worthy of spending the rest of my life with you. If you'll have me."

"What are you saying?"

"I'm saying, marry me, Winnie Darling. Tomorrow, as planned. Be my wife. Be my heart. Be my everything."

"Just like that?" she hiccups. "You're not mad at me? You don't want to yell at me for not believing in you? In us?"

"Oh, I was mad, Winnie. But do you remember when we first met, and I told you that my family had a communication problem?"

"Yeah." She furrows her eyebrows, and I kiss the V it causes between her eyes.

"Remember I told you that I overcompensate because of it?"

She's nodding, but still not understanding.

"My family has taught me a lot of amazing things, but the most important thing is how to love, and what it means to love. We will have fights, sweetheart. We will want to throw things at each other sometimes. And sometimes, we'll have to walk away before we kill each other. I don't know if you're aware, but I can be pretty annoying sometimes." She laughs, and my chest begins to unknot itself. "But through all the fights, and miscommunications, there will always be love. I'll fight for it every day. And on the days you question it, I'll love you double. When I met you at the airport, I told you I wasn't ready for my Wendy. But I was wrong, and I knew it the second I saw you. You were always meant to be mine, Winnie. I'm ready to leave Neverland."

"You still love me?"

"Oh, baby. If you have to question it, I'm not doing a very good job of showing you. Yes, Winnie. I love you. I love you today, tomorrow, and next year. I'll love you when you're old and gray. I'll love you until my last breath."

"I love you so much, Colton. I've never felt pain like this before. Losing my mom was the hardest thing I've ever gone through, but losing you …"

"Shh." Her sobs make it hard to understand her, but I don't think I can handle a description of how much those assholes hurt her. Not when I'm so raw and vulnerable. So, instead, I shush her. I kiss her. I savor holding her until her breathing evens out, and Weston's sleepy babbles create the soundtrack to my future. "Come on," I say, lifting Weston into my arms and offering her a hand. "Let's go home."

"Lub Coto. My thupa thupa."

Winnie leans in to kiss his chubby cheek. "Mine too, Wes. Mine too."

CHAPTER 41

ASHTON

*T*o: Pacen@EnvisionSecurities.com

      From: Ashton@EnvisionSecurities.com

Subject: Time to let go

Dear Pacen,

I know you're still checking these emails because I'm smart like that and can follow the trail. I'm not even expecting you to reply anymore, though. I checked this morning. I've sent you 327 messages. You've returned only one.

I've been tempted over the years to call the number. The number I know you'll answer, but I don't. I'm trying to respect your wishes even though I'm not sure how to run this company without you. I hate my father with the passion of a thousand suns for putting me in this position, but I hate myself more for getting you involved.

We were too young to see and do what was asked of us. I was too scared to do it alone. For that, I'm sorry.

You've been my best friend for over half my life. I never knew you wanted more until that night. The night that changed us. Ruined us. Broke us. I'm sorry for it all.

Our fathers took more than our childhood. They took our future. My father fighting to do what's right. Your father fighting to do what's easy. I wish we'd known then that we're more than their mistakes.

I've been waiting for you, Pacen, because I thought for you to heal, you needed to face the monster that tried to destroy you. I wanted to give you that chance, but maybe seeing your father pay for what he's done isn't how you heal. I just wish I knew how to make us right again. Your friendship has always mattered to me, Pacen.

Anyway, I'm writing today to tell you that your father is no longer a threat. He can't hurt you or my family ever again.

I hope that brings you some sort of peace.

~Ash

I hit send, then turn up the volume on the flat screen TV that takes up an entire wall of my office. I watch as Macomb is escorted into a black SUV in handcuffs and chains around his legs.

Every news outlet in the world has picked up this story. Pacen would have heard about it eventually, but I felt like I owed it to her to let her know it was my doing. I put him away as much for her as for my family. With the evidence I've given the FBI, he'll never be a free man again.

Now, I can only hope Colton will forgive me. Family is all I have left.

EPILOGUE

COLTON

"*Y*ou ready for this?" Lochlan asks at my side. He's standing up for me next to all of my brothers because they couldn't get over themselves long enough for me to choose a best man. So, I chose none of them.

"Loch, I've been waiting for her my whole life." I turn to my friend, who's apparently shooting laser beams from his eyeballs. Following his line of sight, I punch him in the arm.

"What the hell is going on with you and Tilly?"

Without a care in the world, he shamelessly glares at my sister-in-law. "Nothing," he eventually grunts. "We've just run into each other a few times."

"So you've said. Remember what you told me the first time I saw your sister?"

Another grunt from the neanderthal. If it wasn't so close to home, I'd laugh. I've never seen Loch this worked up before.

"Well, the same holds true for my family. Preston would kick your ass if you hurt her."

"I'm not going to hurt her," he mumbles, just as the music begins to play.

My jaw drops to the floor as the band plays "Build Me Up

Buttercup". Weston comes barreling down the aisle with Lexi running close behind. When they get to me, I scoop him up.

"Sorry," Lexi groans. "He caught sight of you and took off."

I kiss her on the cheek. "It's okay. He should be down here with us, anyway."

She hugs us both and steps to the other side of the aisle as all my sisters-in-law dance toward us. My own personal flash mob and it has tears spilling down my face. Laughter and extreme love causing all my emotions to overflow.

"At least I dodged that bullet," Lexi stage whispers.

"That just means I get a private showing at home," Easton replies behind my back.

"Guys! Cut the shit. This is my day."

"Sit. Sit," Weston mimics.

"Ah, that's a bad word, buddy. We can't—" I forget how to use my tongue when I spot Winnie standing at the end of the aisle with Preston. He escorts her down the shimmering row and tears continue to stream down my face. Weston pats my cheek, and I laugh.

I'd wanted a big wedding, but I was too impatient to make her mine. And since all my brothers and sisters are standing up here with us, that leaves very few people sitting in the rows of chairs. Looking out at them now, I couldn't care less about any of it. Winnie and the little man in my arms are all that matter.

When Preston hands her off with a kiss on the cheek and a shake of my hand, something changes in me. Staring left to right and then focusing on the only two people that matter to me today, I find my place in the world. Where I was always meant to be. Where I'll spend the rest of my life showing my love in every way I can.

After the events of yesterday, we chose to go with the traditional vows, which is probably for the best because I could barely get those out without crying. I've never been so happy in all my life.

I hand Weston over to Lexi when it's time for the rings.

Winnie's wearing a smile I've never seen before, and it warms my blood.

Lochlan hands me the small box holding our rings and jumps back out of the way. I give him a curious glance, but he gives nothing away.

"Do you have the rings?" the reverend asks.

I nod and open the box. It explodes in a cloud of fine glitter that covers both Winnie and me. I turn quickly, ready to punch Lochlan in the face for ruining her day, when her voice catches my ear through the laughter surrounding us.

"Colton. Hey, look at me." I tear my pissed off gaze away from Loch and find my lady laughing with everyone else. "They ran it by me first. It's okay. They didn't ruin anything, but they knew today would be the only day you're preoccupied enough to get their revenge."

I stare at her, coated in a mist of sparkles that truly make her look like an angel, and I laugh. I laugh until my side hurts. "You were in on it?"

She nods, laughing.

"You know I always get my revenge, right?"

"I'm counting on it." She winks.

We slip the simple bands onto each other's fingers, and the reverend announces us husband and wife. "You may kiss the bride."

It's like I'm in a trance watching Winnie, but the second I hear those words, I kiss her with so much passion, even the flowers are wilting under our heat.

"I'm yours," she says, smiling a beautiful smile meant just for me.

"You are. I love you, CC."

I try to kiss her again, but Rylan yells, "Let's get this party started before my ankles swell and I can't dance anymore."

Winnie laughs. "That's your best friend."

Grinning, I take her hand and we head out to the back patio for a small reception. They thought of everything, and even

Weston is having fun. He and Ada James have matching head-phones on as they chase each other through the crowd.

"This is the best day of my life," I tell anyone who will listen.

As the night goes on, I find myself never wanting it to end, and for everyone to leave so I can do deliciously naughty things to my wife.

A clinking sound drowns out the chaos, and we glance around, searching for the source. Expecting it to be someone yelling "kiss the bride," I'm surprised when I find Ashton standing at the head table, angled slightly to hide his scar, and little Sadie Sunshine, our adopted niece, holding his hand next to him like his own little protector.

Ashton clears his throat and lifts a microphone to his lips. "We usually leave this up to Colton, since he's the showoff and all." Everyone laughs, even Ash. "But since this is his big day, one of us had to do it. I drew the short straw."

There's more laughter, and he takes a sip of water. Speaking for long periods of time is still difficult for him.

"That's a lie," Preston whispers at my side. "I was prepared to do it, he asked to."

I stare at my little brother in shock. He's hidden himself away for so long, and even before his attack, he wasn't the outgoing one.

"We've all taken different paths to get here, but we all started in the same place. Our parents taught us about love and brotherhood before all else, and no one embodies that better than my brother, Colton.

"Sometimes, it feels like we're losing our way, but Colton is the first one to call us on our shit. To bring us back together. To remind us who we are. I may have lost track of that for a bit, but my heart is always with you.

"Winnie, you did the impossible. You brought Peter home from Neverland, and I've never seen him happier. Thank you for loving him with your whole heart, for bringing him back down to earth when he needs it, and for being an incredible addition to our crazy, chaotic family.

"To Colton and Winnie. May you have happy hearts, healthy lives, and love that lasts a lifetime."

A chorus of Colton and Winnies rings out, but Winnie and I are in a race to get to Ashton. Somehow, she beats me and manages an impressive tackle hug. I wrap them both in my arms.

"Thank you, Ash. I know that wasn't easy."

"Thank you for not giving up on me. I'm not right, Colt. Our family will always come first, but I have a lot of shit to work out. I'm sorry my actions hurt you in the past."

"No need, Ash. We're all good, and you will be, too. You just have to learn to let us in."

He nods, gives Winnie another hug, and settles at a table in the corner.

"He seems sad," Winnie observes.

"I think he's exactly what he said he is. A little lost. He'll find his way, though."

"How can you be so sure?"

"Because if he doesn't, we'll draw him a map."

It is the Westbrook way, after all.

353

EXTENDED EPILOGUE

COLTON

Five years later

"You sure you're going to be okay?" Winnie asks again.

"We'll be fine, Mom." Weston grins, holding his new sister in his arms.

"I know you will. I was asking about Daddy." She shoots him a wink, and I hear him snicker.

"Traitor."

"Maybe I should work from home today." Winnie spins in a circle with one shoe on. Pregnancy brain hasn't quite left my wife yet, but it's her first day back to work since Mara was born.

"They're expecting you. Just because your name is on the building doesn't give you special privileges."

"It doesn't?" Wes asks from his spot on the sofa. He's come so far in the last few years. He's truly a different kid, with the same amazing heart. There are still things that are difficult for him, and he'll probably always prefer one-on-one instead of a large group, but he's my son, and he's perfect.

"No. Uncle Preston will be the first to tell you that when

your name is on the building, it means you have to work twice as hard."

Winnie squeaks when she steps on a pacifier. Crossing the room, I place my hands on her shoulders. "You have to go to work, CC. Someone has to make the money around here." Every time I stare into her beautiful gray eyes, I fall in love all over again. Glancing down, I unbutton her blazer and rebutton it correctly.

"You're ridiculous, you know that? And what about you? Are you going to get any work done today?"

"Well, I won't be saving the world in a courtroom, but I do have a couple of meetings this afternoon. We have it covered. Plus, what's the point of having billions of dollars if I can't delegate for dad duty?"

"Did you ever think you'd be a stay-at-home dad?" she asks as Weston giggles.

"I can honestly say it never crossed my mind until I met you, but it's one of the best decisions I've ever made."

"One of the best?"

"Fishing for compliments, Mrs. Westbrook?"

"Always," she whispers, wrapping her arms around my neck. Leaning in, I kiss her deeply.

"Gross, Dad. Come on. Get a room."

Winnie laughs against my lips, but I don't let her pull away.

"The best decision I ever made is a tie."

Her face softens. She's heard this answer before.

"The day I decided to spend the night at the airport so I could get to know you. The night I found you at the hospital and followed you home. The day you agreed to be my wife. The day Weston's adoption came through, and now, the day Mara was born."

"That's a lot of favorites."

"It's the truth, and I'll just keep adding to it." I swat her ass. "Now go do your lawyering so you can get home to us."

She shakes her head. I like to mention she's a lawyer every chance I get. I can't help it. I'm fucking proud of my sexy wife.

"Did you decide what you're going to do about Claire?"

The disgusting waste of space had the gall to show up here a few weeks after Winnie gave birth, begging for her help. Seems she's a new mother as well. The difference is, she got knocked up by a married man. And that man and his wife are now suing for custody of her daughter.

The humanitarian side of me feels bad for her. As Winnie's husband, I wanted to scream at her to go to hell and this is exactly what she deserves.

Winnie wasn't so quick to toss her out and said she would think about it, then scheduled a meeting for her first day back to work.

"When she was here, we didn't talk much about anything but the lawsuit. I know you don't agree with this, but I'm going to hear her out. It's why I wanted to go to law school in the first place. As terrible as she is, she deserves to be heard."

"CC. It's not that I don't agree with you. I'll always stand by your decisions, I just think you need to keep a layer of self-preservation around her."

"I know," she says quietly. "I will."

Pulling her in, I kiss her on the forehead. "Your giant heart is one of my favorite things to love about you, sweetheart." I feel her smile against my shoulder. "Whatever you decide to do, I support."

"Thank you. It will be a game time decision I think. If she can show any kind of remorse for her actions, I'll consider it. If she comes in hot with her normal attitude, I'll show her the door."

"That's my girl."

I turn when I hear the gurgling sound no parent likes to hear. "Gah! Dad. She just pooped, and it's coming out of her shirt. Gross."

I move like I've been doing this for years and scoop my

poopy little mess off my equally messy son and smile. Glancing over my shoulder at Winnie, I grin. "Have a good day, dear."

She laughs as she walks toward the door.

Home never felt so good.

Winnie

Nerves have me shuffling the papers on my desk for the fourth time. Maybe I should have just told Claire to go to hell, but it just didn't feel right. Like a wart that can't be removed, she is a part of my history, and because of that, I'll hear her out. Like it or not, she helped shape me into the person I am today.

The intercom on my desk buzzes. "Mrs. Westbrook? Claire Milford is here to see you."

I press the call button and reply, "Send her in, Macy. Thank you."

With a deep inhale, I stand at my desk and wait for my old frenemy to enter.

The door opens slowly, and Claire enters with her gaze downcast. She has a toddler on her hip, and I have the distinct feeling this isn't the Claire I've always known. She stops halfway into my office and examines my space. It's tastefully decorated but not overdone. It was important to me that my clients always feel comfortable when they meet with me.

"Come in, Claire. Have a seat." My voice doesn't waver, but my hands shake with nerves as I point to the chair across from me.

As she sits, I get the first glimpse of her daughter. She's the spitting image of her mother, but with real blonde hair. That's when I realize Claire is no longer bleached blonde. Her dark hair is pulled into a high ponytail, and she wears no makeup. I'm not sure I've seen her without makeup since the seventh grade.

"Thank you for meeting with me," she murmurs. She has yet to look at me, and I wonder if I'm being played.

"I'll be honest. I haven't made my decision yet, but you deserve to be heard. So, tell me, Claire, why me?"

"Because you're the only person I know who can teach me to be a better person."

I'm caught off guard by her response, but I say nothing.

"I-I, when I look at Tinsley ..." She glances down at her daughter, and I see the first genuine emotion I've probably ever seen from Claire cross her face. Fear. "When I look at her, I don't want anyone to treat her like I treated you. I know this is too little too late, but I'm sorry for how I treated you over the years."

She continues as I raise an eyebrow, "I didn't realize it at the time, or maybe I just refused to acknowledge it, but I was so envious, so jealous of the relationship you had with your mom. It was childish to take it out on you the way I did. I've never been very good at handling emotions, but I hated myself because I never had what you did, which made me hate you even more. It's not fair. It's not right, but it's the truth."

"And you've changed because of your daughter, or because someone might take her away from you?"

Claire flinches but doesn't break eye contact. "That's a fair question, but something changed in me the first time Tinsley was placed on my chest. A sense of belonging, of love. A sense of duty I've never had before. The first time she wrapped her tiny fingers around my thumb, I knew I'd do anything for her. My life has revolved around her for two years. Three, if you count my pregnancy. My greatest fear is that she'll pay for my biggest mistakes. That someone will hurt her just because they can. It made me realize I was worried that someone would treat her the way I treated you."

I watch her closely as she sets down the diaper bag and pulls out a toy for Tinsley, who takes it happily and buries her face into her mother's shoulder.

"The father," I ask. "Did you know he was married when you slept with him?"

She closes her eyes, and regret flashes when she opens them. "Yes, I did." She stands like that one answer has sealed her fate.

"Would you do it again?"

She pauses, staring at Tinsley. "I'll never regret it because it gave me her. But, if I could do it again with someone unmarried and still get Tinsley? I would do it differently, yes." Claire brings the diaper bag to her shoulder. "I've made a lot of mistakes, Winnie. I'm not proud of who I used to be, but I am trying to be better. For Tinsley, and myself." Her lip quivers, and I see a woman in pain. "She's my entire world. I can't lose her because her father has money, and I don't. I wouldn't survive it. I may have been a shitty person, but I am a great mother."

"I believe you." And I do. I took an oath to help those in need. It doesn't mean I have to like them, but she doesn't deserve to lose her daughter because of it. "I'll help you, Claire."

A small sob escapes her trembling lips. "I didn't think you would."

"To be honest, I wasn't sure I would either, but Tinsley doesn't deserve to pay for your mistakes." Tears well in her eyes, but she says nothing. "My paralegal will take down all the information we need to get started, and I'll be in touch after I've had a chance to review your case."

Hugging Tinsley to her chest, she nods. "Thank you, Winnie. For everything. And I know it isn't worth much, but I am so sorry for everything I did for your dad."

"You're welcome. And thank you for that."

"D-Do you think we could get coffee sometime?" She looks so vulnerable. So lost. But Colton's words about self-preservation hit me like a sledgehammer.

"I don't think that's a good idea, Claire. I'll be your attorney, and I will win this case for you, but I think we are past being able to form a friendship. I'm sorry." I don't know why I apologize for that. Setting boundaries with someone who hurt you is healthy, and the right thing to do, but staring at her, I see how alone she is. I almost crack, but the hurt she caused is too deep. I can help her legally, but I need to put up a wall around her otherwise.

"I-I understand. Thank you, Winnie. For being a better person than I've ever been. And for being an example of what I hope Tinsley will see in me someday."

"I hope so, too. I'll be in touch, Claire."

I watch as she exits my office, and even though I'll be working on her case, I feel an old wound begin to heal. I realize, with a start, that I'm not taking on this case for her. I'm doing it for myself, and I'm good with my decision.

That just leaves one more wound to heal. Dennis Tillman. Witnessing firsthand how Colton took in Wes, I know he would never be able to abandon him. But that's what Dennis did. He abandoned me, which makes him no better than my biological father. Maybe some wounds are meant to leave a scar, because not everything can be fixed.

I glance down at the picture of Colton and Wes on my desk, and I let go of the hate and the hurt Dennis caused. I have no desire to reach out to him, but I choose me and my family. I have no room for the pain caused by others anymore. I won't give anyone that power over me ever again.

Colton Westbrook shook my entire world when he entered my life, but he also gave me something more valuable than any dollar amount he's assigned to Weston and me. He's given me the courage to trust and to love. Not only others, but myself. Colton has made me a better version of myself, just by believing in me wholeheartedly, and I know we will fill our life with light, laughter, and more love than I could ever begin to comprehend.

With Colton by my side, I feel invincible. He's the love of my life, and my very own thupahero.

ACKNOWLEDGMENTS

Hello, Luvs!

We've made it to the end of another book! It has been a seriously crazy ride, but I couldn't do it without the help of so many amazing people. That includes you, my amazing readers. Thank you for sticking with me. For reading these crazy Westbrooks, and for supporting me in this journey. You're the best readers in the world, and I am forever grateful to you.

I wouldn't be here without the support of my husband and children. Thank you for supporting me even when it's three in the morning and you find me sobbing over my keyboard.

To Rhon, my right hand, chaos coordinating, emotional support friend, thank you to infinity for always having my back and knowing what I need, usually before I do. I appreciate you more than words can say.

Beth, my biggest supporter, my overused word finder, my friend. Thank you for being in my corner, and luving me anyway.

#TeamAvery, The Luvables, the ladies who make my dreams a reality. Marie, Carissa, Jennifer, Melissa, Jennifer, Michelle, Atlee, and Kia. Thank you for your opinions, your time, and for helping me put out the best versions of my stories I can.

Street & ARC teams, thank you for believing in me so much that you give up time in your busy lives to spread the LUV like glitter. You're all such a huge part of every success story, and I am so thankful you've chosen me.

The Luv Club, is seriously the most amazing group on the interweb. Thank you for embracing my vision for a luving, caring, supportive group and making it so much more than I could have ever hoped for.

Top Secret Chat Group: You know who you are, and I thank you from the bottom of my heart for the support, friendship, kindness, and laughs every day, multiple times a day, even when shouty caps are involved. Thank you for being my people.

#TeamTWSS: Thank you for taking a chance on me. Your kindness and support have meant the world to me. I appreciate you all so very much.

Dark City Designs: Jodi, thank you for bringing my characters to life in cover form.

There For You Editing: Melissa, thank you for teaching me to drop the S at the end of toward, even if it sounds like there's one in my head!

Feed Your Dreams Designs: Karen, thank you for bringing my teasers to life in picture perfect form.

GET TO KNOW AVERY!

I'm a New-England girl born and raised, but now I live in North Carolina with my husband, our four kids, and two dogs.

I write sweet, sexy, small-town contemporary romance because I'm a romantic at heart. My stories are of friendship and trust, heartbreak, and redemption. I try to bring my characters to life and make you feel every emotion I pour onto the page.

I've always been a fan of the happily ever after and the stories that make them, and now I get to write a soul mate for us all. My heroines have sass, my heroes have steam, and together they create the stories you won't want to put down.

Want to hang out with me more? I'm in The Luv Club every day sharing my chaos, my crazy, my life. Pop in to say hi, meet the other luvables, and stay a while. It's the happiest, kindest group on the internet and I'd LUV to see you there!

ALSO BY AVERY MAXWELL

The Westbrooks: Broken Hearts Series:

Book 1- Cross My Heart

Book 2- The Beat of My Heart

Book 3- Saving His Heart

Book 4- Romancing His Heart

The Westbrooks: Family Ties Series:

Book .5- One Little Heartbreak- A Westbrook Novella

Book 1- One Little Mistake

Book 2- One Little Lie

Book 3- One Little Kiss

Book 4- One Little Secret (Coming Soon)

Printed by Amazon Italia Logistica S.r.l.
Torrazza Piemonte (TO), Italy

47342923R00215